SUDDEN STORM

Clark W. Heckert (signature)

A Novel By
CLARK W. HECKERT

This is a work of fiction.
Some events and characters described herein are imaginary
and are not intended to refer to specific people or places.

LIGHT OF THE MOON, INC. - PUBLISHING DIVISION
Design/Production/Consulting
www.lightofthemooninc.com

Dedicated to John U. Heckert,
whose untimely death in 1957
forever changed my life.

ACKNOWLEDGMENTS:

A collaboration with
Alex Shezifi

In 1989, Alex Shezifi and I collaborated to create an action-adventure novel that was to become *Sudden Storm*. Alex provided technical details on weaponry, aeronautics, and life in Russia where he was born, and Israel where he was raised and served in the Israel Defense Forces (IDF). I put my science, engineering, and naval experience to good use while writing the action-packed passages in this work. In the early 1990s, we both were employed in the DuPont Electronic Imaging Laboratory in Wilmington, Delaware. During that time, I was traveling a lot for DuPont.

As *Sudden Storm* began to take shape in the epic novel it was to become, Alex met our first editor Joan Roes while vacationing at the Sunlight Mountain Resort in Glenwood Springs, Colorado. Joan contributed invaluable critique, and at first more than a few words, until with her guidance I developed the style prevalent in this work – thanks, Joan. Despite a flurry of activity in the early 1990s, Alex and I were unable to enlist a committed publisher. From 1991 until 2017, *Sudden Storm* sat on the shelf gathering dust. During that time, our four children graduated from high school and then college. I retired early from DuPont in 1997 and ten years later I began the process of moving to Colorado full time. I loaned a copy of the novel to Charlotte Graham, a local author. After reading *Sudden Storm,* she enthusiastically encouraged me to self-publish. Our friend Betty Rahn also reviewed the book

Alex Shezifi and Clark W. Heckert, Seattle, Washington, 1990.

and became one of my best boosters. Pam, my wife of 45 years, was working on her novel at the time and after she reviewed and edited *Sudden Storm* to her exacting standards, she introduced me to the Carbondale Writers group where I learned the basics of self-publishing. Finally, many thanks to Alyssa Ohnmacht for her work with the layout, design, and publishing of *Sudden Storm,* and current editor Kayla Henley. I wish also to recognize the information contributions from: the late Professor of Geology Robert Woolsey of the University of Mississippi and my friend Hans Rieger, who for many years owned the Alpine Lodge in Aspen. Thanks also to the Defense Mapping Authority, who supplied helpful maps and charts of Vietnam.

• Chapter 1 •

DA NANG HARBOR, VIETNAM
1972

It was a shining hot afternoon that May 8th. The South Vietnamese were preparing to stand on their own. Back in the cool Oval Office, President Nixon was having little success negotiating an end to the conflict in Vietnam. To bolster their allies, the US military was shipping in massive amounts of arms and munitions. On this day, the harbor was so busy that the fully loaded *USS Hancock* couldn't even find a berth at the piers.

She was now at anchor in the harbor's murky water with two small gray craft snugly tied alongside. Aboard the *Hancock*, the heat-weary men in the open hold moved plywood crates into place for the insect-like crane. The operator in the cabin above picked up each load, swung it to port or starboard, and then lowered it into the gray boats below. On the boats, more sweating men struggled to move each load into place. The work was difficult under the glare of the tropical sun. The afternoon rain showers provided no relief from the rising temperatures of the steel decks, but instead created slippery footing and added more moisture to the already stifling humidity. The work was demanding and slow, but by nightfall tomorrow it would be done.

The *Hancock* was scheduled to be underway the following day, cutting cleanly through the blue green water bound for Greece to off-load the remainder of her supplies. There, she was to take on cargo bound for the States. It was to be her last cruise. The *Hancock* would head home to Philadelphia, her birthplace in the spring of 1943, to be her burial ground in 1973.

In Philadelphia, an unceremonious and unsentimental decommissioning would end her active duty. Over the next six months in a nearby dry dock, a wrecking crew was scheduled to strip her refrigeration, electronics, and engineering equipment. What remained would be scrapped and shipped by rail to the aging steel mills of Pittsburgh and Allentown, Pennsylvania.

The *Hancock* had a proud history covering three wars. In World War Two she participated in the Normandy Invasion by ferrying troops and supplies in those first few critical days. Shortly after completing her fourth trip, a British battleship sheared off her bow in a collision. Her valiant crew kept her afloat for forty-eight hours. By then, a seagoing tug managed to tow her into Southampton. Six months later, with a new bow hastily welded in place, she continued to supply the Allied Forces until the conclusion of World War Two. Twenty-seven years of steady service and two more deadly wars followed.

Every six years she routinely underwent an overhaul in the Philadelphia Naval Shipyard. In recent years, the Navy focused less attention on her aging engineering plant. In fact, during her last two periods in the yards, the engineers completed only the minimum necessary repairs to the boilers, while adding more refrigeration, air conditioning, electronic, and communications equipment. These additions increased the load on her aging steam and electrical generation equipment. The chief engineering officer was below diagnosing an over-pressure problem in her number one boiler.

Seaman Second Class Sam Jackson was glad to be below decks taking inventory. He hated the heat, as many big men do. Here, he was in his glory. He could assign the heavy work of moving cargo to his subordinates while taking over his Chief Petty Officer's paper work. With a clipboard in one large hand and a tiny ballpoint pen in the other, he smiled to himself. He had reached the end of the food inventory list. The chief was now ashore, probably getting drunk with some whore. He seemed to have an old girlfriend in every port. Sam was on the refrigeration deck finishing up the food supplies. The cold air of the Reefer Deck was a welcome change from the hot sun topside. Below him, he could hear the low murmur of the cooling water pumps. He was fortunate; his best friend Jack stood a watch in the hot engineering spaces where he watched gages and turned valves in the one hundred and twenty plus heat. Jack's efforts kept the electricity flowing for the refrigeration system he now enjoyed.

Sam ran his hand through his curly red hair, enjoying the way it brushed against his new gold wedding band, and how it neatly rearranged itself to frame his round, wholesome face. The Reefer inventory was complete. He closed the bulkhead door behind him and secured it with a twist of the counterbalanced lever, continued down a short passageway, then stepped through the forward watertight door. He was now in a small cargo hold. The space was originally used as a magazine, but when the three-inch guns were removed, it became a cargo hold. Beige wooden crates and darker brown corrugated cardboard boxes filled neat racks on both the port and starboard bulkheads. The space had a damp and musty smell resulting from a leak around the overhead ventilation hatch. The leakage had started during a recent storm; possibly the huge metal plates of the hull flexed slightly at the old seam where the second bow was attached.

As Sam started his inventory, he noticed the light in the compartment dim. Slowly, it dimmed even more, then finally went out. He stood in total darkness. Throughout the ship, equipment coasted to a stop. The sound died off as if the ship were in a final exhale. Some jerk in the generation room must have lost control and shut down the main generator. Sam waited, expecting the power to return any moment. Power outages were becoming a frequent occurrence. If the power wasn't restored promptly, the steam safety valves would begin venting the excess from the boiler. Sam waited longer than expected in the darkness, again running his hand through his red hair as if to soothe himself. The steam wasn't venting. He reached into his pocket for his flashlight, switched it on, and lit his way to the door.

In the next moment, Sam felt he was moving in a nightmare. What started as a dull roar below his feet grew rapidly into an enormous blast that reverberated through the hull. The explosion hurled Sam backward. The deck beneath him bulged and began heating rapidly. Steam escaping into the corridor slammed the watertight door shut. A large crate containing machinery slid from its shelf and fell against the door.

The closing of the door kept the small cargo space cooler and prevented the scalding steam from entering. For a long minute, Sam stood bewildered in the darkness. A quiet trickling sound was all he heard besides the hammering of his adrenalin-accelerated heart. Suddenly, he realized water was seeping in around the door's gasket. Sam grasped his flashlight and rushed to the door. He couldn't move the heavy crate. No matter how hard he pushed, it wouldn't budge.

Sam heard the undeniable sound of rushing water. He pointed his flashlight at the bulkhead and to his horror, he found several holes near the overhead wires spitting trickles of water. The deck was tilting beneath him. Sounds of equipment falling echoed throughout the ship. Sam could hear water rushing into the space on the other side of the door.

On the main deck, the crew was already preparing to abandon ship. The *Hancock*'s engineering spaces were flooding and her bow was quickly slipping below water. The leaks in Sam's space, which started as trickles, were now spewing water with increased force. As the water rose in the compartment, a painful pressure built in his ears. He swallowed hard, the pressure momentarily relieved. Sam heard the hull nudge the muddy bottom. There was a slow twist to starboard as the *Hancock* settled on her side. A chill went through Sam's big farmboy body. Was this the *Hancock*'s final resting place? Here in the mud of this God-forsaken country? Was this his final destination?

As the ship twisted, Sam fell to the deck. A heavy crate tore loose from the port bulkhead and crashed to the deck, barely missing Sam. It skidded to the starboard bulkhead and split open.

The water continued to rise slowly in the cargo space as Sam cast about looking for some way out. He climbed the leaning ladder to the overhead hatch where he discovered it wouldn't open, and it was welded shut. Finding no escape above, he searched the deck below. He already knew none existed. The only remaining way out was the door and he had already tried it. He knew it was hopeless.

Remembering that sailors trapped in sinking ships during World War Two made tapping noises on the hull, he scanned for a metal object. While searching, he stepped over the open crate. Two pointed objects inside caught his eye. He grasped one with both hands; it weighed nearly eighty pounds. With his suspicions aroused, he spun it around. The atomic emblem became visible in the dimming light of his flashlight. Printed next to the warning emblem was, "ASROC tactical nuclear warhead" in big red letters.

He looked at the crate. ASROC-that stood for anti submarine rocket. They had nuclear warheads. What were they doing in a crate marked "tools"? Someone had made a big mistake! No time to worry about it now, he could tell the chief later. Finding a dogging wrench, he began to rap on the outer hull. He had to escape. He had to make them hear. How much noise could he make? Could they hear him? Were they listening?

Sam realized the air in the compartment was escaping through the same holes that let the water in. Soon, there wouldn't be any air left. He was going to die. The reality of the fact gripped him. He wanted to cry, but he fought back the tears. It wasn't right to waste the last few moments of life. It wasn't easy for Sam; he had no experience with death.

Slowly, the water rose till his head touched the bulkhead. Then he was tilting his nose up to get air. In a moment, he took the last breath available. He held the air till he could stand it no longer. There was a slow exhale, followed by a tremendous desire to breathe again. No air was available. Sam fought the urge to suck in water. At first, it was very difficult, then it became easier. Eventually, he slipped into unconsciousness, his lungs filled with sea water, and his stomach regurgitated. Both of his big hands, the left one with the shining wedding band, and his right, clenched into fists before relaxing. As his body became stiff, his red hair waved gracefully behind his head as it drifted in the water.

Sam died before his flashlight went out. A week later, his decomposing body settled toward the bulkhead where it came to rest in the open crate.

• Chapter 2 •

MOSCOW, USSR
TUESDAY, MAY 12, 1991

Victor Gerisimov, Chief of the First Directorate of the KGB, was carefully studying an intelligence report while savoring a cigar and mug of hot black tea. His office window rattled from a chilly breeze that was beginning to clear the morning mist from the trees in the street below. His heavy frame matched that of his sturdy oak desk, and his office had a well-used and disheveled look rendered by a busy man with little time for fastidious house-keeping. Gerisimov took a long draw on his thick Cuban cigar and exhaled a blue cloud of smoke through yellowed teeth. Half an hour ago, he had received a secret report delivered by diplomatic courier from New York. The news from his Florida agent was very disturbing. Apparently, the Americans were more successful in correcting reliability problems in their underfunded and over-worked Space Shuttle Program than was estimated two years ago.

At that time, the development of the U.S. Global Climate Survey System had just begun. Now one of the six survey satellites was ready for launch. Early calibration exercises were scheduled for mid-summer, but no definitive data would be available until all six units were deployed, and a seasonal benchmark calibration was achieved. The process was a lengthy one requiring several years, but early data could be expected within one year. Development of the system began in 1990 when it became obvious to the scientific world that the earth was experiencing an ominous warming trend. The Americans proposed that an international team be formed to develop the means to monitor the situation and recommend a course of action to correct the problem. Russia had supported the effort by offering scientific facilities and manpower, but almost no funding due to her economic turmoil. Most of the funding came from the U.S., Europe and Japan.

The problem was the Soviets had been secretly engaged in weather modification for three years. This was accomplished by the use of a large, yet nearly invisible, deployment vehicle that delivered a highly unstable yet fascinating mixed gas system (that Gerisimov did not pretend to understand) to the outer atmosphere. Now this system consistently produced low pressure areas on demand. After their first spectacular failure, the Soviet scientists had been able to stabilize the system and deliver moderate weather to the Ukraine. The last two growing seasons were excellent. Russia could once again feed herself. But could the Soviets continue undetected from the view of the Global Survey System? Gerisimov and his science advisors did not think so.

Victor Gerisimov finished reading the report and sat upright, stubbing out the end of his cigar in the large ash tray at the edge of his desk. He drummed his thick fingers on his wooden desk in a nervous rhythm for a few seconds, then snatched the center phone from the array of three to his left. This one connected directly to General Vassily Tuzov's office. It had a sophisticated scrambling device, but like many such creations of man, it depended on trust of those with access to the codes. The technicians who installed the device could easily work for the KGB, GRU, or anyone else with something of value to offer. Gerisimov didn't trust such people.

He dialed and waited. When it was answered he smiled as he spoke, "Vassily Stepanovich, how are you this morning?"

There was a pause. Gerisimov's expression didn't change as he scratched the back of his head.

"I have news for you from far away," he continued.

There was a brief reply from the other end.

"Yes, I will be over immediately. I am departing now."

Gerisimov rose from his desk, switched off his reading light, grabbed his hat and coat from behind his office door and, with a brief word to his secretary, headed downstairs to the basement garage in the First Directorate Headquarters. His feet made rhythmic thumping as he descended, which his driver Sasha heard. By the time he hit the landing, Sasha had quit his card game with the other drivers and had his black Chaika running. Gerisimov tossed his folder inside, climbed in the rear seat, slammed the door shut, and gave instructions to Sasha. With a lurch they were off into the shadows outside.

Sasha wasted no time in traffic. He drove the black Chaika down the lane reserved for official traffic like it was a tank. At times he exceeded 120 kilometers-per-hour. Sasha enjoyed most of his work. He was able to violate any traffic law he desired in order to speed his important passenger on his way. This was great sport for the son of a peasant from a collective farm near Kiev. As he sped down the official lane, it delighted him to see the Traffic Militia stop traffic at almost every corner so his official car could proceed without interruption. What he didn't like was maintenance. Years ago drivers didn't maintain the cars they drove, but now a more cost-conscious government reasoned drivers had too many free hours, so they were expected to perform maintenance. It was dirty work, and frequently there were no spare parts. Sasha had on several occasions stolen parts from other official cars. It was a common practice.

Gerisimov thought of the impending meeting with General Tuzov. This was bad news. Tuzov had friends in very high places who were counting on the success of the Soviet Space Program. They were benefiting from the success of recent harvests. The prospect of the world discovering the Soviet weather modification system would be received like an icy wind from Siberia.

Gerisimov was aware of both the Russian technological advances and failures. From the start the weather modification system, now called the Harvest Satellite, had its problems. The first time it was used in the fall of 1989, the low pressure area that was to bring warming winds to the southern Ukraine wheat had produced a devastating ice storm. Despite the efforts of the Red

Army to help farmers, two thirds of the crop was lost. Russia nearly starved that winter. After six months of intense study, the system was modified to produce a more moderate, but helpful, effect. The scientists braved another test. It was successful, and now the system had worked well for nearly two years without detection by the West. Recently, the same Soviet scientists that had stabilized the system had devised a means to deceive the Global Climate Survey System so the Soviet weather modification program could continue undetected, but their approach required the construction of six shadow satellites that would be deployed in the vicinity of the survey system satellites. To be successful the Soviet system had to be in space before the U.S. space shuttle delivered its six payloads. Failure to do so would most certainly result in discovery of the Harvest Satellite system. While the current economic and political crisis persisted, Russia couldn't exist without the Harvest Satellite.

The Russian deception program had recently developed a snag when the American scientists had changed the design of the stratospheric probe that measured the concentrations of carbon dioxide, methane, nitrous oxide, chlorofluorocarbons, and other gases thought to accelerate the hot house effect. Since several Soviets were on the team, the design was readily available, but fooling the sensors required an eleventh hour retrofit of the Soviet shadow system. That put the Soviets behind schedule. Then the Soviet Vega rocket, the work horse of the program, developed a problem in its third stage rocket firing mechanism. It had undergone some redesign to provide a smoother start-up. This new system had been proven in extensive ground testing, but had failed dramatically in recent launchings. The Americans were gaining an impressive lead.

The Chaika rounded the turn in front of Dzerzinski Square and came to an abrupt halt in front of the KGB headquarters. Gerisimov got out. He entered the building and showed his identification to the guard behind the large desk in the hallway. A moment later he was admitted and took the elevator to the third floor. The general had a large office down the hall behind the desk of an especially attractive dark-haired receptionist. She was dressed in a low cut yellow blouse and western style jeans.

"Hello Larisa," greeted Gerisimov. It was his usual custom to pause by her desk and engage her in idle conversation while he would gaze at her ample bust, but today he breezed past assuming he would be admitted immediately to the general's office. She looked up and smiled at him.

"Go right in. The general expects you," she chirped to his back as he passed.

General Tuzov was waiting inside. He was tall and trim for a member of the Russian elite. He made frequent use of the private gym in the basement of the KGB headquarters. He was especially adroit in the game of basketball, where his height was an advantage. He enjoyed competition and played well on teams with men ten years his junior.

Tuzov was proud to have risen to his position through hard honest work. He started as a District Commander of Border Guards and through his persistence rose to Chief of the First Directorate. He had done well for each of his bosses, despite his personal opinion of his superiors. As he rose higher, he had not succumbed to the temptation of delivering favors for members of the Politburo. He was known as a man of conviction. That reputation was helping him to rise further.

Gerisimov entered the general's office, seated himself in front of the general's desk, opened his folder, and passed him the report in its special plastic envelope.

"I'm afraid it's bad news. It comes from Cape Canaveral, from one of our better sources. It looks like the Americans are getting the Global Survey program off on schedule," said Gerisimov quietly.

General Tuzov opened the envelope, removed the report, folded the cover sheet marked "Secret" back, and concentrated on the text that followed. As he read, he occasionally scratched the lobe of his right ear with his thumb and forefinger. After a few minutes, he grunted loudly and looked up at Gerisimov.

"How confident are you this information is accurate?" asked Tuzov.

"Very confident, I'm sorry to say. It comes from our most reliable source in NASA. We also have satellite photographs that show they are readying for the final series of launches," replied Gerisimov.

Deep in thought, Tuzov stared out his picture window at the morning sun for a moment. Then he turned to Gerisimov.

"I believe it is best I take this news to the Defense Minister immediately. He will not be pleased."

Tuzov thanked Gerisimov for his promptness, and after a few words about his young daughter whom Gerisimov had met a year ago, Gerisimov departed. While the conversation between Gerisimov and Larisa floated in through his door, the general was left alone with his thoughts.

He was aware of division in the Politburo. The new Chairman of the Central Committee of the Communist Party, who would probably replace Gorbachev after his pending departure, in some ways had proven to be more conservative. If there was any striking difference, it was his reliance on the Red Army to enforce economic policy.

Victor Panfilov was the grandson of General Panfilov, who in World War Two managed to stop the German invasion at the gates of Moscow. He was immensely popular among the Russian public. Of course he had his detractors. They made up a one-third minority in the Politburo, yet they rarely voted against him.

Panfilov wanted better relations with the United States. Jointly, the two countries were negotiating the total dismantling of their intercontinental ballistic missile systems. These systems were quite possibly obsolete because neither nation believed that war between them was inevitable. The appalling state of the Russian economy was the most troublesome. Food and supply shortages had many districts straining for independence in a time when collectively they were on shaky economic ground. A year ago, driven by famine and riot, ethnic hot spots had developed in the Baltic states of Estonia, Latvia and Lithuania. Panfilov had no choice but to resort to some of the old guard military force to stop wholesale insurrection. To make matters, worse the oil reserves in Azerbaijan were beginning to show definite signs of depletion. Exploration was on the increase in Western Siberia, and American oil technology, now off the embargo list, was helping, but it would be years before output could be significantly increased. Meanwhile, Russia had begun a program to increase the use of imported oil. To help replenish the supply of foreign currency, the Party had stepped up export of caviar, furs, and vodka, making them unavailable except to the highest level party members. Increased contact with the West in recent years had created a strong demand for almost anything foreign. The result had been an enormous growth in this black market. Cracking down on the market had been difficult, mainly because most of its activities were conducted by low-level party members. Russia did not lack in raw materials, expertise, or equipment, but after seventy years of communism, her people lacked the will to change to a free market economy. In fact, such uncertainty caused the greatest anxiety among the people.

Still, over the years the needs of the people were slowly gaining ground over the need for national defense. Today, the minority in the Politburo favored a less aggressive approach to the defense effort. It was well-known that the Russian army tanks outnumbered the West's five to one. Sometime in the future, there would be a test of strength for the less hawkish elements in the Politburo, but not today. The seat of power still was bent on maintaining a stable Russia through a strong central army.

General Tuzov decided that rather than immediately meet with Defense Minister Lichev he would discuss the new developments with Pavel Nikitin, the expert on the American Space Program at IKI, the Russian Institute of Space Research.

WEDNESDAY, MAY 13

Tuzov had arranged a hasty meeting with Pavel Nikitin in his office at IKI. This was not the custom for the head of the KGB. Under normal circumstances, Tuzov would have sent a car and driver to pick up Nikitin, but because this investigation involved his friend Lichev, he broke with tradition, preferring to make their meeting appear casual. The Politburo meeting was in two days and Tuzov wanted all the background information he could gather on the American Global Survey program. He did not want others to know the purpose of his mission.

As Tuzov entered Nikitin's office, he couldn't help but notice the magnificent photographs of the surface of Venus. These photos were the result of the Soviet Vega program. It was this program that first proved to the world the Soviet Union was taking the lead in space. NASA had no such photos, even today.

Nikitin's office was spacious with two large bookshelves, each two meters in width, whose shelves reached the ceiling. These were nearly filled with reference books and magazines, many from the U.S. Nikitin had a large hand-carved teak desk in the center of his office with several chairs for guests, and a fine teak credenza imported from Indonesia. On the wall behind his desk was a photograph of the American Space Shuttle lifting off.

Nikitin relished the gathering of data. He had volumes of reports, magazine, and newspapers articles collected from the western press. He spent hours studying this information and gathering more from his trips to western countries to arrange joint programs. Dutifully, upon the return of each mission, he submitted a detailed report on his findings. The KGB was first to get a copy of his report.

Nikitin graduated valedictorian from the Moscow High Technical College. His engineering and mathematical skills were superb, plus he had an excellent memory for detail. After graduation in 1972, he received an unprecedented opportunity to attend graduate school at Massachusetts Institute of Technology on the exchange program as part of the spirit of Détente during the Nixon era. His becoming an expert on the American space program had been a natural outgrowth of his experience at MIT.

It pleased Nikitin that he could be of use to the head of the KGB. Normally, Russians who traveled often in the west were watched closely by the KGB. Helping General Tuzov would reduce the chances of future interference.

He had met General Tuzov only once before. That had been for a review of intelligence programs a year ago in preparation for a KGB report to the new Chairman, Victor Panfilov.

General Tuzov entered his office in a rush, not waiting for his receptionist to take his coat. Nikitin was struck by the general's excellent physical condition. His face was only slightly flushed from the three flights of stairs leading to Nikitin's office. Judging from his forthright manner, it was obvious the general had something of importance to discuss.

"Pavel, I have a report for you to study. It is recent information and I want your opinion after you have finished it," said Tuzov, handing him an envelope.

Nikitin took the report out of the plastic envelope and read the contents. The information was not all that new to Nikitin. He suspected as much from the fragmented information he had meticulously pieced together from the foreign press articles he had piled about his office. After a brief scan of the contents he looked up at Tuzov.

"I am sorry to say, I suspected as much. The Americans were slow at first after the Challenger disaster, but it focused their quality control efforts, so now they have perfected a reliable vehicle. With such a fine delivery vehicle, I'm not surprised they are fast closing on us," said Nikitin gravely.

"Is there any way to slow them down?" asked Tuzov.

"Are you suggesting sabotage?"

"Yes, if necessary."

"I know of no agents in position to cause damage to the program internally. That is your department. I do know the Americans have kept tight security around the launches and that the equipment undergoes thorough testing. Sabotage, if not discovered, could be effective, but it would have to be accomplished just before launch. Security is tightest then. If an attempt was made and failed, the chances are nil a second attempt would be possible. In addition, sabotage would have to be to a critical component, one without a backup. Unlike some of our systems, there are few single critical components in the space shuttle. Failure of those components would be great cause for suspicion. We have never done it before and I advise against it now. Unless, of course, no other alternative exists," said Nikitin.

"Then what can delay the program?" asked Tuzov, grasping for something substantial.

"I'm afraid it's out of our hands," replied Nikitin.

"What do you mean by that?"

"The only delay in the American space program on record for the last two years was for weather during the hurricane season last fall. That massive hurricane in September delayed the Americans for two weeks. We do not control their weather. There are those still among us who believe control should be left to a different Power," answered Nikitin.

Tuzov paused for a second, deep in thought while he stroked his right ear lobe. He then smiled an almost boyish grin.

"Perhaps that is what some people think, but then what do they know?" he replied slowly.

The intensity of the moment was broken. General Tuzov continued to probe for possible alternatives, concentrating on each possibility until satisfied he had gathered its significance. In short, there was little the Russians could do at this late stage in the deployment of the Global Climate Survey System program short of an outright act of war.

An hour later he departed, satisfied that he had completely explored all the options.

WEDNESDAY, MAY 13, 6:30 P. M.

In the early evening, Tuzov arrived at his spacious six-room apartment in the Kutuzovsky Prospect high rise, the exclusive home of party officials. His wife was just starting the evening meal as it was Tuzov's custom to come home late. She was in their modern kitchen with its many built-in cabinets and Formica topped counters preparing Tuzov's favorite meal, chicken with cabbage and potatoes, in their microwave oven.

"*Privet dorgiya,*" he called affectionately from the front door.

After a brief word with his wife, he proceeded to his daughter's room. She was busy doing her homework when he arrived, but looked up with a broad smile.

"So, how is the great guardian of all Mother Russia today, Daddy?" she asked.

"I am busy, it is a very big country we have to guard," he smiled at her fondly. "So how is your homework coming?"

"Fine, but I really don't like logarithms and I have a lot of problems to do for tomorrow for that stern teacher Liebermann," she responded, shaking her head.

Tuzov's daughter was fourteen. He had been surprised by her burgeoning adolescence and couldn't get accustomed to the idea of her interest in young boys. But that was what was to come, and even more. Oh, the burdens of a father!

Tuzov had a son, Evgeny, now twenty-eight years old. He studied geology in Moscow and had continued for a doctorate. He now was in the Ministry of Energy helping to plan the development of the vast coal and iron reserves in Siberia. Ten years ago, when Tuzov was chief of the First Directorate, Evgeny had delighted his father when he and Svetlana Licheva announced their intention to marry. Both families were close. Yuri Lichev, the Defense Minister, had recommended Tuzov when he was elected to the Politburo. The nomination was more than a formality, for they were old friends. Lichev liked Tuzov's honest and forthright style and wanted him to represent the KGB on the Politburo to help support his somewhat hawkish politics. The wedding had been spectacular in a Russian way. It was one of the rare occasions when Tuzov got drunk.

Tuzov gathered the background information on the Global Survey program. He picked up his private in-house phone and dialed the Lichev apartment, which was one floor above his. Olga Licheva answered.

"*Privet,* Vassily Stepanovich," she said in a friendly voice.

"I'd like a word with your husband, if you would be so kind to put him on," said Tuzov.

"One moment, I think he is on the balcony feeding the birds … No, here he is," she said, handing the phone to Yuri.

"I have some important news for you. If you are available, I can come up now."

The meeting was immediately arranged. It was not a frequent occurrence, but since there was sensitive information to discuss, such meetings in Lichev's private apartment were appropriate for the two friends.

In a minute, Tuzov left his apartment, taking the elevator to Lichev's apartment. Yuri was waiting when he arrived. They immediately went to the room Lichev used as a den when he was home from the office. Olga brought some marinated mushrooms and a crystal carafe of chilled Stolichnaya.

"I am afraid the news is not good, Yuri," Tuzov began, as he took the glass of vodka offered by his friend. "It seems the Americans are moving on schedule toward complete deployment of the Global Survey program. The details are in this report," he said, taking the report out of its envelope.

Lichev paused, frowning. "When do you think they could begin testing the system?"

"The information indicates they will begin before November and complete it by mid-January," replied Tuzov.

"Which means they will be able to complete their system before the deadline in February. You know we cannot complete the Shadow satellite program by that deadline. It becomes more clear each day," said Lichev, draining his glass. "You know it is very important to Panfilov that we be first. He is insistent about it. What can your people do to prevent the Americans from humiliating us?"

Lichev paced the floor. His failure to deliver the Shadow system in May would now be followed by the Americans discovering the Harvest Satellite system. That knowledge could lead to the full disclosure of the Soviet Stealth Satellite technology. That would be gravely embarrassing to the Soviet government. The news was more than disappointing; it was potentially disastrous.

"We have little chance for sabotage, which, if discovered, the Americans would consider outrageous. I am sure Panfilov will not allow it. Not with the current peace negotiations in progress. He and Savitsky would block such action in the Politburo. We need a method which would not lead the Americans to suspect we are involved," replied Tuzov quietly, his eyes roving the ceiling as if he were looking for electronic listening devices.

"What could you do?" asked Lichev. He stopped pacing and faced Tuzov.

"It is not what I can do, rather it is what our space people can do. You have already seen how dramatic the effect their Harvest Satellite program had on our weather with its unfortunate instability. If you remember, no one in the West suspected we had anything to do with the spectacular low pressure system that appeared from nowhere. It is reasonable then to conclude they would not suspect our involvement when a series of storms arise in the Caribbean during their normal hurricane season. Such storms will definitely delay their launch schedule," replied Tuzov.

Lichev's face brightened.

"Yes! You do have a point. It could be done. But, it is still a delicate situation. We will need the help from our friends on the Politburo. We will have to prepare for the meeting carefully," declared Lichev.

Lichev and Tuzov continued the discussion long into the evening. When they were finished, they each had further preparation and other members of the Politburo to see before the meeting two days in the future. At eleven o'clock Tuzov descended in the elevator. By then his dinner was cold, a problem easily solved by German microwave technology.

FRIDAY MORNING, MAY 15

The Politburo meeting was scheduled for ten a.m. The members would arrive early, except for the chairman who typically came fifteen minutes late. It was disrespectful to arrive later than the chairman. Therefore, the extra fifteen minutes occasionally saved embarrassment for a minister who might be held up in traffic.

Politburo meetings are held in the left wing of the Kremlin building in a large room with thick red carpets and a long mahogany table. There are twelve seats in the Politburo. Behind the seat occupied by the chairman is a picture of Lenin. In the corner is the flag of the Red Army. Each minister has a single vote. The chairman is the tie breaker.

As Victor Panfilov entered, the ministers all came to their feet.

"Greetings, comrades. You may be seated," said Panfilov in a loud voice as he reached his seat.

Panfilov began the meeting by reviewing the agenda agreed upon at the last meeting. There were several programs under review this month. The Minister of Agriculture had his traditional winter harvest summary and summer forecast report. Next, the

Trade Minister had a progress report on the acquisition of computer technology for various internal programs. Then the Foreign Minister, Savitsky, would follow with a report on the disarmament talks. Finally, the meeting would be completed by a report from the Minister of the Treasury.

There was little discussion about the agenda. Tuzov had not attempted to get the Global Survey program on the agenda, but he was prepared should the subject come up.

The Minister of Agriculture rose to deliver figures that indicated there had been a record winter wheat crop. The major contribution was from improved methods used in insect control and improved hybrids developed by the Ukrainian Agricultural Academy in Kiev and, of course, the unusually mild winter was helpful. That conclusion drew a ripple of laughter from the ministers. The projections for the summer harvest were equally encouraging. After an hour presentation and a half hour of questions from other ministers, the Minister of Agriculture took his seat.

Next, Gregory Gushev, the Trade Minister, rose to deliver a progress report on computer technology.

"Comrades, as I reported in January, we had made an agreement with the Digital American Computer Company to purchase two thousand of their high-performance desktop computers called the Proficient Thirty Two Hundred Computer. You may remember in my last report I stressed how important the acquisition of advanced 32 Bit computer technology is for Russia."

The deal with DACC had started while Gushev was on tour in the United States two years ago. He saw the computer's impressive speed and graphics. Strangely, there wasn't much software available at that time. The scientists at IKI Space Center where the equipment would be used would find the lack of software no problem. In two years, Savitsky was convinced Russian scientists could copy and begin production of their own Proficient Thirty Two Hundred Computers.

"I am pleased to report the Americans have begun delivery of the hardware on schedule."

"That's not all they are delivering on schedule," interrupted Tuzov.

"What do you mean by that?" asked Panfilov.

"I have a secret report here that shows the Americans are meeting the deployment schedule for the Global System," he responded.

"Does that mean we are falling behind?" asked Panfilov, his curiosity aroused.

"I am sorry, but yes, it does," replied Tuzov, rising. "The Americans have scheduled a test demonstration in mid-October before we can finish the deployment of our Shadow Defense system. It is possible that during this demonstration they may discover the minor, but obvious, disturbances that our Harvest Satellite System makes over the Mediterranean. Focusing on those anomalies could lead those well-meaning scientists to discover our Harvest Satellite System. Discovery of any one of our stealth satellites will put the others in jeopardy," concluded Tuzov.

There was a general reaction of surprise from the members not already familiar with the report. Panfilov was first to speak.

"I find that disturbing. The intent of our Shadow Satellite program was to prevent discovery of our Harvest Program. When we started, we had sufficient time to deploy our satellites. Over the past six months I've watched what was a comfortable lead dwindle to a miserable second place. Is this the work of a first class space program, one that delivers objectives on schedule, or is it something less than first rate?" Panfilov let the question hang in the air for a moment, then he turned to Lichev. "Minister Lichev, is there some way you can beat the American launch schedule?"

Lichev straightened in his chair and sorted through his notes. His answer was previously prepared.

"I have learned from our space chief, Arthur Savelin, that we are barely able to assure the completion by the end of March next year. I can see no possibility of speeding the deployment any further. We simply do not have enough Shadow Satellite systems completed to put in space. Further, we are not certain that all the problems with our Vega rocket are behind us. Regrettably, I must conclude that if everything remains on its present schedule, we will be too late," replied Lichev.

There was a ripple of comment among the ministers. Lichev reached for the water pitcher and poured himself a glass. Panfilov continued.

"Is there any way to save the program, or do we accept the loss of all the progress we have made over the last two years?" asked Panfilov. There was an embarrassing silence among the ministers. Tuzov cleared his throat.

"There is one way that might slow the Americans down," replied Tuzov.

"Somehow, I suspect you are about to suggest a way," said Panfilov.

"You are correct. It involves some risk, but we know from the first Harvest disaster we possess a weapon that can make very poor weather for Cape Canaveral. Judging from the size of the storm we created during that first Mediterranean experiment, we could easily delay them past the November deadline," said Tuzov.

Savitsky was shocked at the suggestion. He jumped to his feet.

The Foreign Minister came from an old Russian family and was even remotely related to Lenin. He was enamored with Western dress and had a fascination for automobiles and appliances manufactured in the West. He spent much of his time traveling as his position required.

"We must not be involved with manipulating the American weather. It is bad enough we risked our own. If we are exposed, the consequences will be disastrous. All the time spent negotiating the technology exchange with the Americans will be lost. We would be plunged back into the Cold War again with little hope of any change through the rest of the century!"

Lichev and Tuzov had anticipated Savitsky's reaction and had secretly lobbied for votes during the last two days. The majority of the members was already decided. The vote would be close, but both felt with Panfilov's assistance they would have their way.

The subject was argued for two hours. In the end, it was Panfilov who swayed the undecided members with an impassioned speech. He contended hotly that after seventy-five years of being in second place in the eyes of the rest of the world, it was now the Soviet Union's turn to achieve her destiny. The final vote was in favor of developing a plan to use the Harvest System to delay the Americans.

"Then we have agreed that the Defense Minister will develop for our review next month a plan to insure the Harvest Satellite System will not be detected by the west, and the KGB will insure no leaks about the mission of the Harvest Program," summarized Panfilov.

TUESDAY, MAY 19

Arthur Savelin sat in his vast office just outside the large oval reception area at the hub of the research buildings at IKI. His program chief, Vladimir Ustinov, sat in front of his desk. Savelin was reviewing Ustinov's report, which was to be the basis of his response to the Politburo in the morning.

"And you contend the West does not possess the equipment sensitive enough to pick up the satellite on radar, yes?" asked Savelin.

"Absolutely. The West has never suspected we had anything to do with that mess from the first Mediterranean experiment, nor do they suspect the lower level weather modification work we have been doing for the past two years. As for our satellite, the locations and capabilities of their radar systems are detailed in my report," replied Ustinov confidently.

Ustinov was delighted with the recent attention. Eighteen months ago he was promoted to Chief of the Harvest Program. Its previous disaster had made it, in most respects, a dead program. Since he took over, he had worked hard to improve its image. Through careful work, not to mention the exhaustive research completed by the program's former head, he had turned it into a resounding success. Now, he was suddenly in the center of attention with a real chance to prove himself. Ustinov felt this was a once in a lifetime opportunity.

"Do we have sufficient hardware to complete the objective?"

"Yes, we have ample reserves of Xzhylene gas, two launch vehicles, and additional replenishment vehicles. In fact, we have more than twice the hardware necessary," replied Ustinov confidently.

"Are there any permanent effects from the heavy use of the system that could be traced to us?" asked Savelin, his eyes narrowing on Ustinov. This was a critical question Savitsky was sure to ask.

Ustinov shifted his position, and without meeting Savelin's gaze, responded. "You know there are no known permanent effects. The system has been extensively tested in the laboratory by our former chief, Lebedev. He found the cause of the instability. With this new knowledge, we now have complete confidence the system will produce large tropical disturbances and the Xzhylene gas will quickly dissipate in the atmosphere without a trace."

Ustinov's response was not complete. There was possible reason to delay further use of the Xzhylene gas until additional testing could be completed, but by that time Ustinov's chance would be gone. He preferred to take the risk if the gain warranted it.

Savelin was satisfied. He felt confident his young and ambitious assistant would be able to deliver the storms requested. He intended to present a positive report to the Politburo and fully expected the plan would be approved. Most probably, Ustinov would be launching an additional Harvest Satellite in the very near future.

• Chapter 3 •

GULF OF TONKIN
FRIDAY, MAY 23, 1980

Three hundred feet beneath a choppy navy blue sea, the *USS Stingray* was cruising southwest at fifteen knots. She was headed for the coast of Vietnam, having left Subic Bay in the Philippines the previous day. The *Stingray* was an attack submarine. Her primary mission: electronic espionage.

In the wardroom of the *Stingray*, a briefing was just beginning. At the head of the table stood Captain Robert Jessel, commander of Navy SEAL forces, Philippines. At the foot of the table sat Lieutenant Keith Maddox and to his right Lieutenant Joseph Scott. Four other officers sat in two groups across from each other at the sides of the table. They were Lieutenant Junior Grade Allen Winn, LTJG Daniel Dashford, LT Joseph Scott, LTJG William Crawford, and LTJG David Yahner. All six men were Navy SEALS reporting to the captain.

Behind Jessel a large chart of Da Nang harbor was taped to the wardroom bulkhead. Jessel stood about five foot eight with a trim build, short red crew cut hair, blue eyes, and pointed chin. He possessed a powerful energy like an electric light. It was dormant until things got tough, and then the wattage glowed. His reputation as a living legend circulated in the Navy based on the fact that Jessel got things done; one way or another, regulation or slightly non-regulation, he got things done. He had an intent expression on his face as he spoke.

"Gentlemen, I know I have kept you in the dark about the nature of this mission. As I previously told you, we are going to salvage important equipment from a harbor in Vietnam. Now you will get the full story. After I have explained the mission, any of you who wish to back out may still do so. Is that clear?"

The unofficial leader of the SEAL teams, Lieutenant Maddox, a man who did not beat around the bush, spoke first.

When standing, he had a slender six-foot frame, square shoulders, light brown hair chronically worn slightly longer than regulation, a full sensuous mouth that turned down at the corners, all of which gave a first impression of capability. But the eyes showed more than that. Framed by horn rimmed glasses when he wasn't wearing contacts, the pale blue eyes showed the adventurer lurking inside. A man who could be dangerous and a man you wanted on your side.

"Yes, but we all know you well enough, Captain. We know this one is important. You wouldn't have spirited us away in such a secretive fashion if it weren't. Therefore, it's a foregone conclusion, we are all in."

Although Jessel was no longer a ship's captain, his men found it an easy custom to call him Captain, as it was also his rank. Using his first name didn't convey the same amount of respect. Jessel had had a long and successful career; he was not only experienced in intelligence work, but was also a Navy SEAL. He had the ability to bring out the best in men by developing teams. Tonight he was addressing two of his most experienced teams. Each man was an expert in his own way with a proven performance. This job required it.

"OK, enough of the preamble. The area in question is Da Nang harbor." All eyes rose and looked directly at him. The room was quiet. "The prize we are after is aboard a wreck in the bottom of the harbor."

"You don't mean the wreck of the *Hancock*?" interjected Keith almost immediately.

"You got it, Maddox. What do you know about it?"

"I was an advisor in El Salvador when she blew up," Keith answered quietly. "I remember the newspaper reports. Two of her crew drowned and were never recovered. The wreck was pretty much worthless, and I think, there wasn't even a salvage attempt because she was scheduled to be scrapped anyway." Keith smiled slowly at Jessel and raised his eyebrows. "Is my memory right?"

"That's most of it. But what you don't know, is there were two ASROC nuclear warheads left on board," returned Jessel, raising his eyebrows while tilting his head slightly forward.

For a moment the wardroom was silent. Only the sound of dishes rattling in the nearby galley could be heard.

"Ho—ly shit!" was Keith's slow response.

"How could that happen?" asked Lieutenant Scott.

Joe Scott was stocky. He worked out regularly—as he did everything—in a disciplined manner. He had curly chestnut hair and twinkling, expressive green eyes. Joe was a good Navy career officer. He loved the idea of service, duty, and job well done. He never gave up.

"It seems a certain unscrupulous weapons technician in Subic Bay, by the name of Roger Benson, back in '72 foiled Navy nuclear arms security and managed to remove two ASROC warheads and attempted to ship them to an equally sleazy entrepreneur in Greece. The intended receiver was a weapons chief by the name of Steve Warden. According to this chief, who is now in a maximum security prison, they'd planned to sell the nukes to the PLO in Lebanon. But fortunately for us, the plan of these true blue patriots went sour when the *Hancock* sank."

"So the rumors are true." Keith gave a quiet whistle. "I'd heard there were warheads missing years ago, but nothing ever came of it publicly. Must have caused a couple of strokes for the brass at Subic to know some of their warheads were being delivered into the wrong hands."

"Yes, an admiral was immediately retired while the officers in charge were even more quickly demoted. There's been one of those endless open investigations going on for eight years," Captain Jessel added with a note of disdain.

"So this chief, who is in deep shit, wants to end the search by trading talk for a lengthy sentence?" grinned Winn, a tall dark-haired lieutenant from California. He had volunteered for this mission at the last minute. He was to have been married, but welcomed the excuse of putting it off with the announcement that he had been ordered to return to duty on a highly classified operation. His fiancée cried, and then spent the next three days in bed with him, swept away in the patriot emotion of the situation.

"Yes, it seems his buddy in Subic knew the weapons would be missed, so he disappeared without a trace. We still haven't a clue where his ass is, but his buddy's story has some plausibility. We do know a crate marked 'tools' was shipped by an unknown person to Chief Warden in Greece. It was listed in the *Hancock's* manifest. We think that crate still has the warheads in it," said Captain Jessel.

"But are you sure?" asked Keith.

"No, but it's the best lead we've ever had. We've got no choice but to find out. Don't you gentlemen forget the Vietnamese are still our enemy in most respects. If during our investigation we find the nukes, we have to get them back. You will note I said 'have to,' " Jessel added, staring at each man. "Gentlemen, this is a no-fail assignment."

"So, what's the plan?" asked Keith casually after a moment's silence.

"Here," Jessel pointed with a flourish to the chart on the bulkhead behind him. "This is the closest point of approach that we can get the *Stingray* to the harbor. Here is where the *Hancock* sank in approximately eighty-five feet of water. The distance between is approximately twelve miles. We can't take the *Stingray* any farther than this point because we know the harbor mouth is mined. The plan is to use two inflatable boats to move a salvage team up the river under the cover of darkness."

"Don't the Vietnamese have radar?" interrupted Keith.

"There is no land-based radar. The latest satellite photos indicate five swift boats we left South Vietnamese are still in the harbor. They have radar. Also, three Russian cargo ships are currently offloading supplies at the main piers. The cargo ships have surface radar, but it is not likely any will be in use unless they are getting under way. In the event you encounter either in operation, we have installed a radar scrambler on both boats. It can be activated on the first sweep of your position," replied Jessel. "Maddox will lead the first boat and have operational command. Winn and Dashford will crew." Dashford nodded his enthusiastic assent at the assignment. A fairly recent Naval Academy graduate, he was anxious to add to the list of achievements he had been accumulating ever since he shipped out of San Francisco eighteen months ago. "Should they need help, Joe, you will have the second boat," continued Captain Jessel.

"Sounds like you have a pretty good idea how you want this mission to go, Captain. Mind if we make a few changes as we go along? A little improvisation, shall we say?" Keith asked.

"No, not at all. You all know I encourage 'independent thought' in my command." Jessel smiled. "The photos I mentioned are on board for your study, gentlemen, as are charts of the harbor and surrounding area. After we break up here, Keith, you and your men will need to study these further to develop your plan. What I have covered so far is only a rough cut." Jessel gathered his yellow legal pad, pen, and glasses that he had laid on the table in front of him.

"Aside from the possibility of swift boat radar detection, where can we expect fishing boats and sampans to be concentrated?" asked Dashford.

"Good question," replied Jessel. Dashford glowed with satisfaction, while Jessel continued. "At night there are usually two harbor concentrations of small craft here and here." Jessel pointed to two smaller piers on the chart. "There is little traffic after 2200, but by 0500 you can expect several sampans to be on their way out."

"That gives us only five hours to complete the mission. The round trip with our boat will take three hours. Only two hours to extract the nukes." Keith shook his head. "That's awful tight timing, Captain."

"I know, Keith, but if everything goes according to plan," you can make it."

"If ... everything ... goes ... according ... to ... plan," smiled Keith as he repeated each word.

"The backup plan should be for you to break off the attempt

at 0500 and stow the rubber boat in some relatively deserted area. Let's say, for the sake of argument, this swampy area in this back water. Satellite photos indicate the remains of a Navy supply building that could provide cover. You should remain concealed until 2200. Then you can choose to complete your mission or return immediately. I'll leave it to your judgment."

"What should we do with the nukes while we are in hiding?" asked Winn.

"I suggest … as in 'don't bother to come back if you do' … that at no time, do you leave the nukes where the Vietnamese can find them. Bury them, throw them overboard, but do not leave them exposed," snapped Jessel. "Is that clear?" The electricity of the living legend generated sparks.

"What about civilians living in or around the old supply building?" asked Keith, pointing to the outline on the chart.

"We have no indication from satellite photos that there are any, but obviously you must exercise caution approaching the area," Captain Jessel said.

"What's the plan if we are discovered by the swift boats?" Keith continued.

"The best plan is to get to shore and head westward, bury the nukes, and try to find your way back to the coast. Once on the coast, you can use your portable radio gear to communicate with the *Stingray*. We will stand by for at least a week." Jessel paused and cleared his throat. There was an uncomfortable silence while everyone at the table shifted uneasily in their chairs. "That is, should you get into serious trouble."

"By 'serious trouble' do you mean, 'captured,' sir?" Keith asked, again with a hint of a smile.

"To put it bluntly, yes. We will attempt to get you out, but our resources are limited on the *Stingray* and the Vietnamese probably will move you out of the area quickly," Jessel replied in a matter of fact tone.

"OK, Captain, now for the nuts and bolts. How are we supposed to find the nukes and get them off the *Hancock*?" asked Keith.

"I have a complete set of the plans for the *Hancock*," said Captain Jessel, picking up a large parcel of blue prints.

"Interviews with the crew of the *Hancock* indicate the most likely place for the nukes is in a small cargo hold forward on the Reefer Deck. They don't have to be there, so I have brought some under water 'hot spot' detectors to help you locate the nukes by their radioactivity. If you are in the same compartment as the nukes, you should know it," Jessel continued.

Keith frowned. "Do you know what type of bottom the *Hancock* lies on and what orientation she's in?"

"The bottom is mostly muddy sand. I imagine there is a considerable undercut around her because of the tide, so she is probably settled ten feet or so in the sand. To answer your second question, she lies on her starboard side," said Captain Jessel.

"Good. I think with these plans we can devise a way to find and extract the nukes. We'll need some time to get the boats ready because this little adventure will require most of our equipment."

"Time is no problem. The nukes have been there eight years. Another day or two won't matter. Also, you will want to wait for a dark night. There will be a new moon the day after tomorrow, but no forecast yet for overcast conditions. We will probably have to wait a few days anyway," said Jessel.

"OK, Captain, I think we have the picture. I want some time for all of us to become familiar with the area and with the layout of the *Hancock* before we prepare a plan. By day after tomorrow we should be ready to discuss it in minute detail," said Keith.

Jessel knew it was time for him to leave. The men had to create their own plan. He had done his part presenting them with the best information available. That was the easy part. These were hand-picked men—a unique bunch. They had to deal with the missing information, the kind that often means the difference between life and death. For his men, the planning was just beginning, but for Captain Jessel, the worrying was only to get worse.

SUNDAY, MAY 25

Cruising off the coast of Vietnam, the *USS Stingray* neared the location previously known as the Demilitarized Zone. Her course kept her just outside the international limit while barely keeping steerage way at three knots. The sun was just setting on the immense sand dunes of the mile-deep beach of the Vietnamese coast. In the distance, several sampans with their one-cylinder engines peacefully beat a steady slow course southward. The air was calm, and for the first time in a week the sky was overcast. The gently rolling sea presented a tranquil scene suitable for a postcard.

Joe Scott and Keith Maddox paced the deck as they reviewed their plan with Captain Jessel around a compact table in his stateroom.

Keith leaned forward and put his hands on the table. "As you suggested, we're waiting for the first dark night to begin our assault on Da Nang harbor. I'll lead the first boat. Joe will remain at the harbor mouth with the second boat. He will be in radio contact should we need help." He spoke quickly. The sardonic humor of their previous meeting was gone. Keith was getting down to business.

"If things go bad, I will have an M-60 machine gun and a rocket launcher on the boat ready for use. The intent will be more to create a diversion so Keith and his men can get out," added Joe.

Keith continued, "At 2215, we will begin our approach from the *Stingray*. By 2340 we should be entering the mouth of the harbor. Joe will stay behind while my crew and I will continue to the wreck site. We plan to use the portable Loran system to position us within a hundred feet of the wreck. Using the recording fathometer we will find her. We will use a grappling hook to anchor to the wreck and then prepare to dive. We should be diving by 0200."

He unfolded a blueprint of the bow of the *Hancock* and pointed to the bow hatch.

"Our route of first choice will be to enter from the deck hatch and descend the ladderway into the small hold. If for some reason the hatch is jammed or is covered with debris, there is another way aft through the topside watertight door on the port side. We then will proceed down this ladderway to the refer deck. From here we can reach the cargo hold through the watertight door. If both routes fail we will use the torch to cut through the deck around the hatch."

"That will take some time to cut through the outer deck, won't it?" said Captain Jessel frowning.

"Unfortunately, you're right. It will take at least an hour to make a hole large enough for a man to pass through. By then we will be committed to stay ashore for the day," nodded Keith.

"What is your plan if you have to stay the day?" Captain Jessel frowned again.

Keith cleared his throat and explained the plan he and Joe had developed. "The closest, least populated shore is north where, as you can see, the water gets very shallow. The bottom is probably muddy also. If we're discovered we'll just have to throw the warheads overboard and hope the Vietnamese never find them. Assuming we make it to shore, there are large palm trees where the bank is undercut. We plan to hide the boat among the trees and reeds and cover it with camouflage netting. Then we move the warheads farther inland, bury them, and find shelter in the abandoned Navy warehouse. As soon as it's dark again we'll retrieve the warheads and wait till 2200. The harbor will be quiet, and we then make our exit."

"What if things don't go as planned while you are in the harbor?" Jessel probed.

"Keith and I have worked out a message code to be used by our portable VHF gear. If he is in any trouble, he is to use the code words 'aw nuts' on frequency. That's my cue to enter the scene with all stops out. The machine gun isn't worth much but the rocket launcher can take out a swift boat pretty nicely," said Joe with a grin.

"OK, gentlemen, the plan looks good enough under the circumstances," said Jessel, lowering his voice and leaning forward. "There are things I feel I should warn you about."

"What are they?" asked Keith, looking up from the chart while tapping his ball point pen on the pad in front of him.

"First," Jessel again cleared his throat, "if you get captured, I am not sure we will be able to do much to help. We're not really at peace with Vietnam yet and any military action would require presidential approval. In view of our recent hostage rescue fiasco in Iran, I'm not sure our president will want to risk it again. He may be busy with human rights issues somewhere else. Is that understood?" asked Jessel, looking Joe and Keith directly in the eyes.

"That doesn't leave me with a warm and secure feeling," Keith mused, hoping no one noticed his voice faltered ever so slightly.

"Me, neither." Joe shook his head meeting Jessel's eyes.

"I know how you feel, but not every president has the guts to back our people on the edge to the limit. I'm not sure, but I suspect we could come up short if this gets messy, so both of you use extreme care," replied Jessel.

"What's the second thing?" Joe asked, putting his arm across the back of the empty chair next to him, tapping his foot slowly on the deck.

"The second thing is the Chinese. They're massing troops along the Vietnamese border again. Our intelligence feels they might invade sometime in the next month. What that probably means is, the Vietnamese will be on an increasing state of readiness. Obviously, the sooner you get the nukes up and out of the harbor the better," replied Captain Jessel.

"Understood, Captain, we'll keep that in mind and try to get this job done nice and neat the first night. We've got some last minute preparations to complete before we arrive at the departure point, and only two hours to get it done, so Joe and I had better get going." Keith snapped his ball point pen closed and rose.

"Good luck to both of you," Jessel said softly. "I will be here smoking cigars every minute you are out there. My problem is, I don't smoke normally." He smiled at them.

"Thanks, Captain." The three stood awkwardly for a moment, exchanging glances. Then Keith put his pen in his clipboard, gathered up the chart and blueprints, and moved toward the door.

"Keith," said Jessel quietly, "isn't your hair beyond regulation length? The girls may like it but this is a combat—not comfort—assignment. Look the part, sailor."

"Yes, sir, Captain," Keith answered, saluted, and disappeared down the passageway.

Two hours later, the *Stingray* slowed to three knots as she eased up to the surface five miles outside Da Nang harbor. The night was almost totally black with only a few stars to be seen in the mostly overcast sky. In the distance, the lights of the inner harbor could be seen making long glistening trails across the water. As the *Stingray* cut the dark waters, the bioluminescence of the small sea life in the *Stingray's* wake seemed almost too bright, enough to give away the *Stingray's* location. The temperature was still in the eighties and the air hung heavy and humid. The *Stingray's* conning tower rose slowly above the water, and the sea parted over her deck. In seconds, the bridge watch was topside in the conning tower. The *Stingray* was now at dead stop and running silent.

A single sweep of the *Stingray's* surface radar revealed an empty sea. Captain Jessel turned from the radar repeater and gave a thumbs up approval to Keith and Joe for the mission to commence.

Keith, his face blackened for camouflage, was the first man on deck, his wetsuit feet padding softly on the wet surface. In a moment Allen Winn and Daniel Dashford, clad in similar garb, joined him. They assembled wordlessly and inflated their boat while Joe and his crew made theirs ready. Once both boats were inflated, they immediately launched.

Keith's crew first stowed the diving gear, then the cutting torch, two new M-21 rifles, ammunition, diving tools, camouflage fatigues, some food and water, and finally, the electronics.

Keith's boat carried a Loran, VHF Radio, recording depth finder, and hot spot detector. A hot spot detector is used to find sources of radio activity. It contains an advanced scintillator tube that converts the momentum from particles given off by radiation into photons or light. The light is then amplified by a series of photo multipliers till the light energy can be converted into an electrical signal. The instrument is very sensitive.

Joe's crew loaded their boat with a M60 machine gun, cases of ammunition, two M-21 rifles, a LAW rocket launcher, and a radio.

Each boat was powered by a newly developed sea battery that supplied electrical energy for a high torque electric outboard motor. The boats, fully loaded, could do twenty knots in calm seas. Tonight there was a slight chop.

Keith took the lead as both boats floated noiselessly away from the *Stingray*. Captain Jessel couldn't be sure, but he thought Keith turned and waved a salute as he sped away. Jessel wondered if he had sent his men on an impossible mission. Too many things could go wrong. The inflatable boats were so fragile they would sink on the first provocation. If they lost their boats, there was no way home ... if there was any trouble gaining access to the *Hancock*, the hatch maybe, or sand blocking the entrance ... valuable time would be used ...

The darkness soon completely obscured the boats. Captain Jessel walked slowly back to the conning tower as the bridge watch went below. When the last man disappeared, the hatch was secured. Seconds later, the *Stingray* quietly slipped beneath the waves. Jessel smiled to himself, remembering he'd again noticed Keith's hair. It was, of course, still non-regulation length when he donned the hood of his wetsuit moments before.

Both boats made fair headway over the choppy sea. The water became smooth as they reached the mouth of the harbor. Keith slowed to a stop and waited for Joe's boat to catch up.

As he came alongside, Keith whispered, "OK, Joe, this is where you stay." Keith pointed south. "Looks like there is some cover over there on the south bank for you to conceal yourself should a gook gun boat show up."

"Roger. I'll monitor your frequency. If anything comes up we'll give you warning," said Joe. No one was smiling.

"OK good, buddy, you watch the back door, we'll be returning in a flash with the nukes." Keith grinned, changing the mood. They knew the mission wasn't going to be that easy, but both chuckled.

"Hey, Keith?"

"Yeah, what?"

"Take care. Don't let some asshole gook get you!"

"I'll just kick ass and take names!" retorted Keith with a stony face. With that, he slammed the controls into forward and disappeared into the harbor night.

Keith could now see the piers where the three Russian ships were tied. Each was well-lit. To his right, there were two clusters of sampans, several with lights glowing from their sterns as they rhythmically bobbed in the water.

Keith quickly flipped the switch on the Loran. The system used satellites to determine a ship's position by precisely measuring the delay required for the radio beam to reach the receiver. By using multiple satellites, two numbers are acquired, each representing a delay. These numbers correspond to two lines, which intersect on a chart. Keith knew from the harbor chart what numbers were required. He simply drove the boat in the proper direction till the numbers equaled those on the chart marking the wreck.

A half hour later, the Loran's twin digital display matched the wreck numbers. Keith whispered to Allen and gave him the hand signal to throw the marker float overboard. A weight attached to ninety feet of line sank as the float spun on the surface. Keith switched on the recording fathometer with an illuminated LCD display and began to make ever widening circles around the float. When the float was almost out of sight in the darkness, the hull of the *Hancock* first registered on the fathometer. A few minutes later, after multiple passes across the hull, Keith found the bow. He nodded to Dan to drop the boat's big grappling hook overboard.

The hook gracefully disappeared into the darkness below. The anchor line played out for a minute, then went slack. Keith put the electric motor in reverse and began dragging the hook over the wreck of the *Hancock*. With a slight jerk, the anchor line drew taut. Keith immediately cut the motor. The boat swung slowly with the incoming tide, firmly attached to the *Hancock*'s bow rail.

By prior arrangement, the crew had agreed Keith and Allen would be first to go under, leaving Dan to warn of approaching danger. If warning was required, Dan was to pulse the motor three times. Its high pitched whine could easily be heard on the bottom.

They were wearing thin wetsuits, partly for warmth and partly for camouflage. Keith donned his fins, regulator, mask, and tank.

Both men had large buoyancy compensators that could be filled with air to help lift the warheads to the surface. Keith picked up the diving tools. Allen picked up the hot spot detector.

Keith fell backward into the water with a splash. Allen followed. Keith switched on his light, its brilliant pencil beam momentarily blinding him. Da Nang harbor provided far from the best of conditions. The water was cloudy, with visibility of barely five feet. Even with their lights on, Keith and Allen found it easy to imagine Great White Sharks, skates, groupers, and other big and uninvited guests just beyond the limit of visibility. Diving at night under the best circumstances can be a frightening experience.

Keith was the first to find the anchor line. He glanced at his watch, 0200, two hours to finish and start out. He then swam toward the bottom. Allen followed with light and hot spot detector in hand, using his fins to propel himself downward.

When they reached a depth of sixty feet, the water temperature suddenly dropped. They were passing through the thermocline. Here the visibility got better as it extended to ten feet, aided by fresh sea water from the incoming tide.

At eighty-five feet, Keith saw the handrail of the *Hancock* with the grappling hook attached. A large school of fish swam back and forth through the rail, nibbling sleepily as they passed. Keith stopped a moment to orient himself, then they started forward and downward over the sloping deck toward the bow hatch. The deck was now a mass of tangled line covered with sea life. The line was fish netting, likely left from an unlucky fishing boat that had dragged its nets too close to the bow. The fisherman had probably been attempting to catch the plentiful fish that always surround a wreck.

Giving a thumbs up sign, Allen joined Keith and they began to cut the netting with their knives to clear the way to the bow hatch. The black mussels encasing the netting resisted their efforts and slowed their progress. Each section of netting had to be cut before it would release its grip on the wreck. Some of the stronger line was a half-inch thick.

Fifteen minutes slipped by as they finished clearing the netting sufficiently to find the hatch cover. Cutting the hatch clear took another five minutes. Keith checked his watch. There didn't seem to be any way to speed things up.

Using the wrench, Keith tried the hatch. Apparently, it had been dogged down. With great effort, he managed to get the encrusted bolts to turn one-by-one until the dogs finally fell away from the hatch cover. Again, he tried the hatch. It would not budge. He took the crow bar from the bag of tools. Placing one end of the crow bar under the lip of the hatch and grabbing the netting with his right hand for support, he used all the strength in his arms to pry the hatch open. Still it would not budge. Keith, thinking the hatch might be held by sea pressure, put his light on the edge of the hatch while he tried to break the vacuum with his knife. Keith realized the hatch was welded shut!

Close examination showed a bead of weld around the entire circumference of the hatch. Entry through the hatch was hopeless. "Shit," mouthed Keith to himself.

Their air supply was too low to attempt entering the *Hancock* by the watertight door. As the fish continued their lazy circle near the hatch, Keith pointed upwards with his thumb and Allen nodded. Disappointed, they began a slow ascent to the dark surface above. As Keith rose, his light caught the tail fin of what must have been an eight-foot blue shark, proof that his imagination wasn't completely over-active. Unconsciously, he froze until the fin disappeared from sight and he continued silently upward.

Back on the surface all was peaceful. Joe had radioed a warning that a sampan was entering the harbor, but the sampan had passed without noticing the inflatable boat in the darkness.

"Did you get the hatch open?" whispered Dan. He could already see they didn't have the nukes.

"No, the goddamned thing is welded shut! I guess the old heap of rust must have been warped and they couldn't keep it tight. They probably figured it was too old to replace like it should have been," growled Keith.

"Get your gear on, Dan. It's our turn to try the door. I'm going to get a second tank," said Allen as he moved to the stern of the boat, reaching for a full tank.

Allen was not fond of the idea of penetrating the old wreck at night. He knew well enough what lay in wait for them on the Reefer Deck. A friend of his had penetrated deep into a wreck on the Mid-Atlantic Coast in an attempt to collect china from a sunken ship's galley. He found the galley and the ship's china, but in the process of stuffing the china into his bag, he stirred up the silt from the rotten food in the pantry. In the semi-darkness, his friend made the fatal error of swimming upward in the turbid water to a small port hole where the only light entered. In doing so, he was completely disoriented and never found his way. After fifteen minutes in shear panic, his air ran out. Allen was in the recovery party. He found his friend in the pantry the day after he drowned. The crabs had already started on the corpse. He would never forget the sight.

He led the way as Dan followed down the anchor line. He was still carrying the hot spot detector, hoping this time to get some use out of it. Dan had the tools Keith had carried previously. A glance at his watch showed it was 0230. When he reached the Hancock's handrail, he waited for Dan, who was always a little slower in clearing his ears on descent. When Dan arrived, Allen went aft along the port deck till the bulkhead appeared. In the center of the bulkhead, he found the first watertight door. It was tightly shut, the Hancock's damage control party had made sure of that. Dan worked the stubborn dogs with the wrench till each fell away. Allen pulled on the door's handle. It opened, spewing a considerable amount of silt.

Allen took a reel of light line out of Dan's bag of tools. He tied the line to the door handle and started to reel it out as he descended the ladderway. He intended to use the line to guide himself back out of the wreck. Dan followed, holding the line. Visibility was less than one foot. Allen swam downward for about twenty feet. Suddenly, Allen's mask slammed into the silt on the deck at the bottom of the ladderway. His mask filled with water. Immediately, he started choking from the water in his nostrils. He stayed calm with all the resolve he could muster. Then he pressed the purge button on his regulator. That cleared his mouth and nose. Next he cleared his mask.

In a moment of panic, he realized he had lost the reel. Something big grabbed his arm in the darkness! It must be a shark. He raised his light in a vain attempt to protect himself from the unseen enemy. With a rush of relief he recognized the unknown threat to be Dan holding his arm. Relieved, Allen felt childish about his fears. Dan picked up the reel and handed it to Allen with a firm, affectionate punch to his shoulder.

Shaken and breathing heavily, Allen rechecked his bearings. They were on the Reefer Deck. The watertight door leading to the cargo hold should be to the left. He swam left. The door was very thick.

Realizing this must be the door to the walk-in refrigerator, Allen reasoned the small cargo space must be only a short distance beyond.

Dan followed as Allen led the way. Their fins stirred up copious quantities of silt from the rotted refuse. Visibility became almost nil. Fighting thoughts of the paralyzing memories of his treasure hunting friend, Allen felt his way along the bulkhead. At last, he found the familiar shape of a watertight door. Thank God! This time the dogs were not tight, and easily turned with the wrench.

Allen tried to open the door. No luck. He quickly took out the large crowbar and tried to pry it open. The crowbar kept slipping from the metal around the door. Both Allen and Dan tried to pry it open together, Allen using the crowbar, Dan using the large wrench. Still, the door would not open. Apparently, a very heavy object was behind the door forcing it to remain closed.

Looking at his watch, Allen considered abandoning the attempt when he remembered the hot spot detector. He switched it on and pointed it toward the door while he illuminated its dial with his light.

Allen concentrated on the readout while sweeping the detector from left to right. He discovered a slight reading as he pointed the detector toward the starboard side. Something behind the door was radioactive. The warheads must be there!

Again, Allen realized he would have to return to the surface empty-handed. At least the attempt had been partially successful. Now they had confirmed that the warheads were actually in the hold. He turned to Dan and, with a thumbs up signal, he indicated it was time to go up. Carefully, Allen began reeling in the line as he swam toward the upper deck watertight door in the darkness. Dan was right behind him.

Once back over the main deck of the *Hancock*, Allen quickly found the anchor line. As he began his rise to the surface, he switched off the light. It would not do to flash the lights near the surface this late in the morning. Already, things were coming alive in the harbor. In the distance, Allen could hear the low pitched throb of an inboard engine probably moving a sampan out of the harbor with the outgoing tide. As his depth reached ten feet, he paused to decompress. Each man on Keith's team had his own decompression computer. Allen's now indicated a ten minute wait was necessary before he surfaced. Dan, who had spent less time underwater, could immediately surface. Keith was waiting to help him aboard.

"Did you find the warheads?" asked Keith when he got Dan into the boat.

"No," said Dan, wiping the water off of his face. "The watertight door was jammed shut, but Allen got a reading on the hot spot detector that says they're there."

A few minutes later, Allen finished his decompression and reached the surface. Keith had been looking through a starlight scope at a sampan that was making way for the harbor entrance. It was still too dark to be seen by the naked eye, but it would soon be light enough.

Allen slowly climbed aboard, tired from the exertion under water and fatigued by the tension of the mission.

"Allen, we have a tough decision to make. It's getting light on the eastern horizon and we won't have enough time to use the torch and then get out of the harbor. We have to decide whether we stay the day or break off the attempt now," said Keith.

"Keith, I think you can get the deck cut in less than an hour. I'm afraid we'll have to wait another week for a dark night like this and by then the moon will be on the increase, cutting into our working time. We know the Chinese are planning something. Hell, that's got to increase security in this harbor. I'm for giving it one last shot, even if we have to spend the day ashore in this shit hole," said Allen.

"How about you, Dan?" asked Keith.

"I'm for it. I really don't like this night diving bit. Let's get it over with and get the nukes out of there now," replied Dan.

Keith was glad they felt that way. He felt things couldn't have gone any worse below. Now there wasn't enough time to cut through the deck, retrieve the warheads, and get out of the harbor. He didn't want to take the responsibility for staying all by himself. He had a good team. They were both good men and they were committed to completing the job they'd started.

"OK, then we are committed to staying."

Keith picked up the radio. "Sister, this is brother, school is out, baby is still in church."

These were the code words that meant Joe was to return to the *Stingray*; the warheads hadn't been retrieved and they were committed to spend the day ashore.

In a second, Joe's reply came. "Brother, this is sister. Roger, school is out, too bad but good luck, out."

"OK, gentlemen, I think we'd better get the torch equipment overboard," said Keith.

In a minute, the tanks and hoses of the torch system were overboard and sliding down the anchor line. Next, Dan and Keith donned fresh tanks and prepared for the final descent of the anchor line. Keith was forming a plan to minimize their chance of discovery.

"Allen, when we get to the bottom, I'll release the grappling hook. I want you to tie all your diving gear up with your weight belt so it will sink. Then throw it overboard. Dan and I will do the same when we're finished. I want everything associated with diving on the bottom tonight. If we're discovered, I want our cover story to agree with what's left on the boat," Keith explained.

The cover story—worked out by mutual agreement between Keith, Allen, and Dan—was that they were American mercenaries paid by the rich father of an American draftee to find the remains of his son. In keeping with that story they had agreed to avoid the use of firearms.

43

"Next, I want you to take the boat to the north shore as soon as the hook is free. Once you're there, drag the boat into the reeds and spread the camouflage netting over it. Dan and I, if we get lucky enough, will bring the warheads to shore under water. Hopefully, it'll still be dark," said Keith.

Allen quickly got his gear together as Dan and Keith slipped beneath the surface. The way down the anchor line seemed to take forever to Keith. His light, which had shown brightly on the first dive, appeared to be dimmer now. Keith realized the tide had turned while he was in the boat; the outgoing water was very turbid. Visibility was limited to two feet. Dan was close behind, trying not to lose Keith as he struggled to clear his ears.

When Keith reached the grappling hook, he almost tore his suit on the sharp flukes before he realized where he was. The two divers found and untied the torch, hose, and tanks and carefully stowed the tanks on the deck. Keith then attempted to free the grappling hook, but the current on the boat was too strong. Putting both his fins on the encrusted handrail and pushing with his feet while pulling with his hands, he finally managed to free the hook. In seconds, he heard Allen start the motor and head for shore. Now they were alone—on the bottom.

Keith took the torch in his left hand and began reeling out the hose as he led the way along the rail to the beginning of the netting. From there it was a short distance to the hatch. There, he gripped the netting between his knees and pressed the ignition switch on the torch. The torch exploded with a bright orange flame and a massive stream of bubbles. Putting the torch to the deck, Keith found a small crack in the deck plate. There he began heating the edge of the seemingly endless jagged metal. Precious moments slipped away while the torch did its work. As Keith waited, he could imagine the sun coming up and their chances of escaping dwindling. Keith stared intently as the metal at last became hot enough. He carefully fed oxygen to convert the stubborn metal to rust. Slowly, the metal began to burn. It was a tedious process cutting an eighteen-inch diameter hole in half-inch steel. Finally, the last piece was cut away. With a feeling of satisfaction, he slammed his fist on the cut metal and it fell slowly into the darkness below. Keith motioned quickly to Dan that he was going in.

Easing his shoulders, tank, and regulator through the hole, he swam downward in a slow circle with the hot spot detector in one hand and his light in the other. The visibility inside was better, perhaps extending to ten feet. Keith could see racks that once carried cargo on both the port and starboard sides. He shivered. He could not dismiss the feeling that he was not alone. Quickly, he flashed his light around the hold. On the aft bulkhead he saw a large partially rotted crate leaning against the watertight door. Something large, and metallic was inside. Keith pointed the hot spot detector toward the crate. He shone his light on the dial. No reading. Looking inside the crate revealed a large crank shaft for a diesel motor.

Immediately, Keith swung the detector toward the starboard side. Now there was a definite reading. As he swam forward, the needle went off scale. Pointing his light in the direction of the radiation source revealed a smashed and rotting crate. Keith could no longer suppress the feeling of dread. As he swam forward, he shone his light inside. What he saw was so shocking he dropped the light.

It took several seconds to retrieve his light. Keith could feel a cold sweat break out all down his back. He considered making a swift exit, but recovered sufficiently to look again.

Perhaps the most frightening thing in the dark for everyone is the fear of the unknown. Keith had a premonition of what was to come the moment he entered the hold. His mind had tried to build a defense against his fear, but the sight of a fully clothed skeleton, complete with a grinning skull, was too much.

Trying to maintain control, again he returned to the skull. Of course it must belong to one of the men lost when the *Hancock* went down. He had to fight emotions now; it was imperative. Respect for the dead had to be pushed aside. Do what had to be done now and feel about it later.

Keith pointed the hot spot detector at the open crate. He had to change to the least sensitive scale to prevent the needle from pinning itself! The warheads had to be in the bottom of the crate.

He had no choice but to remove the skull and set it aside. He then picked up the bones, including those of a hand with a gold band still encircling the third finger, and set them next to the skull. Knowing time was running out he pressed on.

On the bottom of the crate were two metal objects, about eighteen inches in length. Brushing one of the objects revealed the familiar atomic emblem. These were the missing warheads! Despite his feelings of horror only moments ago at the human remains, he felt a sense of elation. They'd found them!

Triumphantly, Keith lifted one out of the crate. He knew Dan had brought two rope harnesses with them in the bag of tools, but Dan was still on the deck above. Keith grasped a warhead by his right hand and rested the pointed end in the notch of his left elbow. He held his light in his left hand and pointed it at the hole he had cut through the deck, then pushed off the bottom. Kicking his fins with all his strength, he just barely made it. Handing Dan the first warhead, he returned for the second. Using the same method, Keith retrieved it and returned to the hole cut in the deck. Dan was ready with the second harness. Then Keith carefully eased himself through the hole.

Back outside the wreck, Keith took one of the harnessed warheads in his left hand and passed Dan the other. They had seventy feet to swim to the surface, each carrying seventy-five pounds of nuclear warhead. Fortunately, they both had buoyancy compensators that could be inflated from their scuba tanks by a push of a button. Keith and Dan left the tools on the bottom with the hot spot detector as they both inflated their buoyancy vests and rose slowly off the *Hancock*.

As they pushed upward in the water, Keith and Dan released air in the compensators to prevent over inflation that would cause them to rush to the surface. Rising too fast could result in a fatal air embolism as air trapped in their lungs expanded. When they reached a depth of ten feet, Keith motioned to Dan to turn his light off and start for shore. Guided by their compasses, they began the long swim.

Looking upward, Keith could see a dimly-lit surface. Now he was tired. He could tell Dan was too by the way he swam doggedly for the shore. Keith compensated for the tide by swimming west against the current. After a half hour of heavy exertion, he was tempted to go to the surface to see where they were, but the steady beat of a motor suggested a sizeable craft was moving in the harbor. Finally, when he was about to give up hope, the warhead he carried struck the muddy bottom. Keith knew they were getting close now. With renewed energy he swam the last hundred feet to shore.

Keith broke the surface under the protection of a wall of reeds at the water's edge. Carefully, he scanned the harbor behind him. The sun was about to rise above the harbor's eastern shore. One of the five swift boats was moving away from the government piers and heading out of the harbor with its radar antenna rotating.

Keith turned to Dan, who had surfaced a couple of feet to his right. "Good thing we moved the boat ashore," he whispered. "We'd be in deep shit if we were in the harbor now with it as light as it is."

"Jesus. Yeah, you're right. Hey, do you see Allen anywhere?"

Almost on cue, Allen whispered hoarsely from beneath the overhanging trees beyond the reeds. "Hey guys, we are in deep shit! We got some bum information from those satellite snap shots. I think they mixed up this place with some other beach miles away. The freaking shore is crawling with nervous-looking gooks!"

Keith and Dan quickly took off their dripping wet suits, wrapped them around their tanks, and loaded the combination down with their weight belts. The equipment quickly sank as it was pushed away from shore. Allen had camouflaged fatigues ready for them. Unmarked as their uniforms were, they looked like mercenaries. They carried no identification, which was consistent with their cover story.

Keith and Dan accompanied Allen to the top of the bank at the harbor's edge. From a well-concealed vantage point under the overhanging trees, they had an excellent view of the once-abandoned Navy warehouse. In the last week the area had undergone quite a transformation. Where there once had been heavy growth of tropical brush, the ground was now clear. Gone too was the war debris left when the ARVN troops retreated. In its place was a newly constructed helicopter landing field.

Keith studied the movement of Vietnamese troops for half an hour. They were in a hurry to get discarded material in the old Navy warehouse cleared to provide space for the new helicopter equipment. Most of the work was being done by hand. A lieutenant was shouting orders. At first, Keith didn't notice a heavy-set Caucasian who stood in front of the lieutenant with his back turned, but when the lieutenant paused to confer with the uniformed soldier, he caught Keith's eye. Taking a close look through the binoculars, he found the familiar red stars, boots, and cap of a Russian Air Force uniform. "So Russian advisors are also involved. Not too surprising considering all the supplies and equipment they're giving away."

"Probably the Vietnamese have run out of space and now are forced to use the old warehouse, despite its damaged condition," said Allen.

"We'd better get those warheads somewhere safe right away so we don't risk getting them captured," Keith said, rising to his feet.

"I think we'd better get them away from the boat as far as possible."

"Good idea, let's move out along the bank away from the warehouse and look for a good hiding spot. But first we'd better cover our tracks here and walk in the water while we follow the bank."

With available palm fronds, they brushed the traces of their footprints from the soft sand. Unfortunately, the tide was going out. It would be a good ten hours before any tracks they left would be covered by the incoming tide. Keith grabbed one of the harnesses and swung a warhead on his back. Allen hoisted the second warhead. Dan shouldered the field pack in which he had stowed the binoculars, radio, ammunition, maps, and the food he had packed the night before. He also picked up the two M-21 rifles, put one on his shoulder, and passed Keith the other. As they looked away from the harbor toward the mountains to the west, they saw several concrete watch towers left over from the U. S. war effort. The towers strung out along the shore at half mile intervals. Each tower had an excellent view of the harbor and their position.

"We'd better be careful and keep out of sight of the watch towers, just in case they're manned again," snapped Keith.

The team headed westward in shallow water along the bank till they came to a small stream. Rather than cross, Keith suggested following it upstream to the west. It skirted a dry rice field. Looking cautiously through the protective screen of reeds, they could see several workers wearing pointed straw hats in the field at the far corner. They were working on an irrigation ditch. Others were harvesting the dry rice. The Americans quietly followed the stream till they passed the rice field and reached a bridge. It was now the dry season and the flow was shallow. They crept under the bridge. Above them loomed the hillside where the remains of a missile launching site could be seen. Around the base there were concrete bunkers with entrances partially left open when they were abandoned. As quickly as they could, the three men climbed the hill and entered a long tunnel leading to the center of the concrete compound.

"Looks like this used to be a Hawk missile site," whispered Allen.

In the center of the missile compound lay a reinforced slab of concrete that covered the missile launching system. The missiles had long since been removed, but under the slab some of the hydraulic machinery that raised the missile platform remained. Keith and Allen slid the heavy warheads off their backs and sat down to rest. Dan, who had brought up the lighter field pack, moved forward to examine the machinery below.

A moment later, Dan summoned them to view the launch platform. Keith and Allen struggled to their feet and came over.

"Looks like I found something here. All this machinery used to be the hydraulics that raised the rocket platform. If I don't miss my guess, the plate in the bottom of the motor pit covers a hydraulic fluid reservoir."

Dan quickly climbed down the iron stairway on the concrete

wall to the bottom where he moved the remains of a heavy pump and examined the manhole cover on the floor.

"Now, if we just had the tools we left on the harbor bottom," Dan muttered while looking for something to lift the cover.

He spied a two-foot piece of steel pipe and inserted one end in a hole in the cover. By using the pipe as a lever, he tipped the cover plate up on its side.

Dan picked up the cover, cast it aside, and peered below. "Just as I thought, there's the reservoir. I suggest we stow the warheads at the bottom and cover the reservoir cap with the scrap machinery."

"Excellent idea," said Keith. "That way with all the reinforced concrete and scrap metal around, the Vietnamese will have a hard time using detectors to find them. They'll have to be right on top of the cover to get a damn reading."

Allen took a step forward. "After we drop them into the oil, how are we going to get them back when we get out of here?"

"Simple," Dan answered, picking up a ten-foot length of hydraulic tubing. "We just bend the end of this tubing into a hook and snag the harnesses. Then we pull them up."

"Simple, clean, smart," said Keith, picking up a warhead and passing it down to Dan.

"Simple and smart, at least," corrected Allen.

They plopped the warheads in the reservoir, placed the cover over the access port, and piled the hydraulic pump and associated scrap metal on top of the cover.

The three men trudged back to the entrance of the access tunnel. They were all exhausted. It had been twenty-seven hours since they had had any sleep. Keith took out the binoculars and studied the road. To his right it led to the Navy warehouse. To his left, the road passed the outskirts of what was once the large U. S. Air Force base at Da Nang. From there, Keith could see the road led to a major concrete highway that followed a railroad track.

"That must be Highway 1 leading north and south," he said, pointing to the road.

"Probably so. We poured a lot of free concrete in this place during the war years. If it's Highway 1, it leads all the way down the coast to Saigon," mused Dan.

"I've had it. I think we should try to get some rest in the high grass over there," said Allen. "From the higher ground we can observe the road and the harbor. That will give us warning if our boat gets discovered."

Keith was only too happy to agree. His eyelids drooped from fatigue. By the time they reached the higher ground, they were bone-tired. Before they all fell asleep, they agreed to post watch. Keith reluctantly took the first two hours. Dan, and then Allen, would follow. Allen opened the field pack and they ate some rather bland tasting field rations. The day was becoming unbearably hot, and despite the shady spot they'd picked, they were all sweating heavily.

"Who packed for this mission? These rations suck!" complained Dan.

"Get off my case! At least you have something to eat," Allen shot back irritably.

They finished their tasteless rations and almost immediately the two weary men stretched out in the soft grass and fell asleep. Quiet snoring soon rose from the grass where they lay.

Keith spent most of his two hours fighting sleep, trying to observe the off-loading of the Russian cargo ships. The work was moving at a frantic pace. Vietnamese soldiers were usually somewhat relaxed and undisciplined under normal circumstances, but today they were working with a purpose. Could it be the Vietnamese were taking the threat from the North seriously? With the help of the Russians, were they hurrying to bolster their store of supplies?

Finally, his watch finished and he gladly stretched out as Dan relieved him. He, too, fell asleep almost immediately. For almost four hours he slept without moving. In the middle of a nightmare, he awoke with a start. He dreamed he was back on the *Hancock* trapped in the small hold with his air running out. All the while, the skull was laughing at him and the bones seemed to rattle even underwater. Allen grabbed him by the leg and gently shook him awake.

"Eeyowl! Huh ... oh shit! It's you, Allen. What's up?"

"They've found our boat!" whispered Allen. "They're organizing a search party. We've got to get the hell out of here—now!"

Keith rose in the grass high enough to see a party of five Vietnamese dragging their boat over the bank. His heart sank. That boat represented their way back. Now their only chance was to move farther inland, and then north and back to the coast. Keith realized they must act quickly and put as much distance as possible between them and the warheads.

Keith noticed the field workers had left a truck on the shoulder just off the road they were on. He formed a plan.

"Dan, how good are you at hot-wiring an old Ford pickup?"

"Piece of cake."

"Good. Allen, do you think the stacked rice will burn?"

"With it is as dry as it is, you bet it'll burn!"

"OK, while Dan gets ready to hot-wire the Ford, you and I will start a fire in the stacked rice down by the stream bed. Once the workers are distracted, we'll break for the Ford while they're putting the fire out."

Keith and Allen slipped silently down to the stream while Dan crept up on the pickup.

I just hope this damn thing runs, thought Dan as he readied his pocket knife for some fast work.

Dan was an Ohio farm boy from Preble County. He'd learned to drive a tractor when he was eight years old. He'd driven his dad's Ford pickup before he was fourteen. When he finally got his license, he was always hot-wiring his dad's truck on Friday night and cruising down the main street of Oxford, Ohio, with his buddies to admire the university coeds.

Across the field, Dan saw the first wisp of smoke. As he watched the smoke build, he heard Keith and Allen approach from behind. The workers hadn't yet noticed the fire. Suddenly, with a shriek an old woman sounded the alarm. In seconds, all the workers moved to extinguish the fire.

Dan slid inside the Ford's cab. His knife slashed at the wires behind the ignition switch. Pushing in the clutch and turning his wrist, he twisted the bare ends of the wires together. The starter kicked. To his immense relief, the engine caught on the third revolution. There was no muffler, and the engine roared. Dan released the clutch. The truck leapt forward.

Keith climbed in beside Dan. Allen quickly jumped in the bed of the truck with the M-21 rifles. As Dan swung the pickup toward the concrete road, the old woman who was the last to arrive at the fire shrieked again. Seconds later, the search party responded with a volley of shots at the truck. One round went through the rear window. Allen lay flat in the truck bed, not returning their fire.

Once on the road, Dan stood on the gas pedal. The old six-cylinder strained with pre-ignition caused by the poorest of gasoline, but in a few seconds and two gears later, they were making a good sixty-miles-an-hour toward Highway 1.

When they reached the junction, Dan shouted above the smoke and racket of the motor, "Which way?"

"Right! To the north!" shouted Keith.

Keith hoped they would be able to go north and then turn toward the coast. As Dan approached the intersection, three bicycles and two army Jeeps came from the south. Dan downshifted into second with a jerk on the clutch as the rear wheels began to break free of the concrete; he gunned the motor, making the turn on two wheels. His turn forced the lead Jeep to swerve and flip off the edge of the road. The second Jeep managed to avoid the first Jeep and began giving chase. Again, Dan stood on the Ford's gas pedal.

With a little coaxing the pickup managed to make eighty before the highway ascended into the surrounding mountain range. The pursuing Jeep was losing ground fast in the dust. As they sped north, Keith noticed the Vietnamese had started repairing the abandoned railroad that ran parallel to the highway. In places where the bridges had been blown up prior to the U. S. involvement, there now stood new timber and concrete.

At the top of a hill overlooking a railroad tunnel, they came upon a dirt road that led west. The pursuing Jeep was out of sight.

"Dan, take the road to the left. Maybe we can lose those guys!" shouted Keith.

Dan swung the pickup to the left. The Ford lurched forward and began bouncing along on the little-used dirt road. Keith looked back through the cloud of dust. The hillside appeared to waver in the heat of the sun. Keith hoped the heat would disperse the cloud.

"We'd better put some distance between us and that Jeep because the dust behind us is a dead giveaway," yelled Keith.

Dan accelerated hard, but not for long. They continued for about five hundred feet past heavy jungle with large bomb craters every few yards before they rounded a curve and found the road blocked by a recent mud slide.

"Shit, there's no way to get around!" shouted Dan, as he threw the Ford in reverse.

Back on the main road again, they could see the pursuing Jeep catching up fast. Dan pushed the Ford up the hill in second gear. The Jeep had the advantage of increased momentum. Conversely, the Ford, after returning to the concrete road, had to accelerate up a steep grade from almost a dead stop. The Jeep was catching up. As the Ford neared the summit, a soldier in the Jeep began shooting. Keith and Allen ducked, but didn't return fire. Fortunately, the soldier's aim was poor and the bullets passed the dusty Ford harmlessly. In a few seconds, they reached the summit and started down. As it accelerated, the distance increased between them and the following Jeep. Soon, the Jeep was out of sight behind a curve and the shots ceased.

A dirt road appeared to the right, but there wasn't time to make the turn. The pursuing Jeep was still too near to risk the possibility that it, too, was a dead end. They continued north on Highway 1. The road was rejoined by the railroad exiting from a tunnel nearby. Keith wondered how long they could travel without running into Vietnamese army units.

He didn't wonder long. As they rounded a corner, they ran right into a railroad work party. Two large trucks were parked across the highway, completely blocking the road. Next to the trucks was a Jeep with a radio antenna sticking above its spare tire.

"That Jeep following us must have radioed ahead," shouted Keith.

Dan skidded the truck off the left side of the highway, trying to avoid the volley of bullets coming from behind the trucks. He drove the truck across the ditch separating the highway from the railroad bed. With a lurch, the old Ford jumped the ditch and landed on the railroad tracks. All four corners of the pickup bounced wildly as its tires bumped over the railroad ties. As they passed the trucks, Keith was shocked to see bullet holes appear in the door next to him, barely missing his right side. Allen was not so lucky. A bullet from an AK-47 pierced the truck bed and the shrapnel lodged deep in his thigh. He screamed in pain as he grabbed his upper leg.

Dan stayed on the tracks until he passed the trucks. He then swung the wheel to the right. The truck lurched wildly as the left wheels jumped over the rail and sped down into the ditch. Dan down-shifted, his right foot flat on the gas pedal. As the engine suddenly gained in revolutions and torque, the rear wheels slid to the left. Dan attempted to put the truck back on the highway. Slowly, the Ford straightened out and accelerated toward the pavement.

"Made it!" shouted Dan, as the truck struck the pavement with the rear tires burning rubber.

Dan never got to shift into high gear. As the truck roared down the highway, Keith saw a lone Vietnamese soldier with a rocket propelled grenade on his shoulder. He saw the flash of the rocket, but could not remember the impact …

FIFTEEN MINUTES LATER

Keith couldn't hear. There was a loud ringing in his ears. The truck was on its right side, the windshield completely blown away. Dan was nowhere to be seen, but the driver's side of the truck had a gaping hole where there had once been a door. Keith could feel multiple cuts on his face from the glass of the windshield, but when he felt his arms and legs, he was relieved to find nothing was broken.

Four uniformed soldiers were standing around the truck examining the weapons and field pack while others carried two stretchers, each with a body, toward a nearby panel truck. One of the bodies was moving, the other was limp and very bloody. Keith couldn't remember what had happened, nor did he recognize the uniforms or the area.

The soldiers returned and, grasping Keith by the arms, pulled him through the hole left by the broken windshield. More from instinct than logic, Keith feigned unconsciousness as he was carried on the stretcher to the truck. In a moment the doors closed. Inside the truck was almost total darkness.

Struggling to orient himself, he slowly heard the sound of the truck's motor over the ringing in his ears. He tried to focus his eyes. Allen was bending over his stretcher.

"God, Allen, are you all right?"

"My leg is ripped open with some metal sticking in it," his strained voice answered. "I'm not sure what else but there are bad burns on my back," whispered Allen.

"How's Dan?" asked Keith.

"We lost him," Allen shook his head slowly. "Poor guy took a direct hit from the RPG."

Allen had been vainly trying to stop the bleeding from Dan's massive chest wound by holding a makeshift bandage over it. It was now soaked with blood. It was obvious Dan had died in the first few minutes after the truck had started moving. Keith closed his eyes. Allen sat and stared at the side of the truck, his face white.

"I hope we're headed for a hospital because that leg needs something," said Keith, trying not to sound alarmed. The leg looked awful.

"I've been able to slow the bleeding by making a compress out of my shirt."

Keith took the remains of Allen's shirt, tore it in strips, and tied them in a new makeshift bandage. "That piece of metal will have to come out, but for now we'd better concentrate on stopping the bleeding."

"There was Penicillin in the field pack. Too bad they put it up front with the driver," Allen nodded. Beads of perspiration were forming above his lip and he was becoming paler by the minute.

"Yeah, things are going from bad to worse. Hell, we've been

in tight spots before. We'll get out of this shit too. We're not at war with the Vietnamese. They'll probably be decent to us," Keith added with a casual shrug. But he suspected the opposite. Decency wasn't high on their captors' list of behavior traits.

Keith had little confidence in the Vietnamese. He had heard appalling stories of their lack of concern for human life during the war years. He knew he and Allen were of little value as prisoners. Little value unless, of course, the Vietnamese learned about the warheads. Keith knew he would have to choose death rather than give that secret up.

Keith was also aware that the fissionable material in the warheads was old by U.S. standards. That meant the Uranium 235 had decayed enough to produce some very "dirty" isotopes. Should the Vietnamese detonate one of the warheads, those isotopes would create fallout levels many times greater than all the atmospheric tests conducted by the U.S. and the USSR combined. Reconstructing the warheads required a fast breeder nuclear reactor. The Vietnamese had no such facility. Keith was prepared to protect the warheads at all costs.

The truck made several quick turns, slowed, and then came to a stop. The doors were suddenly thrown open. Keith and Allen, blinded by the light, held up their hands to shield their eyes as they were pulled out onto the concrete pad of what must have been the air base landing field.

Six Vietnamese soldiers and a sadistic-looking lieutenant stood in a small ring around the men.

The lieutenant spoke in broken English. "What you do here? You lose war years ago!"

Keith began quietly with the cover story. He was doing a good job embellishing it with incidental details. At first there was a puzzled look on the lieutenant's face, but he quickly grew impatient and interrupted.

"If true, you must go official channels!" he screamed.

Keith ignored the high strung lieutenant and continued. "The father was dying. He was a rich man in the oil business and wanted to lay his son's bones to rest in the family plot before the old man died."

With a wave of his hand, the lieutenant cut Keith off. "You lie, American. You with Chinese. You come make war. We have place for you. Soon you talk truth!"

The lieutenant fired a series of orders to the soldiers, who started pushing Keith and Allen toward an old DC-6 now warming up on the apron. Keith put Allen's arm over his shoulder and helped him limp toward the plane.

"My comrade desperately needs medical attention," said Keith to the lieutenant in his deep authoritative voice.

"Doctor maybe come later. You go now!" he shouted.

Keith eased Allen, who was moaning quietly, into the plane and took a seat. The soldiers bound their hands and legs with thick rope. Allen could not help gasping in pain as they roughly grabbed his leg.

Shortly after takeoff, they passed over the ocean and from there, Keith could only guess that they were traveling north toward Hanoi. There was conversation between the soldiers. Keith knew some Vietnamese from a crash course, not this particular dialect, but enough to gather they were concerned by activity in the north. Allen passed out from exhaustion and spent the two hour flight in a fitful sleep.

Keith then remembered Jessel had said they would be moved immediately. Jessel was always right!

Finally, the pilot cut back the engine and came in low over a city. *This must be the area surrounding Hanoi,* thought Keith.

The plane completed a lazy circle over the small airfield, then came in for a landing. As they touched down, Keith observed many large bomb craters on both sides of the runway. Gifts from President Nixon, no doubt.

The plane taxied to a small hangar next to a new control tower with radar and communications antennas. Keith tried to form a plan. The cover story was the best they could do under the circumstances, but would it hold up under lengthy scrutiny? He knew it would not. He'd have to develop a secondary strategy for when his captors suspected the truth.

The plane came to a stop. The guards rose and untied Keith and Allen. Keith helped Allen down the plane's gangway; Allen was really having trouble walking. Outside, they were hastily pushed to a waiting van. Again, the van had no windows. This time, the ride was only fifteen minutes, but there were many turns, which totally disoriented Keith.

The van stopped and the doors opened; Keith found they were in a garage. As he looked around, he could see the large garage door, which was now closed, and a corridor leading away. Their guards took them to a small office down the corridor. There they were confronted by a short Vietnamese officer with pinched lips and glaring black eyes.

"I am Captain Liem Tran," the officer announced with a sneer. "So you are the two I have heard about. I understand you had a problem in our southern latitudes. If you would be so kind to tell me your names and the name of your travel agent, perhaps I can make some alternative arrangements."

"I want first aid for my friend. He's lost a lot of blood and if he doesn't get some attention, infection will set in," said Keith.

"I am not interested in what I can do for you, I am interested in who you are and who sent you!" Captain Tran retorted.

Keith recited the cover story yet again, with Allen gamely filling in some details. Keith could not be sure if they were buying his story or not.

When he finished, Keith stared directly into the eyes of the officer. "We have given you the information you requested. Now, please, some medical attention."

"Perhaps that can be arranged. However, there is no doctor here. Possibly tomorrow morning after we've had a chance to check out your story," Captain Tran said with a slight smile.

He gave the guards an order Keith didn't understand. After they were led from the office, they passed a series of three iron gates, each with a guard. The shuffle of their footsteps echoed down a corridor with eight concrete cells. They were pushed into the last cell.

Keith looked around the cell. It was about eight feet by ten feet and lit by a single bulb hanging from the ceiling. There was no window, only the door. At the bottom of the door was a small metal sliding partition. Two bunk beds stacked one on top of the other, each with a bare mattress, were pushed against the wet wall. The cell had a damp, urine smell. In the corner was a wash basin and a bucket to be used to relieve themselves. The basin was filled with brown looking water.

"Allen, I think we'd better take a look at your leg," whispered Keith.

Allen lay down on the lower bunk. Keith washed his hands, removed the blood soaked makeshift bandage, and began washing Allen's wound with the water. He was alarmed to find red lines already running along the veins leading away from the wound.

"I think it's time to get the shrapnel out, Allen. Do you think you can stand it if I try?" asked Keith.

"Go ahead, Dr. Maddox," Allen said weakly, "But just remember if you mess it up, I'll sue, and I've got a son-of-a-bitch for a lawyer.

What a shitty place to have to do this, thought Keith. He took off his shirt, tore it in two-inch strips, and made a new bandage. Then he examined the wound closely. Biting his lip, he took a firm hold on the jagged shard with his thumb and forefinger. He pulled. The metal would not budge. Allen gasped loudly. Keith took a deep breath and closed his eyes for a second. Again, he took grip on the metal and pulled hard. This time the metal let go, freeing a three-inch sliver of the old Ford's fender. Allen writhed in pain, gripping the filthy mattress for support.

"God, I'm sorry, buddy. I had to pull that hard just to get it out," Keith explained, trying not to let his voice shake.

Allen's wound was bleeding profusely now. Keith took up the new bandage, made a compress, and pressed it against the gushing blood. After an agonizing few minutes, the bleeding finally began to stop. Keith firmly tied the bandage in place with another piece of his shirt.

With a knock the small metal plate at the base of the door slid sideways, revealing a small metal pot. Keith examined it to find it was filled with a thin, foul-smelling gruel. It was now 1900 by Keith's watch, and they had not eaten since early that morning. There were no spoons provided, but he and Allen tried to eat as best they could with their fingers. Later, the pot was removed and the lights went out.

Keith climbed into the upper bunk, completely exhausted. Lying in the dark, he became aware that they were not alone in the corridor. An unmistakable tapping on the walls could be heard. It might be a code, possibly Morse, but it was too faint to decipher and Keith was too tired to fight the overwhelming need for sleep.

FRIDAY, MAY 26

It was nearly two a.m. when Keith awoke with a start. Allen was in trouble. His leg was throbbing and the pain had spread far up his side. When Keith jumped down from his bunk, Allen began thrashing in delirium.

Suddenly, Allen said, "Keith! We can't make it! There's not enough time to get the nukes before morning! We'll be trapped here."

Allen sat upright. His forehead was covered with sweat. Keith got the rest of the water and made a wet compress. Easing Allen back down in the bunk, Keith applied the compress to his forehead, trying to break the fever. Keith continued through the night, applying cool compresses until morning when he changed the bandage. This time, there was a sickening smell.

The morning meal came. Keith was disappointed to find it resembled "son of gruel". Again, he did the best with his fingers and tried to help Allen eat a bit.

At eight o'clock, a key turned in the door. It flew open and two guards entered. They threw Keith two sets of what looked like gray pajamas.

"Put on, now," the first guard hissed.

Keith put on one set and helped Allen with the other.

"You wouldn't happen to have some fresh coordinating underwear to match these trendy pajamas, would you?" Keith asked the second guard.

The second guard stared at him blankly and motioned for Keith and Allen to move out of the cell. Allen couldn't put any weight on his leg. His face was drawn tight with pain. Keith struggled to help him. "OK, so you bastards don't have any fresh underwear, but do either of you have a shoulder to help us?" growled Keith.

The first guard, not understanding the words but seeing the problem, took Allen's other arm and together, the three struggled down the corridor. Again, Keith was vaguely aware of the inmates behind the other doors.

They were brought into a large room. There was a desk with two chairs in front of it, and an additional on the side. Behind the desk sat a heavy-set Caucasian about two inches taller than Keith. Keith immediately recognized the uniform of a Russian intelligence officer. Next to the Russian stood Captain Liem Tran.

"Good morning, gentlemen," purred Captain Tran. "Apparently we didn't communicate well enough yesterday, so this morning I brought you to Captain Nikolai Pronin. He is very interested to meet such distinguished U.S. Navy SEALS as you are, Lieutenant Keith Maddox and Lieutenant JG Allen Winn."

Keith was shocked. How could they know their names? Could the Russian intelligence be that good? Had they made a slip? Was there someone listening to Allen's babbling outside their cell? This was a bad situation. The Russian already knew too much and he looked like he could devise a way to get the rest.

Captain Pronin asked Keith and Allen to be seated. Keith noticed their chairs were shorter than the others and made of hard wood.

Pronin started by offering Keith and Allen a cigarette. Both refused. Pronin lit up and, as the smoke crawled lazily out of his mouth and nostrils, he said, "As I understand it, you had an intense desire to remove some Vietnamese property from Da Nang harbor. Is that not true?"

"No, we are here to recover the remains of a fellow soldier." Keith's heart beat wildly, but he tried to keep his voice flat.

"Yes, I heard your cover story, but I find it strange you show up in Da Nang harbor with a boat that has no shovel, no supplies, no means of transportation. You want me to believe you are on a mission to recover bones?" Pronin raised his eyebrows.

"We planned to find what was needed as we went along, like the pickup truck. If we hadn't had a problem in the mountains with the work party, we would have succeeded." Keith shot back with his eyes locked on Pronin's.

"Nonsense, total nonsense, as you say, bull crap! Lies—that is all you speak," said Pronin. Leaning forward and purposely blowing smoke in Keith's face, he said, "We know you were after nuclear devices. We also know that you probably hid them ashore before you were arrested."

Keith knew pursuing the cover story any further was now pointless. He leaned back. "My name is Keith Maddox, Lieutenant United States Navy, serial number 75 11 72. As a member of the U.S. Armed Forces, I remind you we have fired on no one and that our governments are not at war. I respectfully request to be turned over to U.S. diplomatic representatives and for my associate to receive medical treatment," said Keith.

"It surprises me one so concerned with the health of his comrade would not be more cooperative. But perhaps with a little convincing this can be dealt with quickly," replied Pronin, rising.

At the door, he summoned someone outside. In a moment, a muscular man with drooping shoulders resembling a great ape entered with a coil of rope in one hand.

"Lieutenant, I want you to meet Dima. He is a simple sort, but he has a specialty. He is the opposite of an orthopedic surgeon, you see. Instead of setting bones, he breaks them," said Pronin.

Keith began to sweat and his knees trembled ever so slightly. His face remained unchanged.

"Dima, this man," announced Pronin dramatically pointing to Allen, "has a problem with his leg. Could you offer some of your expertise?"

Victor took a step toward Allen, who was by now looking gray. Victor took the rope and bound Allen to the chair. Then he grasped the ankle of Allen's wounded leg and, placing his foot on Allen's knee, began to twist the leg. Allen shrieked with pain as tears rolled down his face.

"You fucking animal!" screamed Keith, jumping from his chair.

"This is not necessary if you will just tell us where the devices are," soothed Pronin, as he removed a Colt 45 revolver from his desk and pointed it directly at Keith's head. "It's best that you keep your seat while Dima gives you a little demonstration of his talents."

"Don't tell this shit anything!" gasped Allen, his face contorted in pain.

Dima began his work. He twisted Allen's leg harder, the muscles in his beefy arms and leg straining. Allen shrieked. Dima gave a sudden thrust with his massive shoulders; there was a loud, sickening pop as Allen's tibia snapped.

Keith was sickened. He was going to throw up. Allen, fortunately, passed out.

"I am so sorry this had to happen," Pronin again purred. "If you had just been more cooperative, this unpleasantness could have been avoided. Do you have anything to say now?"

"You bastard, my name is Keith Maddox, Lieutenant USN, 75 11 72, and if I ever get the chance, I'm gonna kill you." retorted Keith. Pronin stared at him.

"You won't live that long, Yank! I'm not through with you, but I am going to give you time to reconsider your hopeless position, a little time alone, while we decide what to do with your broken comrade. Take this one back to his cell!" shouted Pronin to the guards outside the office, as he nodded casually toward Keith.

"He goes alone," said Pronin to two guards who had just entered. Then, pointing to the unconscious Allen, he continued, "We are not finished with this one." Blood was running down Allen's leg now, forming a puddle around his foot.

Keith sat on Allen's bunk. He closed his eyes and tried to think. He was stunned by the Russian's brutality and panicked at the idea of Allen, defenseless in Pronin's hands. How much more could Allen take? Keith knew the answer.

Keith's life experiences had shown him that he was at his best under extreme pressure. This situation was extreme by all measures. Slowly, a desperate plan developed in his mind. He had to find a way to get Allen help.

LATER THAT EVENING

Pronin was furious at Captain Tran. He and his cohorts were complete idiots when it came to modern methods of interrogation. Had they brought the matter of the two Americans to his attention immediately, they would both have been in good health. There would have been no need to rush. Still, the whole affair had gone well. It was pure luck that news of a possible U.S. covert operation had come across his desk. A barmaid in Alongepoe City in Subic Bay had reported a conversation she'd overheard. That scrap of information led eventually to more details, and finally to their names.

Both men should have been cared for immediately, instead, one was allowed to become sickened by infection. That lowered his ability to remain conscious and delayed the process. All he had needed was a little stimulant to speed confession and to keep the dying man conscious. Just a small dose of sodium pentothal, nothing exotic. Then that Vietnamese doctor; God, he was glad he didn't depend on them for medical treatment.

What should have been a routine procedure resulted in complete delirium and unintelligible babbling. The man threw up several times before he went completely comatose. No effort could revive him. Now it appeared the incompetent doctor was going to lose his patient.

The focus was now Lieutenant Maddox. He would not be easy to crack. His only real lever was help for his comrade. But his comrade was fast dying … But, wait … The lieutenant doesn't know it. In fact, for a while, they could fake his condition, mused Pronin.

Picking up the phone on his desk, he first called the Russian doctor stationed in their barracks. Then Pronin called Captain Tran and made a short request in Vietnamese. He hung up and pulled a pack of cigarettes out of his shirt pocket, selected one, thumped it on his desk several times, then lit it and took a long drag. Pronin's mind drifted back to his wife, Natasha. They had recently married and he was looking forward to a new assignment. Relocation might mean adequate medical care for her heart condition. He hoped it would be Moscow, but he feared it would be a station in the field where she could not join him, possibly in the new trouble area, Afghanistan. It would be nice to enjoy the good life waiting in Moscow with Natasha. To Pronin, Natasha represented all things pure in the world. He had not had a pleasant childhood and he bore the scars of many a beating from his alcoholic father. It wasn't until he met Natasha that anyone had ever shown real kindness toward him. Because of her heart condition, their lovemaking had to be gentle. This excited Pronin. No amount of affection was sufficient in his desire to please her. They had spent their two-week honeymoon in Odessa on the Black Sea. For once in his life, he had felt at peace with the world. The contrast between his feelings for Natasha and his brutal methods in intelligence never occurred to him, for life had never been kind.

The American lieutenant entered Pronin's office with a defiant look in his eyes. *This one could be very dangerous when desperate,* thought Pronin.

"Lieutenant, please be seated," said Pronin, offering one of the low wooden chairs.

As Keith took his seat, he continued. "It deeply grieves me that your comrade, Lieutenant Winn, is very sick," began Pronin.

"I'm surprised that he's alive," Keith answered.

Pronin wondered if the lieutenant suspected the truth about the inept Vietnamese doctor.

"There seems to be a very simple matter here. You know where the nuclear devices are and we want them. We are prepared to use whatever means necessary, but I needn't emphasize that you may not recover from the effects of our methods," snapped Pronin.

"After what your Neanderthal, Dima, did to Allen, not too much would surprise me from scumbags like you," Keith calmly answered.

Pronin smiled. "Now lieutenant, we know where your boat was found. You had only had a few hours ashore before you stole the pickup truck. From there, your route is known. You had your little accident with the RPG. You must realize we can find the warheads with our detectors. So all we are talking about is a matter of time, and not much of it for that matter." The Russian gave a short laugh and stood.

Keith listened impassively. He knew that hiding the warheads in the hydraulic reservoir was only a temporary measure. Eventually, with a Russian version of the hot spot detector, the Vietnamese would find the warheads. Keith needed to prevent that, but he also needed more time and room to maneuver.

So Allen hadn't broken, thought Keith. He tried not to think about the look on his unconscious face when he'd been taken from the room earlier.

"If I reveal any information, I first want to be assured of immediate medical attention for Lieutenant Winn," snapped Keith.

"That can be arranged," nodded Pronin.

Keith was developing a plan, one which would gain time and possible opportunity. "I cannot tell you where the warheads are because we buried them in a field filled with bomb craters. There must be a thousand excellent hiding places in this field; I know the right place. But, before I show you, I want to see that Lieutenant Winn is getting proper treatment."

Pronin anticipated the request and had his staff and the Russian doctor standing by for a charade. Little could be done for Lieutenant Winn, but they would make him appear as best they could.

Pronin reasoned that the American was stalling, but he decided to go for the trip south. Once there, he was sure the American would try something. That could be anticipated and overcome with planning. Afterwards, with the right pressure, they could get the location. If they failed, they would just begin a long search. Either way, they would get warheads, then he would work a deal with Captain Tran for weapons the Vietnamese would find more useful. They certainly didn't want these dangerous weapons in the hands of such idiots.

The deal was struck. Keith was escorted to the compound's meager medical facilities.

The whole complex must be underground, thought Keith, noting a pervasive damp and musty smell. *Probably so it can't be located by satellite photography.*

They entered a small, clean room. Around a patient table with clean white linen stood two nurses and a Russian doctor. A bottle of intravenous fluid hung from a hook above the table. A tube of clear fluid led to Allen's right arm.

Allen looked awful. He was unconscious and his breathing was shallow. His wound was covered with a large bandage, but the dressing was red with more new blood. His lower leg was in a cast. The multiple bruises and burns from the fall off the truck were clean, but his color was so bad Keith knew he must be dying.

"You see our good faith," said Pronin, escorting Keith away from the room. "They tell me he is recovering nicely."

Keith knew it was hopeless. Allen would soon be dead.

"First thing tomorrow morning, we'll depart for Da Nang," continued Pronin in a chatty voice.

TUESDAY, MAY 27

Kept in his cell with no window, Keith could only track the passing of time by his watch. When it was 0615, the light went on, the door opened, and a guard brought a complete change of clothing and something that resembled food. Keith ate it all, if for no other reason than to keep up his strength.

After finishing and changing into fresh gray pajamas, he was led down the corridor of eight cells for the last time. As he passed the fourth cell, he distinctly heard, "Help, please help!" coming from behind the door. It was not Allen's voice.

So, there were other English-speaking prisoners here. But he wondered, were they Americans or South Vietnamese captured after the collapse of their government?

Keith did not know. He would never learn.

As he passed the second iron gate in the set of three along the way to the garage, he happened to catch the flash of a watch under the sleeve of the guard. There could be no mistake. It was Allen's watch.

They stole his watch, thought Keith angrily.

He realized the guards, like so many scavengers, had probably taken it off a dead man's wrist.

Keith was led to the garage where the panel truck waited. This time he was handcuffed before he was put in the van. The van left the garage, and soon, sounds of traffic could be heard outside. After several turns, he gave up trying to estimate their distance and direction. A half hour later, they arrived at a major airfield.

Keith only got a moment to glance around after the doors

were opened. In the short distance between the van and a waiting helicopter, he noted the airfield buzzed with activity. Keith caught a glimpse of four MiGs being loaded with rockets. Farther away, five Russian helicopters with engines running were waiting for troops to load gear aboard.

Something is up. Maybe the Chinese have begun another offensive, thought Keith.

He was escorted on board the helicopter. Inside, he found both Pronin and Tran sitting up front.

"I trust you slept well, Lieutenant Maddox. So nice of you to decide to cooperate," Captain Tran gloated.

Keith had nothing to say. He could barely think. *Allen is dead* was all he could say to himself. Showing his anger now would only make any strategy to avenge Allen's death more difficult, and the only way to avenge it at the moment was for him to get out of this. The handcuffs were momentarily removed so Keith could sit down, but then he was again cuffed to the seat in front of him. There was no opportunity to escape. Two big guards took seats opposite him. There was nothing to do but wait for the flight to finish, and think.

During the two-hour flight to Da Nang, Keith made up his mind he would lead Pronin and Tran on a bogus trip in the mountains along Highway 1. Keith remembered there were several places where the road had steep drop-offs. If he could move at all in the car he would try to lunge at the wheel and send them plunging downward to their deaths. He was most certainly going to be killed, and he wanted to be sure they went with him.

Keith recognized the old Navy warehouse when they landed. He wondered if Joe Scott and Captain Jessel were still off-shore waiting for his radio signal. It had been four days; Jessel had promised a week. They probably were still waiting.

An old Chevrolet Impala was waiting at the heliport as Keith exited the helicopter. Captain Tran got right to the point. "OK, Lieutenant, where did you hide the devices?"

"They are not far from here. We didn't have much time, but after our boat was discovered, we loaded them in the truck. Then we buried them in the mountains," Keith explained.

As Keith spoke, he observed Pronin surveying the harbor and surrounding fields. Slowly, his gaze settled on the former rocket launch site.

They climbed in the Chevrolet. Captain Tran took the front seat opposite the driver with one of the two guards in the middle. Keith was seated, handcuffed in the center of the back seat, Captain Pronin on his left and a heavy-set Russian guard on his right. Keith noticed the guard had a large caliber revolver strapped in a holster on his left leg.

As they started down the road toward Highway 1, a troop transport loaded with a work party followed. *Funny, they think a work party will be required to dig up the warheads, that's giving us a lot of credit for our ability to dig without a shovel,* thought Keith. If they only knew how close the warheads were and how easily they could be found!

The Chevrolet made the right turn onto Highway 1 and accelerated heavily up the first grade into the mountains. The road was not empty; they were passing a long convoy heading north. Keith unconsciously placed his feet close to the seat to ready them for a desperate spring at the wheel. He was looking ahead for the grades where he would have his chance.

Pronin observed the American closely. From the position of his legs, he guessed the American was preparing to spring for the driver. A hopeless attempt to kill them all, he thought. Americans are so melodramatic, so predictable.

Pronin had instructed his men to expect such an attempt. His man in the front seat was waiting for the lieutenant to move. Pronin and the second guard together could easily overpower him. Then the real fun would begin. Pronin intended to make short work of the American. He was dangerous; he should be dealt with quickly. He could either give in or die beside the road. It mattered little. The devices were nearby and the sensitive equipment he had requested from Moscow would find them quickly enough.

They had passed the convoy. Now the Chevrolet entered a turn high on the edge of a steep slope. The time was near. Keith was beginning to sweat, his mouth going dry. He readied his feet to spring. The Chevrolet was beginning the turn, its wheels straining against centrifugal force that was trying to push the car nearer to the edge.

Pronin knew the moment was near. This turn was the appropriate point. The American was getting ready. It was in his eyes.

Suddenly, Pronin heard the sound of jets overhead. Next there was a blinding flash and a deafening explosion behind them. Looking back, Pronin could see the men in the work party being thrown from the transport in all directions.

While Pronin's attention was focused behind, Keith began to move. A second jet was making its approach. The road exploded with gunfire as the second jet began a strafing run. A trail of exploding slugs found the Chevrolet's right side.

Simultaneously, wide holes opened in the roof above Captain Tran and Pronin's second guard. The air in the car filled with small pieces of shrapnel and human flesh. The slugs striking Captain Tran and the guard caused them to jerk wildly and killed them both instantly.

The driver was losing control of the car. The Chevrolet's right tires, which were also struck by gunfire, immediately flattened. The driver slammed on the brakes and strained to control the wildly pitching car. They first skidded right then slowly left toward the edge.

Pronin, realizing the car was about to go over the mountain's edge, opened his door and blindly jumped clear. He hit the pavement with a grinding thud.

The last few seconds were not a loss for Keith. When the transport exploded, the guard on his right was momentarily distracted. Keith made a grab for his gun. He would have been unsuccessful but for the sudden death of the guard from the bullets ripping through the roof. When Pronin made his exit, Keith instinctively lunged for the open door. He landed on the edge of the road.

The Chevrolet went over the edge and careened down the mountainside, smashing the thick underbrush of the Vietnamese jungle ahead of it. Gaining speed, it became airborne. While in the air, the heavy engine brought the front end down. It struck a large rock causing the sedan to somersault, slamming on its roof and trapping its occupants inside. As the Chevrolet came to rest, the gas tank began to leak. A small flame appeared from under the hood.

Keith was first on his feet. He had only one thought, to get even with Pronin. He cocked the revolver and charged the Russian, who was now rising to his feet.

Pronin, seeing the American, reached in the jacket of his uniform for the small pistol in the pit of his arm.

"Now you die, Pronin!" shouted Keith, pointing the revolver at Pronin's head and pulling the trigger.

Instead of the expected roar of the heavy, high caliber revolver, there was only a benign click of the hammer. Keith stood dumbfounded, staring into the barrel of Pronin's pistol.

"I anticipated you might try for my guard's gun, and should you be successful, I took the precaution of not loading it," said Pronin with a menacing laugh.

Behind Keith, there was a sudden explosion and a brilliant flash as the Chevrolet's gas tank ignited. Pronin glanced in the direction of the blast. In that instant, Keith raised both of his cuffed hands and threw the revolver with all his might at Pronin's grinning face. He missed. It flew low, but not too low. The heavy revolver struck Pronin's leg, smashing his kneecap.

Pronin, in great pain, fired but missed. By the time he could rise and fire again, Keith had disappeared into the dense Vietnamese jungle.

With no thought other than escape, he ran blindly for fifteen minutes. When he stopped, he listened for pursuers, but heard only his own gasping for breath. There were no soldiers yet. He was free! But could he stay free? The jungle was incredibly dense. He fought his way through tall elephant grass and thorny vines, which tore at his clothing. The sun beat down unmercifully; still, he pushed on to distance himself as far and as fast as possible from the highway. While resting briefly, he studied the surrounding mountains and the angle of the sun. He tried to focus his thinking on survival. Forget Allen, forget Pronin. Survive! He started again in a generally eastern direction.

Back on the road there was pandemonium. The north bound

convoy spread out along the mountain road was severely damaged by the Chinese MiG 21s. Amid burning machinery, there were cries of agony and shouts for help. Pronin was desperately trying to organize a search party to pursue the American, but his knee prevented him from moving quickly. A hundred yards down the road, five troops gathered and were applying first aid to their comrades who had been in the following truck. Pronin attempted to get help from them, but they had little interest in the lost American. It would be three hours before a search party could be organized; by then it was getting dark.

Keith had a serious problem; he was still handcuffed and the gray pajamas he wore were a dead giveaway. Somehow, he would have to find the tools to get his hands free and a change of clothes.

The going in the jungle was tough. Keith had to make several detours around dense underbrush and stop often to get his bearings. His easterly direction kept him on a downhill slope. He was pushing forward against a dense weight of wait a minute vines when he felt the ground give beneath him. Suddenly, he was two feet shorter. He had fallen into an ancient pongee trap. Fortunately, the sharp sticks had long since rotted. Feeling quite stupid, he struggled forward. He would have to be more careful; many of the traps and mines were never defused after the war. Eventually, he found a stream. He reasoned he could follow it to the coast.

When it got dark, he took shelter under a tall tree for the night. He knew that besides the Vietnamese, there were dangerous animals in the jungle, for he had heard stories of tigers from some of the war veterans. He chose the tree because it had a considerable amount of dry foliage at its base. Not completely satisfied, he found and spread a quantity of small twigs to form a makeshift perimeter. Before he retired for the night, he found a sharp stick about four feet in length. The dry twigs were a warning system, the stick the best weapon he could find. That night he slept with his back against the tree.

When morning broke, he was very hungry and still tired. He had slept only briefly. All night the jungle had been alive with sound. There had been several occasions when large animals had passed in the night. There was no way to be safe in his condition.

Before the sun got hot, Keith began his march to the sea. He was very thirsty and did not want to drink from the stream. What parasites were in the water he dared not guess. He knew he could contract dysentery from the dark water, but eventually he would have to drink it to prevent dehydration. When he found a running spring, he decided to take his chances with the water and drank heavily.

By afternoon, he was leaving the mountains and entering the fertile coastal plain. An hour later, he heard the voices of children playing. Keith approached cautiously and found a hamlet. The buildings, all bamboo and adobe hooches, were arranged in a double row along a dirt road. Behind many of the hooches were pens for pigs and chickens. The pens must have suffered from infrequent cleaning for the foul smell of animal manure prevailed throughout the hamlet. It was obvious that the hamlet was very poor because there was no glass in the windows and no evidence of any plumbing or electricity.

Apparently, most of the adults were tending the fields stretching out in the distance. Only an occasional elderly man or woman could be seen outside the hooches, watching the scantily clad children playing.

Keith observed piles of scrap machinery strewn about behind one of the hooches. Also parked behind this hooch was a dilapidated Dodge Powerwagon. There couldn't have been a single piece of sheet metal that was straight or less than half rusted away.

Keith suspected the hooch would have tools. He had to get his hands free. Since the hamlet was empty of able-bodied adults, he decided to sneak inside. He carefully studied his options. What worried him most were the dogs the Vietnamese kept as pets. They could smell a foreigner, especially one who smelled as awful as he must by now. They would be quick to bark. He tested the wind, then moved to his right to approach the hamlet from downwind. When he was satisfied the wind was right, he moved forward. Quietly, he slipped from one hooch to the next till he was in position to break for the entrance of the hooch with the equipment. He made it in one final dash. He was reasonably sure that he had not been observed.

The hooch was a filthy mess. Trash filled its single room. In one corner there was a pile of beer cans. Nearby, there was a rudimentary kitchen with a large steel wok over an open fireplace and a dry sink filled with dirty dishes. Next to the far wall was a single bed with dirty linen. On the wall hung a battered guitar and two hand-drawn sketches of mountain scenes. A single picture torn from an old Playboy magazine was taped above the bed.

Must be the Vietnamese version of a bachelor pad, thought Keith. What interested him most was the hardware piled about the room. He recognized the parts from motors, transmissions, brakes, drive shafts, communications equipment, and even Japanese TV and Hi Fi equipment. Judging from what he had seen outside and around the room, whoever lived here had an interest in the parts business.

Keith rummaged through the hardware looking for tools. To his great joy, he found a set of bolt cutters leaning against the wall. He stepped forward and picked them up. He then got on his knees and placed the chain between his bracelets in the mouth of the cutters. Putting the handles between his legs and pressing his body against them, he applied cutting force to the chain. With nearly all his weight on the handles, the chain finally snapped. At last, but for the exception of the two bracelets, he was truly a free man.

Keith rose to his feet. As he raised his head, he found himself looking at the business end of an AK-47. A short Vietnamese man with shoulder-length hair had ended Keith's brief flirtation with freedom. Keith raised his hands, but said nothing, the frustration and disappointment too great.

The Vietnamese squinted at Keith. "You ... not Russian," he said slowly in Vietnamese. "You American," he said in English.

Keith kept his hands raised. For a moment he studied the Vietnamese carefully, this man appeared to be a complete maverick. The junk strewn all around spoke of considerable familiarity with Americans and their technology. Could he still have friendly feelings for Americans? Keith decided to take a chance.

"Yes, I am American, and I am no friend of the Russians.

"Yes, I see POW. You escape. Good I not government soldier," said the Vietnamese.

The tension of the moment eased. Keith heard the buzz of flies that seemed to fill the hooch.

"I am Lieutenant Keith Maddox of the United States Navy," he announced as authoritatively as possible.

"What you do here? You lost or miss boat long time ago?" The Vietnamese smiled slightly.

Keith paused. This was a delicate question. He decided a little honesty was his only chance.

"My government lost some equipment they wanted back," he replied. "I was sent here to recover it."

"Ah, so you in salvage too. Me big in junk. Once rich. Had family. That long past. Now everything bad." The Vietnamese looked at the ground as his voice trailed off.

Keith was having trouble understanding the longhaired Vietnamese; his voice was flat, giving no inflection to consonants.

"I'm sorry. We didn't want to leave. Come to our country; things are much better there," Keith quickly offered, smiling.

The Vietnamese brightened. "You know way to America?" he asked. "Cousin in San Francisco get rich in roof business. You get me to America, I be grateful."

Keith paused, pretending to consider the possibility. "I need help. I am here to do a job. I will not leave until it is completed. If you help me and if I can get out, you are welcome to join me." Keith nodded hopefully at the wild-looking little man.

"OK." He smiled. "I am Tuan Tran," he said lowering his AK-47 and offering his hand.

Keith shook Tuan's hand while wondering if he was any relation to Liem Tran.

Tuan bowed and offered Keith some coffee, knowing the American would be impressed. While the water heated over a small fire, Tuan found a file for Keith to use on his bracelets.

"You said you had a family once, what happened to them?" asked Keith.

"Near end of war North soldiers in our hamlet. Me taken to

help army. Near DMZ. Things get bad, I try get family out. I get boat take to Manila. My family on boat. Soldiers see boat. All on boat killed by big gun," said Tuan sadly.

Keith nodded sympathetically. With great rattling and mumbling, Tuan produced a steaming cup of coffee complete with powdered cream and sugar.

"This is really excellent, Tuan." Keith smiled, "How do you have access to such supplies?"

"I find," replied Tuan with a twinkle in his eye.

Keith decided he had to trust this funny little guy. "If you could be so kind, I am very hungry and very tired. I need to sleep and eat now."

"OK," he said. "Use bed. I get food."

Keith was finding it a little easier to understand Tuan as he got used to his flat tone of voice. A half hour later, Tuan served a fine Vietnamese meal, complete with many vegetables, pieces of pork and fish over rice. Forgetting all caution, Keith ate ravenously. He had not had a decent meal for the better part of a week.

"Where did you get all this food?" asked Keith.

"It easy," said Tuan. "Much can food from war. Some here. More in mountains."

"Do you also have a radio?" asked Keith hopefully.

"Sure, in mountains also number one good radio," bragged Tuan.

"Then it is very important, if we are to get to America, we get into the mountains first," Keith grinned back.

"We no can travel now. Too many soldiers. We wait dark. Travel better. You need rest."

Keith knew his new ally was right. He had not had a decent night's rest since he left the *Stingray*. He put his head back and fell fast asleep. He slept for six hours without interruption.

When he awoke, he opened his eyes wondering where he was. It was dark. Tuan Tran was busy arranging a very old pair of blue baggy pants and a brown shirt. He placed these ceremoniously on a small table with great pride and flourish.

"Mr. Keef, I find nice clothes for you. You like?"

"Yes, Tuan, I like very much," replied Keith, as he started to pull the trousers on.

"Man at beach say many soldiers look for you. We must go now!"

"There's one problem, Tuan. I must pick up something near the south shore of Da Nang harbor." Keith cleared his throat, trying to sound confident.

"No can do!" snapped Tuan, jumping slightly, causing his hair to float around his head.

Keith was putting on the shirt that Tuan had brought. The trousers were quite tight, but the shirt fit.

"We may have no ticket to San Francisco without this equipment," replied Keith matter-of-factly.

Tuan squinted hard.

"What is equipment, Mr. Keef, so important you get way out to America?" Tuan spoke the words slowly and carefully, looking directly into Keith's eyes.

"Your army wants the same thing my government wants, some big high tech weapons we left here by mistake."

Tuan gave a low whistle. He had guessed Keith's meaning. "You honor me," Tuan tried to enunciate slowly. "I never have high tech salvage before. You lucky man. Stinking North butchers kill my family. Be big man here if I kill you. Sell equipment. I no want stay here. Want go America!"

Keith had found the leverage that would work with this maverick, a ticket to San Francisco. He had to take this shot, even though the guy could change teams any minute. He had no choice. They needed each other.

"Is there any way we can get to Da Nang," Keith paused, "make the pick up," he paused again, "and get back into the mountains?"

Tuan squatted on the floor and thought. After a moment he looked up. "Is one way. Hide equipment in truck. You hide in truck too."

"You don't mean the truck outside do you?"

Tuan nodded. "Look bad, run number one good. All wheels go. Got winch. Me hide lot in truck. You see," he said proudly.

Keith and Tuan stepped outside into the semi-darkness. Tuan pointed to a cleverly concealed compartment behind the driver's seat that didn't look big enough for a man. If he didn't breathe deeply, Keith could fit inside. The space was hollowed out from the seat back. Tuan had removed the springs and replaced them with a sheet metal frame.

"There is going to be a problem hiding our merchandise in your truck." Keith began, as he put his hand on the small man's shoulder.

"How big is merchandise?" Tuan responded.

"Two objects like this." Keith showed Tuan a two-foot space with his hands.

"Can get wet?" asked Tuan.

"Yes, they're built to withstand salt water."

"No problem," smiled Tuan pointing to two empty oil drums. "We put in drums. Fill old oil. I do before. Army no want old oil. Let me go."

Keith laughed and helped Tuan put the two oil drums into the old Powerwagon. Next, Tuan brought several five-gallon cans of old oil that also went into the truck. Again, Tuan went into the hooch and came out with a box of canned food and several cartons of American cigarettes.

"For army," said Tuan smiling.

"What kind of trouble will we get from the army on the road to Da Nang?"

"Here to Da Nang," Tuan held up two filthy fingers, "two barracks. Each have checkpoint now, we at war. We go dirt road, no check until Da Nang. Before mountains is checkpoint. Very bad one. No way round. Bad soldiers. Always search. Take plenty. I hide you good. We get through," said Tuan.

"OK, let's get going."

"I get something."

He rushed into the hooch, returning with a small box. Keith later learned it contained photographs of his deceased wife and two children. That was all he chose to take of his personal possessions from his country.

The following morning, the army arrived in the village. Shortly thereafter, they learned that the American had stayed in Tuan's hooch. They of course confiscated everything inside it.

Tuan climbed behind the wheel. Keith took the passenger's seat. The ignition switch turned. The old eight-cylinder engine cranked slowly for several revolutions until a single cylinder began to fire. After manipulating the gas pedal, Tuan smiled broadly and coaxed all eight cylinders into action. Surprisingly, there was little exhaust noise as the engine began running smoothly. While Tuan warmed the engine, despite its probable ancient condition, there was little smoke rising from the exhaust pipe. If Keith had any doubt about the Dodge Powerwagon, it disappeared the moment the truck started forward.

"It run number one good, long time I work in GI motor pool. Fix truck real good, yes?"

Keith had to smile in agreement that the engine had significant power and belied the appearance of the dilapidated body.

Tuan drove in the semi-darkness with his lights out. The moon was at first quarter and high in the sky, providing barely enough light to guide them on their way. There was a good cement road to Da Nang, but Tuan knew alternative routes, so they drove in silence down dirt roads most of the way.

For two hours they traveled in the darkness. Then Tuan slowed the Dodge and pointed into the distance.

"Da Nang," he said. "All dark for war." Keith could barely see the harbor in the distance; they were no more than a half-mile from the old Navy warehouse. "Do you know the old warehouse that is now near the new helicopter landing field?" asked Keith.

"Sure."

"Farther down the road from there toward Da Nang there is an abandoned missile platform high on the hillside. Can we get near it?"

"I know road. Is bad." Tuan gave Keith a thumbs up sign and a grin. "We make it," he paused, "I think."

"Then go for it!" Keith returned the thumbs up sign.

The road was indeed rough. During the rainy season it had washed out repeatedly. Since there was little use for the back access after the removal of the Hawk missiles, the road was in decrepit condition. At several locations, Tuan got out and attached the winch cable of the Powerwagon to tree stumps and winched the truck up what was otherwise an impossible grade. Finally, after an hour of difficult driving, Tuan stopped.

"We here, Mr. Keef. You see." Tuan shook his head affirmatively.

Keith could barely see the uprights of the missile compound in the scant moonlight. He and Tuan cut through the concertina wire surrounding the rear of the complex. Then he found the rear tunnel. He entered and Tuan followed. It seemed ages since he, Allen and Dan had been there. Now he had returned, but both Allen and Dan were dead. Keith looked down into the equipment pit. The remains of the heavy hydraulic pump were still in place over the hydraulic reservoir. *Thank God,* he thought.

The two men descended into the equipment pit and moved the remains of the pump off the cover. Then, using the same pipe Dan had used, they lifted the cover off the reservoir. Keith picked up the ten-foot length of hydraulic tubing, bent one end into a hook, and began to fish about in the reservoir, attempting to snag the harnesses attached to the bombs. He was lucky. In a second, he hooked the first one and lifted it carefully out of the reservoir.

Tuan could not believe his eyes.

"Small, light and much powerful," he said, admiring the atomic emblem.

Tuan eyed Keith with renewed respect. He had not expected the equipment to be this important, or that the American would be so trusting.

Keith easily removed the second. They each took a warhead and made their way slowly up the iron stairs toward the tunnel entrance. There, Keith hesitated, set his warhead down, and proceeded to the tunnel that led toward the harbor.

"I want to look at the harbor for a second," he said over his shoulder to Tuan.

As Keith carefully stepped out of the tunnel with Tuan following, he was surprised to see a series of lights glaring at the hillside below. There were several army troops working under the lamps waving a small apparatus over the ground in a systematic search.

The troops were working their way up the hillside. In an hour they would easily be where Keith stood.

"They are probably using some form of Russian Hot Spot Detector to search for the warheads," Keith explained to his new ally.

"Mr. Keef, much better we get hell out now!" urged Tuan.

Keith couldn't agree more. They jogged quickly through the back tunnel and placed the warheads in the drums. Next, they poured the oil in.

They both climbed into the Dodge. Tuan quietly followed the road past the missile compound and slowly to the right, down toward the cement road. The old road was completely out of sight to the soldiers below.

When they reached the highway a half-hour later, Tuan stopped the Dodge. "OK, you must hide. We short way to checkpoint."

Keith reluctantly complied. Now he could only trust Tuan. If for any reason the wild little Vietnamese decided not to honor their agreement, Keith had had it. He knew it was his only chance, but he didn't like it.

Tuan cautiously steered the Powerwagon toward Highway 1. There was only light traffic. The sight of the old Powerwagon attracted little attention. Tuan passed the air station complex without incident. Farther down the road they approached the intersection with Highway 1. There they found the first roadblock. Tuan could pick out four soldiers standing alongside the road. They were heavily armed.

"Damn! We got big trouble," grumbled Tuan abruptly.

Keith was struggling to breathe in the cramped compartment. He heard Tuan's muffled outburst and slowed his breathing to listen as Tuan down-shifted.

Tuan recognized an unfriendly army sergeant. On several previous occasions this sergeant had stopped him and demanded part of his cargo as tariff. He was too thorough, and too greedy.

The sergeant stood in the middle of the road and halted Tuan. The old Dodge reluctantly pulled to a stop. He considered trying to run for it, but the sergeant had a Chevrolet parked on the shoulder that could easily catch the Powerwagon.

"Hello, my good friend, Tuan, how is the junk business tonight?" asked the sergeant with a smirk.

"It is not so good. I have little to sell and no buyers."

The sergeant presented a menacing figure leaning into the window of the Powerwagon. He stood about five foot, five inches with short black hair and had a squat stocky build. His breath smelled of whiskey.

"What do you have in the back of your truck?"

"I have some old oil for recycling," shrugged Tuan.

Immediately, the sergeant waved one of his men inside the truck. Taking the top off one of the drums, the man looked inside. He then asked for a stick. Getting one from another soldier, poked it around inside the drum. Tuan began to sweat; he felt the chill of fear all down his spine. If he were caught now, they would shoot him in the head immediately. Meanwhile, behind the large bench seat, Keith was breathless. He didn't know what was going on. What he could hear of the conversation didn't sound good. The strain of keeping his breathing shallow was on the brink of forcing him to pass out.

"And what do I see beneath the seat?" asked the sergeant.

"Personal property," replied Tuan with the proper reluctance.

Keith's heart froze in mid beat. He hadn't understood what was said, but the voices were moving closer.

"Personal property that looks like a carton of cigarettes!" chuckled the sergeant.

"Oh, yes! I forgot! I do have some cigarettes that I found. They are, of course, a gift for you and your men," said Tuan, pulling out two cartons from under the seat and passing them to the sergeant.

Tuan watched the man who had been assigned to search the truck suddenly exit, realizing he might lose out when the goods were divvied up.

The burly sergeant opened the door and made quick work of emptying all the cigarettes and food Tuan had carefully stowed in the truck. He scowled at Tuan, waved him through the checkpoint, then turned to his men.

Tuan headed north up Highway 1 toward the old Demilitarized

Zone. After five minutes, he turned left onto a little used dirt road and stopped. He jumped out.

"Now safe. You get out," he said to Keith, releasing the seat as quickly as possible.

Keith crawled out from behind the seat slowly. He was dizzy and felt painfully stiff. Slowly, he stood and tried to work the stiffness out of his arms and legs.

"I hope we are done with the hide-and-seek bit for the duration. I can't take much more of that!" he said.

"I think we no meet soldiers this road. It go old fire base. It bad locate, no good for war."

"Is that where you have the radio?" asked Keith.

"Not exactly," responded Tuan.

Tuan did not comment further on their destination. Keith wondered where the little man was taking him as they wound along a steep, narrow ravine. It was now after midnight. The moon had set and it was pitch dark. Somehow Tuan still seemed to know where the road was. Finally, after he was out of sight of the highway, Tuan switched on the parking lights. Keith was shocked to see how narrow the road was. Tuan was actually scraping his fenders against the mountainside. The road was washed out at many locations. Miraculously, at each washout, there was a tree or pile of stones that allowed Tuan to proceed. At each washout Tuan passed, he got out and pushed the rocks or logs down into the ravine.

"They come. They go slow," said Tuan.

They approached the remains of a cement bridge. During the war it had been blown up. In its place now stood a wooden trestle of logs lashed together with steel cable. Smaller cross logs covered the bridge. Some of the logs were broken and there were no guard rails.

"You think we can make it?" asked Keith.

"Yeah sure, I make number one good bridges!" Tuan replied reassuringly.

The heavy Powerwagon began to cross the bridge. The timbers creaked loudly. Tuan eased the truck forward, feeling his way. Suddenly, the left front wheel fell in a hole where the cross log had broken. Pushing the clutch in, Tuan revved the engine slightly and eased the clutch out. The powerful eight-cylinder engine strained to raise the front wheel over the next log. Keith unconsciously held his breath. The heavy Dodge surged forward, broke free, and quickly the left rear tire settled into the same hole the front tire had occupied a moment earlier. Keith felt a sickening feeling as the right front tire rose in the air. The Powerwagon began to lean to the left, threatening to fall off the trestle. Keith could only guess, but the ravine must have been deep. Tuan floored the Dodge. The increased torque slammed the right front tire down as the left rear vaulted out of the hole.

Tuan had to use the same maneuver twice more before the bridge was crossed. Keith was breathless when they reached the other side. He had a new appreciation for this small Asian with the quick hands and feet.

Tuan now managed to turn the Powerwagon around. He and Keith got out. Together they fed the long winch cable through a snatch block they attached to a tree. Then they hooked the cable's end to the central member of the trestle. Returning to the Powerwagon, Tuan started the winch, and it soon strained on the bridge member. A moment later the trestle collapsed into the ravine.

"I so sorry. Bridge take three months to build. But no one follow fast," explained Tuan.

"I'm sorry too," nodded Keith. "I hope all this will be worth the effort and we can get the hell out of here."

"No worry. This remote area. Is very hilly, many trees. No helicopter land here. Only land at fire base. We go where there be good view," explained Tuan.

Keith thought for a second, then asked, "Well, just where are we going?"

"You see," chirped Tuan.

After winding the winch cable around the front bumper, they climbed in and Tuan began a slow ascent into the mountains. The sun was beginning to lighten the sky in the east. Tuan turned the parking lights out.

Several miles farther up in the mountains, Tuan turned off the dirt road and into a dense thicket. There he stopped. "From here two mile to entrance. We get bombs from truck," announced Tuan.

Together they poured the oil out of the barrels, removed the warheads, and set them on the ground. Tuan pulled a camouflage cover out of the underbrush that he and Keith spread over the truck.

They started uphill toward a ridge in the distance, each was carrying a warhead. Tuan had a flashlight stuffed in his rear pocket. "You stay close, step where I step. Mines here!" cautioned Tuan.

A feeling of dread came over Keith as he closed the distance between himself and his new partner. The jungle was getting incredibly hot. They had to stop to rest repeatedly as they ascended the hilltop.

Finally, Tuan stopped, "We here, Mr. Keef." They both put their warheads on the ground.

"Where are we? I don't see a fire base, just jungle and hills," said Keith.

"There," he gestured grandly, pointing to what looked like an overgrown rat hole.

Keith inspected the hole. It was well concealed by the jungle overgrowth. When he peered down it, he saw the entrance was filled with water. He looked up at Tuan.

"Is no problem," waved Tuan, heading off down the hillside.

In a few moments, Keith heard the running of water. Apparently, Tuan had opened a valve and now the water slowly emptied from the entrance mouth. "Soon we go in." Tuan smiled.

"What is this place, and where does this tunnel lead?" asked Keith.

"This underground. It very big. Plenty food, plenty supplies. Have generator and communication station," replied Tuan.

"How did you ever find the complex?"

"I no find. I work here," said Tuan, slowly looking straight at Keith.

"If that is true, then just whose side were you on?" Keith asked.

"I want live. I do what necessary," he replied shyly.

Keith thought for a moment. He was beginning to understand. The water soon emptied. They picked up the warheads and entered the tunnel. At first it was barely wide enough to crawl through, then it widened so a man could walk bent over down the passage. Tuan had the flashlight from the truck. He switched it on and lit the way. For a short distance the tunnel was wet, then it rose above the level of the entrance pool and dried as it continued onward.

"Water keep bad gas from airplane out of tunnel. It work good. We stay underground, no get bombed. Now I keep flooded, keep animals, keep others out," said Tuan.

A little farther in, Tuan stopped at a two-inch valve sticking out the side of the tunnel wall. Tuan opened the valve. Once again, Keith heard the sound of water as the entrance flooded.

They came to several junctions in the main tunnel. Keith was amazed, there were tunnels leading in all directions. Some led to large rooms where a man could stand fully erect. Here lay the supplies of war. Judging from the amount of canned food stacked in one storeroom, there must have been enough to supply a platoon for six months. They set the warheads down among the cans of soup and potatoes.

"Now me make generator run," said Tuan.

They proceeded several hundred feet down a small narrow tunnel. At the end was a small room with a Honda electric generator. About twenty gas cans lined up one of the walls. Along the opposite wall was a long row of lead acid storage batteries.

Tuan busied himself with the generator. First, he filled the tank and checked the oil. Not satisfied with the level, he found an open oil can and added some of it. Next, he flipped the choke lever and pulled the starter rope with a jerk while mumbling something to himself. The generator came immediately to life. Keith could not believe how quietly it ran. He noted a two-inch pipe funneled the exhaust, probably to the outside somewhere above.

Tuan threw a large knife switch. Two bare bulbs hanging from the mud and bamboo ceiling filled the room with light. He grinned broadly, gave the thumbs up sign to Keith, and switched off the flashlight.

"I run generator for one hour. Run radio all day. Number one good system," announced Tuan proudly.

Keith followed Tuan hurriedly back to the tunnel. In the main passageway, Tuan led the way to the radio room, which consisted of a space roughly ten-by-twenty feet with a seven-foot ceiling. Around the walls of the room were benches, a strange assortment of electronic equipment piled on top of them. There were chairs arranged at four foot intervals. Possibly, the equipment in front of each chair represented a specific listening station, but Keith wasn't sure. In one corner there was even a captured R390 receiver and a teletype.

As Keith examined the equipment in the light provided by two bare bulbs overhead, he recognized several parts from a Japanese radio with extensive modifications. In addition, he found modified television sets and an assortment of hand-wired circuits, some with transistors and some with tubes. Whoever put this communications system together knew his electronics.

"What do you know about this equipment?" asked Keith.

"I be mechanic, not work on radio," shrugged Tuan.

"There must be some HF gear here," Keith said to himself.

He went along the benches one-by-one. When Keith was in high school, he'd had a science teacher who encouraged him to work for his Ham license. A year later, after much study and some Morse code work, he had gotten his General Class license. Afterwards, he shopped the electronics flea markets and managed to cobble together a station from an old World War Two receiver and a used Heathkit transmitter. He spent many late night hours pounding on his key, communicating with other amateurs all over the world. He still had a box full of QSL cards to show for it. His experience was about to become useful.

He selected a bench where a large Japanese AM radio sat with modifications hanging out the back. He switched on the power and donned a set of headphones. By spinning the tuning knob, the air crackled with signals.

"There must be a good antenna here," observed Keith, his eyes following the coax until it disappeared into the wall.

"Yes, hide real good too," Tuan offered.

If his guess was right, this was the HF receiver. That meant it operated between three to thirty megacycles. These frequencies were ideal for long-range communication, the kind that it would take to reach Jessel in Subic Bay.

He guessed that the numbers on the front dial of the modified Japanese radio had some correlation with frequency, and tuned to five megacycles. Unbelievably, he heard faintly the relentless time signals from WWV located in Colorado. Keith knew WWV sent time signals on five, ten and fifteen megacycles. The military used these signals to synchronize crypto-receiving equipment. How he wished he were in Colorado now, instead of fifty feet below ground, high on a ridge in the Vietnamese jungle.

Satisfied he could operate the receiver, Keith focused on what was probably the transmitter. In front, he found a black box with a calibrated dial on its face. Behind it were two other boxes with more dials and a single meter on each. He guessed the boxes contained a variable frequency oscillator, a low power transmitter, and a power amplifier.

Keith tuned the receiver to 4.2 megacycles, one of the frequencies agreed upon with Joe Scott. Then he switched on the transmitter. It took several minutes for the tubes to warm up. He then tuned the variable frequency oscillator until he heard its harmonic in the receiver. Keith looked around for a microphone. There was none.

"Where's the mike?" asked Keith, looking at Tuan.

Tuan shrugged his shoulders.

"You no see, I no see," replied Tuan.

Keith spied a Morse key on the next table, picked it up and plugged it in. He tuned the transmitter while holding the key down, and watched the meter until he had both the transmitter and amplifier tuned for maximum output. Keith was quickly getting the hang of the equipment.

"Tuan, I have to tell them where we are. Do you have a map somewhere?" asked Keith.

Tuan disappeared for a moment and returned with a map, yellowed with age.

"It's all in French!" said Keith.

"*Oui, m'sieur,* we once French, you forget?"

Keith took a moment to draft a message. He wanted Jessel to

know he had the warheads, to know his location, that Allen and Dan were dead, and for Jessel to use whatever means necessary to get them out, and in a hurry. Of course, the Vietnamese army would have discovered he spent the previous day in Tuan's hamlet. From there they could easily piece together their route into the mountains. They were probably already following the access road. He had to get help—and now.

He and Joe Scott had agreed on a cipher code based on a commonly known constant, Pi. Each letter in the message was to be offset in the alphabet by the cumulative addition of the numbers three, one, four, one, five, nine, two and seven. Then the sequence was repeated till the end of the message. It was a simple cipher, but required no table and would work for a couple of days before it could be broken. He wrote out his message, then translated it letter by letter.

Keith took a hold of the Morse key. His fingers felt cramped and damp, he hadn't used a key for years. Could he still remember the code? He put the transmitter on full power and keyed down. The large tubes in the amplifier immediately went blue. Their massive plates began to glow slightly red. The lights in the room dimmed noticeably. There was a definite smell of ozone in the air. Keith released the key and began a series of Vs (dit dit dit dah). Then he sent the code words, 'Father this is Son', and waited for a response. There was none, only the background racket from distant lightning.

Fighting panic, Keith waited. Slowly, he tried again to send the code words. At last the receiver came alive. It was from Subic Bay. Keith copied 'Son, this is Father, go ahead'.

Controlling his shaking fingers, his heart pounding, he doggedly sent his message, correcting errors as his fingers tapped out the code. When he was finished, the radio operator on the other end sent the confirming characters and went silent. Keith switched off the transmitter and began to wait. He closed his eyes.

SUBIC BAY, THE PHILIPPINES
Captain Jessel was irate. He had arranged for the aircraft carrier

Enterprise now bound for the sea of Japan to immediately break off and make way for the Vietnamese coast. By tomorrow morning she could be in position to launch a helicopter gunship. Joe Scott had volunteered to lead the rescue party and was airborne on his way to the *Enterprise* now. From there, a six-hour round trip was required to retrieve Keith and the warheads. All that remained was presidential approval.

Jessel stood with a recently deciphered message from the president himself. True to Jessel's prediction, he was more concerned about the adverse political consequences of a second raid failure than about extracting Keith. He did not want to disrupt relations with the Chinese by entering into an arena where they were at war. "No" was his answer. Keith would be left with the problem. Keith was expendable. There would be no help from the U.S. military. With time, Jessel knew the decision could be reversed. The problem was, there was no time. Jessel correctly surmised Keith's pursuers were close behind.

Now Jessel had to send his own message. It had been six hours since his radio operator first heard Keith's coded message on one of the chosen frequencies. He owed Keith that much. The problem was there weren't any easy choices. The warheads must not fall into the hands of the Vietnamese. Once that happened, any Third World country that could pay the price could have two nuclear devices. These devices were light enough to be delivered to any major city in an automobile; they were a terrorist's dream. Jessel expected the Russians weren't far behind the Vietnamese. He was half right; they weren't behind at all.

In the hope Keith could render them useless, Captain Jessel had urgently requested advice from the consultants at the Naval War College. They had not yet responded. Jessel was sure that Keith lacked the tools to disassemble the warheads. Attempting to blow them up with conventional explosives or to burn them was equally hopeless. He had no immediate recourse but to wait for the force of reason to prevail in Washington. The president could change his mind. He had done it before, too often.

But Keith's message had an urgency about it. That could only mean he was in immediate danger. What bothered him most was his obligation to Keith; he had sent Keith in, Keith had completed an exceedingly difficult and complicated mission, now it was time to get him out. Jessel couldn't understand a president who didn't back to the limit American forces who were performing on the cutting edge. After all, these brave men took all the risks. Was it too much to ask for rescue? He felt he had to do something. There were other options. They were highly risky, but he could try one. He was a man of action. Action in this situation was better than doing nothing, even if it later proved to be a mistake.

He picked up the phone and dialed a number in Hong Kong. Shortly after the phone was answered, Jessel switched on the scrambler. Fifteen minutes later, he drafted a short message for Keith. He called for the radioman and handed him the message for ciphering and transmission.

Jessel rose to view the water in Subic Bay outside his window. The sun was setting with a brilliant display of red and orange against the mountains. As he watched the sun settle toward the water, he knew in his heart he had just severely damaged his career.

VIETNAM

Near the old DMZ, a convoy of four Vietnamese army troop transport trucks was slowly proceeding in serpentine fashion up a narrow mountain road along a steep gorge. In the lead was a vintage army Jeep with a radio. Mounted on the back of the Jeep was a thirty caliber machine gun.

Pronin sat in the passenger seat of the M38-A1 Jeep, his leg in a cast. He was frustrated by the slow progress the Vietnamese army unit was making. They were following the trail of some peasant junk man who was known to have aided the American. From the beginning, there had been trouble. The road was narrow with numerous washouts, each requiring the troops to shore up the roadbed before they could proceed. The delays had forced them to spend much of the night with little progress to show for it. How he wished he could be ahead with the advance scouting party on foot, but his injured knee prevented his leaving the Jeep. By morning, they had discovered the remains of a fallen wooden trestle. It took four hours for a D4 bulldozer to be brought up and to fill in the ravine. Finally, they began moving again.

The pain killer used for his surgery had quickly worn off. All night his knee had throbbed relentlessly. He didn't have to be in pursuit of the American; there were other Russian advisors available, but it was personal. The American had severely damaged his knee. He intended to catch him, and to see that the American paid dearly for this humiliation.

Pronin knew a Vietnamese army unit was preparing to board a Russian helicopter for transportation to a deserted American fire base not more than two miles ahead. The Russian suspected the American was nearby. There once was a tunnel complex hidden on the ridge above. That would be a real possibility for the American. They would look for him there.

The Jeep had been in motion for the better part of an hour since they had passed the old trestle. Progress was slow as they worked their way up a steep grade. Abruptly, the tracks of the Powerwagon disappeared. Pronin's driver stopped and put the Jeep in reverse. Backtracking about a hundred feet Pronin spotted the tracks of the Dodge leading into a dense thicket. There the dilapidated Powerwagon rested, covered by a camouflage tarp. There were two oil drums and a dark patch of oil on the ground. At that moment, the Russian troop transport helicopter rumbled overhead, making its way to the deserted fire base.

Keith still didn't know what to make of Captain Jessel's message. He had checked his cipher three times and found no mistake. It read: "You are now a free agent. Do not anticipate Navy rescue. Extraction scheduled for 2400Z. Be prepared. Good Luck!" What does he mean by "extraction"? The time, 2400Z, that would be noon in Vietnam. Just who was to do the extraction?

Keith and Tuan had turned off the generator hours ago. The lights were working off the batteries as they crouched in the observation tunnel. By looking through a slit in the rock, they had an excellent view of the American fire base. Keith looked again at his watch. It was 1135.

Tuan was scanning the fire base and surrounding hills with a set of field glasses. He straightened suddenly.

"Mr. Keef, soldiers come."

Keith took the glasses. On the road below, Vietnamese troops carrying weapons approached the firebase.

"They must have come up the access road," mused Keith, scanning farther down the road.

A Jeep came into view. It stopped and backed up. "Looks like they have repossessed your truck. How well known is this tunnel complex?" Keith glanced at Tuan.

"Too good. I think it on map.

"Then we'd better get out of here," Keith answered, "and into the jungle—real quick."

Back in the supply room, they each picked up a warhead and slung it on their backs using the harnesses Dan had made. An M-16 rifle and a case of ammunition completed the equipment each carried as they moved as quickly as possible.

"What's the best way out of here?" asked Keith, knowing there was likely to be more than one exit.

"This way," said Tuan, heading down a tunnel just outside the storeroom.

The length of the tunnel amazed Keith. He traveled behind Tuan for the better part of a half-mile before they came to a water trap similar to the one at the first entrance. Tuan quickly emptied the water and they squeezed through the small exit into a blinding sun. When he looked down from the hillside, Keith could see the fire base. The advance troops were just approaching the embankment that made the perimeter. Farther down the road, he could see the Jeep leading the convoy. The vehicles were gaining speed on the better road approaching the firebase.

The beating of helicopter blades far in the distance became audible. Keith and Tuan waited, almost afraid to breathe, hoping it was an American helicopter approaching to rescue them. The sound grew louder. It thundered through the mountain valley. Keith was scanning the ridge when the helicopter suddenly loomed above. His heart sank. The red stars declared it to be Vietnamese. Reinforcements, not rescue, would soon be upon them.

For a moment they watched, paralyzed with fascination, as the helicopter landed and the troops leaped out. Keith and Tuan turned to lose themselves in the jungle. A rock began to slide. It gathered speed and sailed through the air to smash loudly against a boulder. The fresh troops below looked up and caught a glimpse of the two figures disappearing.

Keith and Tuan hit the ground as the first shot rang out. The jungle was being torn to shreds around them. Vietnamese troops fired ferociously into the hillside, pinning the two down. The Vietnamese began a flanking maneuver to the left and right of them. They would be caught with the warheads, the worst possibility of all.

Keith turned to Tuan. He smiled wanly. "I'm sorry, Tuan. Looks like we're not going to get to the States. You're a real good operator, Tuan. I'm proud to have met you."

"I sorry. You trust me. I fail you." He lowered his head and shook it slowly back and forth.

Before Keith could answer, the roar from a Huey gunship suddenly rose above the ridge with its twin miniguns alternately spewing bullets as it passed over the troops on the fire base. The Huey maneuvered quickly in a tight circle over the base, allowing each of the miniguns to fire and then reload in turn. The troops on the ground, caught in the open, were cut to ribbons. The Huey hesitated momentarily to concentrate on the Russian troop transport helicopter.

The helicopter attempted to take off, but before the pilot could get the blades up to speed, a single rocket fired from the pods mounted on the Huey's struts found its mark on the side of the troop transport helicopter. The resulting explosion blew the top and side away. The engine caught fire and a great ball of black smoke rose above the firebase. With the advance troops and the Russian helicopter taken out of action, the Huey concentrated on the approaching troop convoy. Two rockets shot from the Huey's rocket pods. They left behind a twin trail of smoke and flame as they found the radiator of a lead truck exploding with a thunderous roar. Three more rockets followed in quick succession, each taking one of the following trucks out of action. The Jeep avoided disaster and darted into the brush and disappeared. The remaining troops scrambled out of the trucks and fled into the jungle where they returned fire from the brush as the Huey turned into a series of tight circles, using its mini guns continually.

In the seconds that followed, a Bell 212 helicopter rose like a huge insect above the east ridge and landed next to the burning Russian helicopter. Keith could see a handful of armed troops exit and spread out to reestablish the perimeter of the fire base American troops had held almost a decade before.

Remembering Jessel's message, Keith glanced at his watch. It was 1205. This had to be the extraction party. Who were they? There were no markings on the sides of either helicopter.

Keith and Tuan were in a tricky situation. How could they identify themselves without getting shot in the process? Fortunately, the Vietnamese convoy was on the far side of the perimeter. The embankment provided some protection from their fire.

Keith took off the shirt Tuan had given him, tied it to the end of his rifle, and began waving it high in the air. From the perimeter below came a shout. Keith was not sure what it meant.

"I think all OK now. It French they shout, but no Vietnamese French," shouted Tuan to Keith.

Carefully, the two men rose. A soldier on the perimeter waved them forward. With the warheads again on their backs, they ran at full speed toward the perimeter. In the distance, the Huey was having trouble with ground fire. Suddenly, one of the mini guns went silent. The M-60 machine gun started a volley in its place.

Keith and Tuan scrambled up the perimeter battlement. The sound of mortar fire striking the far side of the fire base deafened them. In seconds there would be more incoming rounds, each hitting with greater accuracy on the fire base. A tall soldier waiting on the far side of the battlement took a grip on the harness of Tuan's warhead. He relieved him of the burden, and ran at full tilt for the Bell 212. The perimeter troops were all withdrawing. With shattering explosions, the mortar rounds began hitting the fire-base compound next to the Bell 212. Two of the perimeter troops were cut down immediately.

Keith and Tuan and the tall soldier were the first to enter the helicopter. The pilot already had the blades spinning at near maximum RPM, anticipating immediate takeoff. Eight others followed.

SUDDEN STORM

The transport helicopter rose with a lurch and swung to the east. Suddenly the Jeep, which had hidden itself in the brush, broke into the open, its 30-caliber machine gun spraying a volley of bullets. Some of the bullets found the side of the helicopter. Keith could see a lone figure manning the gun in the back of the Jeep. It was Pronin, his left leg in a cast.

The helicopter rose quickly and was soon out of range of Pronin's machine gun. Keith, exhausted, sank to his knees and looked back through the mud-splattered window. Pronin was fading from sight. He sat in the battered Jeep, his fist raised in the air.

Keith saw the face of Allen in front of him. He heard Dan's quiet voice. Both good men who had followed his orders and believed in their mission. Both dead. "We're not finished yet, Pronin!" hissed Keith.

FORTY-FIVE MINUTES LATER

Keith sank into his seat next to Tuan as the helicopter slipped out of the mountains and proceeded across the coastal plain. The Vietnamese Air Force was not in the air yet.

He learned he was in the company of international mercenaries; they were German, French, Israeli, South African and American. They had been hastily organized for the mission by Saul Segal, a big time Israeli arms and technology dealer. Three of the group of fifteen mercenaries had just died in action. One other in the Huey was wounded.

Passing over the coast and heading northeast just barely above the blue ocean, attempting to evade the Vietnamese radar, the helicopter vibrated heavily as it carried the weary men away from land. However, the Vietnamese were only temporarily foiled, for once alerted, their airborne radar quickly picked up the two departing helicopters. Two MiG-21s were immediately scrambled.

Five minutes later, the pilot of the Bell 212 helicopter spotted the two approaching aircraft and abruptly switched on his radio, said a few quick words, and concentrated on evasive maneuvers. He was making a vain attempt to confuse the Vietnamese pilots, who were now beginning their attack.

Keith was devastated. The MiGs could easily blow them out of the sky with their rockets. The weary men watched, frozen in a moment of horror, as the jets lazily swooped low to lock their missile systems on the heat of the helicopter's exhaust.

Tuan took the small box he had removed from his hooch, opened it, and once again gazed upon the image of his lost family. Keith saw a tear form in his eye.

Miraculously, four Chinese MiG-21s passed overhead with a sudden burst of thunder, their afterburners ignited. Keith felt a sharp impact as they broke the sound barrier and rose in pursuit of the Vietnamese Air Force. Suddenly, the hunters in pursuit of the helicopters became the hunted. They were outnumbered four-to-two. The Chinese pilots pressed their advantage and out-maneuvered the Vietnamese, quickly gaining missile lock.

"We're in international waters. The Chinese rule the skies here," announced their pilot.

The Vietnamese reluctantly broke off their attack and retreated westward.

For the next three hours, the two helicopters lumbered forward toward the Chiungshan airport on Hainan Island. During this strange trip, Keith introduced himself to the nearest mercenary. His name was Charles Berdan; his open face was dominated by a large handlebar mustache. Charley introduced Keith and Tuan to the group. Across from them was a tall wiry Frenchman, Henri Vannier. Beside Henri was a stocky German named Hans Wicher, and next to Hans, an athletic-looking Israeli named Alex Sherman.

Keith was baffled as to how the mercenaries had been organized for the rescue. It was Alex who supplied information.

"Yesterday, an unknown party in your armed forces contacted our embassy in Hong Kong. From him we learned you and your associates had recovered some very hot merchandise. You were about to be recaptured with no hope of rescue by U.S. forces. Our embassy contacted Saul Segal, now doing business in China. You had the kind of merchandise we Israelis and the others have a vested interest in keeping out of the hands of certain hostile parties, like the Vietnamese and their playmates," Alex explained in accented English.

Keith then realized Captain Jessel had failed to get presidential approval. He had been forced to make alternative arrangements to save the mission and his man. Keith knew such a move could only be disastrous for Jessel's career.

"Did the Israeli government pay for this mission?" asked Keith.

"No, the Chinese did," said Hans.

"Just what do they expect in return?" shot Keith.

"Why the bombs, of course," replied Alex.

"What?" said Keith incredulously. "They're U.S. property! No way!"

"They were U.S. property, pal," corrected Alex with a smile. "Lieutenant Maddox, the deal is history," he continued in a business-like voice. Did you notice the Chinese MiGs overhead? We are being escorted. If at anytime we make a break for it, we will immediately be shot down. This operation could not take place without their assistance. No friendly airport exists close enough to Vietnam to be in striking distance. The Chinese have agreed to refuel us in Chiungshan and we have agreed to exchange the bombs for a large sum of money," said Henri.

Keith was speechless.

"Lieutenant, do not be too concerned with what they will do with the bombs. Remember, at their age, they are very dirty. The Chinese are only interested in the lightweight firing mechanism. They will disassemble the bombs and copy the design. Now that your government has established friendly relations with the Chinese, thanks to your Mr. Nixon, you have much less to fear about how they will be used than the Russians do," soothed Alex in a calm voice.

There was some satisfaction knowing the devices would not be in the hands of the Vietnamese; the Chinese were the lesser of evils. Keith was in a no-win situation. His control over the warheads ended when he hastily, and gratefully, boarded the helicopter.

As the helicopter set down in Chiungshan, a Chinese army detachment waited. The helicopters were quickly refueled, and the bombs and a suitcase of money exchanged hands. Within a half-hour, the helicopters were once again airborne, bound for Macao on the Chinese coast.

Three hours later they landed. An Israeli diplomat named Zvi Oren met Keith and Tuan. They were both whisked by auto across the border. The following morning found Keith in a luxurious circular bed in a downtown Hong Kong hotel room with a suitcase containing a large sum of American dollars, his share of the take. The rest went to Saul Segal and the mercenaries. Keith wasn't sure what to do with the money. If he kept it, he intended to make sure Allen and Dan's families benefited, as well as Tuan. But right now, Keith wasn't sure of anything. What had this all been about? Lives had been lost. For what? A strange uneasiness formed in his chest and he knew it was going to be there for a long time. Maybe for the rest of his life.

• Chapter 4 •

COLORADO
WEDNESDAY, DECEMBER 5, 1990

It was a raw morning near the old town of Snowmass, Colorado where Keith first met Anna. He was moving two of his partner's horses from their pasture just below the Snowmass Ski Area to their winter pasture on a ranch south of the town of Silt on the Colorado River. Keith had his tandem trailer hitched to the back of his Ford 4WD pickup, the horses loaded and on the road by seven a.m. The weather had been cold for several days, but now the thermometer hovered at the freezing mark.

Keith made his way down the access road, carefully controlling his speed on the curves. Traction was good and he didn't suspect a problem lay ahead as he turned off the county road and headed north on Highway 82. A Toyota leaving Aspen soon caught up, but didn't pass. Two miles later he approached a sharp left turn under the shadow of a steep mountain. Keith slowed his rig. He noticed that the light blue Toyota followed, slowed, and kept a proper distance. Now a light rain was starting to fall and Keith had the wipers working. Around the corner and out of sight, a yellow Jeep Wagoneer taxi in a hurry to reach Aspen was approaching the turn at high speed after having passed three slower vehicles. The driver entered the turn unaware that the mountain's shadow combined with the light rain had played a dangerous trick on him. The road surface became a sheet of ice. Suddenly the driver felt the Jeep sliding to the left and in panic took his foot completely off the accelerator. This caused the heavy engine to slow down forcing all four wheels to brake. They broke free and the Jeep careened across the double yellow line totally unresponsive to the frantic driver at the wheel. It was then the driver saw the oncoming pickup and horse trailer.

Keith's heart froze. The approaching Wagoneer was out of control. Worse, it was proceeding directly into his path. He aimed the Ford for the shoulder. Beyond the shoulder was a deep ditch. He didn't want to get too close because the incline would topple the trailer. He hit the brakes. Traction was bad and his tires tore at the loose gravel on the shoulder. He was bringing both the truck and trailer to a halt, but the Jeep kept coming. At the last moment the driver found traction and the Jeep lurched to the right. It missed Keith's truck but not the trailer. With a sickening impact the Jeep drove the trailer into the ditch. Slowly the trailer tilted to its right then toppled over on its side.

Keith was out of his truck in a second. His ears were filled with the panicked snorts of the horses now trapped in the trailer. Keith knew he had to act fast. He tore open the doors of the trailer. The bigger horse, a thoroughbred, was thrashing about wildly kicking the trailer bottom while the smaller buckskin trapped underneath the separating partition was struggling to get out from under the crushing weight of the thoroughbred.

The taxi driver was trying to apologize, but Keith had little time for words. His concern was only for Marty's horses. He grabbed a rope from the back of his truck while the taxi driver moved the Jeep on to the shoulder and got out a set of flares.

Keith considered his options. The horses could do themselves considerable harm if they remained inside the trailer much longer. They couldn't get out by themselves; he would have to drag them out. He couldn't do that alone. Quickly he decided to use his truck. In a minute Keith had it unhitched and positioned behind the trailer. The taxi driver was making himself useful by stopping traffic. Keith didn't notice the attractive blonde who parked her

Toyota on the shoulder, got out and carefully approached. A moment later she disappeared behind the trailer and untied the halters of both horses.

Keith took one end of the rope and tied it to the Ford's bumper and then approached the trailer. He noticed that someone had untied his horses, but now his concern focused on getting them out. The thoroughbred would have to come first. Keith reached for the hind legs and was about to fasten the rope about one of the thoroughbred's fetlocks when a hand reached out to stop him. Keith looked up and came face to face with the woman. His gaze caught her long legs, tight jeans, ski jacket, and long blond hair. For an instant he was stunned by her beauty.

"Don't use the legs to pull them out. Tie the rope to their tails. If you use the legs, you'll break them," she was saying.

Keith studied the situation for a second. Her voice was firm and authoritative. She knew what she was talking about. Her eyes—a blue-gray color, not unlike his—were clear and knowledgeable.

There was no time. Somehow Keith sensed she was right. By now the horses had been trapped for about ten minutes. Several large cuts in the thoroughbred's fragile skin could be seen. He feared there were more. Quickly they fashioned a knot in the thoroughbred's tail. Then, Keith jumped in the truck and slowly brought tension on the rope. The woman was giving Keith hand signals while watching the horses intently. The thoroughbred snorted loudly when he felt the steady pull on his tail. Gradually Keith increased the tension on the rope. The trailer was taking a tremendous pounding from both horses' hooves. The buckskin was screeching with fear. Finally, the thoroughbred inched backward out of the trailer. The blonde continued her hand signals as Keith applied gas to the engine. To his great relief the horse was finally out, then quickly got up on its legs and stood quietly next to the woman. His nostrils flared, showing deep red inside due to his racing adrenalin. His eyes rolled back and he shook his head. The woman held his halter firmly in one hand as she reached to soothe him with her other.

The buckskin was pulled out in a similar fashion five minutes later. Then both horses were walked while Keith and the woman examined them carefully for injuries. There were several deep cuts on the thoroughbred that would require some needle work from the vet. The buckskin fared better but was developing some dark bruises from being crushed under the thoroughbred.

"I think both of your animals are in shock," she said in an unusually soft but deep voice. "My advice is to get your veterinarian involved and watch them closely," she said. Keith resolved to stay in Silt for a couple of days to watch them. Now he turned to the woman.

"I don't know how to thank you. I wasn't sure what to do. You were though and it helped a lot," said Keith.

"Well, you're welcome." She smiled, not showing her teeth, but a smile involving her eyes and her whole face. "I've never done it before, but I have a friend who wasn't so lucky. He ruined a good horse. Knowing that, I couldn't just stand by and watch."

"I'm glad you didn't. I gather you know horses," Keith tried desperately to extend the conversation. She was wiping her hands on the back of her jeans and seemed to be looking at the ground for something. He wanted to hear her voice again and to see her smile that came more from her eyes than her mouth.

"I do," she said with the smile again.

Keith extended his hand immediately. "Keith Maddox," he blurted out, as she returned the gesture and he felt a firm grip returned.

"Anna Fletcher. Nice to meet you under not very pleasant circumstances." She still seemed to be looking for something on the ground. "Oh, there they are, my gloves." Anna leaned down and scooped them up. "Well, I'd better be going. I hope the horses will be OK." The smile again.

Keith reached in his pocket and found a receipt. *Anything to write on!* he thought. "Could I have your name and address—in case I need it in connection with the accident—and I'll give you mine," he quickly asked. "I don't have a pen though, do you?"

"I do in the car," she nodded. "Wait a minute. I'll get it." She walked to the Toyota and returned with a piece of paper. "Anna Fletcher, Redstone Inn, room 210. I'll only be here for four more days so I'm not sure how much help that will be. I'll give you my permanent address in New York too if you need me for the insurance mess."

Keith quickly wrote his name and number and handed it to her. "I hope I won't have to bother you, but just in case..." he trailed off.

"Well, you'd better get to your horses," Anna said softly. "I'm glad I could help. Bye." She smiled again and walked to her car.

Then, she was gone. Keith felt slightly breathless. Indeed they had made some connection. He had to see her again—soon. He would see her again.

Just a brief meeting on the road that cold and damp December morning, but Keith found himself riveted by his first sight of her as he looked up from behind the trailer.

Soon after, a sheriff's deputy arrived to fill out the accident report. An hour later with the wrecked trailer towed away, he loaded the horses into a hired van to be taken down to Silt. As he followed the van, his thoughts drifted back to Anna Fletcher. There was something special about this woman that Keith liked.

THAT EVENING

Keith finished with Marty and hung up the phone. Marty was surprised to learn his horses had been in an accident, especially concerned for the buckskin because he belonged to his wife, Sue. He was her favorite horse because he had such a gentle manner. The vet Keith had called was finished with his work. Both horses were sedated and treated for shock. The thoroughbred would have a few more scars to add to the ones he already had. The buckskin might be lame for a week or so, but the injuries were not likely to be permanent.

Keith met Marty and his wife the year after he had come to Colorado. His abrupt discharge from the Navy left him at a loss. He was disoriented and confused. After college, he had planned to spend most of his life in the Navy, but Vietnam had ended that. After he returned from Hong Kong to the Philippines, there had been a hasty but quiet investigation. The officer in charge was a surly individual with a limited vocabulary and a habit of keeping a toothpick sticking out of one side of his mouth. It soon became apparent this son of a bitch was more interested in finding fault than considering the circumstances. Keith rightly felt he was singled out as the fall guy. After all, hadn't the Navy deserted him? What else could he have done?

He objected to the officer's approach and eventually refused to cooperate in the investigation. It was a difficult and bewildering time for Keith. He didn't mention Jessel's involvement and he didn't mention the money left in Hong Kong. In desperation, Keith wrote a letter to his Congressmen. His local senator, a friend of his mother, got involved. Apparently, he struck home. Shortly afterward, the Navy suddenly agreed to drop the case. In return, Keith was to be immediately discharged. Keith felt outraged. He was so incensed by the Navy's handling of his case that he decided to keep the money. After all, it had almost cost him his life and it had cost him his career. Wasn't it rightfully his? But a deeper layer in Keith had been touched. He had lost a certain respect for all those institutions he had revered as a child. He didn't want to play the game. If he had to, he'd play, but with at least some of his own rules—that would make the game fair.

About the same time, Jessel was transferred. Keith wasn't sure if it was because of the Vietnam incident or whether something else was involved. He soon lost touch with his old boss. Actually he wanted to. He never blamed Jessel, but he couldn't live with any of the memories. Two good men dead—and for what? It tortured Keith.

He received his discharge at Treasure Island in San Francisco Bay in the early fall of 1979. In San Francisco he found Tuan Tran who had flown from Hong Kong to meet his cousin. They were struggling to make ends meet because the roofing contractor who employed them only paid minimum wages. Keith loaned them enough money to get started on their own. They made good use of the cash and soon would become well-known for high quality work. Their company eventually prospered and they were joined by other Vietnamese. They were fast obtaining a corner on the market. In recent years, Keith had received a postcard from Tuan. He had remarried and had several children. His company, Keef's Roofing Inc, was prospering.

Keith's life didn't pick up with quite the same momentum as Tuan's. He left San Francisco on a beautiful cool clear day. He took a bus to the airport. He wasn't sure what to do. He could take a flight home to his folks in Philadelphia and then look for a job. Somehow that didn't appeal to him. Almost on a whim, he took a flight to Denver. Perhaps he would spend the winter skiing. While in flight, he remembered Bob Moze, a friend he met in Newport, R. I. at Navy OCS. Bob had a father who lived in Grand Junction. Bob had mentioned his dad had trouble finding help to look after some mining property. In past winters there had been considerable malicious damage done by snowmobilers. He now employed a watchman who wintered in the area. The idea of spending the winter high in the Rockies appealed to Keith. When he arrived in Denver, he made the phone call. To his surprise, he had a job if he wanted it. It wouldn't pay much, but it did come with his own log cabin. He felt events were carrying him along. He liked the feeling for the moment; he didn't want to make any major decisions. He wanted to re-evaluate everything. Alone.

Two days later he met Robert Moze Senior in Marble and they went up the dirt road together in Bob's Jeep. Lead King Basin was where the two mines were located. It was high in the Rockies! Keith soon realized he would be living in isolation and have to snowshoe his way in and out from the small log cabin for most of the winter. Still, the idea excited Keith. He loved the mountain air, the crisp cold mornings, the clear nights, and seemed to crave the isolation. He agreed to give it a try. Robert Senior was delighted.

After taking the job, he went into Carbondale and arranged for a small portion of his sizeable Hong Kong bank account to be transferred to a local bank. He then purchased a rebuilt Jeep CJ 2A from a body shop. The old Jeep was in good condition and had more maneuverability than some of the newer models. What he liked best about it was its stainless steel body. It would never rust out. That afternoon he loaded the Jeep with supplies and made his way back to Lead King Basin.

Keith found life by himself difficult. It had more challenges than he had imagined. Many things he had taken for granted as a child—like a telephone, power, and heat—were not trivial matters any more. Daily life was hard work. Although he collected a large pile of fire wood in the fall, by February his supply got dangerously low. By then, the Jeep was completely buried in snow and useless. Food was a real problem. Each trip out by snowshoe took a full day. On the following day he would return. He kept his trips in and out to a minimum because the narrow road was prone to avalanches. Still, he could only transport what he could carry by himself. He had to plan carefully. He took to making lists to remember everything he needed. That winter, Keith learned the true meaning of the word independence. By spring he was ready to face the world again. The lonely weeks took a toll on his enthusiasm for isolation, with the snow too heavy to travel and the constant effort to maintain heat, water, and food.

His first winter in Lead King Basin was his last. When April arrived, he was desperately tired of snow and thoroughly lonely. It was late in spring when he first met Marty. He was fishing in a tiny lake near Marble, when to his surprise, he heard the drone of a small airplane coming up the valley. As he watched, an old Cessna 172 circled the small field near the lake and then settled down for a landing. With his curiosity aroused, he approached the pilot and introduced himself. Marty Matheson turned out to be a mechanic for a major airline who liked to spend his weekends in the mountains. To do so, he had cleared this stretch of pasture in the valley on his father's property. It now served as a private landing strip. Keith, intrigued by this young pilot/mechanic, eagerly agreed to go up for a spin. The view of the mountains was breathtaking. That was all it took for Keith to fall in love with flying.

That summer he got his pilot's license and bought his first plane. Unfortunately, that same summer Marty was laid off. It was at a bad time, for Marty had just married Sue. Now the newlywed was looking for work. Late that fall, Aspen Air Charter was hatched. The idea was to provide aircraft for major corporations to transport guests to the Colorado mountains from Texas and California. The aircraft would be modified to offer a spacious and relaxed atmosphere. Their clients could conduct business while in transit and their guests wouldn't be subjected to the hassle of being packed into a commercial airliner. Keith would supply the working capital, while Marty would purchase and rebuild a couple of used corporate jets. Marty could fly jets, but once they had contracts they would hire additional pilots. The idea took root immediately. Keith won his first contract from a major oil company before Marty could get the first airplane rebuilt. Ten years later, their company owned twenty aircraft and had forty employees. The first five years had been frantic, but now they were doing well. Both Keith and Marty felt satisfied with their accomplishment, and the partnership was a good one. Keith continued to fly. Two years ago he acquired certification to fly jets and now, on occasion, he flew some of the charters himself.

With the establishment of the business Keith had little time—and strangely, little interest—in developing any enduring relationships with women. Most of his female friends were fun, someone to share a drink with, ski with or to spend a night with. Not much more. Therefore this meeting with Anna Fletcher on a dreary day in December surprised him. He felt absolutely compelled to call her later that afternoon. After he connected to the desk clerk and he gave her room number, he heard the phone ringing her room. She answered in the same soft calm voice, "Hello?"

Keith quickly got to the point. He wanted to meet for a glass of wine or beer, whatever her pleasure, to express his appreciation for all her help. After considering his proposal, she just said, "Fine, what time?"

That was it. The time was set. Their conversation had lasted only seconds, but Keith could feel his anticipation rise. As Keith prepared to leave for the Redstone Inn where they were to meet at six o'clock, he glanced at the mirror. He wore dark blue corduroy pants and a plaid shirt covered by a dark blue sweater. His hair, as usual, was a little shaggy. He smiled and headed for his truck.

When he entered the lobby of the inn, Anna was just coming down the main staircase. Incredibly, she wore corduroy pants too and a beige cashmere sweater that matched. A scarf of cobalt blue hung around her neck. Her hair was loose and straight. She wore almost no make-up. She was five-foot seven and descended the steps gracefully, her posture erect, but relaxed.

Keith ordered a bottle of red wine when they sat down at a table, looking out on the snow-covered red cliffs behind the Inn, and turned his face to hers. Without thinking, he blurted out, "I've been living alone here for almost ten years. There's no woman in my life that really interests me, but just looking at you makes me want to know everything about you."

She smiled and cocked her head to one side. "You sound like a man who could be dangerous. You've been hiding out for ten years." She studied Keith for a moment then continued. "I'll tell you this much: I'm a model, moderately successful but not fabulously so. I hate it, but it pays great money so I keep doing it, especially commercials. I worry about what I'll do when it's over. I live in New York in an overpriced apartment that I share. I like to travel. I like to be outside. I like direct people." She paused. "I like you. You meet so many phonies, but you don't seem phony to me. A little disillusioned maybe."

"Disillusioned?"

"Uh huh." She nodded, with her lips turned down. Suddenly Keith felt all the bitterness and confusion he'd buried after the fiasco in Vietnam rise. He'd planned on an ordinary life. He'd followed the rules. He'd followed orders. For that, he felt like he'd hidden himself away, almost, but not quite, punished for doing his job. This woman saw it even when he couldn't admit it to himself. And she saw it immediately. He stared at the light reflecting off his wine glass. He looked at her hands. He raised his head and looked at her.

"I'd like to have dinner with you," he said quietly. "Then I'd like you to come to my cabin tonight." He never took his eyes off her. It was a frightening feeling to Keith. He felt she already knew him. This all was crazy.

"I'd like dinner," she answered steadily, looking straight back at him. "But I'd like you to come to my room after instead."

"Why?"

"Because I don't want to use up all that time driving around these blasted icy mountains." She smiled. They both laughed and took a sip of wine. He couldn't take his eyes off her.

The dinner was extended foreplay. Neither one of them ate too much. They filled each other in on the mundane facts of their lives; she was twenty-eight, had never married, and had trouble with authority. She resented casting directors, the politics of the modeling agencies, the ridiculous treatment by photographers. She lost work because of it. He was thirty-four, never married and, yes, a little bitter, but satisfied as long as he stayed in the mountains leading a somewhat solitary life. He seemed to realize this for the first time. She seemed to already know it.

Her room had a view of the mountains to the west of the town through the double windows next to the bed. Everything was natural. There was no awkwardness. She had the ability to loosen in him all the pain and loneliness he had felt for so long. Her body felt soft, but he could tell her muscles were toned. This was a meeting of equal strengths with different bodies.

She cried afterward. He was totally surprised. "Please," Anna said. "It's just because I feel so vulnerable now. I'm going to need you now. I'm not going to want anyone else with you in bed—or in the bar—or when you have some stupid accident." She smiled with the tears spilling out of her eyes, and reached for a Kleenex.

"Keith, I have some real problems with men. My father walked out on my mother and me when I was four. You know all the Freudian stuff. I'm terrified of abandonment. Trust is a huge issue with me."

"Don't be afraid of that," Keith said softly, stroking her hair. "That's the last thing to worry about." Certainly, now after he'd found her, he knew he'd never let her down. She could trust him. He kissed her and she responded by pulling him to her, and sliding her pelvis under him. Keith felt a moan rise up from his throat.

REDSTONE, COLORADO, THURSDAY, MAY 16, 1991

It wasn't until May that Anna found a long weekend free. She took the morning flight to surprise Keith. It connected through Denver to Aspen. She would have an extra day in the mountains they loved. They had already managed two ski weekends at Keith's cabin that winter. The snow had been fresh and they had taken wild runs in the deep, fluffy powder. Keith knew they were becoming very close. Most of the women he had known had little tolerance for what he viewed as "his independent ways." Anna was different. His previous love affairs had ended because Keith refused to center his world on someone else. Anna had a life she had built by herself, and she too had independent ways. But like Keith, she seemed to yearn for a steady committed relationship, one where both people agreed on the terms, and honored them.

Keith was immersed in the company books when he heard a car come up the driveway. He glanced out the window and saw an Avis sticker on the bumper just as he heard footsteps on the stairs leading to the kitchen.

Anna met Keith halfway across the living room floor and held him tightly as she kissed him on the mouth. Keith returned the passion.

"So, are you glad to see me or what?" said Anna, with a wide mischievous grin.

"Yes, lady, I am! You're a day early. I've got paper work falling off my desk, but the first order of business is we make love." He was pulling her jacket off her as she laughed and tugged at his sweater. "Second, we take the horses for a ride," shouted Keith, as they ran upstairs, leaving clothes behind them.

"Sounds great! You've got your priorities right! I knew it the first moment I saw you with that horse trailer lying on its side in the road," Anna giggled as they reached his unmade bed. It had been a month since they had seen each other. Neither was in a big hurry to end the experience. A lot that needed to be touched, a lot that needed to be said. It was late afternoon before they ate a late lunch in bed. Anna reached for his hand. "I want to tell you I start to feel less fear all the time with you, Keith. I mean my 'trust factor' hang-ups, you know."

He put his glass of wine down and touched her hair. "Good, Anna, you can trust me. You always can." She buried her head in his chest. Of course the horses had to wait until the next morning.

"Today we do something special," said Keith as they began

to tack up. "We're going to the old marble quarry where I can show you our restoration project. You'll love the ride, the scenery, and the company."

"Sounds good. What are you restoring?" asked Anna.

"An old quarry works. It's where the Tomb of the Unknown Soldier was quarried. You know, the huge slab in Arlington, Virginia. The quarry was abandoned about fifty years ago. Now the town has started a restoration project, and I've been helping," said Keith.

It took the better part of an hour to load the horses into the trailer, trailer them fifteen miles up the valley, and unload them at the base of the road leading from Marble to the quarry. Along the way, Keith explained a lot of the history of the Crystal River valley. He told her again of his first winter there and how, after his business got started, he had chosen land in the Crystal Valley. It was remote, but he wanted the isolation. He built the garage and the log cabin he now lived in five years later when the business in Aspen was doing well.

Anna listened as he spoke. She had heard only the barest details until now. Gradually, he was sharing with her some of the pain and joy of those years.

Keith rode his gelding, a feisty strawberry roan named Apache, while Anna rode Danny, a lively but older bay gelding. Keith was not surprised to find Anna was a skillful rider. She learned to ride in English saddles back east. He kept reminding her to let the western saddle do the work. "Just sit there looking competent," he told her.

"I can do that," she said. "I just did a commercial for Volvo Station Wagons as the mother of four. That's what the director told me to do then."

They both were laughing as they reached the road leading to the quarry. It was a good dirt road, but there were several swollen streams that cascaded across it and had carved deep washouts. Keith explained that in another month the erosion would be repaired, then cars could pass. In the meantime, it was best to go by horseback.

They met Jim Dawson, who was managing the project at the mouth of the largest entrance to the quarry tunnel complex.

"So, is this the Anna I've heard so much about?" asked Jim with a grin, knowing he would embarrass Keith.

"Yes, it is," Keith answered, trying to be casual.

"Well, it's nice to meet you, Anna," he said shaking her out-stretched hand, approval in his eyes.

"It's a pleasure to meet you, Jim. Keith tells me you are restoring the quarry works. I'm just dying to see what you two are up to," she said with a twinkle in her eye.

"It would be my pleasure to show you around," said Jim with a dramatic sweep of his arm. "Afterward, I'll need some help from Keith with the timbers under the main platform. OK, Keith?"

"Sure," Keith answered, glancing in the platform's direction.

Jim took Anna past the makeshift barrier where he had roped off the entrance, then down the steps to a series of tunnels which connected the three major quarry openings. Like Keith on his first tour two years ago, Anna was impressed by the amount of marble that had been removed from Treasure Mountain. Tunnels led in all directions. Some were filled with ice and very treacherous. Below, in the three main quarry sections, a solid sheet of ice covered the water.

"The ice doesn't hardly melt till fall. Then it freezes again quickly," said Jim.

Anna studied the ice for a moment. "How deep is the water?"

"Possibly a hundred feet, I'm not sure. But I am sure a person wouldn't last long in it, not with all that ice," Jim replied.

A shiver came over Anna. She shrugged it off.

"Let's go outside and warm up in the sun," Keith said, putting his arm around Anna, pulling her off her feet slightly.

"Good idea. Then you can do some real work and help me with the timbers," Jim teased.

Anna went outside and sat on a rock in the sun to warm up while Keith helped Jim remove the main supports from under the platform. Jim had new timbers ready to replace the rotted ones, but when they were shoved into place it was obvious there was more work to be done.

"Dammit! Looks like we'll have to get some more timber from the sawmill," Jim groaned.

"If we're going to have to wait till the timber gets here, we'd better put up a more official looking barricade and leave a sign," Keith warned. "We don't want anyone falling into the quarry."

He helped Jim rope off the area. As Anna and Keith left, Jim was busy fashioning a warning sign.

The wind was picking up and the sky was clouding over. "I can't tell if it's going to rain or snow, but we'd better get going," said Keith to Jim, as he mounted Apache and they started down the road for Marble.

Typical of the mountain weather, the rain, when it came, quickly turned to snow, and by the time they reached the truck and trailer there was already a half-inch on the ground. Fortunately, it was only a quick squall and soon passed. Within twenty minutes, the sun came out and cast a golden glow on the mountain south of Keith's cabin just as they turned in the driveway. Keith turned the horses out. He put some chicken pieces in a frying pan to sauté for the dinner he was planning. While the chicken cooked, he made two cups of herb tea. Anna sat on his lap and they watched the colors on Chair Mountain change from a golden yellow to red and then to blue as the light faded and the stars started to come out.

"To the end of a perfect and beautiful day," said Keith, clinking Anna's mug as they sat with their feet stretched out in front of them, secure and warm in matching gray wool socks.

It was also a perfect and beautiful weekend. When she left, Keith felt the pain of loss. When she was there, it was as if she held a mirror and helped him see himself. When she was gone, he increasingly found his cabin an empty place. It was a reminder of the loneliness of the first cabin in Lead King Basin.

Fortunately, he had the freedom to fly, and with that freedom he could see Anna fairly regularly. What had begun as comfort and excitement had become necessity for both of them. Anna had been right. But no longer was it just Anna who was vulnerable.

• Chapter 5 •

BAIKONUR COSMODROME
WEDNESDAY, JULY 31, 1991

Sergey Mikailovich Lebedev stood with clenched fists as he stared through the plate glass window at the large high resolution television monitor whose camera was trained on the launch site of the heavy lift Soviet Vega Booster rocket. On top of the booster was the sleek black shape of the Harvest Satellite. Lebedev was in the viewing booth reserved for dignitaries deep in the control center at the Tyuratam Launch Center. Before him was the space vehicle control room where technicians were monitoring the systems on the Harvest Satellite Module. Outside of this control room were two other rooms where engineers and technicians were preparing for the launch of the booster rocket. Again, Lebedev felt the approach of impending disaster. He wiped the perspiration from his forehead and squinted at the launch clock. Sixty seconds to go.

Only once before had he wished for a Soviet rocket failure. The first time, a month ago, he got his wish when the third stage failed. That rocket also carried a Harvest Satellite. What a shame to have spent the majority his career working to improve life in Russia, only to discover the product of his efforts could make things so much worse.

Lebedev watched his younger replacement, Vladimir Ustinov, who was bent over the master control console. By his closure of the master initiation switch, the final launch sequence began. There was an air of cautious optimism about the room because this time, the third stage ignition system had a new design. It had successfully passed all tests prior to this launch. Vladimir was reveling in the prominent position gained by his recent promotion.

Lebedev was an observer, no longer assigned to the launch crew since his demotion. Because of his long service in the space program, he was allowed to watch from a room provided for important Soviet dignitaries. Lebedev joined the Soviet space program a year after the close of World War Two. He was Chief Rocket Engineer on the first Russian Sputnik launch. Subsequently, he rose to Director of Research for the first Russian Manned Space Station Program. At his request, he was transferred to the Harvest System shortly after the preliminary research on Xzhylene gas at IKI; the Russian Institute of Space Research proved that it was possible to moderate Soviet weather.

Ustinov was now satisfied the huge rocket was ready. He began the final launch sequence. Ten seconds to go. Lebedev knew the eyes of the Politburo were now focused on Ustinov and his crew as the remaining seconds counted down to zero.

The Harvest Program had begun in 1967. Its intent was to create tropospheric disturbances, which would bring warming winds in winter and, in a similar fashion, rain in summer to the wheat fields in Central Asia. He had started the program on his 42nd birthday with high hopes for success. His vast experience in research, and his ability to supervise the efforts of others, helped him rise to director of the program. It was called the Harvest System because its primary intent was to improve the Russian wheat harvest. Two years ago he was proud to be the Program's director, but that was before the spectacular failure of the Mediterranean experiment—spectacular because it caused a massive ice storm which almost completely devastated the Ukrainian wheat crop in the winter of 1990. In an era when the Russian economy was straining to import oil to fuel its growing population of automobiles and heat and fuel its apartments and factories, a wheat crop disaster requiring more imported grain from the USA was not well received by the Politburo. Lebedev was immediately demoted, and the younger more politically ambitious scientist, Vladimir Ustinov, was promoted to Harvest System Director.

As the launch commenced, an enormous tongue of flame erupted from its base. Shortly after lift off, so much dust and debris was flying that the view of the rocket was momentarily obscured. Soon, Lebedev felt the booster rocket's low frequency vibration inside the launch command center.

Ustinov was quite proud of himself. Life had been good to him. He had a fine *dacha* outside Moscow and a functional Volga automobile, similar to a Mercedes, except for maintenance, which he acquired by climbing in the ranks of Russian scientists. Ustinov had finally achieved a lifestyle he enjoyed. To maintain it he had to please his superiors. In the past he had suppressed unpleasant information and altered facts to make himself appear more efficient. A month ago, he took a risk when he suppressed a particularly alarming portion of Lebedev's research report. The aging scientist had suggested that full scale use of the Harvest System might destroy the Earth's protective ozone layer.

The Energia rocket was rising now and moving to the east as it gained altitude. Within seconds it was beyond the view of the television camera. Soon, the booster separated and began to fall to the earth while the second and third stages continued upward.

Ten minutes later, the second stage completed its burn. Now Ustinov concentrated on the monitor as the third stage was about to begin. Seconds later, the room reverberated with Russian shouts of joy. The third stage ignition was successful! Today would be a good day for Ustinov. Now the Harvest System was once again continuing its string of achievements. By successful operation of the Harvest Satellite over the Caribbean, the Soviet Shadow Satellite program had a chance to be complete before the Global Survey Program. Two months ago, Ustinov agreed to launch a Harvest Satellite for the purpose of disrupting U.S. Space Shuttle launches. Ustinov, quick to seize an opportunity to gain recognition for himself, had immediately ordered a Harvest rocket assembled for deployment.

The first launch had sustained an ignition failure in the third stage, and was unable to achieve stable orbit. Next, the Harvest

Satellite began to break up in the outer atmosphere. Ustinov, fearing the worst, had ordered its destruction. A large amount of debris fell to the ocean off the west coast of Nicaragua. The clean-up effort by the Soviet trawler fleet was in full swing. The failure had been an embarrassment to Ustinov, but he had rapidly assembled a second rocket with a newly-designed firing mechanism. He had gambled on the new firing mechanism and he had won.

With the third stage burn complete and a stable orbit achieved, Ustinov turned to congratulate his subordinates. "Much better this time, comrades!" he said, as he hugged and slapped the back of the man next to him. He continued around the room congratulating each man and woman in turn. "Comrades, we must make an announcement to all members of the launch crew and to our comrades at our remote ground monitoring stations." With a flip of a small switch on his console he began speaking into a microphone.

"This is Vladimir Ustinov, Director of Harvest Systems program. At 12:30 p.m. this afternoon our huge Energia booster rocket successfully launched a Harvest Systems satellite. The launch was a spectacular display of Soviet rocket superiority. The Harvest Satellite is in perfect orbit to commence its mission. You all are to be congratulated for the success after the effort and sacrifices you made for our country. This satellite will be used for the betterment of life in the Soviet Union and will help us maintain our technological superiority over the Americans. I want to thank each of you."

When Ustinov turned from his console, his gaze focused on the man behind the observation window. Lebedev did not share in their joy.

Ustinov no longer trusted the old man. When the Harvest System caused the ice storm, he had disappeared into the laboratory. The aging scientist had worked day and night for four months in the low pressure laboratory until he had isolated the cause of the system's instability. When he emerged, he appeared ten years older. Sadly, he admitted the system was seriously flawed. His results conducted on the expensive American mixed gas analysis equipment had identified the problem. The model used in initial experiments did not account for several features, which became dominant when scaled up for the Harvest Program. These features were difficult to control in the laboratory, and almost impossible to control in free space.

That explained the failure, but Lebedev had studied the problem further and found that a byproduct of the breakdown of Xzhylene was chlorine gas. He then contended free chlorine in the outer atmosphere could absorb the Earth's protective ozone layer. He had continued his tests during the past two growing seasons and reported a two percent reduction in ozone over central Asia. But is a two percent reduction of any significance? Many factors beside the Harvest Program could account for such a loss.

Ustinov had reason to question Lebedev's results. During the last two years, the equipment used had somehow remained on the American embargo list. The thin membranes, which were critical to the measurement system, were not available. Soviet-manufactured thin membranes had to be substituted for the American membranes. Soviet membrane technology was far behind the American technology and, therefore, test results tended to be non-repeatable, casting doubt on Lebedev's supposition. There was no time to wait for further tests. The Harvest Satellite had to be used immediately. Still, Lebedev was adamant about his conclusions, so adamant that Ustinov suspected his former boss was unstable. Ustinov had cause to notify the KGB. Lebedev was now under observation.

Ustinov now concentrated on the orbit data. In a little over ninety minutes the Harvest satellite would be making its first pass over the Caribbean. The Soviet space tracking station in Cuba had his approval to feed the satellite trajectory data and initiate descent of the first canister. If the Harvest Satellite worked properly and did delay the Americans, his position would be secure. Realizing he had been on his feet for some time since the successful firing of the third stage, he took his seat behind the controller's console. As he glanced again at the launch clock, he noticed Lebedev had left the visitors booth. Ustinov was glad he had the foresight to have the old man watched.

Lebedev was desperate for a way to prevent the planned release of Xzhylene gas. Since the launch was successful, it would only be a matter of weeks before damage would begin. He had to find a way to prevent that from happening.

As Lebedev made his exit from the Space Center, he passed his former systems research laboratory. There, his eye caught a familiar object. In the center of the large display room stood the first prototype of the Harvest satellite.

Previously, the Russians had experimented with modification of their own weather. The world outcry against the program was so intense that the Soviets were forced to keep any further research top secret. Early in the Harvest Program, Lebedev had specified the satellite must be impossible to detect either visually or by ground- based radar. The Soviet chemists had spent years developing a super-high-strength plastic coated by a special non-metallic paint, which made the satellite invisible while in orbit.

The system worked well, thought Lebedev. Even the crippled orbit of the first rocket had gone undetected by western radar. It worked so well that Lebedev's men had to develop a miniature homing device to guide the supply ships which the Harvest Satellite periodically required for replenishment of Xzhylene canisters. To prevent hostile forces from activating the homing device, an electronic security circuit was incorporated.

The prototype of the Harvest Satellite had a functional homing system security device, except for the access code. But the access codes were still available to him.

Twenty minutes later, Lebedev entered the underground electric tram and took a seat in the rear. Several technicians who were just getting off their shift climbed aboard as the tram was about to leave. The doors closed and the electric motor began to quietly gather speed as the tram headed for the Cosmodrome's outer perimeter. Lebedev held a small case containing the remains of his lunch, and a poorly insulated Russian Thermos bottle. Hidden in the Thermos, under a half-cup of cold coffee, was the miniature prototype security device programmed with the current access code and recent orbit data for the Harvest Satellite. In his mind he was developing a desperate plan. He would get word to America. The Harvest Program must be stopped.

He knew his results in the low pressure laboratory were correct.

Xzhylene did break down into chlorine gas. Lebedev often read western newspapers. A week after the Mediterranean experiment, he found the report in the *London Times* describing a reduction in the ozone layer over Eastern Europe. Soviet scientists were too busy recovering from the massive ice storm to gather any ozone test data. It was then that Lebedev suspected the breakdown. Four frantic months later he had proved it, at least to himself.

Lebedev rose as the tram came to an abrupt halt. Thirty steps outside the station was the last security check. He slowly made his exit, so as not to be forced to join the front of the line. So far none of the guards at previous stations had inspected his Thermos bottle. He was fully aware that beneath a half cup of coffee was a plastic bag containing enough evidence to convict him of treason. Such activity would most certainly lead to execution, despite his once highly respected position. Trying not to appear nervous and willing his body not to perspire, he approached the guard. He casually raised his identification badge. The guard, recognizing Lebedev, was about to wave him through, but when he saw the small case he halted him.

"Comrade, open your case for inspection," the guard ordered in a commanding voice.

"It's just the scraps left from my lunch," Lebedev said apologetically.

The guard proceeded with his careful inspection of the paper, pieces of bread, and cheese from his lunch. *This guard is too efficient,* thought Lebedev. The guard picked up Lebedev's Thermos and opened it. To Lebedev's horror the guard stuck his finger into the liquid. He then raised it to his mouth and licked some of the fluid. "What, no vodka?" the guard laughed.

"No, not today. There is an important launch so we must be at our best," Lebedev responded, trying desperately to appear at ease.

Lebedev wondered why these former farm boys, brought to the Cosmodrome and trained as guards, thought everyone in Russia drank as heavily as they did. Lebedev only drank on social occasions, and usually in moderation. To drink vodka while working at his job was unthinkable. The guard nodded, handed Lebedev his case and Thermos and turned to the next man. Lebedev was free to leave.

Moments later he was coaxing his aging Volga out of the small parking lot at the Space Center. From habit he noted the official black Volga that was following close behind as had become customary for the last month.

Getting the security device out of Russia was not going to be easy. He had to devise a method to conceal the homing device better than the one he used this afternoon. He had to find an accomplice, someone allowed to leave Russia.

Forty-five minutes later, Lebedev arrived at Tyuratam airport. The drive had been longer than usual. Traffic around the Space Center had grown much worse in recent years. Russians by the thousands were becoming first-time car owners. The noise and pollution generated by so many stinking cars was worse than the Fifties and Sixties in America. Russia was not yet concerned about air quality. Today there had been a serious accident when a driver had collided his bus with an official Zil when he refused to yield. Lebedev had to wait, stopped in traffic for nearly a half hour. On a good day the trip could take as few as ten minutes. The theft of the security device would soon be discovered. As he waited in traffic, he knew he was losing valuable time. He glanced in the rear-view mirror, noticing that his KGB tail had just lit a cigarette as he waited for the traffic to move.

A half hour later he was able to use his rank to commandeer a seat in the Aeroflot Tyuratam to Moscow Shuttle. It was Saturday afternoon. He had small quarters outside the Space Center, but it was customary for officials of his rank to spend the weekend in Moscow where he had a modest apartment. This weekend he would be sure to visit relatives, take in the ballet and return on Monday with a good excuse for his travels. One could not be too careful when one was watched by the KGB.

Once, long ago, Lebedev had smuggled information out of Czechoslovakia right under the nose of the German SS troops. Before the war, he had met two young musicians in Vienna where he attended the university. Lebedev had considered his violin a hobby, but he enjoyed the diversion of playing with the others on

Friday nights. After the German occupation, Hitler wanted to promote the idea that culture still survived despite the war. He reestablished orchestras in large cities such as Prague, Vienna and Budapest. He then required regular performances for the German occupation army. By chance, all three musicians were recruited in different locations. Because they were constantly on tour, they had an excellent opportunity to observe the German army.

Taking great personal risk, they developed a complicated code based on variations of classical music, music they all knew from memory. By passing coded information in the form of sheet music, their risk of discovery was greatly reduced. To this day the code had never been broken.

One member of the old trio, Gustav Lentz, could only be reached by a post office box in Innsbruck. After retirement, Gustav had bought a small hostel high in the Austrian Alps on the edge of a large glacier. The other, Rudolf Madacheck, emigrated after the war to America and now lived in Philadelphia. Using the old code, Lebedev planned an attempt to reach both.

The key man in his plan was to be his old friend Joseph Halperin. Four years ago, Joseph had applied for emigration to Israel. Times were better in recent years for Russian Jewish emigrants. After years of waiting, he had finally received permission, and was preparing to leave shortly. The problem was that Joseph lived in Sokolniki on the north side of Moscow, some distance from Lebedev's apartment. It would be necessary to make this trip unobserved by his KGB constant companion.

Lebedev's flight to Moscow was uneventful. As he expected, the moment he left the curb in a cab at the airport a black Volga pulled out from behind in quiet pursuit. The KGB in Tyuratam had radioed ahead for his escort. Lebedev instructed the driver to take him to his apartment.

The driver, noticing the black car behind, said seriously, "Are you in trouble, comrade? It seems we have uninvited company."

"I am a senior researcher at the Tyuratam space center. We are working on top secret space projects. From time to time the KGB follow us just to be sure we keep in line. Today must be my turn," Lebedev explained casually.

The driver just grunted. Lebedev couldn't tell if he believed him or not. How he wished it was that simple.

Lebedev's apartment building was in a complex constructed in 1905. It was concrete faced with large blocks of stone, had four stories, and long creaky wooden hallways. Originally there had been no plumbing or electricity, but in modern times such conveniences had been installed, along with an elevator. The heating system was steam supplied from an aging plant two blocks away.

"Hello, Nadezda Petrovna," Lebedev said politely. "How is the family?" knowing her son and daughter-in-law were a great distance away working on the Trans-Siberian Railway.

"I don't know. They don't write, I don't read, and they rarely ever call, but I guess they are all right," she snapped.

The crone shuffled her feet and retired again to her tiny office. Lebedev knew she could be a problem. Age had not affected her hearing or dimmed her eyesight, and she was quick to report anything out of the ordinary.

Lebedev took the creaky elevator to the third floor and entered his austere two-room apartment. He had collected little furniture in his life time. He had never married. Textbooks and technical data he had gathered over the years filled much of the apartment. Quickly he went into action. First he wrote his urgent message in the Bavarian dialect they used in Vienna. Then he converted the message to a variation of an old familiar song. A song that he, Gustav, and Rudolf knew well. In the same fashion he and his comrades had used almost forty-five years ago, he burnt the German version and put the ashes in the trash.

Next, he carved a small hole in the back of his old violin. He removed the security device from the anti-static carrier box, discarded the box, and wrapped the device with aluminum foil. The device itself was smaller than the top of a common thumbtack. It was originally designed by a Japanese company to protect software from being indiscriminately copied, as was the habit of western computer enthusiasts. It was to be sold with expensive software. The software required the presence of the device. Without it, the software could not be used.

Lebedev's men had tested the device in their laboratory, and when satisfied it suited their purpose, they simply copied it. Lebedev used a small amount of black shoe polish to darken the foil, and with contact cement glued the device inside his old violin. He closed the small hole, glued it shut, and wiped the excess away.

He knew he must get both the sheet music and his violin to Joseph that night. In the process he must lose his tail. He would explain to Joseph that he was attempting to sell his music in the West through two old friends and to share with them an old war souvenir. He would prevail on Joseph to hold the violin in Israel for the first of his friends who came to claim it. He chose not to tell Joseph the importance of the mission, knowing Jewish emigrants were often searched and Joseph would become hopelessly nervous. Although he felt pangs of guilt at placing Joseph in such a vulnerable position, Lebedev knew it was of the utmost importance to get the device out of Russia. It simply had to be done. He would not worry about Halperin once he got to Israel. The KGB would not likely penetrate Israeli security.

FOUR HOURS LATER

After midnight, Lebedev's apartment building was mostly darkened, with only a few lights shining from isolated windows. Lebedev was in the basement, having stealthily sneaked past the concierge on the first floor. Had she known he left his apartment at this late hour, she would have notified the KGB immediately. She most certainly knew he was under observation. With a flashlight he lit the way under the stairs past plumbing and electrical distribution systems to the back wall. In a musty trench he found what he was seeking, the crawlspace provided for the complex of apartment buildings that would lead to the central steam plant.

Lebedev planned to crawl along the service tunnel to the steam plant. From there he would continue to a building four blocks away. Once out of the tunnel, he would change his clothes because the crawl space would be filthy. He would then dump the soiled clothing in the trash and once on the street outside, he would use the Metro.

Lebedev found the service tunnel confining, hot, and cob-webbed, but passable. In a half hour he emerged from a similar tunnel four blocks from his start. He was certain his tail would not suspect he had left his apartment. He had waited until he usually turned his lights out to prepare for bed. Once satisfied he had not given indication to the man outside anything unusual was about to happen, he had crept down the back stairs, which also functioned as a fire escape. He felt reasonably certain the concierge had not heard him pass softly by her doorway.

Lebedev continued down Minskaya Street until he came to Grechko Boulevard. From there he went three blocks until he reached Ploshad Pobedi, Victory Square, and then entered the brightly lighted Metro station with the same name. Twenty min-utes later he got off at Sokolnicki Station, took the long escalator up to the street, and a short walk later put him in front of Halperin's apartment. He walked around to the rear entrance, quickly jimmied the ancient lock mechanism, opened the door, and entered a short hallway at the base of the rear staircase. He closed the door behind him and slipped upstairs. At the first land-ing he knocked softly on a door. He knew Halperin kept late hours and hoped he would still be awake. In a moment the door opened.

Halperin was pleased, but astounded to see his old friend, es-pecially in the middle of the night.

"My goodness, Sergey, what brings you here at this late hour?" he asked, frowning, pulling Lebedev into the dingy apart-ment before closing the door gently.

"Old friend, you are leaving Moscow soon and I fear we may never have the chance to be together again," replied Lebedev.

Lebedev explained his other reason for coming. It was one of his better performances. He rationalized the late hour by saying, "You know, Joseph, it is risky for someone as prominent a Russian as I am to be seen with a dissident as notorious as you."

Halperin was genuinely proud that he could help his lifelong friend. He took the music carefully in his hand, promising to mail it the moment he got to Israel. He held the violin on his lap as Lebedev proposed his plan. When his explanation was complete and he was satisfied Halperin understood what he was to do, though he hadn't been told the real importance nor the risk involved in the delivery of the material, Joseph and Sergey sat down to share old times over vodka, as two old friends who were parting ways. Both knew it was for the last time.

By Russian custom a vodka bottle, once opened, must be finished. It was three hours later when the Moscow sky was showing signs of morning that Lebedev left the apartment house. His instincts honed by the war years, now dimmed by vodka, gave no warning as his picture was repeatedly taken.

SUNDAY, AUGUST 4, 1991

Nikolai Pronin sat behind his wooden desk at the secret KGB headquarters in Tyuratam. He had a serious problem. Someone had removed an important electronic device, potentially damaging to the security of a top secret military satellite system.

His superior, Teslov Socknat, a man who did not fare well under pressure, was visibly alarmed when he received the news. Pronin was immediately assigned the problem and swift results were expected.

Socknat had chosen Pronin for the investigation because of his reputation for tenacity and boldness of action, despite a recent disappointment. This was the opportunity Pronin was waiting for to prove himself. Solving this case would help him to get that promotion and a transfer to Moscow. In Moscow, medical treatment would be better for his beloved Natasha. Everything would be better in Moscow.

Recently, Pronin's fortunes had taken a turn for the worse. During an investigation of a student dissident demonstrator who was particularly defiant, Pronin had used one of his favorite, but somewhat cruel, methods. The student was not in good health, and under the stress of Pronin's methods, he caught pneumonia and died a week later. Unfortunately, the young man was the grandson of a great war hero. Now the grieving family was exerting pressure to have Pronin punished. Pronin did not fear banishment for himself; much of his career had been spent in undesirable posts such as Vietnam and Afghanistan. Natasha, who suffered from chronic angina and required constant medical treatment to keep her weakened heart from failing, had to be in Moscow where treatment would be much better. Perhaps they would even risk surgery.

Pronin stepped outside the office and addressed his stocky secretary.

"Katrina, could I have the file on all employees who are under observation at the Space Center?"

"Yes sir, just a moment," she replied. She walked with no sense of urgency down the hall in the direction of the file room.

Moments later, she returned with a manila folder containing nineteen separate files. Each was an individual on the KGB watch list.

Pronin examined each file intently. There were technicians who were suspected of selling state property on the black market, engineers seen at the wrong place at the wrong time, heavy drinkers who talked too much, and relatives or friends of known criminals or dissidents. Lastly, a case where a young former subordinate had reported his demoted boss as unstable and possibly dangerous. The subordinate probably meant to further discredit his boss.

This last folder caught his curiosity. Pronin called, "Katrina, bring the whole file on Sergey Lebedev."

Katrina took longer this time because the more extensive background files of suspects were kept in the basement where there was more space. The KGB kept so many files it was almost impossible to find storage space for them all. When she returned, Pronin was surprised by its size.

Inside were almost two hundred pages of text relating to Lebedev's long and faithful service to the Soviet Space Program, and before that, his heroic service in the Czech underground during the war. Pronin was about to put the file down and return to the others when he remembered something. Reaching into his desk, he pulled out copies of the passenger lists for last weekend's flights out of Tyuratam Airport. His memory was correct; Lebedev had left on a flight to Moscow Saturday afternoon. Could Lebedev have reason to steal the device? He certainly would know what its purpose was and its value. Suddenly, Pronin realized if the device were in Lebedev's possession, he could easily find a way to get it out of Russia. The potential damage, should he defect, could not be dismissed.

He turned to his phone and dialed a familiar number. "Have Sergey Lebedev picked up and brought in for questioning when he leaves his quarters at the Space Center employees' hostel," he said.

His next call was to Moscow. Lebedev's movements there would have to be investigated.

THURSDAY, AUGUST 6

The interview began when Lebedev was escorted into Pronin's office by two husky agents at eight o'clock Thursday morning. Pronin dismissed his agents with a wave of his hand. "Please sit down," he said to Lebedev, as he remained seated.

Once seated, Lebedev realized his chair was a couple of inches lower than Pronin's and made of hard wood. He was not feeling well this morning. For months now he had a nagging pain in his stomach, especially before mealtimes. Because of this meeting with Pronin, he had missed breakfast. He resented Pronin's arrogance and the condescending manner with which he addressed scientists. Pronin hadn't even stood up when Lebedev had entered. Lebedev wished this unpleasant interview could be over so he could get back to his laboratory.

Looking around the room, Lebedev found the walls almost bare except for a picture of Mikhail Gorbachev, President of the Soviet Union. what kind of a man keeps an austere office such as this? Has he no imagination? No desire for color? Is his life as drab as these walls? No, this was the type of man who would have already decided Lebedev's guilt before he arrived. He was dangerous, as dangerous as any of the SS troops he had seen during the war.

Pronin stared at the old scientist for a moment, then reached into his shirt pocket. "Would you like a cigarette? They are imported," offered Pronin, taking out a pack of unfiltered Camel cigarettes.

"No, thank you. I don't smoke anymore. I had walking pneumonia for so long I once lost part of my right lung. I quit smoking then. I don't miss it," Lebedev responded politely.

Pronin took out a cigarette, put it in his mouth, struck a match with a fingernail, lit his cigarette with several short puffs, blew the match out, and deposited it in the heap of butts in a round ashtray on his desk.

"I have brought you here to ask some questions about your work at the Space Center," Pronin started. He inhaled deeply, looked directly at Lebedev, and began a long, slow exhale. A cloud of smoke filled the room.

Lebedev, stifling an urge to cough, replied, "Our work is going well. We have successfully launched a top secret satellite, which can greatly improve our chances of beating the Global Climate Survey System."

"I have a report here from your superior which states you have made disparaging remarks about the administration of your Harvest program, and that you have questioned the wisdom of the Politburo."

So Ustinov has been supplying this pig with information, thought Lebedev. Not too surprising considering his former subordinate's past record. He should have anticipated Ustinov and kept his mouth shut, but he had been too busy with his work to pay much attention to the movements of his boss.

"Reports of any such statements must be greatly exaggerated for the benefit of the informer," Lebedev answered wearily. "I have a long record of loyal service and you know it. I am a loyal party member and find it insulting you even suggest I could be involved in such activities!"

"Yes, I had considered the possibility that your new boss might have a personal motive in the matter, but there is a bigger issue here than your possible indiscretions." Pronin tapped his foot on the floor to add emphasis to his words.

"What might that issue be? It must be urgent for you to bother someone as important as myself. You know I have critical research to complete at the Space Center," Lebedev said, taking the opportunity to remind this younger man that his position was one of prestige and possible powerful connections.

Bending forward, and in a lower voice, Pronin said, "There has been a theft of State property, specifically an electronic device used in the satellite your laboratory designed."

"And what was the device?"

"I believe it is called a security device for the homing system used by replenishment ships."

Lebedev's face was blank. His gaze at Pronin revealed nothing.

"What do you know about this device?" asked Pronin.

"I know little really, only that it enables vehicles to approach the satellite system and to dock, when normally it is almost invisible."

Pronin considered Lebedev's response for a moment as he thought Lebedev's face grew slightly red.

"Come now, Comrade Lebedev, we know better than that, because our Space Center records show you accessed the computerized file for programming such a device Saturday afternoon just before you left the Space Center for Moscow."

Lebedev was not shaken by this comment. He knew they had records of the equipment use, but not the actual work completed.

"In my work I often use the programming equipment. In fact, several times this month I used the equipment for the same purpose. I am experimenting in the low pressure laboratory, and each experiment requires a new program."

Lebedev knew their records backed his claim. Pronin continued, changing the subject.

"I see you went to Moscow for the weekend. What was the purpose of your trip?" asked Pronin.

"Your records must show that I have gone three out of the last four weekends. I like to spend the weekend in Moscow. It is a privilege granted to me as part of the benefits of my position. Surely you can understand that," shot back Lebedev.

Pronin was visibly irritated by the last comment. "Yes, but what specifically did you do while in Moscow?"

"I visited my sick Aunt Hilda, who is now hospitalized, and went to the Moscow Ballet production of *Giselle*. Your man followed me to both places. Why don't you just read his report?"

"Is that all?"

"Yes."

"Then how do you explain these? You were repeatedly photographed entering and leaving your associate's apartment, though you knew he was a dissident about to leave Russia."

Pronin was now standing and leaning over with his chin jutting into Lebedev's face.

Lebedev was internally shaken. He had not suspected Halperin's apartment was under surveillance. He had been caught when Halperin's vodka had made him careless. With a supreme effort, he kept his face blank, showing no emotion.

"I was saying goodbye to an old friend. He was leaving Russia, and we probably will not see each other again. Is that what this is all about?"

"No!" shouted Pronin. "What this is about is this small case found in the trash of your apartment. The same case the Space Center uses to protect sensitive electronic parts such as your security device. I suppose you have a simple explanation for that too?"

Lebedev did not move. He showed no emotion. He stared at the box in Pronin's hand for a moment before he spoke. "Those cases are very common, your people have found the case for the transistor I used to fix my ailing radio. You know how unreliable the Russian models are. I purchased the device at the Russian Space Institute last month and had occasion Saturday night to fix my radio," lied Lebedev.

"Then tell me, Comrade Lebedev, why did you leave your violin case at Halperin's apartment. Did the violin case contain more than a violin? Was that your plan? To smuggle the security device out of the USSR through Israel?" snarled Pronin, slamming his fist hard upon the desk.

Lebedev stood to face Pronin. He tried not to show that his knees were shaking slightly. "No. My friend had long ago asked if he could have it. I gave it to him because he was leaving and I had no use for it." He pointed his finger at Pronin. "You are wrong! Dead wrong! I am an old and loyal Soviet. I have never strayed from my duty. I am innocent of whatever you think I have done, but now that you have made your intent clear, I suggest you think twice before going any further. I will be missed by noon at the Space Center. My absence will be reported. You know I have important friends at the Cosmodrome and the Soviet Space Research Institute. By to-morrow morning, your superior will be speaking to both Arthur Savelin and Roald Sagdayev personally about my welfare."

Staring at Lebedev, Pronin saw the raw determination from the aging ex-guerilla fighter who had lost little courage since the war years. Pronin knew it would be difficult to get any information out of Lebedev. Pronin knew he was right. Lebedev was guilty. Now he wished he could use the methods that worked so well in Afghanistan. With time and the right drugs, he could easily break this man, despite his courage. Unfortunately, such methods were inappropriate, considering Lebedev's high position in the scientific community. Pronin straightened for a moment, giving Lebe-dev a cold stare. "All right, you deny it. I will let you go today, but we will meet again, and when we do, I expect you will have more to say than convenient excuses, Comrade Lebedev."

With a little foot pressure on a hidden switch, Pronin summoned the two agents.

"Take Comrade Lebedev back to the Space Center," said Pronin. The agents each took an arm and ushered Lebedev roughly out of Pronin's barren office.

Moments later, Pronin entered the office of his superior, Teslov Socknat.

"I believe Lebedev is our man. He was not shaken by my interrogation, but I strongly believe he is hiding something," said Pronin.

"And the whereabouts of the electronic device?" asked Socknat.

"Departed for Israel with Joseph Halperin. I would like to further interrogate Lebedev, but use more convincing methods."

Socknat thought for a moment. This was a difficult situation. Pronin had recently embarrassed his department with the student dissident with the unknown heart problem and the bad politics that were continuing to follow.

"No ... not this time, Comrade Pronin. It is better we try to recover the device in Israel. I think it is time some of our Arab friends repaid us a favor. We can deal with Lebedev once the device has been recovered.

• Chapter 6 •

SATURDAY, AUGUST 10, 1991

The *USS Hank* (DDE506) was cruising through the placid blue waters of the Pacific Ocean fifteen miles off the Nicaraguan coast. Twenty fathoms beneath her keel was the coral bottom of the Guardian Bank. The *Hank* was one of the newest American destroyer escorts. She had two five-inch gun mounts one fore and one aft, two 50-caliber machine guns one on each wing of the bridge, ASROC (Anti-submarine Rocket), the latest air, surface search and weapons control radar, the latest sonar, and aft of her two stacks, a platform that bristled with electronic intelligence antennas.

Between the two stacks and in the center of her ASROC deck was a square gray box ten feet on a side temporarily welded to braces on the deck. On the top of the box were seven antennas, each devoted to a different frequency span. Inside, a team of four Navy Beach Jumpers manned communications and recording equipment.

These four men reported to Lieutenant Commander Joseph Scott, a Navy SEAL with a long and excellent service record. Besides the gray box of communications equipment, Scott had a one-man mini wet sub, scuba gear, air compressor, decompression chamber, and an assortment of especially deadly underwater weapons, all stowed neatly below decks. Commander Scott had two SEAL divers assigned as crew for the sub. Scott and his men were anxious to use the equipment.

Six days ago the *Hank* left San Diego harbor to investigate an unusual build up of Russian trawlers off the west coast of Nicaragua. Satellite photos revealed roughly fifty ships engaged in organized search patterns with more ships on the way.

Two days outside of U.S. territorial waters, two Russian trawlers appeared and began to shadow the *Hank*. A day outside the search area, the Russian shadows began to intentionally obstruct the *Hank's* course, first by forcing her to yield in agreement with the international rules of the road, and then twelve hours outside the search area, the Russians started aggressively blocking the way, forcing the *Hank* to constantly change course to avoid collision. Now the *Hank* was a lone U.S. warship in the midst of a vast armada of Russian trawlers. The *Hank* had been at General Quarters for more than two days.

A hundred feet forward of the ASROC deck inside the *Hank's* Combat Information Center, a status review was in progress. A crew of five men manned four RADAR repeaters and maintained a large clear plexiglass status chart showing active radar and sonar contacts. Standing in front of the status board were the CIC watch officer; Radar Chief Gary Martin; Lieutenant Commander Joseph Scott, commander of the beach jumpers temporarily assigned to the *Hank*; Lieutenant Commander Darrell Shannen, operations officer; and Commander John Stewart, the ship's Executive Officer.

"I don't believe it!" growled an exasperated Martin. "There are too damn many Russian trawlers. It's impossible to track them all! We're concentrating only on those closer than ten miles."

Shannen shifted his position to study the dots on the radar repeater for a moment. "Jesus, how many are there?"

"At least a hundred," replied Martin. "Each operating in its own search territory throughout a long rectangle roughly measuring ten miles by one hundred miles."

"The racket on Russian UHF frequencies is intense. We're recording everything we intercept, but with all this activity we've got real difficulty keeping up," Scott added, shaking his head.

"What they're looking for must be damn important. I've seen smaller concentrations off both our coasts, but nothing this big," added Stewart. "What do you guess is the objective?" he asked, looking at each man in the group.

Shannen shrugged, "Best guess, Darrell, is that the Russians have lost something important, something they want back real bad. It's here in these waters either floating, or on the bottom."

"Like the satellite that hit Canada back in '82," said Chief Martin.

"Or like the sub we got near Hawaii with the Glomar Explorer," continued Shannen.

"Could be either, but we've neither indication from NORAD that one of the Russian birds is in trouble nor word from CincPacFlt that one of their subs is missing. No, gentlemen, this is strange," Stewart added, shaking his head.

Radioman Second Class, Harry Lauderback, entered the room and handed Commander Stewart two messages. Stewart turned to take them, paused a moment to read both, and turned back to the group. "That was a message from Commander Submarine Forces Pacific Fleet. Ivan's got one nuclear and two conventional subs in our immediate area. Apparently, they're after more than flotsam."

There was a momentary silence among the group. Commander Stewart observed their reaction and then continued. "The second message is from CincPacFlt. He's not leaving us alone any longer. The aircraft carrier *USS America*, two missile cruisers, and six destroyers are headed this way. ETA is forty-six hours."

"Good," grunted Chief Martin, showing the strain of little sleep for the better part of three days. "I'll be glad when this shit is done so we can relax."

The *Hank* began to tilt heavily to starboard. From the bridge of the *Hank* came loud voices issuing sharp commands. The conning officer, Lieutenant Commander Jim Shirley, attempted to avoid a collision by passing aft of a Russian trawler. Shirley realized too late that the Russian trawler was dragging bottom rigging. The rigging was now fouling the *Hank's* two huge propellers. The rigging drew taut and began straining with audible popping noises. Now the crew on the Russian trawler was scrambling in all directions. The rigging didn't withstand the strain for long. With an enormous crack it parted. The backlash caught a Russian seaman in mid-section and nearly severed his body in half. The *Hank's* propellers were now fouled by the remainder of the bottom rigging.

Before the rigging parted, Commander Shirley halted both engines. The *USS Hank* was drifting almost dead in the water.

The captain of the *Hank*, Toby Bidderman, peered through his field glasses at the aft deck of the Russian trawler. He could see four men gathered around their comrade. Soon they carried his limp body below decks.

"That poor bastard's a goner," the captain said to Commander Shirley. "We've got an international incident on our hands. Let's hope they keep cool about it."

The Russian captain was swinging his ship in a tight starboard turn. Captain Bidderman could see two crew members scrambling to pull a tarp off a large caliber machine gun on the bow.

Turning to Shirley, he said, "Load both guns and lock the director's radar on the trawler's bridge."

In seconds the crew leveled the *Hank's* two five-inch guns at the trawler. The director was in radar lock. Both breaches were loaded. The automatic loading systems were ready to spew projectiles in rapid succession. In an instant the *Hank* could reduce the trawler to sinking scrap.

As the trawler approached the bow of the *Hank*, Captain Bidderman could see the frustration on the face of the Russian captain as he stared at the *Hank's* guns. In a single gesture he raised his fist to the American captain. Bidderman stared back defiantly. The port lookout used a different gesture.

The trawler passed harmlessly down the *Hank's* port side. The Russian captain was satisfied further contact would be fruitless. Commander Shirley returned to the problem at hand. "Captain," he asked, "request permission to try to cut the rigging by using the engines?"

"No, remain DIW. Watch the Russians and be ready to move if necessary, but give them the impression we've broken down." To the Petty Officer the captain said, "Have officers Stewart, Shannen and Scott summoned to the wardroom."

In a moment, the Captain turned and descended the ladder heading for the wardroom, leaving Lt. Shirley on the bridge.

FIVE MINUTES LATER

Once all four men had gathered in the wardroom, Captain Bidderman, addressed them. "We know the Russians had a big head start in this operation, at least a week. We also know the Russians started in deeper water hoping to clear international waters first. Now, what does that suggest?"

"That they haven't got it all," said Commander Stewart.

"And what's left is within the territorial waters of Nicaragua," said Scott.

Captain Bidderman nodded. "My assessment also. We're probably too late to find anything outside the international limit. However, a large search area remains just inside the limit."

"Just a second, are you suggesting we enter Nicaraguan waters?" Commander Stewart interjected.

"No, not with the *Hank*, but with the equipment Commander Scott brought aboard. Assuming, of course, Joe, you and your men are willing to volunteer for the mission."

Joe and his men were itching for the chance. Now it appeared they would get it. Years ago Scott had been involved in a clandestine operation, but he had seen no action. He had watched as three other men pushed off into the dark of a humid Vietnamese night. Keith Maddox was the only one that ever made it back. Scott tried not to be too enthusiastic as he responded, "I'm game when it comes to risky business. Especially if the risk appears worth it, as it does here."

"Good. When can you be ready?"

"If necessary, in an hour."

"Excellent. It'll soon be nightfall. We're drifting on an inshore current. I want to anchor just outside their thirteen-mile limit. Here's the tricky part: I want the mini-sub over the side under the cover of darkness. I don't want the Russians suspecting what we're doing," Captain Bidderman stated calmly.

"We could use the spotlight on the signal bridge to blind the

Russians' night vision. It has the added benefit of temporarily disabling infra-red scanning equipment," suggested Commander Stewart.

"Good idea," said Bidderman. "Joe, how good is your team at night navigation?"

"The sub's got a good gyro compass and computerized dead reckoning gear. Navigation is a breeze, but using search lights at night would be a dead giveaway," disagreed Scott.

"Then the best plan would be to begin your search in the morning," Bidderman added hastily. "You could slip overboard in darkness and by the time you get inshore there will be enough light to see the bottom."

Scott nodded his head in agreement, "OK, Captain, the only thing that remains is where to search."

Bidderman took out a large chart and spread it out on the wardroom table.

"Here, gentlemen," said Bidderman, pointing his finger, "is where we are. And here is an area where the Russians are just beginning to search. It's roughly five miles inside the territorial waters of Nicaragua. Joe, can you and your sub make the distance?"

"I think so. The sub's top speed is five knots. Cruising speed is three knots. Taking into account the two knot current now bringing us inshore and remembering it will be against us on the return trip, I think we have enough charge in the batteries and air in the tanks."

"How long will you have to search?"

"Between the sub's twin 700s and the double 100s for each man, assuming we don't go below forty feet on our way out or on our way back, we'll have ninety minutes," replied Scott.

"Great," said Captain Bidderman, "Any problems with the plan?"

"Yes," Scott answered quickly. "The bottom time is excessive. If we operate the search at eighty feet for that long we'll be in two-stage decompression. That means we can't surface. The problem is in daylight we can be seen. If we're discovered, they can run us over with their propellers or worse yet, drop explosives!"

Bidderman was equally quick to respond. "If they try to run you down, Joe, I'll use the *Hank*. If we risk an international incident, so be it! We must find out what the Ruskies are up to. Can you signal if you're in trouble?"

Commander Scott straightened. "Sure, we have a radio beacon float. You could monitor the frequency and use the *Hank's* directional antennas to find us," he said.

"Good. Then, gentlemen, I suggest we get the wet sub over the side and catch some sleep. We're going to have a long day tomorrow," said Captain Bidderman, rising from his seat.

SUNDAY, AUGUST 11

The Pacific was dead calm. There was no breeze. The sun was about to rise above the horizon; the sky away from the rising sun was a dark blue to black. The *Hank* seemed almost too quiet with her main propulsion system shut down. Sea birds rose high and swooped low to gather scraps of garbage thrown over after the morning mess. The *Hank's* crew spent the night on port/starboard alert watches, allowing each man four hours of sleep. The *Hank* was again at General Quarters as she swung gently about her anchor.

Commander Scott found his wet suit too hot in the warm tropical air. As always when he suited up, he longed to jump into the cool water below as quickly as possible. Finally, he and his two men, Lt. William Larson and Lt. Peter Walters, were ready. Fully suited and with their double tanks on their shoulders, they jumped fins apart into the clear ocean below. A moment later, Larson and Walters were aboard the wet sub and beginning the checklist for departure.

Commander Scott swam aft, and then with a saw, cut the two-inch hawser of the Russian rigging fouling the *Hank's* propellers. When the *Hank's* propellers were clear of rigging, Commander Scott swam forward and climbed into the pilot seat of the wet sub. Satisfied his crew had completed the checklist, he threw the forward switch and headed inshore in the dark water at three knots. The only light was from the instruments on the operator's console and the occasional bioluminescence of a passing jellyfish.

Commander Scott kept his depth at forty feet to remain below the Russian trawlers. Behind the men was the inevitable telltale trail of bubbles. To minimize the possibility of discovery, Commander Scott occasionally changed course to avoid an approaching trawler.

He kept thinking this was like any other mission. It wasn't his first mission into the unknown, but a growing feeling of dread remained as he scanned the dark surface above. Should they be discovered, Scott wasn't confident Captain Bidderman could get the *Hank* into action soon enough to save his crew. Besides, his wife Lori in San Diego had no idea what he was doing. Shortly after rising he had drafted a note to her and the kids. A nagging fear had started then and he hadn't been able to shake it. This was silly. Wasn't this what they were waiting for? Hadn't he and his men trained for just this kind of work? He was glad they were underway. No time to worry; they were in action. Both men in his crew were experienced; it was their first mission under hostile circumstances, but Scott was certain they would prove themselves.

Two hours later, the wet sub arrived at the search area. Scott glanced at the fathometer. It read a steady eighty-seven feet, indicating a hard flat bottom, excellent for the search. Scott descended to eighty feet. There in the blue green light, a sandy bottom, dotted occasionally by coral formations, appeared. Sighting a coral head large enough to conceal the sub, Scott let it settle on the bottom.

The three divers switched from the wet sub air to the air in their double tanks, picked up their spear guns and lights, and swam off by prior agreement in directions each 120 degrees apart. Commander Scott headed inshore, his two men heading offshore into slightly deeper water. Each man was to proceed outward for forty-five minutes and return. Their tanks had sufficient air for two hours, giving each man a half hour of reserve air. They knew they were already deep into the decompression tables and that they could not rise to the surface without a lengthy decompression. If they failed to find the sub on the return leg and had to surface, a fatal case of the bends would result.

For a half hour Commander Scott continued his inshore course with little more than an occasional parrot fish, grouper, or school of bait fish for company. Then a long shadow passed overhead. Looking up, he saw a ten-foot hammerhead shark cruising above him. Scott loaded his speargun with one of his five explosive tipped spears and activated its compressed gas canister. The shark moved closer and arched its back with the obvious intent of attacking. At point blank range Scott fired. The spear point entered the shark's mouth. It penetrated upward until the explosive charge disintegrated the shark's primitive brain. The lifeless shark slowly sank as a stream of blood floated through the water.

Knowing blood in the water would bring trouble, Scott swam away from the fallen shark. In seconds, gray sharks gathered around the hammerhead and started tearing at its flesh.

While making his hasty exit, Scott came upon a strange object. On the bottom was a white sheet with strings attached. He realized he was looking at a parachute. Following the lines to their base revealed a large black object in the sand. Swimming closer, Scott found a barrel about three feet in diameter and five feet long. At one end was a cone-shaped shroud from which the parachute apparently was deployed. At the opposite end was a corroded metallic coating with a half-inch hole in it. Striking the barrel with his knife resulted in a dull thud. Commander Scott easily turned it over to examine the underside. There in the middle of the bottom, was a single metallic identification tag. Close examination revealed Russian lettering.

Joe almost shouted through his regulator. "Is this what all the fuss was about? ... Why?"

He took out his knife, separated the plate from the tank, unzipped his wet suit jacket, placed the plate inside, and zipped his jacket.

Now back to the sub, he thought. He checked his air gage. Only 825 lbs of air remained! Barely enough to get back, just barely enough. Scott calculated the distance he had traversed, avoiding the sharks. He would have to conserve his air. He now was on a new heading hoping the return course would prove shorter.

Suddenly, out of the darkness, an enormous object appeared

on the ocean bottom. Directly in his path lay a sub, a big sub! Commander Scott reasoned it must be Russian. He was alone and exposed. He turned to flee, but before he got fifteen feet, a party of six Russian divers appeared on his right. They were using two scooters to ferry the barrel-like objects. By their reaction, Scott knew they had seen him.

A moment later Commander Joe Scott was swimming flat out, desperately seeking cover. Behind him he could hear the high pitched whine of the Russian scooters. In a large coral head he found a low cave and entered. Seconds later the first of the Russian scooters arrived. The diver, knife in hand, prepared to enter the cave. By his actions Scott knew he meant business. He loaded his spear gun and waited. The Russian approached, wildly flailing with his knife. Scott didn't hesitate and fired his speargun directly into the Russian's chest at close range. The tip penetrated the Russian's rib cage, then exploded with a nasty crack, stunning Scott. The force of the explosion blew away a large chunk of flesh from the Russian's back. Blood and debris permeated the water. The Russian momentarily reacted with shock and indignation, then sank limply to the floor of the cave.

One down, five to go, Scott thought.

The first Russian's two companions were not far behind. Each was armed with a deadly speargun. After witnessing the demise of their comrade, and not wanting to repeat his mistake, they approached Scott cautiously. Seeing a long column of bubbles rising from behind the next coral head the two approached from different sides expecting to catch the American between them on the far side.

Scott had released a blast of air from his mouth and while holding his breath, he moved under the bottom edge of the coral head.

When the Russians reached the far side, they realized they had been fooled. But it was too late. They came face-to-face with Commander Scott, who was ready to fire. They both raised their spear-guns. The first Russian to fire missed as he took the full blast of a spear tip in midsection. The second Russian, momentarily blinded by the bubbles exiting from the first Russian's gun, also missed the American. Now Scott's knife flashed and cut the second Russian's air hose. It spewed air. Gasping for air while trying to hold the two ends together, the second Russian ascended toward the surface.

Commander Scott noted the gray sharks beginning to gather again.

Now the three remaining Russians approached. Joe loaded his final spear, grabbed the second Russian's scooter, and headed in the general direction of the wet sub. Looking backward, he could see the Russians were not gaining.

Maybe he could make it. There could still be enough air in his tanks. Maybe he could keep ahead.

For ten minutes the scooter continued in the direction of the sub. Slowly, Joe realized the motor speed was decreasing. Maybe the Russians knew the batteries were nearly exhausted. They were now gaining on him. The scooter was slowing rapidly. Soon, its battery would be dead. Looking back, it was obvious the Russians would overtake him.

This is it … This is the end. I'm going to die here. I'm not going to get home to my wife. Oh God, Lori, I'm sorry, he thought.

As Commander Scott turned to face the enemy, his speargun ready, his air supply ran out. The approaching Russians saw him straining to suck air from his empty tanks. They stopped and waited out of range of his spear-gun. They knew he was in trouble, but they also knew his spear gun was deadly, so they waited.

He swam desperately for the surface. If he had made it, he would have died from the bends. But he blacked out twenty feet from the surface. The Russians didn't bother with his body and let it float away. It remained trapped and decomposing in the wet suit for a week before the bloated remains washed ashore.

Back at the wet sub, Lieutenants Larson and Walters were in a dilemma. Commander Scott was overdue. Both men, after completing their search without finding anything, had continued using the air in their double tanks. Now the air was exhausted. That could only mean Commander Scott was also out of air.

After switching back to the sub's air, they waited for an additional five minutes and then, reluctantly, Lieutenant Larson took the controls and began heading for the *Hank*. Ninety minutes later they discovered a Russian trawler approaching at high speed. It became apparent the Russians' intent was to crush both men with the trawler's propellers.

Lieutenant Walters immediately released the radio beacon float. Lieutenant Larson drove the sub below the depth of the trawler's propellers.

The Russians sighted the float, retrieved it, and smashed its antenna. Now they concentrated on the divers with a different tactic. They dropped grenades. The first explosion nearly crushed the two men while rupturing their ear drums. Lieutenant Larson struggled at the controls, fighting acute vertigo from the cold water now in his middle ear. The sub veered to the left, straightened, and picked up speed as Lieutenant Larson switched to full speed. A second grenade went off, but at greater distance. The effect was deafening, but Lieutenant Larson remained in control. Bubbles filled the water. The sub, being deeper in the water, was impossible to see from above. Lieutenant Larson attempted to keep away from the trawler by constantly changing course. This frustrated the Russians, who began throwing grenades at random into the mass of bubbles rising to the surface. With each successive concussion, Lieutenant Larson had greater trouble remaining conscious. They could not last much longer.

The USS Hank, upon receipt of the beacon signal, raised anchor and entered Nicaraguan waters at flank speed. In ten minutes the Hank arrived at the scene, pointed one of her fifty-caliber machine guns at the Russian trawler, and strafed the bridge. The trawler immediately withdrew.

Captain Bidderman's crew retrieved Lieutenants Larson and Walters. Both men were in serious trouble. They were immediately placed in the recompression chamber with the corpsman. After picking up the wet sub, the Hank departed for international waters.

To Captain Bidderman the loss of Commander Scott and the injuries to Larson and Walters would have been worthwhile had they found what the Russians were after, but that was still unknown. Even more puzzling was the lack of Russian public protest about the loss of one of its sailors and the attack on its trawler.

• Chapter 7 •

FLORIDA
FRIDAY, AUGUST 16, 1991

John Whiting could hardly believe his eyes. He worked the evening shift at the Hurricane Center in Coral Gables. From this station the massive storms were routinely tracked throughout the hurricane season. Until tonight, the season had been mild with only a few tropical depressions. Each one dissipated before acquiring hurricane status. This evening was a different story. Before him was a large screen showing the computerized summation of satellite pictures taken from multiple passes over the Caribbean. Near the center of this screen, just a hundred miles south of San Salvador Island in the Bahamas, was a major low pressure system. What astounded him was the rapid growth of the storm. It hadn't been there when he started his shift eight hours ago.

Shortly after he began his work, the first weather bird had relayed a photograph showing a small tropical depression. By the time the second weather bird relayed its pictures, the depression was widespread and organized. On his recommendation, the dispatcher had approved the flight of the Hurricane Watch 409, a weather observation aircraft. The weather service used aircraft to gather data on tropical storms. This storm was of particular interest because the conditions, as monitored by multiple ground and satellite-based systems, were judged not conducive to the generation of a tropical depression by the weather service's four Cray computers. In an era when the weather service was gaining confidence in its prediction capabilities, this storm was an anomaly. An hour after takeoff, 409 reported its approach on a massive cloud system. They were climbing to thirty thousand feet to fly above the weather. That report was two hours ago. They had not been heard from since. In another hour they would be due to return.

John began to draft the warning messages. First he had to inform the maritime services, then the wire services, and finally, NASA at the Kennedy Space Center. The Coast Guard Station on San Salvador at midnight had reported winds with gusts exceeding forty knots. It was time to brief his boss and to get the station geared up for a major hurricane watch. He handed the evening secretary the message drafts for transmission. John sensed his long evening was going to stretch into an even longer night.

With the messages sent and his boss notified, John started down the hall for his fourth cup of coffee since his shift began. Suddenly, the teletype came to life. As John waited, an updated report came from San Salvador. The winds had reached 110 miles-an-hour. John knew this sudden storm was a full-scale hurricane. The flight of 409 would certainly confirm it. John scanned the computer listing for names already selected for hurricanes. This storm would then have the name Alvin since it was the first of the season. As he poured a cup of coffee left over from the day shift, that was so stale it had a definite oil slick on the surface, he wondered what had happened to the flight of Hurricane Watch 409.

Two hundred miles east of the hurricane center in Coral Gables, the four-man crew of Hurricane Watch 409 were struggling along at eleven thousand feet in a rebuilt P3 Orion. Two hours ago they had lost their primary and secondary navigation and communications equipment. Despite these problems, the pilot, Tom Jackson, had been determined to gather as much data on the storm as possible. He knew from first sight he was watching history in the making.

Never before had he encountered weather that towered above sixty thousand feet. Evil streaks of lightning constantly flashed throughout the massive cloud formation. Shortly after they entered the wall of clouds the plane had been driven upward by the denser, moisture-laden air then driven back downward seconds later. Powerful bolts of lightning twice blasted the plane. The hull had absorbed most of the shock, but the external antennas were burned away. As a result, they lost both the navigation and communications equipment. The radar remained operational. Before the crew could recover from their surprise, a strong down draft pushed the plane downward on a stomach-turning ride for fifteen thousand feet. Tom had required assistance from his copilot to pull the plane out of the almost vertical descent. The engineers never designed the P3 Orion to withstand such forces, but somehow the plane had survived.

During the following half-hour, Tom managed to climb back to thirty thousand feet in the blackness. There had been heavy rain and lightning all the way. The high altitude air was turbulent. He alone had insisted they continue into the center of the storm. His navigator and copilot had already seen enough. The plane continued to pitch, climb and dive suddenly in the turbulent air. The electronics technician monitoring the storm, a timid flyer to begin with, was overcome with motion sickness and filled several barf bags while struggling to keep from bumping his head on the instruments above him. Despite all their problems thus far, none of them was prepared for what was to come.

When the P3 Orion entered the relative calm of the center of the storm, the air turbulence, ceased. Tom had taken occasion to relieve a well battered-bladder, the natural result from drinking two cups of coffee before takeoff. He had left his copilot, Bill Simpson, at the controls while he made use of the head located aft of the weather monitoring equipment. On his return he noticed the electronics technician, Art Benson, was bleeding. He had hit his head on the chart recorder mounted above him. He took pity on Art, and he broke out the first aid equipment and offered him a bandage.

"How are you doing now?" asked Tom.

"I think my head will be all right. Head wounds always bleed more than they hurt. My stomach is much better now that the plane has settled down. But I'm afraid I'm not cut out for this kind of flying. It's my nerves, Captain. I get so uptight! I think I'm getting too old for these hurricane missions. After what we've been through tonight, I don't think you'll see me out here again."

Tom wasn't surprised. Art was the father of four children; his youngest was less than a month old. He had too many people depending on him for this kind of work.

"By the way, there are some real strange readings I'm getting each time we drop a probe. I'm not sure if the equipment hasn't gone haywire after all that lightning," said Art.

"Oh? What are you getting?" asked Tom.

"Well, look at the outside temperature! We're at forty thousand feet. The temperature should be around zero degrees Fahrenheit, but instead it reads nearly fifty. That's way too hot!"

At that moment Tom heard Bill.

"Tom, I think you better look at this!" shouted Bill.

Tom hurried forward.

"What's the problem?"

"It's not a problem, but look!" Bill answered dumbfounded.

Bill stared at the altimeter. The readings were steadily increasing. The old P3 aircraft was rising above fifty thousand feet and accelerating upward through no effort of its own.

Tom took the controls and immediately throttled the engines back to idle. The rate of ascent slowed, but didn't start downward. Tom was baffled. Something was sucking the aircraft upward with such force the plane kept rising without power. Tom was aware the P3 Orion wasn't designed to fly above forty thousand feet. He advanced the throttles and put the aircraft in a shallow dive. He then reduced cabin pressure and ordered his crew to use the emergency oxygen. Slowly, the plane started downward. Twenty minutes later and fifteen thousand feet lower, he eased the throttles back. Then they turned for home and entered the massive wall of clouds from the storm.

Back in the clouds, things immediately got rough again. The heavy droplets of rain suddenly turned into hail. The size of the hailstones increased at an alarming rate. Tom further slowed the engines and put the nose down in an attempt to lose altitude rapidly in order to reach the warmer air below the hail. His descent was not fast enough; as the plane passed below twenty thousand feet, the left side of the windshield cracked from the impact of multiple hailstones. Fortunately, it was not broken, but they lost cabin pressure. Tom again reduced altitude over the next half hour to eleven thousand feet and reduced speed to ease the strain on the windshield.

They continued at eleven thousand feet, making slow but steady progress toward the mainland. When it looked like they were about to exit the worst of the storm, they were dealt a final blow; another lightning bolt took out the radar. Fortunately, the engines were working satisfactorily except for a slight vibration in number one. The navigator attempted to dead reckon their way to Nassau.

They expected to emerge soon from the thick wall of clouds surrounding the storm. Tom wasn't sure where they were. He only hoped they had enough fuel to get to a major airport. He was studying the fuel gages, trying to estimate their maximum range, when the warning light for the port engine flickered on.

REDSTONE, COLORADO, FRIDAY, 23 AUGUST, 1991

It had been almost a year since Keith had met Anna. The charter business the summer of 1991 was very busy. He would be glad when Labor Day weekend, with its complicated schedule, was finished. Finally, he would have a few weeks of relative leisure before the hunting season began in earnest.

Keith was taking advantage of some recent cooler weather to help Jim Dawson with his quarry project. He had just returned from a long day where he and Jim had finished removing the remaining support beams from the platform at the main entrance. This platform led to the connecting tunnels, and it stretched out over the water. With the rotten beams removed, the platform could barely support itself. Joe had ordered steel I-beams to replace the removed timber, but a union strike was delaying shipment. In the interim, they had used temporary beams to support the platform and had roped the area off to keep out intruders. Jim was expecting to spend the month of September in Denver and Washington on a fundraising campaign.

As Keith entered his cabin, he checked the recorder for messages. It was partly used to record messages and partly to screen out unwanted calls. Today the message was urgent. It came from John Wells, his father's next-door neighbor in Philadelphia. Keith's father had suffered a mild heart attack Saturday evening.

Keith immediately picked up the phone and dialed John's number. He answered promptly. Keith's father had been in a concert when the pain began, but he completed the evening performance and then was rushed to Saint Elizabeth Hospital. He was lucky it was only a mild attack. Of course, it was foolish for him to have delayed. He was now resting in the Coronary Care Unit. John gave Keith the number of his father's doctor. Another call convinced Keith that he should fly east.

He called the airlines to reserve a flight to Philadelphia. He could arrive by midnight. Next, he called Marty to reserve one of the older Lear Jets. Hastily, he packed a suitcase and was on his way to the Aspen airport. Keith would soon learn he was going to arrive just before the season's first hurricane.

The Lear stood ready on the apron of the Aspen airport runway when he arrived. Keith thanked Marty for his help, climbed aboard, and efficiently completed the pre-flight checklist with his copilot, Joe Clement. He contacted the tower and requested clearance for takeoff.

After waiting five minutes for a Mountain Express Jet to land, Keith was cleared for takeoff and moving down the runway. As he rose above the valley and began a slow turn to the left over the Snowmass Ski Area he admired the extra power the twin rebuilt Pratt & Whitney engines gave the old plane.

For a moment, he gazed down on the ski area. The upper elevations had a light covering of snow. He smiled, remembering the relaxed days skiing with Anna the previous winter. Much to Keith's delight, she had found the deep snow lighter and easier to ski than she had ever expected. She was fast becoming a confirmed powder hound. On each day they skied until they were completely exhausted.

In his mind, Keith transported himself back to his cabin. At dusk, they always built a fire in the stove and opened a bottle of her favorite wine, St. Julien, along with whatever food was available, for they were always ravenous when they burst into the cabin. Before they cooked dinner together, they made use of the Jacuzzi. Curiously enough, Keith was more sexually aggressive when almost every muscle in his body was tired. Anna responded with equal verve. The sexual bond between the two was very strong and it was equally important to each of them.

A flicker on the instrument panel caught his eye. The oil pressure wasn't holding steady on the port engine.

"Better have Marty check the port engine when you get her back to Aspen," remarked Keith.

The Lear had seen many years of service and was smaller than the newer planes. They had considered selling it before Marty found a new use for her. He modified the craft for high altitude cloud seeding and had a standing contract with the University of Colorado to conduct rainfall enhancement research. She was now Marty's pet project.

The flight to Stapleton Airport took forty-five minutes. The air traffic was heavy as usual. Keith had to wait fifteen minutes in the landing pattern. After landing, he hurried to his connection while Joe took the Learjet back to Aspen. Timing was tight, but he made the gate just as it was closing.

Four hours later, he arrived in Philadelphia. After a thirty-five-minute cab ride downtown to Delancy Street, he was home. The old tree-lined street had long since become gentrified with the revival of downtown Philadelphia. When Keith was growing up here, the street was sprinkled with professionals, working families and middle class couples. Now the property values were astronomical; many of the houses had been rehabilitated while the others seemed to be consistently maintained. Keith's father still lived in the classic brick townhouse with black trim. It was a strong reminder of his now deceased mother. Her voice echoed through the empty rooms. The loneliness gripped Keith. The coldness of the rooms prompted Keith to pick up the phone to see if he could visit his father in the hospital immediately. No luck. Visiting hours were over for the day.

The next morning dawned two hours early for Keith. The wind was rising outside. Large raindrops were beginning to fall and streaks of lightning filled the air. He turned on the small kitchen radio. The weather report contained a storm watch. There was considerable excitement about the sudden storm that had risen from almost nowhere to become a major hurricane in ten hours. Its center was now one hundred miles southeast of Cape Hatteras and moving rapidly north. Damage in Florida had been severe with tides ten feet higher than normal. Power was out in over fifty thousand homes in Florida and Georgia. North Carolina and Virginia were bracing for the onslaught. A planned launch of the space shuttle Discovery had been postponed.

Travel to the hospital was difficult. The streets were beginning to flood and traffic light malfunctions were causing gridlock. When he arrived at the hospital, Keith found his dad in good spirits and resting comfortably. His condition was serious, but could be successfully amended with bypass surgery. It was scheduled in two weeks. Despite his problems, his dad was already demanding to get out of the hospital.

Later that afternoon, the storm reached its peak. The television showed scenes of serious beach erosion in Atlantic City. By evening, the storm center was predicted to pass east of Long Island. He called Anna in New York, filling her in on the latest turn of events. After absorbing the surprise that Keith was in Philadelphia, not Colorado, Anna listened to the news of Keith's father's heart attack. "Oh, Keith, I'm so sorry. Would you like me to take the train down to Philly? I can do that if you want me to."

Keith was stunned. He'd never expected her to offer this. He felt exactly as he had that first night in Colorado, that she knew what he felt and what he needed before he did. He was feeling damn scared. Alone. He didn't want to be alone right now.

"I'd like that, Anna. How do you know what I need before I know?"

"I guess I drink the right wine, Keith, and I make friends fast with the right people. And I love you."

"I love you, too. Come as soon as you can, Anna."

By the following morning, the storm cleared. When Keith

opened his eyes, he studied the morning sky. Long ago his grand-mother had recited an old seafarer's poem:

"Red sky in morning, sailors take warning.

Red sky at night, sailors' delight."

This morning the wind was calm, but there was a brilliant red glow from a mackerel sky. If there was any truth to the saying, they were in for another storm.

Keith dialed his cabin in Colorado to get his messages. There were two. The first was from Marty. He had postponed a charter from New York due to weather, no surprise. The second message was quite different. The voice was from out of the past. At first he didn't recognize her voice. Suddenly it dawned on him. It was Lori Scott, Joe Scott's wife! She sounded distraught. Keith had kept in touch with Joe after he had left the Navy. Joe was now a lieutenant commander stationed in San Diego. Keith's mind wandered back to the dark night in Da Nang when Joe had given the thumb's up sign as he went on the mission that would mean the end of his own naval career.

He decided to wait two hours before returning Lori's call. It was too early in California. Keith made breakfast and tried to read the newspaper. Most of the front page was devoted to the freak weather. Finally, he felt it was a decent enough hour and dialed Joe's number. The voice at the other end was faint and frightened.

"Keith," Lori sobbed. "Joe once told me if I ever had any trouble and he wasn't around, that you could be counted on to help put things straight. I know Joe had great faith in you. Well, Keith, I'm in terrible trouble now." She started to cry uncontrollably. Finally she managed to whisper, "The Navy says Joe is dead."

Keith was in shock. He gripped the back of the kitchen chair with his left hand. How could this happen to Joe? The thought of his dying didn't make sense. His heart pounded with a sense of foreboding. During the next few minutes Lori tried to explain all she knew about Joe's last mission. It wasn't much and she was too upset to talk further. Keith decided he should fly to San Diego. He dialed Anna's number, and got her answering machine. He heard his voice leaving the message. It didn't even sound sane to him. "Don't come tomorrow. Something's come up. I'll explain everything later. I'm going to San Diego. I'm sorry, but it's really important. I'll call you later. I love you." He was relieved in a strange way that he didn't have to explain the ominous turn of events. Until now, their life together had been discovery, passion, and joy. Passion and joy. How would Anna react? It wasn't just that simple. He hung up the phone and stared at it for a moment.

SAN DIEGO, SUNDAY, AUGUST 25, 1991

The sky was clear and the weather wonderfully warm when Keith landed. Lori was there to meet him. Judging by the dark circles around her worried eyes, she hadn't slept well in a week. She cried and seemed to collapse against him as he hugged her. Keith waited for his luggage while Lori haltingly tried to relate what she knew.

Three weeks ago Joe was suddenly called out on a secret mission. Joe had not revealed his destination. She later learned from one of his crew that something was up in Nicaragua, something involving Russians. He spent three days getting his equipment and men ready to board a destroyer. She thought it was called the *Hank*. Then they departed. There was no further communication from Joe.

One afternoon last week, Joe's commanding officer and the base chaplain appeared at her door. Joe was missing and presumed drowned in a routine salvage operation. He had been clearing the fouled propellers of his ship and disappeared without a trace. Lori was appalled to learn they couldn't locate his body. The Navy theorized he was either trapped by the suction of the ship's pumps and drowned, or attacked and killed by a shark.

Lori found both stories close to ridiculous. Joe was too careful. He would never have gone under the ship without a safety line.

Then, the letter came. He had written it just before leaving the *Hank*. The tone implied that much more than a routine salvage mission was involved. Between the Navy's explanation and the letter, Lori felt something was terribly wrong.

When they arrived at Lori's house, Keith greeted her parents, who had come to be with her. Her two children were outside sitting with a teenage babysitter. They were strangely subdued, sitting beside her as she read from a book.

Keith turned to Lori and smiled. "Let's have a cognac and take a look at the letter. You sit there." He pointed to a soft chair by the glass doors leading to the backyard. The children started to ride bikes. Lori watched them for a moment. She sank into the chair and looked surprised when he handed her a big tumbler with a small amount of the amber liquor in it.

"Keith," she laughed weakly, "you used the wrong glasses." Her eyes filled with tears, but a trace of a smile remained.

Keith came to the chair and knelt beside it. Awkwardly he put his arms around her and they stayed like this for a full minute. When he looked at her face again, she was still smiling slightly and had stopped crying. She was able to talk now.

They began by discussing the facts of Joe's death. During the long silences they sipped brandy from the oversized glasses. Keith's mind raced back to his own experience with the brass after returning from Vietnam. He knew there was one person who might be able to get the facts on this bizarre tragedy. Robert Jessel, Admiral (Retired).

Lori searched through a desk drawer for an address book where Joe kept the numbers of his military connections.

"Here it is," Lori said, with her finger on the name. "I remember Joe mentioned that old Jessel had some mysterious small company, Global Oceanic Discovery, that did work for the U.N."

Keith dialed the number of the company headquarters in Washington and learned Jessel was in Hawaii, but was headed back to Washington. Keith spent a half hour trying to locate Jessel in Hawaii. Finally, the familiar gruff voice spoke across the miles and years. "What's up, Maddox? You in more trouble?"

Keith wasn't smiling. He filled Jessel in on the death of Joe and the suspicious manner in which the whole thing was being handled.

"I think I could make a stop in San Diego, Keith. Maybe we can clarify some of this. See you and Mrs. Scott tomorrow." He hung up, leaving Keith with the portable telephone in his hand, standing outside Joe Scott's house in the bright California sunlight. Lori, still sitting in the chair with the cognac in her hand, was looking through the open French doors at him.

MONDAY, AUGUST 26, 1991

They met for lunch in the Officers' Club at the air base. Lori held onto Keith tightly. Jessel was still his feisty old self. He stood only five-foot six, but what he lacked in height he more than made up with his manner. He still had the booming voice that commanded respect. He was accustomed to giving orders and naturally assumed control of any situation. His hair was graying slightly now, but he was in excellent health due to frequent exercise and a careful diet. Admiral Jessel immediately embraced Lori and offered his condolences.

Turning to Keith he said, "It's good to see you again after all these years, Keith. I understand you're doing well in the charter business and that you do some of the flying yourself! I also notice you still don't like to pay barbers, Maddox!"

"It's good to see you too, sir," replied Keith, wondering how Jessel knew about his business.

They sat down at an isolated table to discuss Joe's death over beer and sandwiches. Jessel hadn't wasted any time in San Diego. He had contacted friends in CINCPACFLT headquarters and had a partial understanding of the circumstances surrounding Joe's death.

"My information from a very good source suggests more than a routine operation was underway down south when Joe died," said Admiral Jessel, keeping his voice down.

"What exactly was going on?" Keith asked.

"I'm not sure because it's classified, but I do know that Russian trawlers were involved and that they were very busy for a short time off Central America."

"Do they know where his body is?" asked Keith.

"No, and they don't expect to find him. Seems it may have drifted inshore where the Navy can't legally go," replied Jessel.

"What shore?" Lori gasped at the thought.

"I'm afraid Nicaragua. Our relations there are pretty poor," said Jessel.

"Is there any way to find out more? The Navy doesn't seem to be of any help. I don't understand. Was he just expendable?" asked Lori in a voice choked with emotion.

"Possibly there is a way to find out. My ships can go where the Navy sometimes can't. One of my ships, now under contract with the United Nations for a geological survey, is headed for Nicaragua. Since the contract is administered by the U.N., it won't be hampered by our country's poor relations. The trick will be to investigate without arousing suspicion," replied Jessel.

TUESDAY, AUGUST 27, 1991

Keith flew to Panama City in the Canal Zone shortly after leaving Lori and Admiral Jessel. The admiral's ship, the *Prevail*, a World War Two mine sweeper now an underwater geological survey ship, was in transit through the Panama Canal. Admiral Jessel was a strong advocate for safety. As CEO, he periodically required independent audits of the methods used in their work. First, he set Keith up as an independent consultant, contracted to conduct a safety audit on their submersible procedures, and then sent orders for the crew to cooperate with Keith's requests.

When Keith arrived on the *Prevail*, the ship's captain, Bill Wiley, welcomed him aboard. Keith presented Jessel's letter of introduction. After reading the letter, Wiley asked him to complete his work as soon as possible so they could get on with theirs. He and his crew, mostly Americans, were nervous about working so close to a potentially hostile shore. The Nicaraguan government understood their work could provide much needed support for their national treasury, so officially they were on a friendly and helpful mission. Still, while in their waters, it was not appropriate to engage in activities outside of their charter. The real purpose of Keith's visit was not mentioned, but the captain's meaning was clear. Keith lost little time in getting started with his work.

Eight hours later he was completing his initial study of the compact submersible. It consisted of a crew chamber six feet in diameter. A titanium sphere with walls four inches thick encased this chamber. Through the wall of the sphere was a single access port for the crew to enter. All the control cabling entered through two separate pressure fittings. The rest of the *Crab*, as it was affectionately called by its crew, was constructed of lightweight stainless steel and aluminum, except for the cigar-shaped skids slung underneath. The skids contained the heavy batteries that powered the submersible and provided ballast.

There were two main propulsion motors which each powered a directional tunnel drive. In addition there were four positioning motors used to maneuver the craft. By adjusting the speed and direction of thrust of both the positioning and propulsion motors, the crew could steer the *Crab* with relative ease. The *Crab* had two video cameras located on the bow and stern of her saucer-shaped outer hull. The bow camera was mounted on a directional pedestal with a good viewing angle of the two mechanical arms. The arms were equipped with a hand-like gripper and a utility basket conveniently located on each side of the outer hull. Inside, there were two operator's positions, one for the *Crab's* pilot, the other for the manipulator of the arms. A third seat, which folded, was provided for a single passenger. The *Crab* was equipped with a sensitive side-scanning sonar and a magnetometer. There was only one small porthole made of thick glass in the center of the bow between the two arms.

Keith had gotten the Cook's tour by the *Crab's* two operators: a short Italian named Tony Palermo, and a squat German, Fritz Wickmann. Both men were thoroughly familiar with the operation of the submersible. Keith suspected they resented the interruption of their work. That was understandable, as his presence suggest the home office didn't completely trust them with the expensive equipment. Keith explained it was simply an insurance requirement, an argument they could understand.

Tony explained the original purpose for the *Crab* had been to service oil rigs in the North Sea. For ten years she had faithfully maintained the deeper rigs in the frigid north. Now the range and versatility of the *Crab* was no longer considered state-of-the-art. Jessel's company had acquired the *Crab* at a fraction of her original cost.

In 1988, the Navy considered the *Prevail* no longer safe for use in the frigid waters of the North Atlantic. Admiral Jessel's company bought her in 1989. Since then the *Prevail* had been through a major overhaul in dry dock. The *Crab* was also refurbished and pressure-certified to eight thousand feet.

Keith hoped to get his "audit" work underway the following morning in the waters off the western shore of Nicaragua. The *Prevail* was continuing work started by the United Nations five years ago. A previous survey had located gold deposits off Costa Rica. Now they were hoping to find placer deposits off Nicaragua. During lunch he met the on-board team of geologists. They were friendlier. When Keith asked a simple question about their work, the head geologist, Bob Maxwell, took the time to explain their mission. They were seeking deposits of gold. The west coast of Central America was particularly interesting because there were submarine concentrations of gold, which, in ages past, had undergone primary and secondary enrichment.

"I've often wondered how this process of enrichment occurs?" asked Keith.

Once started, Bob felt obligated to explain the process at length. Over sandwiches and iced tea, he explained the process began from submarine volcanic activity during the Tertiary Period, or age of the dinosaurs, millions of years ago. Those early siliceous lava flows carried background values of microscopic gold. As the volcanic activity continued, seawater penetrated the fractured rock, which became super-heated and super-concentrated to the extent it readily dissolved all the gold it encountered. The gold solution eventually rose to exit submarine vents via fissures and fractures in the rock. By rising, the super-heated brine came under less pressure. It boiled off, leaving its load of gold and silica as native gold in quartz veins.

Once these veins were raised above sea level by the interaction of the geological plates, they were immediately attacked by the relentless forces of weathering which provided the second order of concentration by the removal of all rock constituents soluble in the acidic tropical rainwater.

Wave action along prehistoric shorelines further concentrated these deposits. Over several hundred thousand years of the Ice

Age or Pleistocene Period, ice levels in North America reached a mile thick and the sea level dropped as much as three hundred feet worldwide. As the ice rose and melted, two major hesitations in the moving sea level occurred. They were at sixty and ninety feet below the present level. During these periods, the wave action weathered and effectively washed away the lighter material at the shoreline, uncovering the heavier material of the bedrock and its gold. At these two levels, the team hoped to find gold.

"That's fascinating. I asked a simple question, but now I feel I could get a whole course in geology here," said Keith.

That brought a resounding laugh from the group.

"I'm sorry. We don't often get visitors, and I'm afraid I am also a college professor. It's difficult to break the habit of teaching," Bob said, his blue eyes twinkling.

The group rose and left the wardroom to get on with their work.

Keith busied himself with the charts of the surrounding water provided by the Nicaraguan government. He studied the satellite pictures Admiral Jessel had gotten from his associates in the Defense Department. These were high resolution shots of the area during the period when the *Hank* was investigating the Russian activity. Their search was confined to a rectangle ten miles wide by one hundred miles long. Most of the rectangle lay in international waters. Near the middle, the rectangle extended over the continental slope and dropped to a depth exceeding five thousand feet. The charts supplied by Nicaragua indicated a submarine canyon extended into a deep cut in the wall. It was at the bottom of this canyon that Keith felt the most likely prospects existed for finding anything, now that the Russians had finished their search.

In keeping with Captain Wiley's wishes, Keith wanted to make his stay on the *Prevail* short. He requested the opportunity to conduct his audit the following morning. Captain Wiley readily agreed. He didn't question the location Keith had chosen. Early the following morning the *Prevail* would be resting at anchor near the edge of the continental shelf with the *Crab* ready to be deployed by the *Prevail's* single cargo crane.

That evening, the ship's cook served an excellent meal in the wardroom. The entire crew could be served in just two sittings. The civilian crew was one third the size the Navy required when the *Prevail* was a minesweeper. The major reason for the reduction was automation of the engineering power plant and electronic navigational equipment installed while the *Prevail* was in dry dock.

After dinner, Keith decided to get some sleep. He knew the following day would be a long one. The test dive was scheduled for 0800. That meant the crew would be up and making preparations by 0530. About midnight, the *Prevail* dropped anchor in 120 feet of water. They were inside Nicaraguan territorial waters.

WEDNESDAY, AUGUST 28, 1991

The sun rose at 6:12 a.m. Keith had been up before five. He finished studying the log of the *Crab* and had taken some notes. He requested help from the *Crab's* technicians. They had gone below and emerged a half hour later with a box full of hardware that was loaded into the utility baskets of the *Crab*. Keith had explained to the *Crab's* operators that the purpose of today's dive was to thoroughly check the ship's procedures for use of the submersible. His examination of their log showed they had previously used the *Crab* at depths approaching six thousand feet. This gave him cause to request a deep dive in his audit. It was unusual for an audit at such depth. After his explanation, Tony and Fritz stared at each other momentarily. This was to be a very thorough audit.

Keith went below and ate a hearty breakfast with the two crew members. Thirty-five minutes later all three climbed into the *Crab*.

Fritz took the pilot's position, Tony the manipulator's. Keith assumed the folding passenger's seat. The order was given to swing the *Prevail's* crane and lower the *Crab* into the water. A minute later, Keith saw the water cover the single forward porthole. The ocean was calm and spectacularly clear. Keith could see a lone diver struggling to detach the *Crab* from the crane on the TV monitor. Both Tony and Fritz were busy with the pre-dive checklist. To be consistent with his cover, Keith carried a yellow legal pad. He was busy taking notes.

Fritz was in contact with the *Prevail* using underwater telephone Gertrude. He and Tony had completed their checklist and were preparing to dive. Captain Wiley gave his permission. Fritz turned the *Crab* toward the continental slope and put the nose down. He then purged the ballast tanks overhead. The *Crab* descended nicely over the edge of the shelf. Suddenly, the shore current pushed up the nose of the *Crab*. Fritz had anticipated the onrush as he passed over the leading edge of the slope, and soon had the *Crab* in control.

"OK, Mr. Safety Audit, what is it exactly you want to see us do with this thing so we can get back to our work?" asked Fritz.

"I want you to act as if this was a normal descent. That includes all communication with the surface. I've planned a set of exercises on the bottom. When they're complete and we surface, I'll be out of your hair," replied Keith, not taking the bait.

Keith watched the single porthole forward. The water color was changing from blue-green to dark green, and finally to black. They were descending at a rate of two hundred feet per minute. At this rate, it would take twenty-five minutes to get to the base of the slope.

Tony switched the headlights mounted underneath the bow and stern of the *Crab*. Immediately, the cameras came into focus.

"Can you follow the bottom of the canyon on your way down?" asked Keith.

"Sure, but it isn't the way we prefer do it. Trenches like these have mud slides. It's not safe," replied Fritz.

"Let's make an exception, I want to see the bottom as we descend," Keith answered, trying to sound casual.

Now Fritz was showing signs of irritation. It was bad enough he had to put up with this intrusion from the home office, but now the guy who was supposed to be a safety inspector wanted to attempt a high risk descent over the edge of the continental shelf by taking the submersible into one of the deepest canyons he had ever seen. Fritz was determined to school this intruder. He put the *Crab* down as low as he dared and continued headlong down the narrow canyon at cruise speed.

Keith was slightly amused. By irritating Fritz he was getting a closer look than he expected. They were now skimming barely five feet off the bottom. From time to time Fritz had to veer to the left or right around a large boulder. When they encountered a mud slide, he was forced to bring the nose up suddenly. Even though Fritz was a skillful operator, the ride inside was a little rough.

"Keep your eyes on the monitors and the magnetometer. If you see anything out of the ordinary, sing out," said Keith.

"What do you mean out of the ordinary? Everything is out of the ordinary here," laughed Fritz.

"Yeah, what kind of an audit is this anyway?" asked Tony.

"This isn't an audit," Keith told them. "I can't say more, but I'm here on Jessel's orders. We're looking for something man-made."

Fritz and Tony gave Keith a knowing look. They were both well aware their boss was into many different ventures. Occasionally, there was an air of intrigue about a portion of their work. Suddenly, Keith had two willing shipmates aboard the *Crab*.

"OK, so we are looking for something man-made, any idea what it is?" asked Fritz as he steadied the *Crab* after passing a towering boulder.

"No, we don't have much of an idea," Keith shook his head. "But a month ago the Russians were very interested in picking up something in these waters. I figured by the depth and narrowness of this trough, the Russians may have stayed clear of the mud slide areas. Maybe they overlooked something."

"If you don't mind my asking, what makes you so interested in finding what the Ruskies lost?" asked Fritz.

"No, I don't mind at all. A good friend of mine is listed as MIA. He was here trying to find what the Russians were after. I'm not leaving him here—whether he's dead or alive—without at least an explanation for why he didn't come back."

Their depth passed three thousand feet. That was equivalent to ninety-two atmospheres. Keith figured the pressure at that depth was fourteen hundred pounds-per-square-inch.

They were long past the maximum depth for sonar Gertrude with the *Prevail*. They were on their own. Outside, the canyon walls showed little sign of life, except for the occasional deep sea fish whose body was often distorted by a large mouth and sharp teeth. For a moment, Tony turned off the lights while Fritz stopped the *Crab*. Many of the fish, which seemed dull in color under the *Crab's* bright lights, were bioluminescent in the darkness. Moving on, there was a sand flow that covered the base of the cut. The sand relentlessly sought the bottom of the wall in the same fashion water seeks the ocean.

Tony methodically worked the camera from right to left, sweeping the canyon walls as much as possible while Fritz concentrated on following the main channel downward. So far, the search had revealed nothing. Now the canyon walls were getting steeper. Fritz slowed the descent of the *Crab* as the walls closed in. "Looks like this might be the end of the line."

"Keep going while you still can," urged Keith, concentrating on the monitor.

"No way, man, I think we'd better stop or else we'll get stuck," Fritz said.

Keith was about to agree when his eye caught sight of a dark object. "Wait, I see something!"

Already, Tony was maneuvering the camera and lights for a better view. There in the blackness, partially buried in the flow of sand, was a large black object bigger than a fifty-gallon oil drum. Over the drum was a light covering of silt.

"Bingo!" Tony cheered. "That could be it. Looks like only a month's worth of silt on it."

"Of course it could just be a used Ruskie oil drum," Fritz cautioned, "sunk while they were searching here."

Keith wasn't sure, but this object looked more like a pressure tank than an oil drum. He could think of no reason the trawler fleet would need such a tank. He wanted a closer look. "Tony, can you get one of the arms to grab it?"

"Yes, but Fritz will have to bring us in sideways so I can get the arm around to it," replied Tony.

"I'll turn us around. I make no guarantees. This is very tight," said Fritz.

Using the positioner motors, Fritz maneuvered the *Crab* sideways in the tight canyon and managed to get the submersible in close enough for Tony to reach the object with the right arm. By the time Tony could get the arm close enough to grip the end of the object, the bow and stern of the *Crab* were rubbing against the canyon walls. Tony moved the camera and starboard light to get a better view of the object. Fortunately, there was a lifting hook on its near end. Tony clamped the three-fingered gripper securely around the hook.

"OK!" yelled Tony, "let's get out of here!"

Fritz directed the main thrusters downward. Next he reached for the release valve to blow the ballast tanks. Slowly, the air filled the small tanks on the outer hull above the crew chamber. He applied power to the thruster motors.

The *Crab* started to rise. The arm extended fully then took a strain on the object. The suction from the fine sand and dirt resisted the pull from the *Crab*, bringing it to a stop. Fritz reversed the thrusters momentarily to lower the *Crab*. Then using the momentum of the submersible to his advantage, he tried to jerk the object from the silt. This time he was successful. The object tore free of the bottom trailing a huge plume of silt.

"We got it!" exulted Fritz.

"Great! Let's go topside!" shouted Keith.

The *Crab* rose rapidly, with the craft leaning to starboard from the added weight of the tank.

Keith shifted his feet to keep from sliding off the folding seat. He was about to suggest they proceed more cautiously when there was a sudden, tremendous strain on the right arm. The craft's upward movement came to a twisting halt, slamming its passengers against the overhead equipment. Now the *Crab* hung motionless, with its starboard side down, twenty feet off the bottom of the canyon.

"Goddammit!" shouted Fritz, as he fell from the pilot's seat and slammed his head on the magnetometer housing.

"Scheisse, I'm bleeding!"

Fritz grabbed a handkerchief from his pants pocket and tried to stop the bleeding from a cut around his right eye. The handkerchief fast became dark red. Keith moved to a position near Fritz where he could see a large welt growing on his forehead, just above a laceration which traced his eyebrow.

"Tony, throw me the first aid kit!" shouted Keith.

Tony released the first aid kit strapped near his seat, and handed it to Keith. He opened it and took out some gauze and a chemical cold pack. He broke the interior seal of the cold pack and placed the gauze over the cut, then applied cold pressure to the wound.

"Besides this cut are you all right?" asked Keith.

"I'm OK, I think. I bet my eye will swell up bad. I may not be able to see out of it soon. I wasn't paying enough attention to the load. Should have had my seat belt on. I hit my head on the magnetometer."

"Keep holding this compress on your eye. I think the pressure will stop the bleeding and keep the swelling down." Keith turned to Tony. "What's holding us up?"

"I can't see, but I think there are some small ropes leading into the darkness on the other side of the tank."

"Can you bring the arm in so we can get a better look," asked Keith.

Tony concentrated on the controls for a moment. Then he maneuvered the lights and the camera.

"Oh, shit!" said Tony.

"What?" asked Keith.

"We can't control the right arm. The control cables were broken by the strain. You can see them hanging from the arm. Worse yet, I can't get the hand to release the tank!"

Keith eased Fritz out of the pilot's seat. He aimed the port thruster upwards and applied power. The *Crab* began to right itself. Then he purged the ballast tanks. The *Crab* started to settle toward the bottom. Keith did well maneuvering the *Crab*, having watched Fritz at work. "Tony, can you get the left arm around to release the right arm?" asked Keith.

"Negative, the left arm will never reach. Best I can do is reach about half way down its length. The control cables are broken beyond that point," replied Tony.

"OK, I'm going to rotate the *Crab* and try to see what is holding the object to the bottom." Keith started to move the craft as he had seen Fritz do previously.

"Easy on the power," said Fritz. "She's a little tricky at first. Best not to be in a hurry and take longer than you think you should. If you get her moving you can flip us easily."

Keith eased the power controls on the motors one at a time. Slowly, the *Crab* rotated clockwise till the back side of the tank was revealed. There, in the silt, was an array of thin, but strong lines leading into the darkness beyond.

"A parachute! That's what's on the other end!" exclaimed Keith.

"No wonder we couldn't get it off the bottom!" said Tony.

"That thing must be snagged in a dozen places!"

"Can you get the left arm around the tank and reach the lines?" asked Keith.

"I don't know. I'll try," said Tony.

Tony maneuvered the submersible's left arm toward the lines. It fell two feet short.

"Nope, sorry."

Keith maneuvered again, this time bringing the port side up away from the canyon wall, then rotating the *Crab* to the absolute limit against the wall. Tony tried again.

"No, that won't do either, I'm still missing it by a foot," said Tony.

Fritz observed the efforts from his seat beside the controls. "We'd better come up with a way to reach the lines and cut them or else we're going to be stuck here forever," he remarked.

"There's no way to reach them from here," Tony shook his head. "We're helpless in this position. We're also too deep to contact the *Prevail*. We're in big-time trouble!"

Keith spent the next hour repeatedly trying different angles, but Tony could not get the left arm close enough to the parachute lines to cut them. Fritz had been successful in stopping his bleeding, but his eye was quite swollen and threatening to close. He was applying a second cold compress. They all knew their resources were dwindling. It was Fritz who finally made the assessment.

"We have enough power for another hour of operation and enough oxygen for two more hours. If something doesn't happen fast this might be our last stand."

"If we could only free that grip of the right arm! It's like a vise," said Tony.

Just then Keith remembered the equipment he had placed in the utility basket. "I assume you both are familiar with seismic charges?"

"Very familiar. We've been using them a lot lately," replied Fritz.

"I thought we might find something stuck on the bottom. So before we left I put six charges in the utility baskets. Possibly we could blast our way out?" offered Keith.

"No way! If we use charges we could wreck her hull, and at five thousand feet we sure as hell don't want to do that!" Fritz argued.

"OK, but what if we only use one charge and save the rest?" Keith suggested.

"Maybe one," said Fritz. "But it is still really risky."

"Is there any way we could get the right arm to release by detonating one of the devices?" asked Keith.

"There might be a way. Let's see," replied Tony, who moved the lights and camera to focus closer on the right arm.

"There! See the large cotter pin in the elbow? If we place one of the charges between the main support rods, the explosion just might shear the pin off. At least it's worth a try," said Tony.

"Just hold on," interrupted Fritz. "Don't you realize we're in the bottom of a very steep and unstable canyon? One blast could easily bring the whole canyon down on us. Then we'd never get out."

"Well, I agree, Fritz, we could easily bring more trouble," Keith looked at him. "But if everything remains the same, in two hours we'll be dying anyway. We've got to try something."

Reluctantly, Fritz gave in to Keith's plan. Tony picked up one of the charges and placed it between the support rods of the right arm. Then he armed the device. Fifty seconds later there was a deafening boom inside the *Crab*. Silt stirred up everywhere. In the distance, a rumbling sound could be heard.

"Damn! I think I hear an avalanche!" shouted Fritz.

Tony could barely see the right arm. It was not severed by the explosion, but it was no longer locked in a rigid outstretched position. Keith took immediate advantage of the slack the bending of the right arm provided. He maneuvered so Tony could reach the lines of the parachute with the cutters in the gripper of the left arm. Small boulders began bouncing off the hull. The distant rumbling sound was growing louder.

Tony was having trouble cutting the last of the lines. Keith again maneuvered the *Crab* closer to give Tony a better view. Silt sliding down the canyon walls was beginning to pile up on top of the *Crab*, weighing it down. Finally, the last of the lines was cut. Keith applied full power to the main thrusters and blew the ballast tanks. The *Crab* and its cargo broke free of the bottom.

"Tony, grab the drum with the left arm!" shouted Keith above the background rumble.

Tony moved the left arm to grasp the parachute lines at the attachment ring on the far side of the object.

Suddenly, a huge boulder rolled beneath the *Crab*. In its wake there was a tremendous vacuum which sucked the *Crab* downward behind it. Keith fought to keep the craft upright. Behind the boulder was a huge glob of mud that threatened to engulf the small submersible in its path. The headlights of the *Crab* were now completely blinded by the turbid water. Keith felt they were falling. He was expecting an impact. It came with a strong jolt as the *Crab* hit the canyon floor, causing the skids to plow a furrow deep in the sand and silt. Keith was no longer in control. The submersible started to tilt forward. Keith maneuvered the main thrusters to stop the *Crab* from pitching over.

"Watch out! If she goes over you will lose power. The batteries aren't built to be inverted!" shouted Fritz, straining to keep his seat.

Keith was not fast enough and couldn't stop the *Crab* from beginning a slow somersault. As it turned over, the lights dimmed and the thrusters slowed. Then the *Crab* landed on its back like a helpless turtle. The mud slide caught up and began to push the *Crab* farther down the canyon. Keith couldn't estimate how far the *Crab* continued its headlong slide on its back. The electrical system went completely dead. In the darkness the crew became unwilling passengers in a hellish roller coaster ride downward.

"Shit! This is it. We are done for!" shrieked Tony, trying desperately to untangle himself from all the loose gear around him.

As the *Crab* continued its upside down ride, the submersible continued to gather speed till it slammed its stern against a large boulder. The impact sheered off the lights and camera with a screech of tearing metal. It also caused the *Crab* to complete its somersault. The *Crab*, now upright, rather than continuing to tumble, began to accelerate straight downward as if falling into an abyss. The batteries began to function; power was returning to the electrical system. Keith felt a sick falling sensation in the pit of his stomach. He was fighting to keep the *Crab* upright. Any second he expected another impact, but miraculously they kept floating downward. When he dared, Keith studied the output display of the side scan sonar. It was useless in the close confines of the canyon, but now it began to register a separation from the canyon wall. After it recorded a hundred feet separation, the water became clearer. He had complete control of the *Crab*.

He maneuvered the *Crab* farther from the wall and out to clearer water. He studied the depth gage. Apparently there was a drop-off at the end of the canyon. The fathometer showed the bottom was four hundred feet below. They were at 5,600 feet. The mud slide had sucked them down six hundred feet! The hull of the *Crab* was well designed. Despite all they had been through, there were no leaks.

Keith aimed the thrusters downward to propel the *Crab* to the surface. He guessed most of the air in the overhead ballast tanks would have emptied while they were upside down, so he opened the air valve to blow the ballast tank again. There was only a low hiss. The compressed air tanks were empty.

"You'd better drop the load if we want to see the surface again. That tank is too heavy for us to make it," said Fritz earnestly.

Keith did not want to lose the tank, not after all they had been through getting it. Besides, the right arm probably wouldn't release it anyway. He studied the monitor, looking for motion.

"There! See that plume of silt falling? We must be rising! The tank can't be that heavy!" shouted Keith.

"Don't be so sure; silt always settles," said Fritz.

But they were rising. In the next fifteen minutes they rose one hundred and fifty feet. However, all the resources in the *Crab* were getting dangerously low. This was not the first time Fritz and Tony had been in such a position. Once before they had spent twelve hours on the bottom while they waited for rescue from a second submersible.

"If we want to make it, I suggest we shut down all the electrical systems except for life support. We barely have enough oxygen for an hour of normal operation. That can be stretched to about three hours if we all just take it easy and relax," said Fritz.

Keith and Tony switched off all the motors and electronics except for the equipment, which supplied oxygen and purged the carbon dioxide in the crew chamber. In the darkness, they tried to make themselves as comfortable as possible. Without the heaters working it was getting cold. Keith passed the time by studying the bioluminescent fish that occasionally came into view through the thick glass porthole. Every half hour he switched on the light over the depth gage. At first their progress was hopelessly slow, but as the air in the ballast tanks continued to expand, the *Crab* accelerated gradually toward the surface. The last thousand feet took twenty minutes. When they reached the surface, Tony opened the hatch and let in the fresh sea air. It had taken nearly three hours to surface.

They each took turns sticking their heads out of the hatch as the *Crab* rolled in a calm sea. Keith couldn't remember a time when sunlight ever looked better. When it was his turn at the hatch, he climbed out and dove into the ocean to inspect the tank.

Much to his surprise, he discovered it was made of lightweight plastic. Its color was a dull black. At one end there may have been a metallic seal, which must have corroded quickly in the water because only a trace of the metal remained. There was only a small identification plate in the center of the cylinder's side with some Russian lettering on it. Keith was certain the tank and its contents represented a significant find, but he wasn't sure what it was. He found a rag in the *Crab* and stuffed it into the ruptured seal. Later, he replaced the rag with some quick drying epoxy.

In the first few minutes on the surface, they all developed severe headaches. Keith was to learn it was a natural consequence from oxygen starvation experienced on their ascent. In a couple of hours the headaches passed, but the memory of the downward plunge of the *Crab* would never be forgotten.

Tony used the radio to signal the *Prevail*, and she immediately headed in their direction.

"I think I owe you two fellows a drink as soon as we get into port!" said Keith.

"You sure as hell do!" was the quick answer. "That was some audit you did down there. You may have to buy us a bottle each!"

Keith didn't mind. *More good men,* he thought. *Just like Joe. And Dan and Allen. Damn this world.*

THURSDAY, AUGUST 28, 1991

Shortly after dawn, the *Prevail* put into port in Poneolya, Nicaragua to receive a replacement arm for the *Crab*. Admiral Jessel wasn't disappointed by the loss of the submersible's right arm and rear camera; instead, he was delighted by their find. His company, Global Oceanic Discovery, quickly arranged for the delivery of a spare from the original equipment manufacturer. The replacement arm was crated and already on its way to Managua. Keith's work with the *Crab* was complete. The *Prevail* could begin its contract for the United Nations the next day.

Jessel's company found it difficult to ship equipment directly from the States to Managua. To insure the crate would not be delayed, G.O.D. shipped it by way of Mexico City, using the name of a Mexican equipment manufacturer for cover. Captain Wiley had orders to place the tank the crew of the *Crab* had retrieved in the crate and ship it via Mexico City to Jessel's headquarters in Washington. It would then be thoroughly analyzed by the Defense Department. If the replacement was delivered promptly, they could be underway by the following morning. Keith wanted to use the short stay to search for information about Joe.

Two hours later, after the crew had cleared and washed the decks and stowed the equipment below, Captain Wiley assembled the crew on the fantail for a briefing. He explained that the political situation in Nicaragua was essentially stable. The government had achieved a shaky truce with the rebel forces and incidences of violence were uncommon. He reminded them it was wise to travel in groups while ashore, and to return to the ship before dark. The government was cooperating with their efforts and promised to arrange military escort for the work party to be sent to Managua, ninety miles away, to get the *Crab's* replacement arm. He also pointed out the Russian trawler, which was tied alongside the pier twenty yards from the *Prevail*.

"I do not expect any trouble from the Russians. They tend to stay by themselves and get drunk and happy. They will respect our U.N. contract. Likewise, you are to treat them with respect. I don't want any incidents. Is that clear?" Captain Wiley looked at each man to be sure there was no misunderstanding. After three months at sea, the crew was anxious to blow off a little steam. Five minutes after Captain Wiley finished his speech, the first party went ashore, heading straight for the nearest bar.

Keith was not ready to go ashore immediately. Prior to Keith's departure, Admiral Jessel had assembled an impressive amount of material. Along with the satellite photos provided by Jessel's friends, there was a complete weather analysis for the period the *USS Hank* had been active just outside Nicaraguan waters. Included in the weather analysis was a tidal chart. By calculating the currents on the day Joe was reported missing and estimating the wind speed and direction, Keith thought it possible to predict where a person lost near the *Hank* might drift ashore. He assumed Joe had inflated his life vest. If Joe had failed to do so, all bets were off. The most probable point for Joe to reach land was a five-mile stretch of beach ten miles north of Poneolya.

Keith could search the beach by himself, or in the company of some of Captain Wiley's men, but first he felt it prudent to check with the locals for information. After all, it wasn't uncommon in a country racked with civil unrest that people didn't report things that might bring too much official attention.

The moment he left the gangway and stepped on the pier, he was besieged by teenagers trying to sell him cheap wood carvings and leather goods. Keith begged off in some Spanish he had picked up in southern California.

When he reached the end of the pier, he found a street that led toward the center of town. The main street of this town of almost fifty thousand people had a row of establishments almost five blocks long. They served drinks and provided instant intimate companionship to the few lonely sailors who chose to dock at Poneolya. Some of these establishments hadn't fared well in recent years, and the windows and doors were boarded up with cheap plywood.

He passed a bar from which loud rock music flooded into the street. Glancing inside, he recognized several members of the *Prevail's* crew. Each had a seductive, highly made up girl in tow. An attractive woman at the entrance encouraged him to enter, but Keith decided to explore the street further.

At each street corner he found a soldier in uniform. Apparently, the government wasn't tolerating any violence in the port area. Keith noticed Chico and Charlie's Bar, where the music was from a percussion band, and the sound of billiards knocking could be heard from the rear.

Once inside, he saw that the band performed from a small platform along the left wall. Of its four members, two played guitar, another shook a tambourine, while the fourth sat on a box-like instrument and played a set of keys over a hole in the box with his right hand. There was a long curved bar beyond the band platform. Behind the bar stood a bartender with a wide handlebar mustache. Next to the bar sat an incredibly obese bouncer. In the front of the room near the band was a square dance floor surrounded by several tables and a row of booths along the right wall of the room.

The pool table was in the rear of the room. Around the table were four Caucasians holding pool cues. Keith knew immediately that they were Russians. One of them was in an officer's uniform. An uneasy feeling came over him. He could not shut out the face of Pronin every time he saw a Russian in uniform. He was about to turn when there was a tug on his right arm. To his astonishment, he was dragged to a booth by a middle-aged woman barely five feet tall.

"*Una cerveza,* sailor boy?" she asked, with a pleasant smile revealing incredibly crooked teeth.

Keith reluctantly accepted the beer and slid further into the booth. In a moment, she returned with his order. She was accompanied by a young girl, barely sixteen, with long lustrous black hair.

The woman passed Keith a glass and a bottle of Dos Equis. "That will be a hundred Cordobas."

Keith had no Nicaraguan money. He took out his wallet.

"You take dollars?" he asked.

"Dollars good here. Two dollars, please," she said quietly in English.

Keith took out two ones and placed them in her hand. He wasn't surprised the good old dollar still had value in Nicaragua.

"You lonely, sailor? Lolita give good time, good talk. She know little bit English. What you say?" she asked. Lolita lowered her eyes and moved her hips seductively as Keith glanced at her.

Keith expected the offer, but he wasn't interested.

There was a loud roar of laughter from the pool table. The Russians were playing eight-ball. One of the Russian sailors had just sunk the little black sphere accidentally while trying a side pocket shot. The officer was the winner and apparently the better player. The game was over. Each Russian downed his drink. The bartender automatically refilled their glasses and they immediately settled into another game. Keith wondered how long they had been at it. He turned to the woman.

"I don't mind buying the young lady a drink if she will get lost. I'm here looking for information," said Keith in a low voice.

He handed the woman another two dollars. She immediately pointed to a doorway in the back and the girl walked sullenly toward it.

There was a loud crack from the pool table and a whoop for joy. The woman bent forward and lowered her voice. "You want information, you come right place, mister. What you want?"

"I want to know about something that happened about a month ago on the waterfront." Keith stared into her black eyes.

"You want to know about Russians. They're here. You ask

them," she said, turning and pointing to the pool players. The Russian officer glanced in Keith's direction, then bent forward over the table to concentrate on his next shot. He was skillfully clearing away the balls.

"No, not the Russians," Keith replied hastily. "I'm interested in someone who might have swum or floated ashore."

"What's this someone to you?"

"A friend."

"The police. Why don't you ask them about your friend? You could save trouble?" She spat out the words.

"I'm looking for a source who might be reluctant to go to the authorities," he told her, quickly laying his hand on her arm.

"OK, I know some people who might know. What it worth to you?"

Keith took out a twenty and passed it to her under the table. She smiled and leaned forward to whisper.

"Fishermen much restricted by government. Can't go out far. Catch little. Hurt many families. They fear the government. Man named Manuel at fish market, end of Baja Street, third booth. Say Maria send you. He tell you what you want to know."

A hand grasped her shoulder. Maria stiffened. Keith looked up to see the Russian officer standing before him with a cue in his hand and a sly grin on his face. "You play pool?"

Keith fought the urge to rise suddenly. After all, he had not been threatened. Slowly he moved from the booth seat and stood. He was slightly taller than the Russian.

"You want to play pool?" Keith returned cautiously with a sheepish grin. The Russian nodded his head, slowly smiling. "All right then we play pool," Keith replied agreeably. He went to the wall where the spare pool cues were hung and chose one that was relatively straight. The Russian officer waited patiently for Keith to break. The other three Russian sailors stood by the bar. The band started another song. Maria returned to the table where Lolita and two other young girls were passing time by playing cards. Keith carefully chalked his cue while studying the table. It was not in the best condition. The felt showed signs of wear and there were places where it had been damaged by abuse. The

Russian officer had placed the balls in a tight rack at the other end of the table.

Keith lined up his shot. He preferred to play an open game of eight-ball. A professional would try to keep only his next objective free, but Keith was not a professional and neither was the Russian. Carefully, but with considerable force, he broke the rack. The cue ball caught the center of the rack at just the right angle to spread the balls. As he had hoped, the three ball sank in the corner pocket.

Keith studied the table. "Five ball corner pocket," he said pointing his cue. He sank the five ball and next the two ball, but when he tried a side pocket shot on the one ball off the cushion, he found the cushion was quite dead and he missed his shot.

The Russian took his turn. He skillfully sank the nine, eleven, twelve, thirteen and fifteen balls, but when he tried a double cushion shot on the ten ball he missed, leaving Keith in good position for the six ball.

Keith promptly sank six, leaving himself in good position for the four and seven. They both fell in quick succession, but again the dead cushion left Keith in poor position for a shot on the one ball. He tried a two cushion shot for the right side pocket. The cue ball struck its target, but the one ball caught the edge of the pocket and settled into a small groove next to the cushion. Keith stared at the ball. *What kind of a table is this anyway?* he thought.

The Russian laughed at Keith's expression while measuring his shot on the ten ball, a long corner pocket shot. He sank it with a resounding crack, the cue ball returning to his end of the table for a simple shot on the fourteen ball. After a moment's hesitation, he sank the fourteen ball, but the cue ball drifted behind Keith's one ball, leaving no simple shot on the eight ball. The Russian studied his position carefully, trying to determine his simplest option. He straightened and took the chalk for his cue and looked at Keith carefully. "You with the U.N. ship?" the Russian prodded.

"Could be," Keith returned. "Are you with the Russian trawler?"

"Yes, the communications officer," the Russian stated proudly with his broad smile.

"Why does a fishing boat need a communications officer?" Keith grinned back.

For an instant, the Russian looked alarmed. Then he smiled again, took a deep breath, bent and took his shot.

"Why are Americans wandering about onshore when their contract is for offshore survey work?" the Russian countered. The cue ball found the eight ball, but failed to sink it.

Keith ignored the question and sank the one ball and the eight ball in rapid succession, finishing the game. He was anxious to leave, but the Russian insisted on sharing a drink. He raised his glass and challenged Keith to the best of three games.

Keith felt trapped, but reluctantly agreed. During the second game, Keith learned the Russian's name was Slava Maslov and that his ship had been at sea for the past six weeks. Slava won the second game, leaving Keith with two balls on the table.

In the third game, Keith did no better till his second turn. He then sank his last four balls in succession, leaving the eight ball and two of his opponent's. The problem was his opponent's balls stood between the cue ball and the eight ball, making a straight shot impossible. Keith studied the table carefully. Short of a three cushion shot, there was little hope of sinking the eight ball. The cushions had proven to be unreliable. Keith gripped his cue. He would try the impossible. "Eight ball corner pocket," he announced.

The Russian snickered.

Keith squinted at the cue ball, sliced the lower right corner sharply with his cue putting considerable spin on his shot. Like magic, the cue ball curved around his opponent's balls and struck the eight ball, sinking it in the corner pocket. There was a gasp of amazement from the Russians, and then a cheer.

Slava graciously raised his glass to Keith and he downed it in one swallow. "You play pretty good game," he said, frowning.

"I usually play on a better table, but you play a good game yourself. Listening to you, I can't help wonder what has kept you and your crew so busy in these waters," ventured Keith.

The Russian officer was immediately reminded with whom he was playing. "What we Russians do here is none of your concern."

Slava glanced at his companions, and then looked directly at Keith.

"Was it looking for something you lost, perhaps?" pressed Keith.

"You know what I think? I think you ask too many questions. I have enjoyed playing with you, but it is better you leave now," warned Slava.

Keith turned and strolled outside. The sunlight seemed overly bright and he was forced to squint as he made his way back to the ship. At the end of the first block, he glanced behind and saw the Russian officer talking to the soldier outside the bar. Keith knew he was the subject of their conversation.

Back on the *Prevail*, much of the crew was ashore in the bar with the loud rock music not more than five hundred feet from the pier. From the *Prevail* Keith could hear their high-pitched voices drifting on the breeze.

Three members of the ship's kitchen staff were returning. A young man Keith had met the evening before who washed dishes and did other menial tasks was having his problems. Weaving his way halfway up the gangway, he paused to retch over the railing. The kid was suffering from heavy drinking after a prolonged stay at sea. This was not his only torment. Pepe, the Filipino cook, was shouting at him while shaking his head and waving his hands.

"If you can't make it, just who do you think will! We've got thirty hungry people to feed tonight and I don't think they give a damn about how bad you feel. Just who the hell do you think you are getting drunk when I need your help getting food from the market!"

Keith approached Pepe and suggested the fish market as a place to procure his supplies.

In ten minutes they were on their way in an old Ford taxi. Pepe felt honored to be accompanied by a friend of the company president. As Keith might have suspected, the local militia provided escort. A pleasant young soldier about eighteen with a crew cut and a thin mustache was assigned to accompany them.

The youth chose a dilapidated Ford from several waiting taxis. The driver naturally turned out to be his cousin, Carlos Caballo, who had a suicidal approach to driving. There were few street lights in Poneolya and some didn't work. When they came to an intersection, Carlos would thrust the old Ford forward with a certain arrogance. In most cases, the show of force worked. When it didn't work, he slammed on the brakes and swore heavily in guttural Spanish.

They made several stops, getting supplies for the ship. Eventually, they came to the fish market on Baja Street. Along the street was a row of neat homes where the families of fishermen lived. The fish market was in the center of the pier. Each day as the boats arrived, a group of women gathered to clean the catch. They washed and gutted the fish, throwing the entrails and blood into the water. The smell of rotting fish was everywhere. There was a considerable amount of activity around the pier, as the boats had already unloaded the morning's catch and the captains were gathering their crews to leave for the evening.

Pepe began searching the row of six small shops for fresh catch.

Keith went to find Manuel. He was pleased to see the soldier agreed to stay next to the car to guard the supplies and to talk to his cousin, the driver.

In the third shop, he found an elderly woman standing in front of a counter. Behind glass, under the counter, were large trays filled with fresh grouper on ice. When he asked in Spanish for Manuel, she apparently didn't understand him, as she cupped her hand behind her ear. Assuming she was hard of hearing, he raised his voice. After repeating himself three times and still getting nowhere, a large man with big shoulders and tattooed arms came from behind the door to a small storeroom in the back.

"Don't mind her. My mother is deaf. You look for me?" the big man asked.

"I am, if you're Manuel," said Keith.

"I'm Manuel. What can I do for you?"

"Maria from Chico and Charlie's Bar said I might get some information here," replied Keith.

"That all depends on what you want to know."

"I am looking for information about the body of a diver that might have washed ashore a month ago." Keith felt a shot of loss by his use of the word body, but it was time to face the facts Joe was most probably dead.

Manuel looked thoughtful for a moment. Then he shook his head. "*No, señor,* I have heard nothing of such things."

"Is there someone here who might know?" Keith ventured hopefully.

"No, you try the militia? They know these things," Manuel returned sympathetically.

Keith knew the American Embassy had been trying for the past four weeks without success. It looked like he too had found a dead end. Keith stepped away from the counter while Manuel turned to serve two women that had just entered the booth.

Keith decided to leave the market area where the fish smell was overpowering. He would find fresh air farther up Baja Street. He passed the soldier and his cousin standing near the Ford. The two men were in a heated argument and didn't notice him as he passed by.

Keith strolled slowly up the street thinking of Joe, oblivious to the fresh breeze and the sinking sun. He was deep in thought when a young boy rudely interrupted him.

"Hey, mister, you want some dirty pictures?" shouted the youth.

The boy held a cardboard box in his hand. Inside the box was a series of small brown envelopes. Keith wasn't interested in the boy's wares, but a flash of metal on the boy's wrist caught his eye.

"I don't know, let me have a look," replied Keith.

The boy was delighted to show his prospective customer a sample. Keith bent over the youth, pretending to look at the pictures while studying the boy's watch carefully. Keith paused, as if to consider something. Then, he looked the youth straight in the eyes.

"I tell you what, I'm more interested in a watch," Keith offered.

The youth stopped, studied Keith, then took the watch off his wrist.

"How much you give for this watch with the funny face, mister?" he asked.

The youth let Keith have a closer look at the movement. Keith examined the back. It was engraved with three initials J.T.S. His hand began to shake slightly. Those were Joe's initials. The coincidence was too great.

"I like this watch just fine. How much you want for it?" Keith asked quickly.

The youth paused, considering a price. Finally, he tried for an amount he thought was impossibly high, hoping to bargain from there.

"How about fifty dollars?" he piped.

"I'll take it," said Keith, producing two twenties and a ten. The youth, delighted with the sale, took the money and handed Keith the watch. Keith took the watch and examined it carefully. The crystal was scratched more than he expected, and he wasn't sure, but the band had a funny smell about it, perhaps from a strong cleaning solution. Keith could feel a certain dread building within. His hands began to sweat and his mouth was going dry. He must have more information, but he would have to be cautious. The boy could be scared easily. Perhaps if the boy had Joe's watch, someone had found his body, and had more of his equipment.

"I am also looking for scuba equipment. You know where I could buy some?"

The youth seemed puzzled, and tilted his head slightly. "What is scuba?"

Keith reopened his wallet, found his certification card, and showed the youth a picture of a diver on it.

"Oh, diving equipment," said the youth with a knowing smile.

"What about diving equipment?" Keith persisted.

The youth studied Keith for a long, indecisive moment. There was more here than just a watch, Keith was sure of it, but the boy was street wise and wary of strangers.

"Maybe I help you, mister. You follow," he said.

The boy led the way down a narrow alley. It emptied into a wider street on the edge of town, which led back to the waterfront. At the end of the street was a rambling and decaying pier where several aging fishing boats were tied. The boy continued with a bouncy gait, leading his customer down the pier to a fishing boat about twenty-five feet in length, which also served as living quarters for the captain.

He jumped down to the boat from the pier and knocked on the weathered cabin door.

A short, deeply tanned, and wrinkled man with graying hair opened the door. Seeing the youth he smiled. When he saw the boy's box, the smile disappeared. "You've been out selling dirty Don's pictures again, Geraldo! You are a disgrace to your father. He would blister your behind if he were alive!" He grabbed the cardboard box.

Only then did the aging seafarer notice Keith.

"Why do you bring a stranger to my boat, Geraldo?" he bellowed.

"*Tio* Pedro, he wants to buy some diving equipment. I think you help him," the boy replied meekly.

Pedro studied Keith suspiciously.

Keith held up Joe's watch. "I am sorry to bother you, sir. The initials on this watch Geraldo sold me are the same as my friend who was lost while diving here a month ago. Do you know anything about such a diver?" asked Keith.

The expression on Pedro's face hardened slightly.

"I know nothing. I am a fisherman. That's all."

Pedro took Geraldo by the arm and pulled him inside the cabin. He tried to slam the door but Keith stuck his foot in the way.

"Look, mister, I don't want trouble," Pedro pleaded.

"I'm not here to cause trouble. I'm looking for a man who once saved my life. I just want to find what happened to him!" Keith shouted.

Pedro relaxed his grip on the door. "Maybe I know, but if I tell you, you no go to authorities?" pleaded Pedro. Keith could see the fear in Pedro's eyes. He felt sorry for the old man.

"You can count on it," replied Keith softly.

Pedro opened the door and turned to Geraldo. "You stay inside and keep door locked. I talk with you later." Turning to Keith he said, "I'm sorry, it is impossible to watch kids all the time. Times weren't always bad, but the government restricts our fishing and we no longer can make a good living. Soon the bank will take my boat. Geraldo tries almost anything to make money. His mother ran off shortly after he was born. I've tried to raise him since my brother was lost at sea with his boat five years ago. It isn't easy."

"I'm sorry, it must be difficult," replied Keith sympathetically, as he followed Pedro's slow pace down the pier.

Pedro led the way up the narrow cobblestone street along the weathered and abandoned buildings. Keith wondered where he was heading. They came to a modest Catholic church built from native stone and mortar. Behind the church was a small, but well-tended graveyard with a view of the ocean and the setting sun. The parishioners were poor, the tombstones simple, but here and there flowers were planted by faithful relatives, and the grass was kept well-watered. In the center of the graveyard, Pedro stopped in front of a fresh grave with only a small wooden cross for a marker.

Pedro looked at Keith; he could feel the sadness in the man's eyes.

"This diver washed ashore near here. I was gathering conch and find him. He was in bad shape, the crabs, you know. We did not want trouble with the authorities. We were afraid the body would attract attention. The authorities do not trust us. We gave him a Christian funeral and buried him. I keep the watch and his equipment, but not the wet suit. I'm sorry, we were too afraid to do more."

Keith felt a deep sorrow. He had come a long way, secretly hoping Joe had made it. He knew he was only fooling himself, but still the truth hurt.

"Was there any identification on the body?" Keith asked, idly kicking his shoe in the soft ground.

"Oh yes, around his neck. I hide on my boat. Come," urged Pedro.

Back at the boat, Pedro produced a set of I.D. tags on a light chain. Keith examined them with a faint hope they weren't Joe's, but they were.

Keith wasn't sure why he asked the next question. "Was there anything else?"

"Yes, strange thing inside wet suit with Russian writing," Pedro replied.

In a moment, he returned with a piece of plastic about three inches by five inches. Keith immediately recognized it as identical to the one on the tank he, Fritz, and Tony had brought up off the canyon floor the day before. So Joe had found a similar object somewhere and had died trying to get back to the *Hank*.

Keith left Pedro with a small roll of money for his assistance. Enough for him to keep his boat and some for Geraldo to keep him off the street. Pedro could hardly believe his good fortune, and promised to help the people who would come to transfer Joe's body.

By the time Keith made his way back to the fish market, an hour had passed. The young soldier and his cousin were helping the cook fit the supplies they had bought into the Ford. The soldier gave Keith a dirty look, as he suddenly realized he hadn't seen him for some time, but since he had returned and they were ready to go, he made no issue of it.

Later that afternoon, Keith finished a long conversation via satellite with Jessel. In the morning, he would meet with Lori to explain that Keith had found Joe in Nicaragua. Keith also scheduled a morning flight out of Managua. There would be another hair-raising ride to Managua with Carlos, but he would be in Mexico City by noon and San Diego before evening. The staff at Global Oceanic Discovery was making arrangements with help from the U.S. Embassy in Managua to have Joe's remains flown to San Diego.

Keith still had one debt to settle. He met Fritz, Tony, and Pepe and took them with his military escort of the afternoon to the best bar in town. Keith bought all the drinks for his newfound friends. The owner was delighted to keep the margaritas flowing and the band playing. Keith got soundly drunk in the memory of an old friend.

In the morning, Keith paid little attention to Carlos' driving. A tequila hangover made the ride tolerable.

• Chapter 8 •

SAN DIEGO
FRIDAY, AUGUST 30, 1991

Keith stayed in San Diego for two nights and one day. He spent most of his time with Lori. She mentally wandered from the past to the present. Keith sensed it was a natural and needed release. They talked haltingly of the first time she met Joe that summer in San Francisco at a party thrown by an old roommate. She felt drawn to him at first sight. After engineering an introduction to him, he called a day later. It wasn't long before they were spending weekends sailing, or up in the mountains at Yosemite. Six months later they were married. The life of a Navy wife wasn't easy. Of the ten years they were married, Joe had spent almost five at sea.

In turn, Keith talked about their experiences at OCS in Newport, Rhode Island where he and Joe first met. Keith, admittedly, was a brash kid with a big mouth. He was fresh out of college and looking to the Navy for adventure. They were roommates. Joe had a steadying influence on Keith, often keeping him out of trouble. They worked well as a team studying maneuvering problems and navigation theory while polishing their shoes late into the evening during those long weeks at OCS.

One Saturday night near the end of the program, Keith stayed out late drinking at a local night club called Hurley's. It was July, and he was wearing an immaculate white uniform, not by choice, but by OCS requirement. Keith hadn't been drinking for some time. That night, he learned the exaggerated effect clean living and exercise has on alcohol tolerance. When he left the club to find his car, he was drunk. He subsequently tripped and fell in the gutter, bashing his nose, skinning his knee, and trashing his uniform. In seconds, it was a filthy and bloody mess. Despite his condition, Keith maneuvered his sporty Mustang like a homing pigeon through the complex of narrow cobblestone streets back to the base. The Marine at the gate lost his composure when he saw the errant Officer Candidate. Getting through the base gate was the easy part. Keith knew he must report in at the quarterdeck of King Hall before going upstairs to his company quarters. The desk was manned by Officer Candidates like himself. They would go strictly by the book. He would be on report. Keith's record at OCS was far from spectacular. Reporting in at the quarter deck in his disheveled condition might have brought an end to his very short career.

Joe had recently been selected company commander. Joe had no special reason to help Keith, but he tossed him a shirt and pair of trousers out the window. By this time Keith's nose had stopped bleeding, the new uniform covered his scrapes and a sock tied over his knee kept the bleeding in check. He reported in at the quarterdeck without incident. Luckily, no one questioned the smell of whisky on his breath. A few moments later he passed out in his room. In the morning, he threw his soiled uniform in the trash and thanked Joe for his help.

As they neared the end of OCS, there was an opportunity to sign up for SEAL training. Both he and Joe jumped at the chance. They were more interested in the skills and excitement the SEALs offered than the more career-oriented shipboard billets. Six months later, they met Captain Jessel for the first time. A couple of years later, they both requested and received positions in Jessel's command.

Both he and Joe had expected the position would last for quite a few years, but that was not to be in Keith's case. Through the years, he and Joe had kept in touch with occasional phone calls and cards. Now he hoped he could help Lori continue life without Joe.

To that end, he encouraged Lori to go back with her parents to Utah for a couple of weeks. Then, when she felt better, she planned to return and clean out the house and maybe move back east with her sister. Jessel had offered to arrange a job for her in Washington if she wanted.

When Keith got back to his hotel, he called his answering machine in the cabin at Redstone. There was an urgent message from his dad in Philadelphia. Strangely, nothing from Anna. From the sound of his father's voice, he was very agitated. That was bad for his condition. Keith immediately dialed Philadelphia. After five rings, the voice of his father was on the other end.

"So where the hell ya' been? First we hear you're going to visit the wife of an old friend in San Diego, then you disappear off the face of the earth for a week. What's going on, son?"

His dad still hadn't gotten used to his lifestyle after all these years. Keith gave a brief description of his adventures as a consultant for Global Oceanic Discovery.

"Now that I've explained my week, what has you so excited?" asked Keith.

"Son, you remember the time I spent in the Resistance during the war and how we passed messages by secret code?"

"Yes, Dad, you've told me many times."

"Well, there are only three of us that know the code. We never discussed it with anyone, even after the war. We had codes and some secret words. One such word we rarely used. It meant we were to risk everything, even death, to pick up a priority message. I just received a telegram from my Russian colleague which came by way of Israel and used this code word. I know this has to be really important. I am supposed to pick up a package in Jerusalem. You know I will have my surgery this week. The point of this lengthy discussion, son, is I want you to go in my place."

Keith was totally drained, both physically and emotionally, from the past week's activities. He wanted to get back to the mountains and his business. But his father was insistent. Keith tried to refuse, but finally gave in. At least he would fly to Philadelphia to discuss the matter. That would give Keith an opportunity to see Anna. He really needed to talk with her. She represented a whole different way of life to him that he felt ready to accept.

He hung up the phone and dialed her number. No answer. No machine to take the message. *Strange,* he thought.

SUNDAY, SEPTEMBER 1, 1991

Morning in Philadelphia was cool and clear. The debris from the storm of the previous week was for the most part cleaned up. The coast of New Jersey was particularly hard hit. Keith rose early and read the details in the morning paper over coffee.

Keith visited his father at Graduate Hospital during morning visiting hours. Rudolf was feeling better since his heart attack, and more argumentative. Still, he was in no shape to travel. Open heart surgery was scheduled in two days. Keith found it impossible to convince his father he should wait for the package to be mailed to him, or until he could recover from surgery. He grabbed Keith's hand tightly and looked him straight in the eye. "Keith, you must do this. You must, do you hear me?" Keith sensed his father needed this done more than anything else he could do for the old man.

In frustration, Keith left the room to walk down the hall. He stopped at the pay phone and dialed Anna's number. He had tried to call once from San Diego, as well as the night before. The phone rang seven times before there was an answer. It was not Anna, but her roommate, Katherine, who answered.

"Hi, this is Keith. Could I speak to Anna?"

"No, sorry she's not here, Keith. She's on an assignment and won't be back until next Monday. Is there anything I can do?"

"I guess not. No, wait a minute, where is she working?"

"Ahh, I think she's in Israel. Let me check." There was a pause. "Yes, here I have it. She's staying at the King David Hotel in Jerusalem. I can give you the number. Do you want it?"

Keith could hardly believe what he'd heard. "No, I already have it, thanks. I'll give her a call."

Suddenly, Keith saw the trip to Israel in a different light. Perhaps there was a way to sort this all out to everyone's satisfaction.

The thought of surprising Anna in Israel and getting his father's business accomplished was tempting. His father was relieved, and calmed down immediately when Keith told him he would go. That was a good sign. *Already, something good was coming out of this trip,* thought Keith.

TEL AVIV, ISRAEL, MONDAY, SEPTEMBER 2, 1991

The Boeing 747 swung low over the ground as it came in for a landing at Ben Gurion Airport. The plane had left New York late the previous evening. Keith decided to treat his body to a reasonable amount of room for the long flight. He purchased a first-class ticket, expecting to finally get some sleep. Shortly after takeoff, he was served a champagne steak dinner. When the meal was finished and the china removed, he discovered that Star Trek VI could be selected on the TV screen on the back of the seat in front of him. He succumbed to the temptation to watch. Three hours after the movie finished, the sun came up over the horizon. It was three a.m. Keith's time, but he couldn't sleep anymore. The plane continued to fly across Western Europe until the blue Mediterranean came into view. By early afternoon, they were about to land. Keith had little more than four hours sleep to show for the flight.

The weather was almost perfect as the 747's wheels touched the runway, leaving a cloud of blue smoke. Much easier than skimming over mountain tops and dodging fog and clouds, reflected Keith. Minutes later the plane taxied to the terminal building.

The first stop for the passengers was Passport Control. Young Israeli security forces who wore their shirttails hanging over their trousers and sneakers for shoes manned the area. The shirts covered their weapons and the sneakers provided agility.

Keith casually answered the customary questions from an attractive young female security official who checked his passport. Finally she smiled and said, "Welcome to Israel. Enjoy your stay."

Keith waited a few minutes by the carousel for his bag, forming a plan in his mind. In New York, luggage was carefully examined before the passengers boarded the plane. He had no items to declare and the officials waved him through customs.

Keith walked out of the terminal building toward the Avis Rental agency. The weather was very much like southern California. No wonder so many movies were filmed here. The weather must be perfect most of the year.

The young woman behind the Avis desk spoke perfect English. She seemed to anticipate his questions. He rented a Ford Cortina and got maps and a set of directions for Jerusalem.

The route the girl gave him was a narrow two-lane road that passed several camouflaged fuel tanks before he reached #1 Speed Road. This interstate-like highway led eastward to Jerusalem. Keith noticed the coastal plain was very fertile and well irrigated. There were many orchards as he got farther from the populated area around Tel Aviv. Little wonder after leaving the desert, the early inhabitants referred to this area as the land of milk and honey.

The highway started to climb up a long winding valley. As the altitude increased, the terrain became drier. The hills had the same appearance as the foothills outside San Diego. Alongside the road were the rusty hulks of armored transport trucks, remnants of the violent history of twentieth-century Israel.

Eventually, the road led to the outskirts of Jerusalem as it reached the end of its climb to the highlands that overlooked the desert to the east. Keith took a right on Hertzel Boulevard then a left on David Wolfson to Ruppin Road. Once on Ruppin, he made good progress on the wide pavement as he passed the Knesset, the Israeli Parliament, on his left. Following his map, he made his way through the traffic toward the Old City and the King David Hotel just outside. He left the car for the valet and made his way wearily to the front desk. It was quarter after three local time. Keith was exhausted. He checked in, happy to find they had his hastily-made reservation, and let the bellboy carry his bag to his room on the sixth floor.

Once in the room, the youth opened the drapes and pointed out the features of the room with its TV and bar. Keith handed him a couple of dollars as he left, and closed the door himself.

For a few minutes, Keith stood looking out the window at the ancient walled city below. There, amongst the stone and dust that made up the streets and houses, were the remnants of kings, prophets, philosophers, poets, fools, engineers, artists, slaves and beggars. Men who had lived and died, leaving behind a lot of man's recorded history in this compact city. How much of that history is fact and how much is fiction is a time-worn controversy responsible for much of man's hope? Keith mused further as he watched the traffic snarl below his window. Because of man's intolerance for his fellow man, much of man's misery was repeated from generation to generation. Take too much religious fervor, add some fanaticism and mix in modern weapons, and you have a recipe for a world of hurt, reflected Keith. He gazed at the mysterious, beautiful city in awed silence.

TEL AVIV, BEN GURION AIRPORT

A tall man with the long gray overcoat, who walked with a slight limp, was nearly the last passenger to get off the plane from Copenhagen. He knew he was entering Israel at great personal risk. He had spent too many years abroad in countries where Russia was trying to expand its influence for his picture not to be on file with Israeli intelligence. He carried a Norwegian passport under the false name of Peer Ericsson. His business reason for entry was to negotiate a contract for army helmets manufactured in a kibbutz in Lower Galilee.

Pronin was very worried about his wife, Natasha, whom he had left in Baikonur. In recent months, her heart had grown weaker. Now she tired easily and spent much of her time resting in bed. They both knew she needed the operation soon. After long deliberation, Natasha had finally consented to open heart surgery. She had a great fear of operations because, when she was a young girl, her mother died during a routine operation to remove a breast. The cause was listed as heart failure, but her father claimed it was caused by an overworked and inebriated doctor using antiquated equipment with an under-trained staff.

The following year, Natasha contracted rheumatic fever. Her father was an engineer for the town power plant and often worked late. That evening, he worked much later than usual. When he came home to their cramped apartment, the old woman looking after her had put her to bed early. She was trying to keep her fever down with cold compresses. He immediately wrapped her up and rushed her to the local hospital forty kilometers away. It was fortunate that he had acted quickly, or she probably would have died. As it was, before the antibiotics took effect, one of the valves in her heart was damaged.

She never fully recovered. As the years passed, the valve's function worsened. The resulting heart failure taxed her heart muscle so that she could no longer put off the operation. Medical treatment in Soviet Russia had come a long way since her mother's death; still, she delayed the inevitable for as long as possible. Finally, they had scheduled the operation in Moscow. It was to be in two weeks. Afterward, Natasha hoped to convalesce in Moscow because there were excellent rehabilitation facilities there. His transfer would make it all possible.

Now he had to make the trip to Israel to recover the security device and whatever information was carried by Halperin to Israel. Natasha could not face open heart surgery alone. Just when everything was set, the plan was ruined by Lebedev's treason. Pronin had the opportunity to make or break his career in the next day. Success would guarantee not only his promotion, but a transfer to Moscow. Failure would mean banishment to a very cold assignment in the Northeast, an assignment he knew Natasha would not survive.

Pronin approached immigration and Passport Control carefully, hoping not to attract any attention to himself. He stood quietly in line behind the other passengers. When it was his turn, he handed the official his passport. Pronin realized that the security people were well-armed. If he were recognized, there would be little hope for escape. The official looked closely at Pronin and at his passport.

In Copenhagen, his luggage had been examined carefully and probably x–rayed thoroughly as well. He had no need to bring weapons or explosives with him. Palestinians in Jerusalem would supply what he needed. He was confident the odds of discovery were small. Still, he was taking no unnecessary chances.

The official smiled, stamped the passport and said, "Welcome to Israel, enjoy your stay," in accented English.

Pronin just nodded and strode forward to pick up his luggage. Behind him, the official turned to the next person in line.

He had previously arranged assistance from a terrorist group headed by a Palestinian named Hassan Habashi. Several members of this Marxist organization were trained in East Germany before the two Germanys were combined. For many years they had been supported by the Soviet Union. *Now it was time to repay the favor*, reflected Pronin.

As he passed out the exit, he followed an attractive female tourist dressed in tight white shorts and a body shirt who had an exquisite suntan. His eyes studied her swaying hips critically. Despite the intriguing view, the thought of betraying Natasha never entered his mind. He walked to the taxi stand just outside the terminal building where he hailed a cab.

"Please take me to the American colony in Jerusalem," he said getting in.

Pronin thought again of Natasha. How she would like the warm weather here, for it was almost as nice as the time they had spent in Odessa that first summer they were married.

His leg even felt better in the warm weather. Lately in winter, or when there was an approaching storm, it ached unmercifully. His knee had undergone a series of operations after the disastrous affair in Vietnam. He had bravely endured the pain of a shattered knee cap to pursue the capture of the escaped prisoner.

Pronin couldn't help wonder, as he proceeded up the valley from the coastal plain toward Jerusalem, the reason why the Israelis had been so successful in their wars against the Arabs. He couldn't understand the Americans' fatalistic desire to back them. It was probably because so many of their population were Jewish. By their greater numbers and arms, the friends of the Soviet Union should have overcome the Zionists and the Americans long ago. But that discounted the tenacity of the Jewish people and the treachery of American cunning. Pronin had seen plenty of the Jewish persistence in his own country.

He had previously booked a room in the American Colony

Hotel. It originated from a hospice with a history dating back to the time of the Crusades. Now it was a luxury hotel, two blocks from the Old City. Tomorrow he would meet with Hassan and his two Palestinian assistants. One day was all he would need to spend in retrieving the security device from Halperin. *How surprised the elderly Jewish emigrant would be to see him in Israel* he thought, chuckling to himself.

6:20 P. M.

Keith was feeling much better. He had requested a wake up call for 6 p.m. hoping to get a few hours sleep before surprising Anna. He was dressed in white slacks and a dark shirt as he sat waiting in the bar on the first floor of the hotel. A group of businessmen was having cocktails before dinner. They must have started early because they were laughing loudly at a rather rotund, bearded man's jokes.

Keith ordered a margarita and took a seat by a small table in the back. He waited patiently, listening to the pop rock music that floated through the bar.

About fifteen minutes later, there was a disturbance as a group of women and two men arrived in the lobby and made their way toward the bar. The heads of the businessmen all turned as the three women entered. In the lead was an attractive blonde who was obviously irritated about something. As they passed, taking no notice of the man alone at the table, Keith caught part of the conversation.

"... and then the dumb photographer notices he loaded the wrong film! Can you believe that!" the blonde continued in a loud voice, shaking her head.

The three women took seats at the bar. The bartender, after finishing a brief conversation with another patron, made his way past the bottles and beer mugs to take their order. One of the men in the party was obviously a photographer because he carried his equipment with him. The women were no doubt models, judging from their makeup and appearance. The first two women, one with straight black hair, the other with curly red hair, both ordered. As the blonde was about to order, the bartender interrupted.

"Someone has already ordered a glass of St. Julien for you," he said.

"A what ... who?" she responded, not completely comprehending.

"I believe it's your drink," said Keith from behind.

With a huge smile, Anna whirled around, and found Keith returning the smile. She immediately fell into arms that wrapped her in a tight embrace. Totally oblivious to their audience, they kissed. The businessmen, models, and photographer all clapped lightly. Laughing, Keith gave the thumbs up sign behind Anna's back without breaking the kiss.

A few minutes later, after all the necessary introductions, Keith and Anna sat down together.

"What are you doing here, Keith? I mean, I've been furious. I have to tell you. You call me, tell me your father's had a heart attack, you're upset, and the next thing I know I have a message on my machine that you're leaving for San Diego. It's all pretty cloak and dagger to me. What are you doing, trying to play Indiana Jones or something? Is that what you are? Or are you the Keith I know and love?"

"Maybe I'm both," Keith said. "We'll talk about it all later, OK? Just say I'm here because I couldn't live any longer without seeing you." He lowered his voice and leaned towards her. "Let's be glad for this moment, our wine, and each other, Anna."

She smiled knowingly and raised her glass to him.

It was the following morning when Keith finally told Anna the real circumstances behind his arrival in Israel. He wanted the surprise to make the moment magical and did not want to diminish the effect.

In a few moments they excused themselves and hastily left the bar for Keith's room. Keith noticed envy in the eyes of the businessmen as they passed.

Keith and Anna studied the view from his window of the Old City, with its separate quarters, churches and mosques. They turned to each other, losing themselves in a long embrace. Keith could feel her warmth as she pressed herself against his right thigh. Not surprisingly, Keith felt warm and overdressed.

"If I'd known you were going to be this glad to see me, I wouldn't have dressed so formal," he said.

"Well, that's a mistake we can correct easily," replied Anna.

They took turns slowly undressing each other. Anna first took off Keith's shirt. Next, he took off her turquoise cotton tank top. Her breasts were completely bare. Keith gently kissed her nipples. He learned long ago not to rush a woman into bed. The secret was to understand her pace and, if possible, get her to take the lead. Her climax is the more difficult to achieve; therefore, if love-making is to be a shared experience, her needs must take precedence. Once Anna's need was satisfied, Keith knew he would follow. The real goal they shared was to try to make it a simultaneous event.

Naked to the waist, they embraced again. Keith could smell a hint of her perfume as his passion rose. In a few seconds, Anna deftly undressed Keith. She drew her finger gently over the scar on his thigh that he had received from his Navy injury. Keith undid Anna's belt and slid her skirt and panties down over her hips. Soon, they were both naked. Rather than retreat into the bed, Anna took Keith's hand and led him to the shower.

She turned on the water. Keith took the soap in his hand. The water with its warmth seemed to melt away the weariness of Keith's travel and the irritation of Anna's work. They took turns washing each other, using more soap than was needed in erogenous places. When they were more than clean, Anna turned off the water, and Keith picked her up and carried her to the king-sized bed. She was ready for him and responded with real passion. Keith knew there was no need to wait. With a suitable preamble for an appetizer, and then a change of position for effect, they skillfully satisfied their desires together.

Later, in the quiet twilight zone found after sex, as they were both about to drift off to sleep, it was Anna who asked the philosophical question.

"How many centuries do you suppose people have been having sex on this very ground?"

Keith could only guess.

TUESDAY, SEPTEMBER 3, 1992

Morning in Jerusalem dawned clear and cool. The sky was a deep blue. Anna was up at 7 a.m. Keith, who wasn't accustomed to the local time, spent part of the night trying to fall asleep. Now he felt no desire to get up, but he had a mission to accomplish and Joseph Halperin, the man who sent the telegram, would be waiting. Over breakfast he and Anna discussed what they would do when Keith finished his business.

Anna was sure her company would complete shooting the swimsuit catalog on location by the Dead Sea sometime that afternoon. Afterwards they planned to go browsing in the small shops of the Old City. Anna was looking forward to showing Keith around Israel. After Jerusalem, they would spend a couple of days taking the long drive to Masada, and then continue to Eilat for more sun and some scuba diving.

Keith finished his breakfast with Anna in the hotel, kissed her goodbye, and went outside to get his car from the valet. A few moments later he was again in traffic heading for the Immigration Center on Levi Eshkol Boulevard. First he made his way to the old Jaffa Road, and then, turning on Natan Strauss, he followed the connecting streets to the Immigration Center. Keith found that the center was used by recent immigrants as a residence until they could find suitable accommodations elsewhere. It appeared much like a hotel with a large reception area on the first floor. The building was noted for its stone architecture. He parked his car in the lot across the street and entered the building.

The receptionist was an attractive red-head with long curly hair who couldn't have stood taller than two inches over five feet. She was conversing in Hebrew with an elderly gentleman. When Keith asked for Halperin's room, she immediately replied in English.

"Mr. Halperin is in room 222. On the second floor. Just upstairs and the sixth room on the left," she answered.

When he knocked on the door, there was an answer from the other side. In a few seconds, an elderly man with a slight stoop opened the door.

"Hello, I am Keith Maddox. I'm the one who sent the telegram. As I stated in it, I'm here because my father is in the hospital," said Keith, extending his hand.

The old man looked at Keith for a moment and then said "You are bigger than I imagined … I am sorry. I am Joseph Halperin … My English not good … but I so happy you come. My friend Lebedev ask me bring things for friends," he said with a heavy accent.

"I assume it must be extremely important for Lebedev to request my father to come in person," said Keith, entering the room when Joseph gestured.

"I not sure why. He is a man of … ah … mystery. He very important Soviet space scientist."

Joseph had very little in his room. He was not allowed to take more than two suitcases from Russia, and almost no money. Now, after a lifetime of service in Russia, the Soviets agreed to let him spend his retirement in Israel at his own expense. He went over to a small desk and took a thick folder of papers out of a bottom drawer. "Here is package to give your father," said Halperin, handing the folder to Keith.

Keith took the package and examined the contents. Inside were possibly twenty pages of hand-written sheet music. The calligraphy was carefully inked in. Keith could tell by the way the music was notated that the author spent a great deal of time creating the copy. Keith thought the music was possibly familiar, similar to music his dad had tried to teach him on the piano in Philadelphia. That was before he asserted his right to go outside and play baseball rather than practice music. He had done little with music since.

He took off his sport jacket and sat down to study the music further. Joseph took the coat and went to his closet. He returned with a violin that had seen many years of service.

"He wanted your father to ah … have this violin. He said a … souvenir of war. Lebedev not play much. So he want to give to your father," said Halperin, placing his hand on Keith's shoulder.

"Did Lebedev say there was any problem or some emergency?" asked Keith.

"No … nothing when I see him last. Ah … strange, he risk to

see me when I get permission to leave. Look bad, but he impor-tant ... I think he need not worry," replied Halperin.

This all seemed very strange. The message relayed to his fa-ther indicated a desperate situation, yet here the messenger did-n't seem to be aware of any emergency. Keith took a careful look at the violin. It obviously had seen better days. Considering its condition, Keith could hardly believe it was worth the effort to carry it out of Russia, much less require that someone come to Is-rael from Philadelphia to pick it up.

"Ah yes, a note for father," said Halperin turning back to his desk. "Here."

Keith took the note. It was written in longhand. It simply said:

> *Dear Rudolf;*
> *The violin is a gift. I hope it will help*
> *you to play the music as it did in the old*
> *days.*
> > *Your old friend and comrade,*
> > *Lebedev*

The short note gave no clue as to what the meaning of either the sheet music or the violin was. He knew enough about his fa-ther's associates to know there was a considerable amount of in-formation in the music. He carefully gathered up the sheets and returned them to the envelope. It was obvious that Halperin did not understand the music was a code; therefore, any further ques-tioning was of no value. Keith thanked Halperin for his assistance.

"Well then, if you ever come to America, Mr Halperin, please look us up. I would be glad to show you around. This is my busi-ness card. It has my address in Colorado on it. You already know my dad's address in Philadelphia," said Keith.

"Ah ... would be nice to go America, but ... I get settled here. Thank you just the same," replied Halperin.

Keith shook the hand of the old man, left his room, and de-scended the stairs to the lobby. The receptionist was still there. She waved and smiled as he passed.

Back in his hotel room, the package of music he had received captured his curiosity. If a man as important as Lebedev took the time to create such a volume by hand, there was a good reason. He felt the music should be decoded soon, but decided there would be enough time to do it after he and Anna spent a couple of days sightseeing.

He had eaten a quick breakfast that morning with Anna. It was not his policy to indulge himself in front of a weight-conscious model. As he was about to leave his room for a bite to eat, he realized he had left his sport jacket in Halperin's room.

That morning, Pronin entered the Old City and found a coin shop on a narrow cobblestone alley. It was a modest but popular business that bought and sold coins often dating back to the Greek period. The owner did quite well on the tourist trade. As a sideline, some of the coins were mounted and sold as expensive jewelry. Because of the quality of the workmanship and because the coins were guaranteed to be authentic, many of the professional guides patronized his shop. They brought with them their rich customers. The coin shop had a back room, as all shops of its kind do.

When Pronin entered, there was another customer talking to the owner. Shortly, he was met by an attractive young dark-haired lady wearing bright red lipstick.

"May I help you?" she asked.

"I would like to see something in old Roman coins," he replied.

She took him to the back of the store. There was a long glass display case. Inside the case were three shelves with many antique coins spread out artfully on red velvet.

"The top shelf is principally Roman. What period would you like to see?"

"Anything around the first century A.D.," he responded.

The young lady expected his response, and continued a casual conversation until the other customer left. Then the owner opened the back door and led him down a short hall to the back room. Inside, Pronin found Hassan and two other young Arabs.

"Hassan, sahbi!" greeted Pronin, happy to meet an old friend.

The two men hadn't seen each other for five years. Pronin had visited East Germany on an inspection tour in the fall of 1987. He had met Hassan as he was completing training. Prior to that, Hassan was a petty thief in a refugee camp in the Gaza Strip. He had no living parents. His father was one of the first to be killed in an Israeli air raid during the Six-Day War. During a riot in 1987, which ended when Israeli soldiers were forced to open fire on the unruly crowd, his mother had been struck and killed by a stray bullet. With support from the Russians, Hassan had found focus and purpose for his life after that. Hassan now carried the passport of a dead garage owner who, while visiting in Jordan, refused to cooperate with the PLO.

His two associates, both Palestinians, were from Ramallah. Their names, Abu Musa and Abu Nidal, were taken in memory of two guerilla leaders killed in a spectacular commando raid on Tripoli. They were barely eighteen years old. All three were armed with Russian-made AK–47s and grenades.

"Ah, Comrade Pronin, it is good we meet again. Everything is set. As you can see, we are dressed as janitors. We even stole a trash truck for transportation," said Hassan.

Pronin began the explanation of the operation. It was fairly straightforward. Pronin would confront Halperin in his room. The old man would be easily persuaded to return the stolen Russian property.

"When I am finished, I will signal you from his window. I will terminate Halperin. Your job is to make his demise appear to be a random terrorist attack. That shouldn't be too difficult for men of your experience, especially with your vast demolition expertise, yes?"

The plan was set. In a few minutes they had exited the Moslem Quarter by way of Herod's Gate.

Keith had finished his lunch, a falafel, and was on his way to Halperin's room to recover his jacket. At the moment he was rounding the corner of the Jaffa Road onto Natan Strauss, the receptionist inside the Immigration Center was becoming increasingly alarmed.

Five minutes ago the cleaning staff had arrived to pick up trash. She did not recognize the three Arab men, nor did she know of any reason why they should carry a trash barrel into the building. The Immigration Center had its own equipment. They had proceeded immediately upstairs, leaving the first floor and the lobby trash to wait. This was strange. The five years she had spent in Israel had taught her to be suspicious. She now turned to her boyfriend, Dov Shahar, a member of the paratroopers, who had arrived just after the men went upstairs.

"Dov, I think something is wrong. I don't recognize those three Arabs who went upstairs. They are wearing the right uniform, but the cleaning staff was here yesterday and aren't due again until Wednesday," she whispered.

Dov took his Galil, an Israeli-made automatic rifle, off his shoulder and rushed upstairs, taking the steps two at a time. Meanwhile, the receptionist cleared the lobby and called the Magav, the Israeli Border Police.

At the top of the stairs, Dov listened for voices. There were muffled sounds coming from down the hall. He moved forward past several rooms before he determined the sound was coming from a room on the left. There, he heard a muffled call for help. Dov reached forward and tried the door. It was locked. Dov moved to one side of the door and shouted.

"Open up!"

Barely had the words left his mouth before the door was riddled with a wild spray of bullets from inside. Most of the slugs missed Dov because he had moved, but two rounds struck his right side, one in his shoulder the other in his right lung. As he fell he returned fire, systematically sweeping from right to left before he was overcome by pain.

There was a moment of silence before someone in the room edged the door open from inside. The room was a bloody mess. Three bodies were sprawled in the middle of the room. Halperin had taken the worst of the blast from the young Israeli, but the two young Arabs were also fatally wounded. The face of Hassan was first to show in the hallway, followed by Pronin. Hassan turned, grasped a timed incendiary device from the trash barrel, set the timer, armed the firing mechanism, and placed it next to the pile of bodies. He was not troubled by the fact that his two assistants were still alive.

The two men made a hasty exit down the stairs to the lobby. Hassan still carried his AK-47. The lobby was vacant. They scrambled outside and ran into the street toward the stolen trash truck parked on the other side. At that instant, the second floor window erupted with a loud explosion that shattered the glass and filled the room with smoke and flame.

Keith had just parked his rental car in front of the Immigration Center when he heard the sound of automatic weapons. He looked up to see two men leaving the building on the run. Suddenly, a face from the past flashed into view. It was older now and the hair was thinner and graying, but he felt sure he recognized the big man. A strange feeling of rage gripped Keith. "Pronin!" he shouted.

The tall man in full flight for the truck took one quick glance in Keith's direction. There was a dramatic moment of recognition as their eyes met. In the next instant, Hassan, realizing the Russian had been recognized, leveled his AK-47 at Keith and blasted away. He climbed aboard the truck, and a second later it roared to life. Pronin jumped inside as it began to speed away.

Keith had lunged to safety behind his rental car. Hassan was too late in firing at Keith, but the slugs from the AK-47 splattered the side of the rental car, disabling it. The radiator was leaking, a large cloud of steam was forming, and the left tire was flat. Keith, except for a scratched knee and elbow, was unhurt. The trash truck was now roaring down Levi Eshkol Boulevard. As Keith watched, it made a right and headed toward the Old City. Keith could hear a siren. In a moment, an Israeli Border Officer in a Jeep arrived. Keith ran to the Jeep. "They just drove down that way to the right," he shouted at the officer.

As the officer yelled to his driver, Keith jumped in the back of the Jeep. The officer was surprised by Keith's interference. "I know one of the men who is responsible for this attack! He's a Russian son-of-a-bitch!" shouted Keith.

The officer was busy keeping his seat as the Jeep veered wildly around the corner toward the Old City, trying to dodge traffic and gain distance on the trash truck. He was about to order Keith out of the Jeep, but changed his mind, preferring to press the chase.

The truck approached an intersection clogged with traffic due to a red light. Up ahead, the truck was slowing down.

"Try to move up on his left in the center lane, I'll take out the driver," shouted the officer, readying his Galil.

For a moment, it looked like it would be easy to catch the trash truck. There were four cars stopped at the traffic light at Shimon Hatzadik Street. The trash truck was trapped in the right lane. As the Jeep approached cautiously on the left, the truck suddenly roared to life, swerved to the right, and accelerated down the sidewalk. It blindly sped into the intersection, striking an oncoming van. The van was impacted just behind the cab, its momentum pushing the truck sideways. The truck was not disabled by the wreck, but swerved around the wrecked van and continued up the avenue, and then veered left into a narrow alley.

The Jeep followed, its siren blasting as it rounded the smashed van to follow the wild course taken by the trash truck. They were approaching the Old City. The streets were narrow and the roadbed rough and unpaved. The driver was having trouble keeping the Jeep, with its high center of gravity, under control as it rounded several corners in hot pursuit. Abruptly, the truck lurched into a very narrow alley.

Pronin couldn't understand why Hassan had chosen this alley. It was so narrow it would not let the truck pass. Besides, the alley appeared to dead-end about a hundred yards farther ahead where it was blocked by a large wall of rock.

Hassan had a plan. He was no stranger to this alley. Long ago, he had spent many afternoons playing in this neighborhood, back when Jerusalem was partially Jordanian territory. Now he drove the truck forward, oblivious to the narrowing walls. With a tremendous screech of tearing metal, he wedged the truck hopelessly between the alley walls. Pronin was almost ejected through the windshield.

"What the hell's the matter with you, Hassan? We're stuck!" yelled Pronin.

Hassan said nothing, but grabbed a fire extinguisher from behind the driver's seat and smashed out the windshield. In a second he was out through the opening and down in the alley. Pronin was right behind.

"Have confidence! I know a way out of here!" shouted Hassan, as he began the dash down the alley.

Pronin made good time over the rough surface, despite his knee. Soon they reached a rock wall. Off to the left at the base of one of the last buildings that made up the alley wall, was a small opening barely wide enough to allow a man to pass through. Hassan was through the opening in a flash. Pronin, because of his considerable bulk, took longer to squeeze through. When he reached the other side of the wall, he found a small private garden that probably dated back to the time of the Crusaders. The garden was well-tended and well-watered.

Hassan, desperately trying to remember the layout of the cave that he knew led from under the great rock wall back into the catacombs of the Old City, paused for a moment. The problem was there would be no light, and they would have to proceed by feel in the darkness. He waited a moment for Pronin to catch up. He arrived, breathing heavily. "Stay close to me and hold on!" Hassan shouted.

Hassan abruptly bent forward, entered the cave, and headed inward to the left in the dim light. Hassan was moving slowly by feel alone with Pronin inching along behind.

Keith and the officer approached the wedged truck carefully. At any second they expected return fire. The truck made an excellent barricade. Keith dropped to the cobblestone road. By peering beneath the truck, he could see two sets of feet quickly retreating down the alley.

"They're getting away," said Keith as he dove under the truck and began crawling toward the other side.

The officer instructed his driver to wait by the Jeep. He followed Keith. In a few seconds Keith was on his feet. He was just able to see the last man, who he was sure was Pronin, disappear through a narrow exit. Keith and the officer ran all out for the same opening. Keith prudently let the officer lead because he was armed. On the other side, they found the garden. The two fugitives were nowhere to be seen.

Catching his breath, Keith carefully examined the garden grass as if he were tracking a deer. The ground was moist from the automatic sprinkling system, which had just finished its cycle. He found the footprints of the heavier man leading toward the large rock wall. As he approached the wall, the small entrance to a cave appeared at its base. There were wet footprints leading inward.

"Over here!" whispered Keith to the officer.

They peered together into the dark entrance of the cave. Taking a flashlight from his belt, the officer bent forward and said to Keith, "Follow me."

They were in a confining tunnel heading downward. As Keith studied the walls, he could see the cave was not a natural formation because there were many chisel marks. At some period in ancient times, the tunnel had been laboriously carved out of the solid rock. They moved forward for about five hundred feet, taking several curves. The deeper they went into the ancient tunnel, the more primitive the stone work became. At each intersection they had to study the area carefully for alternative tunnels. As they were rounding a particularly sharp curve, Keith thought he heard the sound of footsteps on the hard surface a short distance ahead. They must be gaining on the two men. Apparently, they did not have a flashlight either and the darkness had hampered their progress.

A major intersection presented two tunnels. One led forward, to the right and upward, the other to the left and downward. There was no way to determine which way the two fugitives went.

"You take the right, I'll take the left," volunteered Keith.

"No, you're unarmed and have no light. If you catch up to them, it won't be good. I'll lead and we'll take the left," the officer replied.

Keith, for the lack of a better alternative, followed. About two hundred feet farther down the passage, they suddenly came to a blank wall. There once had been a tunnel which proceeded farther, but the ceiling had caved in and the passage was tightly sealed.

Retreating back in haste to the intersection, they flew down the right tunnel. It led upwards for about three hundred feet. There was light ahead. Keith and the officer charged forward. At last, they rushed through a narrow entrance into a roped-off area at the base of a parking lot. At street level they stopped. The officer shook his head, realizing they were in the parking lot of the Rockefeller Museum. Their quarry was nowhere in sight.

Little could be done. Keith dashed toward the street, hoping to see something. The officer took out his radio and called for backup. In a few minutes, two trucks arrived. The officer quickly ordered the additional officers to search the area.

There was a large crowd at the bus station next to the museum. Keith held little hope they would find anything now.

After a fruitless half hour, the commanding officer called the search off and walked over to Keith.

"I am Offer Lavi," he said, extending his right hand.

"Keith Maddox," said Keith, shaking his hand.

"How do you know these men?"

"I'm not positive, but the tall man looked like a Russian bastard I met twelve years ago in Vietnam," Keith answered.

"I must ask you to come with me to the local Magav office," Offer explained apologetically.

"I don't mind. They shot my rental car. I need to call the rental agency to report the good news," replied Keith.

Offer asked his driver to bring the Jeep around. They headed for a stone building on Elezar Hamodai street.

Keith followed Offer inside. There was a considerable amount of activity. As Keith headed down the hall toward Offer's office, he was astounded to hear a familiar voice from down the hallway.

"Keith Maddox! I don't believe it!"

"Well, hello there, Zvi!"

It was Zvi Oren, who had been involved with the mercenaries in Keith's escape in Vietnam.

"Shalom, Keith. Don't tell me your Navy has lost nuclear devices on Israeli soil!" he laughed.

"No, but I think my rental car was retired by an Arab who was in the company of Pronin, the Russian agent you might remember that caused me such grief in Vietnam," replied Keith.

The smile deserted Zvi's face. "You don't mean here in Jerusalem?"

"Yes! Not more than a half hour ago. And his Arab buddy was

packing some potent fire power! They just blew up the Immigration Center," replied Keith.

"There were actually four involved. Two burned bodies and the Russian immigrant were found in room 222," interrupted Offer.

Keith was shocked. It had not occurred to him that it was Halperin's room that had blown up.

"I know that old man. Poor old guy, his name is Joseph Halperin," Keith told Zvi.

"Seems you know a lot about what happened. Perhaps we should talk."

Keith followed Zvi into his office. There he related the events that had occurred after he arrived at the Immigration Center. He did not mention his visit there earlier in the day, or the purpose of his trip. He had no intention of revealing the fact he had the package of music in his possession, or that it was connected to an old World War Two code. The package was now safely stowed in the hotel safe.

"What you say about this Russian, Pronin, bears further investigation. I will get in touch with our intelligence people and get a trace on this man. Where will you be staying while you are here in Israel?" asked Zvi.

"We, that is, my girlfriend and I, are planning to take a couple of days to go sightseeing. We will probably spend a day at Masada and a couple of days at Eilat, diving."

"Please notify me before you leave. We will put out an alert for this man at the airport and all the border crossings. We might get lucky. A man of his size with his limp should be easy to spot," said Zvi.

"Don't be too sure. He is a dangerous adversary. I should know." The sight of Pronin's distorted face looking back at him flashed into Keith's mind. This was not the end of Pronin and he knew it.

Keith spent the afternoon at Jerusalem's Via Dolorosa following the stations of the cross. It was overwhelming to actually be in the location where history was made so many years ago. At each location, he paused and tried to imagine the scene of that fateful day. The children playing in the cobblestone streets, the shops, and the patrons crowding one another made it easy to imagine the sudden commotion caused by the procession of the prophet Jesus with his tormentors and believers in tow. If imagination wasn't enough on this Friday, as on most every Friday, there was a procession of priests dressed in black robes who were tracing those fateful steps.

It was after six when Anna returned to the King David Hotel. Anna looked at Keith, who was uncharacteristically moody.

"Why the long face, Keith? Did something go wrong today?"

"The man I went to see this morning was killed in his room this afternoon." Anna gasped and covered her mouth with her hand. She seemed paralyzed, but ready to hear more. "I watched the killers escape after they blew up and burned the Immigration Center. What's worse, I know I recognized one of them," Keith continued.

She nodded her head slowly to encourage him to go on.

"Do you remember, I once told you there was a Russian involved when I was captured in Vietnam?"

"Yes, but that's impossible, he couldn't be here!"

"Well, one looked very much like him. On top of that, he turned when I shouted his name. Can you imagine the gall of that bastard doing his dirty work here in Jerusalem?"

He took some time to explain the events of the morning completely. He gave most of the detail, even meeting with Zvi Oren. He did not dwell on the significance of the music he had picked up earlier.

There was little Anna could do to console Keith. They ate a late dinner in the hotel and, before going to bed, watched the hotel movie channel.

Leaving early the next morning, they first took time to visit the Church of the Nativity in Bethlehem. The experience was more than Keith had expected. To his surprise, he found the old stable was really a cave rather than the wooden frame stables so often found in churchyards in America. The experience brought a dose of reality to all the stories told again and again each year throughout his Christian upbringing.

The magic of the Holy Land still held its appeal for Keith, but the trip towards Masada was spent in gloomy silence. It wasn't until Anna suggested they take a swim in the Dead Sea that Keith began to come out of his shell of doom. They stopped at a resort, especially designed for the purpose of bathing in the salt water, with a hot spring inside the building. Although he had heard about the Dead Sea for years, Keith was quite surprised by the buoyancy of the salty water. He laughed when Anna took a copy of Cosmopolitan Magazine and sat Indian style in the water, her buttocks barely below the surface of the salt-laden water. The position was unstable, and despite considerable effort, she fell over backwards with an amusing flop punctuated by, "Oh, shit." Soon they were both trying to duck each other below the surface of the murky water. Afterwards, they gladly took a long soapy shower.

A half hour's ride southward brought them to Masada. The mountain fortress could be reached by cable car, relieving visitors of much of the work of getting to the top. On the way up, Keith learned the Roman fortress was built on high ground left behind by erosion as the western plate rose above the fault that formed the Dead Sea valley. The high ground towered 1,500 feet above the Dead Sea and stood alone, separated from the plateau to the west. Keith had never seen a better natural fortress. The approach to the top required the opposing troops struggle up nearly vertical walls. The defenders had a distinct advantage, with plenty of rocks to throw down on the opposition. There was an impressive system for storing dried food supplies, and an elaborate cistern system used to supply water to the defenders of the fortress.

During the ride up, Keith could not shake the feeling they were being followed. He carefully examined each passenger in the cable car, but didn't notice any of the nine or ten other passengers acting suspiciously. Still, the feeling persisted. They began to walk the relatively flat surface at the top of the fortress cliff, which measured almost three hundred by six hundred meters. As they climbed through the partially restored, yet still elegant, remains of Herod's palace, Keith kept looking over his shoulder. Several times he thought he caught a glimpse of someone darting out of sight as he looked back. Feelings from many years ago in the jungles of Vietnam returned.

Despite his uneasiness, Keith found Masada awe-inspiring. The view below from the Eastern Gate of the Dead Sea, with the dikes and channels of the Dead Sea works clearly visible, made quite a sight. The fortress was first constructed in approximately 100 B.C. King Herod turned it into a luxury retreat around 30 B.C. Around 70 A.D., nine hundred or so Jewish Zealots held out against ten thousand Roman soldiers. The miles of piled rocks still remain, forming the circumvallation wall and eight camps, which the Roman forces built to contain the Zealots at the base of the fortress. The confrontation continued for years. The Jewish Zealots had sufficient food and water, but in the end, the Romans used Jewish prisoners to build a great ramp up to the west wall of the fortress. The Zealots would not use their catapults against their own people. Eventually, the Romans successfully breached the fortress's west wall. The Roman victory was an empty one, as the Jews chose to commit mass suicide rather than be taken by the Roman horde.

Keith had just left the Synagogue of the Zealots when two Israeli F-16 fighters on patrol along the Israeli eastern border flashed past. When they approached the fortress, both pilots raised the right wings of their aircraft in honor of the Zealots' struggle. Keith could clearly see the star of David on the wing and fuselage of the planes as they passed overhead at subsonic speed. Keith gained a deeper appreciation for the past and present Jewish struggle in Israel.

Following his instinct, Keith suggested they walk down the Snake Path, the alternative to taking the cable car to the bottom. Anna reluctantly agreed. The serpentine path provided excellent visibility of the hillside. They were not alone on the descent; still, Keith could not identify anyone who appeared to be following them.

Anna was taken aback by Keith's anxiety, but decided to ignore it. He had chosen to become involved in this crazy scheme without consulting her, so he would have to handle this himself.

Instead, she was absorbed in the history of Masada in her travel guide. Much of the walk she spent reading it aloud to Keith.

They reached the parking lot in late afternoon. Keith opened the car door for Anna, then climbed in the driver's seat. He swung out of the parking lot and accelerated south down the road to Eilat on the Red Sea. While driving, Keith continued to watch the rear-view mirror. At one point, a car approached rapidly from behind, but before long they were passed by a young woman in her twenties driving too fast in a Mercedes convertible. Darkness approached. There was little traffic and they continued southward to Eilat without incident.

They arrived after dark at the King Solomon Hotel. Keith immediately called Graduate Hospital for news of his father's operation. He managed to get a resident who said the operation was complete and his father was resting in ICU. There were no complications and his prognosis was good. Tomorrow morning he should be well enough to answer the phone.

Keith wanted to show Anna some of the best diving in the world. His company travel agent in Aspen had arranged for a diving tour through an organization called Underwater Sports International. Their business provided diving equipment and transportation along the shore of the Red Sea in the Sinai Desert. From their vehicles, divers could simply walk into the Red Sea for some of the best reef diving in the world. The Israeli government had supported the effort during the Sinai occupation. Recently, the Egyptian government had realized that the reef was a natural resource and began punishing offenders who used grenades to fish the reef, causing terrible ecological destruction and killing many of the reef's inhabitants.

They intended to spend three days diving in the Red Sea. They found the beaches in Eilat were quite cosmopolitan. Half of the beach allowed topless bathing. Anna, despite her striking appearance and excellent figure, declined the opportunity. Keith found the sun deepened his high altitude tan and, slowly, he began to relax. Only once in the compressor shack of the dive shop did he feel he was being watched by a rather feminine looking Arab who was near the transport van. After his tanks were filled, he found that the doors to the van had been left open. Immediately, he suspected trouble. He checked his equipment, especially his air regulator carefully for sabotage, but found nothing. Next, he checked Anna's equipment. Still nothing. Keith was beginning to think all his worries were groundless.

They enjoyed the opportunity to use a rented underwater camera and separate electronic strobe. The equipment manufactured by a well-known Japanese camera company was excellent. The internal design of the camera allowed auto wind and focus while the strobe metered the right amount of light for each exposure. This was truly point and shoot underwater photography. Keith found it easy to get the best photographs he had ever obtained underwater. The blues and reds of the coral and sea life were brilliant even using high speed film. In Eilat there was a 24-hour photo shop, which allowed him to get his film developed for review after dinner each day. There was little more he could have asked for.

Reaching the reef from the beach was a trivial matter. There was no surf and a few strokes brought both Keith and Anna into superb reef diving. Anna had obtained her diving certification in Florida during a spring vacation while still in college. She had done little diving since. Keith was a veteran diver, having filled three books before he gave up keeping a dive log. In the past, he had logged more decompression dives than he cared to remember. Much of his diving was done in full wet suit and with double tanks in the North Atlantic and Pacific. Diving in the Red Sea was a pleasant departure from the more strenuous wreck diving he was used to.

At one point early on the first day, Anna, who was fascinated by the fish in the reef, found one with striking colors on its fins. As she approached and stretched her hand out, Keith, who fortunately was watching, pulled her back. He later explained there is a principle often true underwater, the more striking the coloring of a fish, the more deadly. In this case Anna was examining a lionfish, whose spines are quite poisonous.

They were planning their third day of photodiving when a young man dressed in casual clothes appeared at their hotel room door.

The stranger held up his identification.

"I am Deni Landa. I work for Zvi Oren. I am here to invite you to a meeting with Zvi and, for your convenience, I have a plane waiting at the airport."

Keith realized the invitation was a polite way of summoning him. He also knew Zvi must have made progress in his investigation. Hoping to hear news of Pronin's pending capture, he was anxious to leave immediately.

Anna looked slightly annoyed at the change in plans. After fifty minutes in which they had to pack, return the photo equipment, and check out of their hotel, they were airborne on their way to Sde-Dov airport near Tel Aviv.

The meeting was brief. Zvi confirmed that a video camera at the Tel Aviv airport immigration had recorded a man who looked very much like Nikolai Pronin, a Russian KGB agent, entering Israel under the name of Peer Ericsson. Zvi had sent a bulletin to all border crossings requesting they stop anyone matching the description, but his message arrived a few moments late at the bridge across the Jordan River. Pronin had escaped.

"I am very sorry to report we were unable to apprehend your old enemy. I am also disturbed to find out from the receptionist at the Immigration Center that you visited earlier that morning and that it was Joseph Halperin you visited. You did not mention this before; could it be there is more between you and Pronin than you have revealed, my friend?" asked Zvi.

Keith took time to reflect on the situation before he replied. He wanted to reveal more about his reason for being in Israel, but first he had to get the message decoded before he would share that information with an agent of a foreign government. He decided to take no chances.

"Joseph Halperin was a friend of my father's. I promised to visit him while I was vacationing with Anna. She invited me to join her after she finished shooting. The fact that Pronin was here, doing more of his bloody work is coincidence," Keith told him in a confidential tone.

This was not the response Zvi was hoping for, but he tried not to show his disappointment. "I will accept that answer for now, but do not underestimate this man. Our folder on him contains plenty of details. He is one tough bugger. He has been involved in Vietnam, Cuba, and Afghanistan. We have reports that say there has often been torture and murder associated with his work. He is a very ambitious man who has plenty of field experience. I'm not sure if it is relevant, but he is now head of the security forces at the Baikonur Space Center. If there is any more to this story, you might save yourself a lot of grief by being more open with us." Zvi looked at Keith and then sighed.

Something in the back of Keith's head started to click.

"You needn't remind me of his capabilities. It was Pronin who was after me when we were snatched out of Vietnam and he was the one who tortured to death my associate Allen Winn … No, I doubt there is significance to his showing up in Halperin's room after my earlier visit. Except, he comes from Russia and knew a friend of my father's. He certainly didn't reveal anything to me. I would guess Halperin left Russia with some information that the KGB didn't want loose in Israel, but I can't speculate on what it could be," responded Keith.

The meeting ended abruptly. Zvi wished Anna and Keith the best of luck. As Keith left, Zvi reflected that it had been over thirteen years since they had last seen each other. "Come back and see us more often," Zvi invited. But he didn't expect to see Keith again in the near future.

• Chapter 9 •

PHILADELPHIA
MONDAY, SEPTEMBER 9, 1991

Rudolf Maddox lay quietly in his bed. Two days ago he was in Cardiac Surgery ICU and now he was in a semi-private room on a cardiac surgery floor. His doctor felt he was making good progress. Soon, he would be going home. Yesterday he had a roommate, and today the other bed was empty. He had a private bathroom, which he was finally able to use. The room also had a small window with a view of the alley between the hospital buildings. The first day, an attendant had arranged for the color TV to be turned on for a minimal rental charge. The previous two evenings he had caught the news on CNN. Early this morning the heating system came on, possibly for the first time since the previous spring. A musty smell filled the over-heated room. After lying in bed so long, Rudolf was tired of resting, and bored stiff.

Now the PA system broke the silence, a sure sign morning had arrived. Soon, the aide would bring breakfast, or something that resembled breakfast. He hoped they would finally cook something that had taste. So far the food was very bland. What he missed most was salt. Salt gave everything flavor. How could the doctors expect a person to go on eating without flavor? He had always been a heavy salt user, always would be.

Today would be better than the previous two days. Today Keith would arrive. He left a message shortly after picking up the package in Israel. Rudolf had seen on the evening news that there was an incident in Israel. It was listed as a minor random terrorist act, but it alarmed Rudolf that it occurred in the Immigration Center where Keith was to have met Halperin. To his relief, Keith called the next day. This morning he would finally get a chance to see what all the fuss was about and what his old friend Lebedev had sent.

He was not alone in the room. A man wearing the white jacket of an intern entered and stood at the foot of his bed. "Good morning, how are you doing today?" he inquired cheerfully.

"You must be new," Rudolf smiled. "I don't think I've seen you before."

"I am a resident doing rounds for Dr. Lang because he had an emergency. So, are you feeling all right, Mr. Maddox?" he asked, picking up Rudolf's chart to study it.

"Much better now that I am allowed to get out of bed occasionally. I do feel some pain around my incision, especially when the nurses make me cough, or when I breathe deeply," Rudolf replied.

"That can be expected. I see from your chart that your pain has been with you for some time. Dr. Lang has given orders for relief," said the resident, with a faint accent Rudolf couldn't quite place.

The resident produced a syringe, filled it from a small bottle, and injected the clear fluid into the membrane in Rudolf's IV. Soon the fluid entered the vein in his arm.

"There ... that should ease your pain,"

The man left the room. Rudolf was trying to recognize the accent. It was faintly familiar, definitely eastern European, but he couldn't quite place it.

Where was that aide with my breakfast? See there, my stomach is growling, he thought. *Damn! I want to be finished with breakfast when Keith gets here.*

Rudolf reached for the nurse's button. As he stretched out his arm he started to feel drowsy. *Strange,* he thought, a moment ago he was wide awake, and now he felt as if he could easily fall asleep. *I guess I'm not as awake as I thought.*

Again, he stretched out his hand, but had trouble finding the call button.

My hand is shaking so. Why am I so drowsy? I can barely keep myself awake ... Something must be wrong ... Shouldn't sleep like this ... Got to get the nurse ...

He was barely able to press the button before the room appeared to take a series of somersaults around in his head, as if he were rolling downhill. Slowly, his mind passed from a blurred and spinning vision of reality into the blackness that lay beyond.

FIVE MINUTES LATER

Keith was on his way up the elevator. He carried the package he had retrieved from the safe of the King David Hotel two hours before their plane left Tel Aviv. His curiosity was highly aroused. Could it be that Pronin was after this package? Translating the code might answer that question. The anticipation grew as he reached the fifth floor. His dad was in room 515. He paused at the nurses' station to ask directions. At that moment, there was a commotion down the hall. Suddenly, two residents and two nurses pushing a heavy cart with IV bags hanging from an attached pole ran past.

Keith stepped out of the way to let the team pass, then found the nurses' station. A stout woman, with the name Sarah Henderson clearly visible on her ID badge, looked up and smiled.

"Hello, I'm Keith Maddox. I'm here to visit my father. Could you tell me which room he is in?" he asked.

The smile disappeared.

"Oh ... Well I'm not sure exactly. I need to ask someone. If you will just wait here a second, Mr. Maddox, I'll be right back," she said rising.

She left the station and proceeded down the hall. In a minute she returned with Dr. Lang, his father's physician.

"I'm Keith Maddox. How is my dad doing?"

"I am deeply sorry, but your father just suffered a relapse. We are trying to revive him. The Code Blue team is working hard, but he is not responding."

"Oh, no!" gasped Keith, hardly believing his ears. His brain simply couldn't comprehend the situation.

"If you will please wait in the lounge with Mrs. Heissler, our head nurse, I will return as soon as there is a change in his condition."

Keith walked slowly to the lounge, shaken by the news. The head nurse did her best to help Keith while he waited. She left for a moment and returned with two steaming cups of coffee.

"We don't let patients drink coffee because it is not good for the heart, but the staff always keeps a pot brewing. I thought you might like some, wouldn't you?

"Yes, thanks."

"Do you take cream and sugar?"

Keith was deep in thought.

"Oh, I'm sorry, cream only."

She quickly mixed the cream in his coffee, leaving the second cup black for herself. Keith impatiently waited for Dr. Lang to return. He remembered a time fifteen years ago when he wondered what it would be like when his father was gone. In those days, he very much depended on his father's advice. That was before his mother died and the charter business started taking up all his time. Over the years, he lost all of his childhood dependence on his father. Recently, their association was limited to one visit a year and a phone call a month. Now, even that would all come to an end if the team down the hall failed.

Keith spent one of the worst half hours in his life waiting. Finally, Dr. Lang returned. When Keith saw his face, he knew the truth. He didn't have to go into much detail. Dr. Lang suspected his father probably sustained a blockage in the new vessels grafted to his heart, resulting in a fatal infarction. There would be an autopsy. It would no doubt confirm Dr. Lang's suspicions.

Keith left the hospital feeling like he was in a dream. Somewhere in his mind, he knew there would be funeral arrangements to make and the lawyer to contact. He would have to arrange his father's things, and the sale of the house. Keith was weary. He had been going nonstop since he first flew to San Diego weeks ago. He decided to go to his dad's house, break out a six-pack of his dad's favorite beer, and get a little buzz on in memory of the old man. He was grateful that long ago, when he was old enough to realize all the trouble his parents had gone through raising him, he had told them how grateful he was. Knowing he had verbalized his feelings helped him immensely as he fought the overwhelming pain rising in his chest and throat. Despite his living in Colorado, he still felt a closeness with his father. Now that was history.

THREE HOURS LATER

Keith parked his rental car in front of the stately brick row house. Delancy Street is one of those streets in Philadelphia that has a row of sycamore trees on each side. It was not yet fall, but dry leaves blew down the sidewalk in the brisk wind. Two children, a boy in a red jacket and a girl in pigtails, both about seven years old, were roller skating down the sidewalk. They passed Keith with a loud clatter from the rough surface. He paused to watch for a second, remembering days like this when he was eight or nine—playing on the same sidewalk.

He turned toward the front door. It was ajar. He had locked it before he left for the hospital. How could it be open now?

Keith pushed open the door to find the house in complete disorder. All the drawers in the living room were pulled out. Books from the bookshelves were tossed on the floor. The mess was worse in the upstairs, especially in the bedroom. Clothes from the two dressers were piled in a heap. The closet was completely emptied with many of his parents' treasures strewn about.

Keith noticed that the revolver that his father always kept loaded and in the closet was in the midst of a pile of his mother's jewelry. He checked the silver in the corner closet in the dining room. His mother's best silver, which she used to hide in the attic when they went away on trips, was still there, untouched.

The mess was appalling. Why would someone go to the trouble of pulling everything out of the drawers, yet leave the valuables untouched? Could this just be some kind of juvenile vandalism, or was there a motive for all the mess?

Keith checked the back door in the kitchen. It was shut and locked as he had left it after taking the garbage out the night before. The breakfast dishes were still in the sink, but the drawers of the sink and the cabinets showed signs of a hasty search. Even the freezer door was ajar. He shut it.

Keith chuckled to himself sadly. There was a time when a wise neighbor revealed his secret for keeping his vacation cash safe. He always left his wallet in the freezer compartment of the refrigerator. Better than American Express, he had proudly exclaimed, no self-respecting thief would look for cash in the freezer. Well, this one must not have any self-respect, he reflected.

Keith noticed the old violin he had received from Halperin lying on the kitchen table. In his haste, he had forgotten it that morning. No surprise the thieves hadn't stolen it.

The phone rang suddenly, breaking Keith's concentration. He reached for the phone near the refrigerator. "Hello?"

"Keith, is that you?" came Anna's worried voice.

"Anna, yes, it is me." He paused, trying the words for the first time. "My father died." The words silenced both of them.

Finally Anna spoke. "How? What happened?"

"I can't believe it … I was almost there. They must have called the code just as I was coming down the hall. They don't really know what happened. He was recovering and doing fine. Then something just went wrong."

"Keith … I'm so sorry. I want to be with you. I'm coming down there now."

"No, not right now, I've got a mess to clean up here. That'll take a couple of hours. Then I'd like to come up to New York and be with you, if it's OK? I just need to get away from here—too many memories."

"Come up as soon as you're ready, Keith. I'll wait for you."

Keith couldn't talk anymore. He hung up and went back to the task at hand.

There was no sign of break-in at either the front or back door. Every drawer in the house had been pulled out, but no valuables taken. The whole house had been thoroughly searched.

Someone was looking for something. Could it be something

his father had? Something someone wanted kept secret. How could they know he had just died? Possibly they were taking advantage of his being in the hospital. What could he have that someone would want so badly?

Back upstairs in his old bedroom, which now was his father's den, he found records strewn about. His dad saved every check he ever wrote and kept every receipt. His records filled three filing cabinets. In these cabinets were old letters from friends, family albums, and even some war mementos.

As Keith sadly went through the mass of papers on the floor, trying to make some order out of the chaos, he found a picture of his dad's old war buddies, Lebedev and Lentz. All three had been honored for their work in the Czech underground. The newspaper clipping was old and faded, but it showed all three clearly. He studied the face of Lebedev for a moment. "What was so important that you had to send it in that music I picked up in Israel?" he wondered.

Next, his eyes fell on a letter from Gustav Lentz. Keith had heard about Gustav when his father told stories about their college days. Gustav was quite a ladies' man. He even went so far as to have an affair with a professor's wife, but in the end he never really could settle down. As Gustav grew older, he became more of a recluse. He finally married, but there were no children. His wife died in an avalanche while crossing a high mountain pass in mid-winter. It had been dry that fall, followed by heavy snow after Christmas. The snow that clung to the ridges had no stable base. Unfortunately, Gustav and his wife chose the wrong time to cross to his mountain chalet. They were both buried, but Gustav was able to dig himself out and escape. Recovery efforts found his wife in late March, following an exhaustive search. Afterward, Gustav moved permanently into his chalet. He came down to town only once a month for supplies.

Keith picked up the letter. It was dated 11 July, 1990. He looked through the pile for the letter's envelope. A pack rat when it came to letters, his father always kept envelopes with foreign stamps. He'd intended to find out if the stamps were worth anything to collectors. Someday, he planned to get around to it. Well, someday never came. Still Keith could not find the envelope. There was a paper clip on the letter. It was his father's habit to attach the envelopes to the letters with a clip. The clip was there, where was the envelope?

The envelope was missing. Could it be that was what they were searching for? Why? Could the missing envelope and the ransacking of his father's house be somehow related to the package he picked up in Israel? If so, why would an envelope from Gustav be of any importance?

It struck him like a thunderbolt—there would be a return address on the envelope! Gustav was the only person outside of Russia who could translate the music, since his father had died this morning. They were trying to find Gustav!

Keith sat and stared in front of him. His father's death had not been from natural causes. The realization made everything fall into place. If they were after the package he had picked up in Israel, then it was apparent they were prepared to kill for it. Isn't that what happened to Halperin? If that were true, then is it out of the question for them to get to his dad? After all, Halperin had his father's address. They could have gotten it before Halperin died.

Keith stood up. It was dangerous to stay in this house with the package outside in his rental car. Time to move out. Keith made phone calls to Dr. Lang's office and to his father's lawyer. He packed his suitcase.

Just before leaving, he picked up the violin Lebedev had saved for his father. He locked the front door, placed his suitcase and the violin in the trunk of the rental car next to the package, climbed inside, and headed for the Walt Whitman Bridge and New Jersey. Soon, he was speeding up the New Jersey Turnpike while the sky darkened by the clouds from an approaching hurricane.

TWO HOURS LATER

Keith arrived in the parking garage beneath Anna's apartment just as it began raining large soaking drops. The sky was black with intermittent flashes of lightning. Keith was glad he didn't have to brave the heavy rain outside. *Nice to have an inside garage,* he thought.

When he knocked on Anna's door, she opened it almost immediately. She looked deeply into Keith's eyes for a second, and then put her arms around his shoulders. He was speechless; there were tears welling up in his eyes. Sobs came out of his throat involuntarily. They stood embracing in the doorway for several minutes, clinging to each other.

"Thanks for being here."

"I'm glad I could," she said, taking his hand and leading him into the living room.

"Can I fix you a drink?" she asked, smoothing his hair and leaving her hand resting on his forehead.

"Yes, and make it a strong one."

In a few moments, Anna had made a vodka tonic for herself and a stronger one for Keith. When she returned to the living room, Keith was seated in his favorite easy chair, his head in his hands. She touched him on the shoulder and handed him his drink. He downed a large portion mechanically.

"Anna, I can't be sure, but I think all the things that have happened lately are related to the package I picked up in Israel. I'm sure the package is responsible because the two people associated with it are now dead. Halperin was killed by a terrorist attack, but it wasn't a random act, because I saw the Russian, Pronin. Now, before I can get the package back to my dad for translation, he suddenly dies. I think someone killed him, but I don't have any proof of it." He paused and swallowed the last drops of his drink. "Wait, there's more." His voice was dead serious.

"Just a minute, back up, that was all too fast for me!"

Keith repeated the story more slowly. Then he continued. "While I was in the hospital, someone ransacked Dad's house, but they took nothing of value. My God, Anna, it's the package they're after! Whatever information is in that code, they're willing to kill for it! I was lucky not to be at the house when they arrived. I never suspected they were coming!"

Anna began to understand what Keith was saying.

"Anna, I think they are now after Gustav Lentz. He's the only one that can translate the code. He lives high in the Austrian Alps without a telephone. I've got to get to him before they do. As soon as this weather clears, I'm going to Austria." He grabbed her hands. "But in the meantime, I want you somewhere safe."

"Where would that be? Am I in danger by just staying here? After all, this is New York, not some foreign country. Russians can't just go around here knocking people off, you know!"

"Yes, this is New York. Do you know how many hundred Russians or Russian agents are in this city presumably associated with their embassy and the United Nations?"

"No, I don't!"

"Well the point is, someone got to my father, so it's possible they could find you."

"You don't know that. You only suspect it! But you want me to go into hiding, while you go off to Austria! Just what am I supposed to do? Lock myself in some closet and pray the Commies don't get me?"

"OK, you've made your point." He stood up and put his arms around her. "I don't want anything to happen to you. All I'm asking you to do is go somewhere for a little while where they can't find you. That's all."

She looked at him and thought a minute. "All right. I've got some time off. Maybe I'll spend it with my folks, or better yet, I can get a jump on my next assignment by going to Aspen early. I could stay in the cabin and wait for you!"

"I like the idea of Aspen, but not the cabin. They might look for you there. It would be better if you stay with Jim Dawson and his wife. They are always happy to have guests, and I'm sure under these circumstances they would agree."

Keith picked up the telephone and dialed Jim's number. Vicki Dawson answered. Jim was working up at the quarry again. Keith briefly explained the situation. Vicki agreed immediately that Anna should come as soon as possible.

With Anna's safety assured, Keith decided to try to book airline reservations for Austria. He called several major airlines, but could not find an opening before Thursday. It was Wednesday afternoon; both Philadelphia and New York airports had closed hours ago due to high winds from the approaching hurricane. It would be days before the backlog was cleared out. The agent on the phone sounded very tired. This was the third time a major storm had disrupted eastern air traffic in five weeks.

Keith hung up, satisfied there would be little opportunity to get a commercial flight in the next few days. He called his charter service in Colorado. As he suspected, one of the company planes was grounded at La Guardia. Foul weather had forced a group of New York businessmen to cancel their marketing seminar in Colorado. The plane was a Cessna fitted with long-range tanks. It had sufficient range to get to Ireland from New York. In a few minutes, he had made arrangements to have the plane ready. He could leave at the first opening in the storm.

As Keith left Anna's apartment for La Guardia, the rain became heavier. His headlights cut a blazing path through the downpour. The gutters were beginning to fill, and at a low section of the road at the first underpass, the storm sewer had overflowed and the water was deep. The underpass was part of a major through route. Keith didn't know an alternative. In his haste, he decided to brave the high water. The water was deeper than he expected. His rented Nissan Stanza was low to the ground, and the water started pouring in around the doors. He would have preferred his old Jeep CJ-2A. Twice in the underpass he felt the engine falter as the water splashed about the motor compartment, but each time it faltered, the Japanese ignition system managed to overcome misfire and kept the Nissan moving. When he emerged on the far side, there were almost two inches of water inside the car.

Back on the parkway, Keith discovered the New York drivers, who usually drove at a breakneck pace despite overcrowded highways, had wisely reduced their speed below fifty. The rain overpowered the wipers, making visibility poor. Keith was now in the far left lane, peering intently through the momentary slices of clarity behind each traverse of the wipers. Suddenly, a large van in the opposing lane threw a tremendous shaft of muddy water that hit the Stanza, totally blocking Keith's vision. An instant before, Keith saw an object in his lane. He wrongly assumed it was a piece of rusted exhaust pipe. The next time the wipers cleared the water, there wasn't time to swerve around it. Keith held the wheel steady, hoping to straddle the object. Too late, he realized it wasn't a piece of pipe, but some sort of gear box. Never mind how it got there, it was a little too big for the Stanza to straddle. Keith slightly altered his course to avoid exposing the vitals under the engine, but the object struck the right side floorboards with a bang and thump. There were at least two following thuds before it made its exit under the rear bumper. To his surprise, the Japanese car kept running without difficulty, but there was a hole in the floor board beneath the passenger seat. When he regained control of the car and changed lanes, he noted the water from the underpass was running out the hole. Nice improvement. He smiled to himself.

As he approached the airport, the rush hour traffic—delayed by the flooding—further slowed his progress.

It took two hours to get to the bizjet terminal at La Guardia. When he checked in with the maintenance crew chief, George Taylor, the plane was ready.

Keith first met George when he contracted with Jetserv for service at La Guardia on the company's jets. George was a lanky six-footer. His father owned a small airfield near Bridgton, New Jersey. He was an excellent mechanic, having spent most of his youth fooling with his dad's airplanes. He had only one vice: he liked to chew tobacco. Keith was inclined not to notice, hoping he wouldn't spit in front of customers. Tonight, George had stayed late to get the plane ready for Keith. "Not that it'll do you any good," George shook his head. "The weather's supposed to be bad for at least twelve hours."

"Any chance there'll be a break before then?"

"It's a bloody mess out there, man! The radar looks like pure hell! I don't see you gettin' out o' here before late tomorrow morning. But anyway, she's ready, just like you asked. That's the best I can do," sighed George, passing Keith the maintenance manifest for his signature.

"I appreciate the help, George. This is an emergency. I'm going to stand by and make a break at the first chance." Keith signed the manifest.

Keith carefully checked the Cessna in the hangar himself. It was one of the planes they had rebuilt the previous year, and was in excellent shape. The engines had fewer than two thousand hours each. Keith had flown it from Aspen to New York several times to spend the weekend with Anna. Even in bad weather, it should make Shannon, Ireland in about five hours.

Keith needed a copilot for the flight. He knew the two pilots spent nights in the local Holiday Inn, just outside the terminal. There was a phone in the hangar. Company pilots were required to leave a phone number where they could be reached. He dialed the hotel and asked for Joe Carter. Joe was out, but because the weather was bad he hadn't left a number with the desk clerk. The clerk ventured they were probably at his favorite bar in Manhattan, but he wasn't sure where. Keith left an urgent message, hoping Joe would get it.

There was little to do but wait. He needed sleep badly, so he decided to check into the hotel, but not before visiting the weather center.

This was a small room with two operators present at most times. Behind the front desk was a large radar screen showing the composite image from many separate radars, clearly depicting the approaching storm. In the right hand corner, a noisy impact printer churned out weather bulletins. Mary Sullivan, from whom he often got his pre-flight weather information, recognized Keith as he approached. Mary was updating the weather center's plot of the hurricane's track on a wall map.

"Hi, Keith. You're not trying to get to Aspen tonight, are ya?" she called out in a cheery voice.

"No, ma'am, not tonight. But I'm trying to get to Ireland as soon as I can," he laughed.

"You … Going to Ireland? Is this an international expansion of the charter service?"

"No, Mary, this is private flight." Keith lowered his voice and frowned. "It's an emergency."

"I doubt you'll get clearance before tomorrow morning, Keith, unless … " she said hesitating.

"Unless what?" he urged.

"Unless you get real lucky and the eye of the storm passes over the airport. You might get clearance then," she cocked her head to one side and smiled.

"What're the possibilities?"

"Slim to none. The storm seems to be heading inland now. Unless it turns out to sea, the eye will miss us completely. But don't give up hope. The last two hurricanes we've had blew up real big like this one over the Caribbean, but when they pushed northward past Florida, they pooped out. Once that happened, they turned out to sea and died. In short, it's my guess it could happen," replied Mary.

"OK, I'll be at the Holiday getting some much-needed rest. Please call me the moment anything changes," said Keith.

"Is this really as serious as you said?"

"Yes, it is!"

"Then you can count on me to call," Mary smiled reassuringly.

TWO HOURS LATER

Keith slowly woke in the hotel room. For a few seconds, he didn't remember where he was. Sleep was calling him back under the covers, but something was different. The room was quiet. That's it, he realized, there wasn't any wind buffeting the building. Earlier, the wind had howled around the window frame. He was out of bed with a bound. Checking his watch, he found it was eleven o'clock. The timing was right.

Suddenly, the phone rang. Keith picked it up.

"Hey, hot shot, you got lucky! You've got probably forty-five minutes to get outta here. If ya hurry, you can make it," crooned Mary into the phone.

Keith made it to the bizjet terminal in record time. Mary was ready with the latest weather information. "Good luck, Keith, you got about fifteen miles of clear air outside the airport, then it will be real rough until you can climb above it."

George already had the plane outside the hangar. The engines were running. "Where's your copilot?" George asked in his usual stiff tone.

"Don't ask. I tried to get Joe. I'm going alone," Keith told him in a tone that didn't ask for any reply.

"Well, good luck, Lindy," said George, smiling perhaps for the first time in years. "You've got more guts than I do."

Keith raced through the pre-flight checklist. He was familiar with the plane, but he had not yet flown it in bad weather. Now he wondered how it would respond with the heavier long range tanks on the wing tips. George was outside removing the chocks from the wheels. Keith took a moment to monitor the ATIS (Automatic Terminal Information System). The recorded message said the wind was dying down and the visibility was improving. As Keith began to move, he contacted ground control.

"La Guardia ground, this is Cessna 731 Alpha Sierra at bizjet terminal ready to taxi for departure."

The controller was obviously surprised to hear his request. "Ah … roger, Alpha Sierra, taxi to intersection Bravo, turn left, hold short runway 31. Tower frequency 118.7."

He reached the end of the runway, switched to the tower frequency. "La Guardia tower this is 731 Alpha Sierra ready for takeoff, transatlantic flight 184."

A moment later the tower responded.

"Roger, Alpha Sierra, cleared for takeoff. Wind 300 at 15. Right, turn at 2000. Contact departure on 120.8."

As he turned off the taxiway onto the runway, the landing lights showed the long cement slab under a light rain. Ahead of him stretched the amber landing lights into the darkness. Keith would have less than five minutes of calm air after takeoff. He tightened his seat belt, then eased both throttles of the Pratt-Whitney engines full forward. After a momentary hesitation, the engine whine began to increase and accelerated down the runway.

I will never get over the exhilaration I get from the rapid acceleration of jets, thought Keith, as he was pushed back into the pilot's seat. "A few seconds now and we'll make takeoff speed. OK rotate, nose up and gear up."

The Cessna was airborne and climbing steeply. Keith kept the engines at full power as he switched to the departure frequency.

He could clearly see the immense cloud formation ahead in a moonlit sky.

"New York departure, this is Cessna 731 Alpha Sierra, at 2000, squawking 1200, transatlantic flight 184."

New York responded almost immediately.

"Roger, Alpha Sierra climb to flight level 270, heading 030. Storm center at 240 heading 060, 25 miles. Next contact Gander control at 121.7."

Keith requested a series of vectors from departure control, which would keep him in the clearest weather till he was approaching twenty-seven thousand feet. He could monitor the position of the storm clouds on his radar screen. After returning to a westerly course, he was sufficiently above the storm to request a vector toward Albany, New York. This course would take him away from the more violent northeast corner of the storm.

With the first lurch, the Cessna encountered the turbulent air at the wall of the eye. Keith had dimmed the cabin lights before taking off. The flashes of lightning cast dark shadows about the cockpit, and temporarily blinded his night vision. The air was rough, but not as rough as he had anticipated. As he passed through twenty-six thousand feet, there were a few severe bumps when the aircraft dipped so violently it caused the dishware in the cabin to jostle about. In general, the flight so far was little worse than might be encountered along any strong front. After an hour, Keith was vectored toward Montreal.

The air was much calmer now. The storm center was five hundred miles southeast. The ground was still covered by heavy overcast and rain, but at twenty-seven thousand feet, Keith finally had smooth flying. He set the controls on autopilot and reached into the cabin for a cup of coffee from the pot he had left warming before takeoff. Finally he had a chance to relax. Now if he could just keep awake for the next five hours.

"Gander control, this is Cessna 731 Alpha Sierra, transatlantic flight 184 at flight level 350 request vector instructions."

"Roger, flight 184, climb to 420 heading 070. Next check Greenland control at 120.9."

Two hours, three cups of coffee, and a couple of Rolaids later he could see the clouds clearing below. He had passed the northeast edge of the storm.

Mary was right, it was dying quickly. The weather bulletins now indicated the hurricane was out to sea and losing force rapidly. It was morning and the sun was shining brightly through the windshield, so brightly in fact, Keith could feel its unusual warmth. Keith knew he must get some sleep before heading to Salzburg.

It was eight a.m. when he touched down in Shannon. He taxied to the fuel depot immediately. Fortunately, the airport would accept his Exxon credit card, because he carried little cash. A half-hour and eight thousand pounds of fuel later, he parked the Cessna at the edge of the fuel depot and went aft in the cabin. He wasn't flying to Austria without at least four hours of sleep. He set his watch and made good use of one of the comfortable passenger seats.

TUESDAY AFTERNOON, SEPTEMBER 10

Keith advanced his watch. It was three o'clock local time in Salzburg. He had a lot to do before nightfall, with many miles to travel. From experience in Colorado, Keith knew it was unwise to explore unfamiliar mountain roads after dark. He paid for a tie down near the fuel dock, planning to refuel upon his return. With the plane safely parked, he set out to get a rental car.

At the Avis desk, he found a pleasant young woman dressed in a red uniform. Keith's German was adequate, but after a moment of stilted conversation, she switched to English. Keith took a Ford Escort equipped with snow tires.

Out on the road, he turned south toward Werfen. Salzburg was located just a few kilometers from the edge of the mountains. Keith was driving up a valley with mountains on both sides. He knew enough about different mountain ranges to know they each have personalities. The Rockies of Colorado, for instance, are primarily ocean bottom thrust up long ago. Much of the rock of the Rockies is soft and crumbles easily, making climbing treacherous. In addition, there are steep slopes covered with loose rock, or scree. Once a climber slips on the flat rocks of the Rocky Mountain scree, he may not stop till he reaches the bottom. That makes for some of the most dangerous rock climbing in the world. The mountains in Europe, in general, are of harder rock, which provides better stability. In contrast to the Rockies, the rock strata is often on edge, providing excellent hand holds for climbers.

Keith made two stops outside of Salzburg. The first was at a restaurant where he got dinner. The second stop was at an outfitters shop. There, Keith purchased light hiking boots, a down jacket, a pair of stretch jeans, a day pack, and a set of crampons. Keith hoped he would be on the glacier early the next morning. He needed to be warm and have good traction on the snow.

It took the better part of an hour to get to Werfen. He turned right toward Bischofshofen. The sun was setting when he reached Bruck, where he turned left and moved quickly up a long valley for Neukierken am Grossvenediger. He had phoned ahead to a lodge recommended by the agent at the car rental agency. The lodge was rustic, but comfortable, with several cabins built around a parking lot. Each cabin had a splendid view of the mountains, but it was too dark now to appreciate it.

In the main lodge, where the owner served a continental breakfast, there were rooms for rent. Keith had reserved one with a shared bath. The trees were just beginning to change color outside the small curtained window. With the weekend approaching, rooms had been hard to find.

The first order of business was to arrange for a guide. Keith learned long ago the dangers of venturing alone in the mountains. His first year in the Rockies he had helped the Mountain Rescue Team retrieve a body from Frigid Air Pass. A lone backpacker had stepped off the trail to take a picture and had slipped on the snow and fallen over a precipice, breaking his leg. He had warm clothing and food in his pack left by the trail, but he could not reach it. No one knew where he was, so it took a week to find him. By that time he was long dead.

Johann Clausen, the lodge owner, suggested his son-in-law, Helmut who worked for the local power company, and was a guide on weekends. When he met Helmut, he liked him right away. Helmut was trying to buy a house for his growing family and was saving all the money he made as a guide. Keith was pleased to hear Helmut's excellent English as they chatted about his work at the power plant, and Keith told him he wanted to go to Gustav's cabin.

"Too bad you weren't here last week," said Helmut.

"How come?" asked Keith.

"Gustav was here for dinner and spent the night before getting his supplies. I haven't seen so much interest in him in years."

"Really? How's that?"

"That's where the other party wanted to go yesterday. I wouldn't have cancelled, but they were so impatient. I couldn't be sure I could get away from the plant. Besides, I don't think they were experienced climbers," said Helmut.

"How much experience do you require?" asked Keith.

"Not that much, but they acted like city people, all their gear was new, and they wanted to leave immediately."

"Where were they from?"

"I'm not sure, but they were German, possibly leftover DDR from the look of their clothes."

"Were there any Russians involved, possibly a big fellow with a limp?" Keith urged.

"No, there weren't. Good thing too, or I'd never take them. I don't like Russians."

"That makes two of us," Keith said. He liked this young mountaineer. Helmut had good judgment and understood the prudence of waiting until conditions were favorable before venturing out on the glacier.

It was soon settled. Helmut would guide Keith up the glacier and over the pass to the chalet where Gustav lived high in the mountains. Before going to bed, Keith packed the folder containing the music, extra socks, and a sweater in the bottom of the day pack. It was only then that he remembered Lebedev's old violin was still in the trunk of the rental car back in New York.

WEDNESDAY, SEPTEMBER 11, 3:25 A.M.

Keith was startled awake from a deep sleep by a sharp rap on his door. Helmut had agreed to get Keith up at 3:30 a.m. They had to be on the glacier by first light. By making good use of the morning, they could get to Gustav's lodge while the snow was hard. By early afternoon, the snow would be soft, making further travel difficult and dangerous.

Keith reluctantly rose and took a quick, hot shower. He shaved the stubble beard he had grown on the trip from New York.

A few minutes later, he quietly slipped downstairs. Helmut already had strong coffee brewing. There were fresh baked rolls with sausage and fresh orange juice waiting on the table. Keith was fully awake and ready for the mountain after the tasty breakfast.

Helmut had his 4WD pick-up truck warming up. The outside temperature was -2 degrees Celsius. The drive to the base of the glacier took about an hour. The road up was one of those that wound upward around the steep side of the mountain. There were endless hairpin turns, each barely one lane wide. Fortunately, there was no descending traffic this early in the morning. Helmut's truck was equipped with a set of halogen lamps mounted on its roof. They provided excellent visibility, even in the tight turns.

They arrived at the glacier's base by sunrise. There was a small parking lot and a hostel nearby. The mountain air at this altitude was colder than it was when they started.

The water exited the glacier's base with a roar as it pitched headlong down a steep slope into a pool of glacial blue brown water. From the amount of silt in the pool, Keith knew it was an active glacier. At this end, the glacial ice was black from the sand and dirt carried down the mountain by the glacier. Underneath, huge sections of blue ice were exposed. Helmut felt it safer and easier to skirt the glacier's base, rather than try to cross the blackened ice.

Keith and Helmut put on their packs and started on the gravel strewn earth along the edge of the glacier until they passed the huge sections of ice. About a half-mile farther up, the surface of the glacier was covered with snow. When they walked on another half-mile, Helmut judged the snow would be strong enough for them to walk on. They both put on their crampons. Helmut took the lead and began walking on the snow while looking carefully for cracks indicating any sign of weakness. Keith wisely followed about forty feet behind.

"Farther up we'll have to use the rope, but I think this area is safe enough to go without. Just don't get too close to me. I'll need you to pull me out of any crevasse I might fall into," said Helmut with a half-serious laugh.

Keith could see the snow field they were on angled upward for about a mile. Then it rose steeply where the descending flow of the glacier caused the ice underneath to break up considerably.

"We'll have to be very careful when we reach the rough section ahead. There are many dangerous snow bridges there. I will try to avoid them," promised Helmut.

Keith knew a glacier was really a river of ice. It could move as much as a foot and half per day. When its course or descent angle changed abruptly, huge cracks would appear. In such sections, deep crevasses would form. Early in the season, snow masks the crevasses, but now in early fall, the snow covering the crevasses is weakened and treacherous.

They were making good time on their approach. Keith was grateful he was in good shape. All that exercising was paying off. He was finding the past week's lack of physical activity hurt his stamina little.

Forty minutes later, they approached the first steep rise. Huge sections of blue ice showed from underneath the snow cover where the glacier passed over several steep ledges. Large crevasses were apparent where the ice was exposed .

"The safest approach here is to the left," advised Helmut.

"How long do you think it'll take to get to Gustav's hostel from here?"

"You're in good shape. At this pace, we should reach Gustav's by one o'clock. That's good because this bright sun will make the snow soft by then."

"Now that you mention it, do you have any sun block?" asked Keith.

"Yes, good idea," said Helmut, reaching in the pocket of his jacket for a tube of lotion.

"Thanks. I've had my share of high altitude sunburn," said Keith. His face already had some color from the flight to Shannon, and that was after the bright sun in Eilat.

The left approach was not a simple one. It required Keith and Helmut to tie themselves together. Keith didn't have to be reminded to keep his distance as they crossed the first wide crevasse by climbing over a jagged chunk of ice jammed between the two walls. He waited for Helmut to cross before moving. Then it was his turn. He started up the ice. As he reached the middle, the ice below cracked suddenly. Fortunately, the ice Keith was on wasn't involved. Quickly, and slightly shaken, Keith joined Helmut at the far side.

Soon, they came to a section where Helmut had to straddle a knife-edged mound of ice with a sheer drop into a crevasse on both sides. Once he got to the far side, he set his ice axe and held the rope for Keith. After a couple of minutes of careful scrambling, Keith made it to the other side.

"That's the worst of it," Helmut said with a smile. "From here it's pretty much open snow."

They took a few moments to enjoy the view. The sun was shining brightly on the valley they were climbing. Down below small gray clouds hung lazily over the valley. In the distance, Keith could see the vibrant fall colors of the trees. The tourists in the sleepy village at the base were probably just getting up.

Helmut turned and moved toward the saddle between two jagged peaks that formed the pass through which they would have to travel. It took a good two hours of steady climbing to reach it. Every fifteen minutes or so they paused to catch their breath. Occasionally, they would hear chunks of ice breaking off the glacier and tumbling below. Finally, they reached the top and rested.

"I don't know if you know it or not, but here is where Gustav lost his wife. They had just scaled the pass when there was a snow avalanche from that ridge," said Helmut, pointing upward to the right.

Keith studied the mountain face for a moment. There was still a small drift clinging to the top. In winter, he could imagine a huge cornice forming. Below the small drift was a slick sheer funnel that would carry snow directly toward where they were standing.

"Yes," he nodded solemnly, "I heard about the accident from my father long ago. He told me it was months before they found her."

"This is true. My father helped with the recovery party. They tried three times unsuccessfully to dig her out. Each time a storm drove them off the glacier. They were afraid she would get trapped in the ice and not melt out for years, but in early spring they brought her body down." Helmut sighed.

Looking southeast toward Gustav's chalet, Keith searched the valley below. "Where's Gustav's place?"

"He's located off to the left above the snow," replied Helmut, pointing. "You can see it from here; look above that boulder field where it extends slightly into the glacier."

"Ah, I see it now."

"The snow will be soft from here on. We'd better get across now before it gets any worse," warned Helmut. "When we get to the chalet, we can stop for lunch."

"OK, let's go."

As they passed from the shadow of the nearby peak into the brilliant sunshine, the snow became very wet. Keith noted they were leaving footprints six inches deep behind them. Again, he kept his distance while they were roped together. Because this slope had southern exposure, it was more dangerous than the snow they had ascended earlier. It was tough going in the soft snow; they had to rest more often, even though they were descending.

Keith's boots and jeans were getting wet. Good that he'd packed extra pairs of wool socks, he thought. His new boots were beginning to take their toll on his feet. Too bad he hadn't had the foresight to throw in a pair from the cabin that were already broken in. His feet were beginning to chafe at the heel, which would certainly cause a blister.

It was just after one o'clock when they reached the edge of the large boulder field that lay below Gustav's chalet. At the edge of the snow, they took off their crampons and made their way about four hundred feet up the rocky slope to a stone building nestled into the hillside.

In front, they found snow-covered stone terrace, which was the only level ground outside the chalet. Keith noted the massive timbers that supported the steep metal roof. The chalet was modest, but very sturdy.

"By the construction, I'd say a lot of work went into this building, especially getting those timbers up here," observed Keith.

"They came from the other side of the mountain by cable winch. If you look at the ridge above, you can see Gustav still uses the cable to move supplies. But you are right, they were a lot of trouble. The chalet was built during the war. Germany used it briefly to house troops. I think it was built late in the war when they felt Italy would fall. There was some thought the pass might be used by the Allies, but it was not," explained Helmut.

Keith went to the door. Finding it unlocked, he opened it. Inside was a small dining area with a large wooden table adjacent to the kitchen. On the wall above the table, a climbing rope was strung through an ancient set of pitons. In the center of the wall hung a rifle, old enough to have been used in World War I. The kitchen contained a large wooden cook stove.

Helmut followed Keith inside. Together, they searched for Gustav. Keith looked in both bedrooms; each had four military bunks with clean linen. Both rooms were empty. So was the bathroom.

Helmut decided Gustav was probably visiting friends in a nearby lodge. For Helmut, "nearby" was within eight miles.

They went back to the dining area and shared the lunch Helmut had prepared in the morning. As they were finishing, the door opened. Keith remembered the picture of the three men in his father's file. The face of the man who now stood before him was covered by a long beard, but the expression around the eyes was the same. He was dressed in a pair of climbing shorts, wool socks, and a wool shirt. He wore sturdy hiking boots and carried an ice axe. Gustav put down his pack and greeted Helmut warmly in German. Keith could not catch the meaning. Helmut switched to English.

"Gustav, it is good to see you again so soon, and I brought someone to see you," said Helmut, turning to Keith.

"I am Keith Maddox, my father is Rudolf Madacek. He changed his name when he came to the States," said Keith, not yet able to use past tense when referring to his father.

"So you are Keith!" Gustav nodded in approval while shaking Keith's hand. "Yes! You look a little like your father, but you are bigger!"

"Yes, my mother always said it was the vitamins they fed me, but there were big men on my mother's side, so I come by my height naturally," said Keith.

"I am happy we meet after all the years. What brings you all the way up here?" Gustav asked.

"Didn't you get a telegram from Israel?" Keith asked.

"Yes, I got a telegram, but it was only last week when I got to town."

"What did it say?"

"Well, it was strange. Your father and I have an old friend in Russia. In his message he used the old code words asking us to come to Israel. I was planning to leave soon, but I still have people with reservations and I have to close the chalet for the winter," Gustav explained.

"So you don't stay here for the winter?" Keith inquired.

"Oh no! Not any more. When I was younger, I did. For many years after I lost Helga I stayed here, but I am too old now and the winters are too harsh! Now I spend winters closer to town," replied Gustav with a laugh.

"I can understand that. This is a remote location, but the view of the mountains is breathtaking. It certainly rivals the view I get of Chair Mountain from my cabin in Colorado. But I'm afraid this is not exactly a social visit. Some trouble started after my father got the same message. He was in the hospital so he asked me to pick up the package, which I did.

"How is your father?" asked Gustav.

Keith avoided answering. "Well, I think that package triggered something. There was trouble in Israel. Halperin was killed."

Gustav, noticing the expression of pain on Keith's face, pressed gently for an answer. "Yes, Keith, this is terrible. But your father—he is well?"

Keith shook his head. He said nothing for a moment. He raised his head slightly and looked directly at Gustav. "My father is dead," he said sadly.

There was silence in the room. The old man was visibly shaken. He couldn't reply, but shook his head.

"No ... no! I thought that was all finished with the war. How could this happen after all these years?" He covered his face with his hands.

"It's a long story," said Keith, taking a deep breath and sitting down. It would take the better part of two hours to cover all the events leading up to his arrival. As Keith began his monologue, Helmut finished his lunch and prepared to leave.

"I have friends on the other side of the mountain. Yesterday I promised I would spend the night at their house. Then I return to the lodge in the early morning. The sun is going down, so I must be on my way," explained Helmut, as he rose to leave.

Gustav and Keith rose and shook Helmut's hand at the door. Helmut stepped off the terrace and started steadily up the boulder field with a quick stride. In a few minutes, he turned and waved, then disappeared over the first ridge.

Keith and Gustav returned to the warmth of the cabin. Keith continued his recent tale. He stopped when it was necessary to explain his father's death. Gustav waited patiently for him to continue.

"I always had hoped I would see him again," Gustav said quietly. "Now that is all passed ... I am so sorry. Your father was a brave man. I think you were very close. This is ... " he paused, trying to find the right word, "Terrible. You think the damned Russians are involved? That is tragic!" Gustav went on wearily in a voice heavy with sadness and concern.

"Yes, the Russians can be real bastards," Keith continued, trying to control his voice, relieved to be off the subject of his father. "We should decode the music immediately." He paused again. "I think it may explain the reason why my father was killed."

"I don't know ... It's been a long time since the war. The decoding process is tedious. My eyes are not much good for reading any more ... But I will do my best," Gustav told him, taking out his reading glasses and opening the package Keith had carried in his day pack.

Gustav labored over the music for hours. When the sun set on the western ridge, Keith lit a kerosene lantern and placed it on the table next to Gustav. The lantern gave the chalet an orange glow and cast dark shadows about the room. Finally, when it was completely dark outside, Keith lit a second lantern in the kitchen. Searching the pantry and the icebox outside, he found some ingredients and prepared a dinner of bratwurst and sauerkraut. As he served Gustav his dinner with strong coffee, Gustav looked up with surprise.

"Thank you, Keith. I can use the food and the coffee. This used to be your father's favorite meal. I see it has been passed on to the next generation. I'm getting the translation, but it is slow. I am unfamiliar with some of the words. I'm afraid I've forgotten some of the reference music that makes it hard to decipher. In two places so far I guess at the meaning," said Gustav with a sigh as he put down the music, rubbing his forehead.

Keith was very interested in how the code was constructed. Gustav took off his glasses and closed his eyes. Then he began eating his dinner while relating how the code had evolved. "In short, it went this way ..." Keith was fascinated. It was so simple! Yet, to the casual observer it was indistinguishable from normal sheet music.

It was ten o'clock when Gustav finished his explanation. He then turned to the music and began again. He was less than half way through Lebedev's masterpiece. As the evening passed, Keith increasingly felt the strain and fatigue of the past weeks. Twice, he heated coffee on Gustav's stove. Each time Gustav gratefully accepted his cup and bore down on his translation.

He translated the old German dialect into English, then passed Keith his work. Keith read the first portion.

WARNING, RUSSIAN STORM DEVICE IN OP-
ERATION OFF USA EAST COAST. INTENDED
TARGET IS CAPE KENNEDY TO DELAY LAUNCH
OF GLOBAL ENVIRONMENTAL SURVEY PRO-

GRAM UNTIL RUSSIAN SHADOW SATELLITE PROGRAM CAN HIDE EFFECTS OF HARVEST PROGRAM, WHICH MODERATES UKRAINIAN WEATHER.

STORM DEVICE UTILIZES SECRET GAS, XZHYLENE, TO CREATE LARGE LOW PRESSURE AREA. REPEATED STIMULATION IS REQUIRED IN DAYLIGHT TO CREATE PROPER EFFECT. SYSTEM CAN BE CONTROLLED BUT IS EXTREMELY UNSTABLE AND CREATES DANGEROUS STORMS.

DANGER EXISTS AS XZHYLENE GAS DISSIPATES IN THE UPPER ATMOSPHERE. LABORATORY TESTS INDICATE XZHYLENE BREAKS DOWN INTO CHLORINE GAS. CHLORINE IN SUFFICIENT QUANTITY TO COMPLETELY ABSORB LARGE AREA OF OZONE LAYER.

I HAVE LOST INFLUENCE HERE. UNABLE CONVINCE AUTHORITIES DANGER EXISTS … U.S. ACTION REQUIRED TO HALT OPERATION.

SATELLITE NOT DETECTABLE BY RADAR. VISUAL CONTACT LIMITED TO TWO MILES. SOVIET CLOAKING DEVICE IN OPERATION. SECRET HOMING DEVICE INSIDE VIOLIN. TRANSPONDER DEVICE FREQUENCIES 2854 IN, 2954 MHZ OUT, 5 WATTS ERP. INSTALLATION INSTRUCTION FOLLOWS

Gustav hadn't gotten much further.

Keith stared at the message, dumbfounded. The violin! That seemingly worthless piece of memorabilia held the key to the Soviet security system?

"Shee-it!" said Keith, remembering it was left behind in the damaged rental car.

"What do you say?" Gustav inquired politely, looking up.

"There's a problem with the violin, but I think we can find it … I hope."

The events of the past weeks were beginning to make sense.

The Russians, after years of food shortages, had resorted to secretly modifying their weather. Their recent harvests were a testimony to the success of the system. But modifying the world's weather is potentially dangerous and something that would require the world's agreement, for it would affect all nations. The Russians had done it in secret and they intended to keep it a secret. Finally, fearing they were falling behind in the race to hide their system, they were trying to better the odds. They were using a dangerous weapon, one they didn't fully understand. Lebedev had risked a lot sneaking the message and violin out of Russia. Halperin had died because he carried the message. His father died because he could translate it. Logically, he and Gustav would be next on the Russians' list. Keith didn't like the fact he was in Austria so near the Russian border.

Somehow, he had to get this information to the State Department. But how? He had no influence there. It could be weeks before they could be convinced. At the rate the Russians were creating storms, the ozone layer could be long gone. Again, one name surfaced that could help: retired Admiral Jessel. He would know how to make them listen. He must get hold of Jessel immediately!

The more Keith pondered the situation, the more convinced he was they should leave early the next morning. Gustav wanted to continue translation of the message, but Keith felt they would need rest before leaving, and Gustav was already too tired. He agreed to make it a night. Keith put the music and its translation back into his day pack.

It was well after midnight when Keith lay down on the bunk above Gustav and fell into a fitful sleep.

NASA LANGLEY RESEARCH CENTER, HAMPTON, VIRGINIA
MONDAY, SEPTEMBER 9

Ron Read PhD and Senior Research Physicist for NASA, was furious. His morning was a disaster and now it promised to get worse. His team was conducting simulated zero gravity tests on the SVR (Service Vehicle Robot) in the vast swimming pool in the basement of building 25. But the testing was behind schedule, and to make matters worse, last week a serious leak developed in the robot and the electronics flooded. Immersion in water wouldn't normally have presented a problem, but in a last minute modification, his team had inadvertently ruptured a hermetic seal. The resulting malfunction took a week to isolate and diagnose.

The pressure was on. The program was viewed as a high priority for NASA. The SVR system weighed less than one third of a manned vehicle and therefore had much greater range at reduced cost. It was expected to be the maintenance workhorse of the American space program. Ron was under intense pressure to get the program back on schedule. His crew had responded by working around-the-clock and weekends until the job was finished. There was a good prospect they might make it, but only if everything continued to go smoothly.

What Ron didn't need now was an interruption, but that was just what happened. Sometime early in the morning, a truck arrived at the loading dock with a crate. Shortly thereafter, a message came from an old friend, Archibald Canning. He was a full bird colonel in the Air Force, who had done Ron numerous favors in the past. Apparently, one of his past favors was being called. Archie had a piece of hardware he wanted thoroughly examined. What Ron didn't need now was the military brass pushing work on some sort of space junk. Unfortunately, favors were favors and Archie had kept his crew intact during the cost-cutting era of the Seventies through special contract work that continued through much of the Eighties. He had little choice but to respond positively to the request.

Ron had made a career in space materials research. To support his work he filled a lab with sophisticated equipment. The military paid for the majority of the equipment under their contracts. As a result, no group knew more about materials used in space exploration than Ron's. Ron was familiar with the Stealth Program, and had tested many of the materials used to reduce the spy satellite's susceptibility to radar detection. Ron was also aware that the Russians were working on a Stealth Program of their own.

Although they were probably making some headway, he doubted they had anything approaching the American materials. His curiosity was aroused when he learned the crated object was Russian, but from the cylindrical shape he instinctively felt it would provide little of interest.

Ron stared at the SVR, attached by a tether to the full scale mockup of the Service Vehicle, as it glided below in the clear water under the control of his crew. This robot was probably the most sophisticated ever developed for space. It was capable of accepting commands in English and accomplishing those tasks much as a man would, but it was highly precise in its work and far more consistent than a man. Once trained, it did not require the constant attention of an operator, except, of course, when it malfunctioned. The series of tests was coming to the critical point. Previously, the SVR failed to coordinate its two arm-like devices because the visual input it received from a miniature solid state charge coupled array had confused its pattern recognition system. The problem had been tentatively traced to software. A fix was quickly identified and was now under test. Almost as if jinxed by his watching, the robot began a series of loops counterclockwise with its arms locked in a frozen position while it began wrapping itself helplessly in its tether. The fix was not working!

Ron slammed his fist against the observation window in anger. There would be more delays and more effort required to catch up. He reluctantly started down the corridor, ignoring the sharp pain in his fist. A moment ago, Archie had arrived and was now in the VIP conference room. It wouldn't do to keep him waiting.

The VIP conference room was in the front of the building on the ground floor. The building was new, having been built five years ago, and had the high tech appearance, which required lots of glass and open space similar to buildings in Silicon Valley.

Ron took the elevator up to the ground floor. Once the elevator door opened, he passed in front of the reception desk, with its potted plants and hanging ivy and strode into the conference room.

Inside waited Colonel Archibald Canning. "Good morning, sir," said Ron, offering his hand. He thought of Colonel Canning as Archie, but rarely used his first name in conversation.

"Good morning to you, Ron. And you don't have to be so damned formal either," replied Colonel Canning, shaking his hand. "I appreciate your being available on almost no notice despite your busy schedule."

"Oh, no problem for an old friend. I wasn't that busy," lied Ron with a smile.

"Nevertheless, Ron, I know how things go in the crunch phase of equipment prove out and how the unanticipated can occur," Ron's smile didn't change, but he wondered if the colonel knew just how far he was getting behind, or whether he was speculating. Ron noticed the coffee system in the conference room had been replenished. The receptionist customarily loaded the drip system whenever Colonel Canning visited, knowing he preferred to discuss business over morning coffee.

"Would you like a cup of coffee?"

"Yes, thanks."

Ron filled two of the styrofoam cups, gave one to Colonel Canning, and then they both sat down at opposite sides of the large mahogany table.

"What I've got for you today is a curious piece of Russian hardware for your crew to examine," began Colonel Canning. "But first a little background."

Canning switched off the lights and slipped a disk into the image projector at his end of the conference table. Almost instantly the image was read from the disk and a medium resolution satellite photo was projected on the overhead screen. He described the summer build-up of the Russian trawler fleet off the west coast of Nicaragua. The series of photos that followed showed the trawlers in organized search patterns systematically sweeping the ocean. He then followed with some high resolution photos of the Russian nets straining to bring on board their catch. By the shape of the netting, it could be inferred they were recovering some cylindrical objects. Once the objects were on board, the crews wasted no time getting them below. The next sequence of photos showed how the Russian trawlers continued their search into Nicaraguan waters, and then finally dispersing when the search concluded. Then he switched to a series of photos that were obviously taken on board a ship. They showed a black cylinder about the size of a fifty-five-gallon drum with the remains of a parachute attached.

"This is the equipment we want your people to examine closely. Don't be fooled by its somewhat mundane appearance. If the Russians are interested in it enough to deploy almost their entire Pacific trawler fleet, you can be sure it's important."

Ron wasn't impressed, despite the elaborate Russian deployment. He found it difficult to believe the Russians were really interested in what appeared to be an over-grown tin can. He believed there must be some mistake in what he had just heard. There was a helpless sinking feeling in the pit of his stomach. Colonel Canning was too good a supporter to deny him any reasonable request. The question before him was the upcoming list of tests reasonable in view of his present circumstances?

"So, what do you want my people to do with this equipment? Or perhaps better stated, what should we be looking for?"

Canning paused for a moment, collecting his thoughts. *Now it begins,* thought Ron. *Now when I have no time to spare, the colonel will come up with a hopelessly long list of required tests.*

"From the physical appearance of the object, I would say it successfully completed reentry from space with only minor damage. It appears to be made of a unique plastic composite material with great resistance to heat. There may be other properties about this plastic we know nothing about as well."

Ron suspected his worst fears would be realized. The colonel's budget could definitely afford the freight, but Ron's forces were severely strained, especially in view of the mess he just witnessed in the basement.

"There is one other thing I forgot to mention," continued Colonel Canning.

"What's that?"

"The seal on the cylinder was ruptured when the equipment was found on the bottom, but our diver had the good sense to plug the hole before the cylinder was brought on board. Some of the original contents still remain inside. You may want to pump the contents out before you start your tests."

Ron knew this was not a request, rather, it was precisely what

Colonel Canning wanted accomplished. *Great, more tests,* thought Ron.

"I suggest you give the plastic material the same series of stress tests you gave some of the materials we've been developing for our military satellites. Let's face it. It's not often we get a piece of Russian space material to examine. Considering how badly they wanted this stuff back, I bet we'll learn something."

There was silence in the room while Ron considered the request. This couldn't come at a worse time. He couldn't pull a single member of his team off the SVR. There was too much attention on the program and too many questions to answer about delays as it was. The only free person was Dan Pedicone, who was just beginning a series of tests on a new low temperature lubricant. Dan was a bit of a problem and an embarrassment to Ron. Ron had originally hired him because he was brilliant when working alone. Unfortunately, he was so exacting in his own work that he could not tolerate even the most simple of mistakes by his co-workers. In truth, one might conclude he was a petty individual who considered all others, with the possible exception of Ron, to be incompetent. It was no secret why Ron had taken him off the SVR last month after he caused such a stink at the progress review meeting. Ron was in the process of trying to find a satisfactory transfer for Dan. If he failed, Ron felt he would suggest to Dan that he resign. Ron didn't like to fire people … for any reason.

OK, if Archie wants us to do some snooping on Russian equipment, then he would assign Dan to the job. Dan certainly had the credentials for the job and had performed many of the tests Colonel Canning wanted, so he was familiar with the routine. Yes, that was the best plan. Dan could run interference for him to keep his old friend from further delaying the SVR progress, and afterward, he would see what could be done for Dan. Ron met the colonel's gaze.

"Colonel, I think I know how to get this work done. I will assign Dan Pedicone. You may remember him from the work he did for you last year."

If there was any disappointment from Colonel Canning, it didn't show in his blue eyes.

"I think we should now go down to the receiving dock, and on our way I'll try to find Dan. Then we can both see what you've brought us," concluded Ron.

Both men rose, Colonel Canning took his disk out of the projector and finished his coffee. The two left the conference room for the back of the building where Dan had an office. The electronic projector shut down and there was silence in the conference room for a few minutes before the receptionist entered and collected the empty styrofoam cups and shut off the coffee machine.

MONDAY, SEPTEMBER 16

Dan stared at the multi-colored curves previously plotted by the laser printer in the radiation lab. Each curve showed electromagnetic reflectivity plotted against wavelength in the microwave spectrum. *Amazing, simply amazing,* he thought. Never before had he seen such a composite material. Lightweight, ideally strong, almost impervious to heat, and now almost invisible to the whole microwave spectrum. Compared to other materials he had tested, this was one for the record books.

What started out as an annoying interruption to a series of tests on the B13/A high-lubricity low-temperature grease he was testing for the Lewis Research Center rapidly became one of the most intriguing assignments Ron had ever given him. It came at a good time too, as Dan was beginning to feel he was losing credibility at the laboratory, and for the first time since Ron had hired him five years ago, Dan was considering looking for a job elsewhere.

It was a week since Dan first set eyes on the black canister in the crate on the loading dock. There, he had met Colonel Canning for the second time. Colonel Canning had been on the phone several times since. He had started with the simple physical tests, weight, tensile strength, dielectric, and thermal properties etc. The results were so impressive he had been astounded. Dan had trouble believing it was really Russian. After all, he had never seen such a strong and heat-resistant material before. So, where had they copied it from? Or worse yet, could they have actually invented it? If so, Ivan really had something this time.

He had immediately scheduled around-the-clock testing and launched into a program to determine how the material gained its amazing strength. Dan had stayed at the laboratory much of the week, eating the food dispensed by the machines in the cafeteria and sleeping on the couch in the reception area. Exhaustive testing on the polymeric structure indicated it came from a family of polyaeromids. The resulting composite must be expensive and quite difficult to manufacture, but it delivered performance. The closest thing he had seen to it was some of the high performance tire cord used in auto racing tires.

But strength and heat resistance weren't the only surprises the composite had to offer. The tests he scheduled in the radiation laboratory were before him now. Colonel Canning had mentioned that if there was a space vehicle that carried the canister aloft, they had not been able to track it on radar. That meant it might not reflect much. If the canister was made of the same material as the vehicle, its reflective properties should be fully investigated. Well, this stuff didn't reflect much of anything, and therefore, it must be almost invisible to deep space radar. Also, judging from its appearance, it should barely be visible to the eye against deep space. Dan judged the pilot of a space recovery vehicle would have to be within a half mile of the canister to achieve visual contact.

His last observation brought an icy thought. *Great material out of which to construct a spy satellite, but I wouldn't want much of that stuff floating around up in space. Not if I was trying to pilot my way safely around it.*

The results were now before him and many of his conclusions were already formed. Dan turned to his word processor. His fingers felt stiff over the keyboard. It was late and he badly needed sleep, but he would have his report on Ron's desk before morning, and then go home to his wife and son for the first time in five days.

AUSTRIA, THURSDAY, SEPTEMBER 12, 4:30 A.M.

Keith awoke bathed in sweat. The chalet seemed very hot. It took him a full minute to remember Gustav had fueled the heater in the dining area and lit it before turning in. The bedroom was now totally dark. His right heel was sore from his new boots. The pain marked the location of a large blister. When he rose, he could just see the first rays of the sun in the east. The first magnitude stars could still be seen. "Star time," reflected Keith, referring to the period in the morning when navigators take star fixes.

He remembered the dream. It was one he had dreamt before. He was in the mountains camped by a lake. After dark, a mother grizzly with two cubs had stumbled across his camp. He remembered the foul smell of her fur as she brushed past. For a moment, he had lain perfectly still, afraid to breathe. Then she turned and her mouth closed on the zipper of his nylon bag, trapping him inside. He seemed to be frozen in his sleeping bag, unable to move by an overwhelming feeling of terror. The bear began dragging him away from the dying embers of his campfire. Suddenly, she tore at the nylon with her long claws, ripping the bag to shreds. Keith remembered trying to feign death. He could feel the hot breath of the bear on his ear. Just before he woke, he felt the stabbing pain in his foot.

Keith was all too aware there was a bear after him, a Russian bear by the name of Pronin. He immediately woke Gustav.

"Gustav, we must get out of here now!" said Keith, shaking his shoulder.

Gustav awoke slowly and rubbed his eyes. He rose with a groan and headed for the bathroom. In a few moments, he returned with his trousers on. They were soon both dressed, and Gustav had packed some clothes.

They went into the kitchen. It was barely light outside. Keith could see the ridges to the east clearly backlighted by the rising sun. The higher peaks to the west were aglow with the orange light of morning.

"I'll fix us a good breakfast for the long hike out of here," said Gustav, going outside to his icebox in the snow bank. A half hour later they heard the faint sound of an approaching helicopter.

"Are there any helicopter services near here?" asked Keith.

"None that I know of. We don't see helicopters in this area often," replied Gustav.

"I think we'd better forget breakfast and get the hell out of here!" Keith snapped.

"Why?"

"I suspect the helicopter isn't particularly friendly, that's why!" Keith raised his voice as he moved from the window.

Carefully, he studied the terrain around the chalet. There was not a flat spot within a mile of the building. Any pilot would have to land near the pass Keith and Helmut had crossed the previous afternoon. The crew would then be forced to move on foot to the chalet. They would be in plain view.

"Gustav," Keith asked, "Do you have a gun?"

"Only the one hanging on the wall in the dining area, but I don't have any ammunition."

"OK, do you have any skis?"

"Of course." Gustav nodded his head.

Gustav produced two old pairs of mountaineering skis. He passed Keith a set.

"See if the bindings can be adjusted to fit."

Keith placed the skis on the floor and put his hiking boots in the bindings. They were too big. He began backing off the adjustment on the cable. Outside, he could hear the helicopter hovering over the chalet. Keith backed the adjustment on both skis fully out. He thought he could jam his boots in to fit. Keith gathered his pack.

The sound of the helicopter moved uphill. With a deafening roar, it landed on the flat of the pass. Two men left the helicopter as Keith and Gustav slipped outside. The taller man had a set of binoculars and a rifle slung over his shoulder.

"I think they have a rifle, Gustav. We'd better use the far side of the boulders for shelter."

"After you," Gustav gestured, as they turned left.

Carrying their skis and poles, they made their way rapidly down the hill. Slipping behind a large boulder, they paused to put on their skis. Keith was barely able to get both feet seated properly. He hoped he could remember how to ski on such old mountaineering equipment. A survey of the slope revealed they would be in plain view of the two men the moment they entered the snow. It was easily forty feet before the snow began to drop, then another sixty feet before they would be out of sight.

"Try to make the edge quickly and change direction often on your way," said Keith, taking a deep breath.

Keith watched the two men approach as he exhaled. When they momentarily looked at the ridge above, Keith lunged forward, his legs making long skating arcs on the snow while his arms pushed hard on his bamboo poles. Gustav was right behind him. The first fifty feet seemed to take forever. Keith changed his direction twice before starting down the first drop. It was then he saw the burst in the snow at his feet, followed by the sharp crack of the rifle. Keith dove forward down the slope to his left. Gustav dove right. The next bullet whizzed harmlessly overhead. In desperation, Keith and Gustav slid forward on their stomachs, their packs barely visible to the two men above. In the following seconds they dropped completely out of sight.

Moments before, the two men above saw Keith burst onto the snowfield. Seeing the fleeing man below, Pronin knew his quarry was escaping. Using the field glasses, he recognized Keith immediately. He raised the rifle and fired a quick shot without compensating for the drop in slope. The bullet went low, hitting the snow in front of Keith. His next shot was more calculated, but it too missed as Keith suddenly dropped low. Another man had entered the snowfield and now both were out of sight.

Pronin ran down the glacier to get a shot at the two men before they got farther. The snow was already getting soft and Pronin's knee was bothering him again. By the time he caught sight of Keith and Gustav, they were out of range.

Pronin shouted to his pilot and started hobbling back to the helicopter. They must stop the men before they reached the glacier's base and the village. The trip up was more difficult than the run down due to the steep incline. The soft snow improved when they entered the shadows near the top. It took a full five minutes to reach the helicopter and get its engine started again. Pronin left the door on his side of the two-man helicopter open and readied his rifle. His pilot had the aircraft aloft and they rapidly descended over the glacier's face. Far below, Pronin could see two men skiing over the rough glacial surface. Farther down, huge cracks of blue ice jutted above the surface as the glacier descended through a tortuous turn to the west. Pronin realized the change in terrain would provide natural cover for the two fleeing men.

"We must catch them in the open," shouted Pronin to his pilot over the roar of the engine.

Pronin shifted his position so his feet hung outside the open door. Leaning forward, he ordered his pilot to swing the craft to give him a better shooting angle. It was a race; both skiers were approaching the edge of the rough area. He aimed at the lead skier. This time, he compensated for the drop angle and squeezed off a single round, clearly hitting his mark, the center of the back of the lead skier. He now swung the rifle to shoot the second skier.

When the skiers saw the approaching helicopter, they renewed efforts to reach the safety of the broken terrain below. Keith was no longer in the lead. The cable behind his left heel had slipped off and he lost ground when he stopped and reset it. Ahead, there were massive sections of ice separated by deep crevasses. Instinctively, Keith moved away from Gustav, knowing there were snow bridges beneath them. The helicopter approached, the menacing roar of its engine getting ever louder. There wasn't enough time.

Keith saw Gustav fall, then heard the crack of the rifle. Knowing he would be next, Keith made a desperate drive for the nearest crevasse. Just as he thought he would make the edge, he lost his left ski, causing him to pitch forward out of control. Scrambling forward, Keith heard a bullet pass by his ear as he tumbled into the crevasse. Too late, he realized it was very deep.

Pronin ordered his pilot to set the helicopter down immediately. The pilot maneuvered the craft uphill about five hundred feet before finding a flat area to land.

Pronin jumped out and ran carrying his rifle toward the motionless body. He had gone about three hundred feet when he suddenly sank into the wet snow up to his waist. To his horror, he realized he had fallen into a small crevasse. He was not familiar with glacial terrain, but he recognized the danger. His pilot was catching up. Pronin shouted for him to keep clear.

"I want you to advance on the left!" he shouted.

"But I am unarmed," his pilot protested.

Pronin pointed his rifle.

"You will advance anyway!" he shouted.

Keith could hear the shouts of his pursuers, but he was helpless. His right ski was jammed across the crevasse. It had saved him from plunging headlong downward, but he hung suspended upside down. He desperately tried to claw his way up the side of the ice with his fingernails, his free foot kicking wildly against the wall.

The pilot was terrified. He realized it was a mistake to follow Pronin down the slope. At any moment the man hidden ahead would rise and shoot. Moving forward slowly, he could hear Pronin following close behind. His feet were sinking into the snow. The sun was bright in his eyes. He was sweating heavily under his dark flight jacket and completely out of breath from running at high altitude. His shoes leaked and icy water soaked his socks. They followed the tracks of the skiers toward the edge of the first crevasse. He knew Pronin was pointing the rifle at his back and he dared not turn to protest.

Keith was just beginning to get a toehold on the ice with his free leg. With care, he attempted to shift his weight to his right foot. The ice failed, causing him to lose his handhold. He swung downward, stopped only by his right ski. The pain in his ankle was intense. How long could he count on it to arrest his fall? He knew it would soon give out. Again, he clawed at the ice, carefully trying to regain lost ground. While struggling, he heard the crunch of ice, followed by a rumble nearby. He realized they must be approaching. Soon, his flight would end. Keith was completely exhausted. His fingers were numb and his right ankle ached from the strain. There was no way to escape now. His fingers refused to work. He was completely out of breath. He needed rest. Defeated, he hung motionless, warming his hands. Any second Pronin's snarling face would appear above him. The bear had finally caught him.

In about two minutes, Keith was ready to try again. Miraculously, Pronin hadn't arrived. Using every ounce of his remaining strength, he climbed hand-over-hand until he grasped the ice at the top edge. Placing his toe in the hole his boot had dug, he kicked his right foot free of the ski. His right leg swung heavily beneath him, almost dislodging his handhold. Gathering all his reserves, he pulled himself over the edge to safety.

But was it really safe? Where was Pronin? He could see Gustav lying face down, a pool of blood forming on the snow. Behind Gustav was a large hole that wasn't there previously. The tracks of their skis showed they had crossed before the hole appeared. Footprints led to the far side. In a flash, Keith knew what had happened.

He rushed to help Gustav, but one quick look proved it was hopeless. The bullet from the high powered rifle had cleanly pierced his back, making a gaping hole in his chest. Gustav had probably died before he hit the snow.

Keith didn't take time to assess the Russian's situation. He immediately adjusted his left ski and put them both on. He carefully made his way to the right, avoiding suspected snow bridges. After traversing for a quarter mile, he began a long descent to the valley below. It took a full two hours to reach the glacier base and the village. His right ankle protested all the way.

Higher up on the glacier, a struggle was in progress. Pronin had seen his pilot plunge downward when the snow had given way. The fool didn't have a chance; he fell a good thirty meters before he smashed onto the ice below. Certainly he was dead. Pronin's fate was little better. When the snow collapsed, he had fallen several meters before he struck the ice wall. Had he not flailed wildly with his arms, he would be below with his pilot. Now he hung precariously on the small ledge.

He was using his rifle to cut snow steps up the icy wall. It made for very slow going. As he dug, his hate for the American rose. Would he ever be free from this nemesis? The flight to Austria was to be the final effort required to stop the crisis created by Lebedev. At least he had the satisfaction of knowing Lebedev had taken his own life before Pronin's return from Israel. Then again, he had cleverly arranged for the demise of Rudolf Maddox. An agent in New York had carried out his orders perfectly. Gustav

Lentz was to be the last link to the old code. Now all his successes could be for nothing. The American was probably fleeing at this very moment.

And then there was Natasha. She was bravely facing surgery alone in Moscow that very afternoon. Again, he cursed the American as he slammed the butt of the rifle against the ice, breaking its stock. He tossed the useless piece of wood below and continued the slow work cutting steps.

It was a full hour before he reached the top. He could see fresh ski tracks leading away from the crevasse below. Again he cursed the American.

Knowing he was racing against time, he set out for the helicopter, carefully avoiding snow bridges. He had no illusions about his ability to fly. That was impossible. But he could use the portable satellite radio stored behind the pilot's seat.

Keith was hot from the exertion in the bright sunshine when he reached the base of the glacier. He had shed his jacket, tying the arms about his waist. His sweat-soaked T-shirt felt cool on his back. It was a "blue bird" day, as a friend in Utah used to say about brilliant, blue cloudless days.

About a mile short of the glacier's base, Keith left the snow and took off his skis. A little-used dirt road stretched out in the distance to a small village. About two miles away, he could see a two-story lodge with a steep overhanging roof and a deck reaching around three sides, joined by three smaller buildings of similar construction.

Keith suspected he was sunburnt, as his face felt warm. He was very thirsty; his tongue felt like leather against the roof of his mouth and his right ankle was beginning to swell. He passed the dirty ice and the blue-green glacial lake at the base. With each step, he felt growing pain in his right leg.

The trip took longer than he expected because he had to rest his ankle often. To ease the pain, he relied heavily on one of his ski poles.

He must have made quite a spectacle for two female sunbathers as he hobbled past. They were obviously out to improve their ample tans, bathing topless in the brilliant sunshine reflected off the snow. Keith couldn't help but pause for a second. Great way to get skin cancer in a place where it doesn't belong, especially if the Russians have their way with the ozone layer.

As he came closer to the buildings, he discovered the lodge had a restaurant next door. Alongside the restaurant was a filling station. The fourth building was a small bus station. He headed for it, hoping he could catch a bus back to Salzburg. He did his best to tolerate the rising pain in his ankle as he entered the building.

Inside, he found a bulletin board with the schedule. The station master sold him tickets, which would get him to Salzburg after midnight.

Keith wasn't sure what to do about Gustav. He wanted to report the killing to the police, but he didn't care to be tied up answering questions when he had to get to Jessel as soon as possible. No, he wouldn't report it until he was in the air homeward bound for Washington.

Outside, he spotted a Pepsi machine. With change left from his ticket purchase, he bought a can to quench his thirst. He took a seat on the bench outside the station. *Pepsi never tasted better,* he thought. He had two hours to kill before the bus left, so he stowed the day pack and his jacket under the bench, intending to get some much needed rest.

From around the corner, a radio broke the stillness of the midday quiet. Searching for the source of the noise, Keith discovered it was coming from an empty police car parked in front of the restaurant. He tried to use his rusty German to translate. It seemed a hopeless effort, considering the poor quality audio and the heavy dialect in use. Suddenly, he recognized the word "Americaner" and "tot". An uneasy feeling crept over him. When he heard the unmistakable syllables of Gustav's name, there could be no mistake. The message blaring over the police radio had to be about Gustav's death. If the police knew it, then Pronin was probably the source. Keith could imagine how that message must read. Somehow, he must get out of Austria before Pronin or the police could stop him. This was a totally different matter. He could no longer wait idly for the bus.

He surveyed the parking lot. Experience taught him long ago opportunities present themselves to those who are observant enough to recognize them. There wasn't much time before the officer who left the car parked by the restaurant would get the message. He must be on his way by then, as he would be an obvious suspect.

Should he steal the police car? Great idea for Hollywood, but not practical. The police car could easily be identified. The other two cars presented opportunity, but closer examination revealed they were locked.

In the distance, the deep throated sound of two-inch headers mounted on a very mud splattered Range Rover approached. Keith watched from the bench as the driver made a sweeping turn toward the filling station. Perhaps he misjudged the curve, because he overcompensated by turning sharply and then, while weaving slightly, aimed the vehicle toward the gas pumps. At the last second, the young driver slammed on the brakes, sliding the oversized tires in place next to the pumps. The driver then opened his door, shouted something to the attendant inside, and trotted toward the back of the station, leaving his car door open. Keith noticed a beer bottle had fallen to the ground when the driver got out.

The attendant came outside, wiped his hands with a cloth, and started the gas pump. To his annoyance, he realized the engine was still running. Shaking his head he muttered something to himself.

A second car approached and parked behind the Range Rover. Three of its four occupants got out and headed into the restaurant. They weren't tourists, more probably businessmen in a hurry, thought Keith. He was looking for an opportunity, but so far there were too many people around the vehicles to provide a good chance.

The attendant finished filling the Range Rover and shut off the pump. He looked in the direction of the station, but the driver could not be seen. The attendant then looked at the driver of the second car, shrugged his shoulders, and went back inside the station. This irritated the second driver, who was blocked from access to the pumps by the Range Rover. He showed his impatience by blowing his horn.

Now, there was an opportunity. Keith picked up his pack and jacket. He looked neither left nor right, but strode directly to the Range Rover. In a single motion, he threw his jacket and pack inside, closed the door, and found first gear. In a matter of seconds, he was outside the service area and heading down the road, leaving the attendant running after him in the dust.

The driver of the second car was annoyed when the attendant left. He had come a long way over the mountains at high speed. He needed to gas up immediately and get moving. Blowing the horn seemed the only way to hasten the other driver out of the bathroom.

Suddenly, a stranger climbed in the Range Rover and drove off. To his amusement, the East German realized he had just witnessed a car theft. The attendant was quick to realize the situation, but was fast being left behind.

The owner exited the bathroom. He glanced up to see his vehicle was gone. Shouting and waving his arms, he confronted the helpless attendant. His slurred speech and uneven foot work revealed he'd had quite a few beers before his stop at the gas station.

It wasn't until his three companions returned from the restaurant with sandwiches that he realized the jacket and day pack he saw thrown into the Range Rover matched that of the description of the man they were seeking.

Keith wasn't sure what was the best route to Salzburg. He knew the route taken by the bus went a great distance west before crossing the mountains and then heading southeast. If only there were a shorter route over the mountains to the north. He searched the glove compartment and the Rover's interior, hoping to find a map, but found nothing. The back seat also contained nothing of value, only a collection of empty beer bottles. Probably the owner was a local and didn't need a map. Keith knew it would be risky to use the main roads, but he had little choice.

Just as he made that decision, he passed a young fellow with a back pack at his feet. Keith recognized the universal sign of the thumb and immediately stopped. The lad trotted to the Range Rover and peered inside.

"*Wohin gehen Sie?*" asked Keith.

"*Ich gehe nach Innsbruck,*" the youth replied.

Keith told the boy to put his pack in the back seat and in a few seconds they were off again. Using his basic high school German, Keith learned that the boy's name was Tomas. He lived just outside Innsbruck and had spent the last week hiking with his friends in the mountains. His English turned out to be better than Keith's German. Tomas was anxious to get home for the weekend to help his father.

Cautiously, Keith pushed the conversation ahead. "I am in a hurry to get to Salzburg to meet a friend and I am not familiar with the roads here. Is there a quicker way than the route the bus takes?"

"*Ja*, but it is a rough road only open in late summer. But you will have no trouble with this car."

"Where can I find this road?"

"Up ahead about five kilometers is a dirt road, which after a few kilometers eventually branches with a fire road leading over the mountains to Neukirchen," Tomas explained, pointing to the north.

"Then I will be turning there. Thanks very much for the information."

"Thank you for the ride, I was getting bored waiting for someone to stop. I will get off at the first fork. The best route for me is to continue on this road."

They traveled for ten minutes along the winding paved road while Tomas described the hike he had taken with his girlfriend, who lived nearby. There wasn't enough time to finish the story before they stopped.

Tomas got out and thanked Keith again. Keith was about to leave, when he remembered the ticket in his pocket.

"Here's a bus ticket I bought but wasn't able to use. Perhaps you can make use of it," said Keith, handing Tomas the ticket and waved.

Tomas was delighted. The ticket could easily be redeemed on

the route to Innsbruck. He waved cheerfully as Keith headed up the dusty dirt road toward the mountains to the north. Keith looked back in the mirror. Tomas was already a hundred feet down the road, but there was a car turning onto the dirt road at high speed.

I certainly hope Tomas was right about this road, thought Keith. He preferred this back road, but he couldn't afford following a dead-end and then having to back track. He had to hurry. Eventually, the police would learn he had a plane waiting at the airport.

Strange, thought Keith, as he watched the car behind gain speed and approach. *Seems as if I'm not the only one on this road in a hurry.* The car behind looked familiar. It was a 4WD Mitsubishi. He remembered seeing a similar one back at the gas station.

Suddenly, Keith caught a flash of something sticking out the passenger's window in his mirror. A second later there was a crash as a bullet smashed through the rear window and exited the Rover by shattering the windshield, leaving no doubt about the intentions of the following car.

Keith downshifted and slammed the accelerator to the floor. The Range Rover accelerated, its four-cylinder engine straining against the grade and altitude. The road led alongside a rushing mountain stream. Heavy dust from occasional traffic and lack of recent rainfall covered the surface. As the Rover gained in speed, it stirred up a copious quantity of dust. The dust made it difficult for the driver behind to see the road, which temporarily kept him too far behind for his passenger to get a good shot. Keith knew this was only a temporary situation. The Range Rover had four forward gears and overdrive; Keith was using them all, making maximum use of the engine torque.

Keith reached the fork in the road. As Tomas had predicted, the upper road led into the mountains to the north. Keith reached forward and threw the Rover into four-wheel drive. The race was on. The road surface was harder, which allowed the following car to see better. The fire road followed a branch of the stream that made several waterfalls over the steep grades ahead. Keith was in first gear trying to get all he could out of the engine. The Mitsubishi was gaining. The driver could clearly be seen. Keith could see the passenger pointing a rifle at the Rover. Keeping his foot down on the accelerator, he began to swerve wildly to confuse the man with the rifle. His next shot barely missed Keith's head. The high-powered slug smashed out the rear-view mirror. Now the windshield of the Rover was completely gone. The cold mountain air rushed into Keith's face, making his eyes water.

Ahead, the road took a shallow dip before rising sharply and turning to the right. To the left, the rushing stream formed a large whirlpool below the road. At the turn, loose gravel covered the road, making conditions treacherous.

Keith kept the Rover in first gear, preferring not to shift into second. Doing so would force him to downshift when he lost momentum in the coming turn. The Rover momentarily dropped out of sight from the pursuing car as it began the short descent.

The driver in the Mitsubishi cursed loudly in German. He had repeatedly tried to overtake the Rover without success. Now the heavy dust that had hampered his approach was gone. The new road was very rough. The driver was unfamiliar with four-wheel drive, but he finally figured how to use the lever on the floor. Now he was gaining with renewed traction. The Rover dropped out of sight momentarily below the hood of the Mitsubishi. *Good,* he thought, *the rise ahead is just what's required*. He slammed the shift lever into second and began accelerating, clearly gaining on the American. Up ahead, he could hear the roar of the Rover's engine, but to no avail. Karl, in the front passenger seat, would soon get his shot. Karl was leaning out the window. The Rover rounded the sharp corner to the right, and Karl was about to take his shot, but the next corner was sharper than expected. Karl lost his balance and missed. The Mitsubishi was losing RPM rapidly. A downshift was required. The driver missed first, the shift lever in his hand vibrating loudly on the gears. He had lost momentum, the Mitsubishi was beginning to coast backwards and picking up speed.

The driver jammed the Mitsubishi into first and stood on the gas pedal. To his alarm, it lost traction and continued backwards with all four wheels throwing gravel into the swirling water below.

The Mitsubishi was approaching the edge. The driver's foot was frozen on the accelerator. Slowly, the edge drew closer. First, the rear wheels started downward, then the front wheels. There was a screech of metal as the under-carriage was momentarily high-centered. Then, the front wheels left the ground. The engine continued to roar at the high end of its power curve as the rear wheels bounced over the boulders that supported the graded road above.

The Mitsubishi made a large splash as it slammed backwards into the whirlpool. Karl screamed at the driver as the cold water began pouring in his window. The car sunk like a rock. The current first turned it on its side, then flipped it on its top. Karl waited for the inside to fill with the icy water before trying to escape. There was a gap between the window bottom and the collapsed roof, almost big enough. He was out of breath and stuck halfway out when he realized the gap was too small.

Keith took four hours to get to Salzburg. To his great relief, his pursuers had dropped out of sight at the first hairpin turn. He was able to keep off main roads for some of the way, aided by a map he'd obtained at a gas station. He'd also found some cloth and wrapped his ankle in ice to minimize the swelling.

Now he focused on the task ahead. He would gas the jet, phone Jessel, and leave quickly for Washington. As soon as he could retrieve the violin, this mess would end.

He was approaching the airport. In the distance, he could see the Cessna. It looked wonderful after the last two days! Damn! There was a police car parked next to it with its red beacon flashing brightly. Somehow, Pronin, or the police, had found out where he'd parked the company jet. Now what to do?

Keith parked the Rover in a fire lane outside the perimeter fence. He took the owner's address off the registration. Later, he would send a generous check for the damage and use of the Rover, but now he focused on the job at hand. There were two police officers guarding his jet. One was inside, the other outside, standing near the ramp, smoking.

Officer Mueller waited impatiently for his partner outside the plane. The young fellow was taking flying lessons and had dreams of flying jets. He had little desire to go inside the jet himself, but for his partner, the temptation to sit in the pilot's seat was too great. He had been playing with the controls for the past fifteen minutes.

Soon, they would be relieved and not a moment too soon, thought Mueller. His feet were getting cramped from standing on the concrete. He shouted inside to Heinz, the ambitious pilot.

Keith scaled the fence and dropped softly to the ground, trying to favor his ankle.

Heinz took his time leaving the plane, lovingly examining the interior. "What a set-up," crooned Heinz. "They even have a bar in the passenger area!"

Heinz descended the ramp and lit a cigarette, the end glowing brightly in the dark near the fuel dock.

"You suppose the pilot will return?" asked Heinz, idly.

"No, I don't. They will probably catch him in the mountains at one of the roadblocks. Still, we'd better keep a sharp watch."

The two men continued to talk quietly in the darkness for a few minutes. Finally Heinz suggested he go for coffee to warm them up. Officer Mueller happily agreed.

Heinz flicked his cigarette in a long arc toward the fence near a trash container. It landed harmlessly on the concrete in the darkness. A second later, there was a brilliant flash followed by an ominous roar. The trash container and the fuel truck nearby were engulfed in flames.

"Sweet Jesus!" was all Heinz could utter.

Officer Mueller ran for the fire alarm. Heinz charged the fire and made a vain attempt to put the flames out with an extinguisher. Keith used the distraction he had set to get closer to the aircraft. He kicked the front chock and pulled the chain on the other chocks, clearing the wheels. Climbing quickly inside, he shut the door.

In seconds, he had both engines running. Outside, Heinz was trying to open the locked door. Keith rammed the throttles forward. The plane began to move. He steered the jet for the taxiway. Heinz was left behind in the roar of the engines, too dumbfounded to use his pistol.

On the radio, Keith could hear the controller giving clearance for a plane to take off. Two commercial aircraft were waiting their turn at the end of the taxiway. In the distance, a fire truck approached. There was no way Keith could expect the waiting aircraft to give clearance so he could make a desperate break for the runway. Already the controller was screaming orders for him to halt. Keith looked at the taxiway stretching into the darkness. There was little wind. Would he dare a takeoff on the taxiway? Was it long enough? What choice did he have?

Keith put the flaps down and prepared the plane for takeoff while gaining speed. He mentally went through his checklist. The plane's tanks were nearly two-thirds full. That was enough to get to England. But what then? Would he be able to continue to Washington, or would the plane be impounded? He might be held for extradition.

The Cessna was now fast accelerating down the taxiway. The aircraft at the end, seeing Keith accelerate and realizing he would not stop, were trying to get clear. To his relief, they made it just as he rotated the aircraft for takeoff. Keith immediately brought the gear up. There was a hangar at the end of the taxiway. He had to climb steeply. The Pratt-Whitney engines were developing full power, pressing Keith back into the pilot's seat. He cleared the top with five feet to spare. Now he must avoid any incoming aircraft. Sure enough, the tower was directing traffic away from approach. Keith pointed the nose of the Cessna toward the west and made a quick exit over the first ridge of mountains.

The graceful plane made the ridge and Keith settled it into the valley beyond while he tried to formulate a plan. Was there an airport in Western Europe where he could land, refuel, and take off for Washington? Keith didn't think so. The alert would be out for his Cessna. He doubted he could avoid NATO radar. It would only be a matter of time before he would be discovered and carefully tracked. When he landed, there would be an unfriendly reception. Perhaps he should have surrendered to the Austrian authorities? But he wasn't ready to give up yet. Could he still avoid detention? Knowing he was an American, they might expect him to fly west or north-west. What if he flew south or south-east?

Deliberating over the alternatives for a few minutes, he rechecked his fuel. Then he banked to the left and kept the Cessna low, using his radar to help steer through the mountains. He was headed for Italy and then the Adriatic Sea. He would take considerable risk flying low in the mountains, but it was his best chance to evade detection. Fortunately, the moon was almost full. Once over the water of the Adriatic, he would keep low until he reached the Mediterranean. Then he decided he'd take a long detour for Israel. If he was careful, there was just enough fuel to make Tel Aviv. Keith was counting on getting help from Zvi Oren.

FRIDAY, SEPTEMBER 13, 7 A.M.

Keith was dangerously low on fuel and completely exhausted. The warning light above his fuel gage had first came on a half-hour ago. Now he was mentally coaxing every revolution out of the rebuilt Pratt-Whitney engines. His navigation gear indicated he was nearing Israeli air space and, not a minute too soon, considering he had less than fifteen minutes of fuel left. Now he had more to concentrate on than simply staying awake.

"Well, let's see how sharp the Israeli Air Force is," said Keith aloud as he squinted into the rising sun.

For several seconds, he stared at the gages before his head bobbed, breaking his sleep-like trance. Sitting suddenly upright and taking a deep breath, he was surprised to see he had two escorts, Israeli F-16s, in close formation.

Keith opened the international frequency on his radio.

"Israeli Air Force, this is 731 alpha sierra, I am declaring an emergency and request permission to land, Tel Aviv. I am low on fuel. I repeat, very low on fuel! Possible only ten minutes, over."

The response was immediate. The Israelis expected their enemies, such as the PLO, to use declared emergencies in suicidal bombing attacks on Israel.

"Cessna 731 alpha sierra, this is Israeli Jet 102 india, Negative Tel Aviv! Permission is not granted. Vector 090 at 50. Follow my instructions and do not deviate, I repeat, do not deviate, immediate retaliation will result."

In less than ten minutes, they flew over a small airport in an undeveloped section of Israel near the Lebanese border. After passing once over the single concrete strip, Keith landed. The concrete was barely long enough for the Cessna, but he managed to stop a hundred feet from its end. Keith shut down the engines and sank back into the pilot's seat, relieved to be finished with the long flight. Seconds later, a squad of paratroopers surrounded the plane.

Keith opened the door, held his hands high, and sheepishly smiled his apology to a well-armed captain outside.

"I'm Keith Maddox, I'm American, and I have an urgent message for Zvi Oren in your security force," said Keith to the captain.

"Perhaps you are, but you will come with us," replied the captain cautiously.

Keith was taken by Jeep to Shin Bet security. This time, the local office was in a wood-frame structure built in 1968 after the war. Inside Keith, wanted to phone Zvi immediately, but first he had to convince the captain he was neither a terrorist, nor a criminal. That wasn't easy. The Austrian police had informed Israeli authorities of his alleged involvement in Gustav's death and of his reckless takeoff in Salzburg. He had miscalculated. Convincing the captain to listen wasn't simple, but after two hours of talking, his request to contact Zvi was finally granted.

Zvi arrived by helicopter a half hour later. He immediately relieved the captain and took Keith aside into a private office.

"You've got a lot of explaining to do, and this time I want the whole story, old friend!" Zvi warned.

"This time I'll give you the whole story, and I have evidence to back it up." Keith pulled out the package of music Gustav had partially translated. He handed the translation to Zvi.

"When I was here last, I didn't understand the significance of this music. My dad, who was laid up in a hospital in Philadelphia, asked me to pick it up. At first, I thought all this World War Two cloak and dagger stuff was nonsense. That was before the attack at the Immigration Center. Still, I foolishly thought it was coincidence. Then my dad died. I found his house ransacked. That did it. I became convinced this music and the message it contained were the cause. I'm sure someone killed my father. I'm equally sure Pronin was behind it. I know he killed Halperin at the Immigration Center and my father's associate, Gustav Lentz, in Austria. I saw him both times. Pronin didn't want this music to be translated and my father died because of it."

Zvi sat and read the message. He took a full five minutes to grasp its complete significance.

"This is a matter best dealt with by the authorities in your country," observed Zvi.

"With your permission, I'd like to make a phone call on a secure phone. There is someone who can be very helpful in this situation," urged Keith.

Zvi guessed it was Admiral Jessel, whom Keith intended to call and gave his permission. Keith dialed the number while Zvi picked up the extension. The phone rang several times before a sleepy voice answered.

"Hello, Admiral, this is Keith."

Jessel was immediately awake.

"Where are you?"

"I'm in Israel, sir, with Zvi Oren."

It took a second for Jessel to respond.

"Ah, yes, I remember him. He was involved in that China deal, right?"

"That's right, but we're not here discussing old times. Do you have a scrambler on your phone?" asked Keith.

"Not here," replied Jessel.

Zvi suggested a solution.

"Can you drive to the Israeli Embassy and contact us on their equipment?" asked Keith.

"Yes, but I'll take at least a half hour," responded Jessel.

Keith waited for Jessel to reach the Israeli Embassy and call, then switched the system on.

"Admiral, after I saw you last, I went to Israel to pick up a coded message for my father. A lot of very bad shit has happened since then."

Keith briefly explained the events in Israel, Philadelphia, and

Austria, leading up to the current situation. He ended by reading the partially decoded message from Lebedev.

"Good God! We've suspected something was mucking up the works in our weather, and no wonder they've had good harvests. This goddamn confirms it! Why, do you realize they are trying to slow down the deployment of the Global Survey Program just so they can save face! Those bastards couldn't stand to be embarrassed by getting their hands caught in the cookie jar. And listen, Keith, we think that canister you brought up off Nicaragua has something to do with the Russian system."

"How could it?" asked Keith.

"I've got a hot shot physicist at NASA, named Ronald Read, working on it. He thinks the canister is part of a deployment system. It has some kind of secret gas in it. Could be that's how they create storms," replied Jessel.

"There's one other thing," said Keith.

"What's that?"

"What does your physicist say about damage to the ozone layer?"

"I don't know. We haven't considered the possibility. I'll get him working on it immediately," replied Jessel.

"Good, I think he will find it causes damage ... Oh! There's one other thing," said Keith.

"What now?"

"There is an old violin I mistakenly left in a damaged rental Nissan Stanza at Continental Rentals by LaGuardia Airport on Wednesday. When I left it, I didn't think it had any value, but now I know there's a Russian security device glued inside.

"OK, we'll check it out. Look, you better get here as soon as possible. The sooner we fully decode that message, the sooner we can bring this crisis to an end. When can you be here?"

"That depends on how much help I can get from Zvi," replied Keith.

Keith could see by Zvi's nod and wide smile that he would cooperate. He hung up and turned to Zvi, who was talking rapidly.

"We still have the problem of the Austrian warrant for your arrest, but in this case I'm going to bend the rules. I think I know a way to get you back to America undercover."

"Good," said Keith as he followed Zvi down the hall.

MONDAY, SEPTEMBER 16

Keith woke with a start. The new Israeli-built West Wind was experiencing considerable turbulence. He was stretched out in the passenger compartment. Zvi had arranged for him to be a passenger on the new jet that was to be delivered to Midlantic Aviation in Wilmington, Delaware. It took two days, but it was the best he could do under the circumstances. Keith was anxious to make up for lost time.

For the past four hours he had been fast asleep. Looking outside the window, he saw the approaching clouds of a major tropical depression.

He limped forward to the cockpit.

"Looks like some weather up ahead," he said, rubbing his eyes.

"Yes, we've been advised to land in Bermuda, because the airports in Wilmington, Philadelphia, Baltimore, and Washington are shut down due to a major hurricane," explained the pilot, Joel Sherman.

"Looks like there will be some delay, but it shouldn't be too bad, possibly two hours and Wilmington will open up again. We'd keep going, but then we'd arrive a little short on fuel and couldn't circle long enough," said Randy Golden, the copilot.

"Damn, looks like a Bermuda layover is in the works," Keith growled as he went aft to get a cup of coffee.

Pouring himself a steaming cup from the pot that had been brewed hours ago, he decided to let the black concentrate cool. Keith sat to adjust the bandage on his right ankle. Before he'd left Israel, he'd had it examined by a doctor. It was sprained, but not broken. Taking the bandage off and examining it carefully, he saw that his ankle had red puffy areas around the joint. He re-wrapped the compression bandage around the sore ankle, hoping to prevent further swelling.

In a few minutes they would be landing. He hadn't been to

Bermuda in years. As beautiful as the island was, he hoped it would be a short stay.

The Israeli West Wind jet made a single pass on Hamilton airport, and landed smartly into a fifteen-knot wind. Storm clouds were scudding close to the horizon, and it was raining lightly.

Keith went inside the terminal building and into the pilots' lounge, preferring not to tempt fate with Immigration. The Bermuda authorities could be looking for him. He searched for a phone booth. Admiral Jessel's number in Washington rang several times before his secretary Betty answered. "Hello, Keith. The admiral isn't here right now. Where are you?"

"Bermuda. I was supposed to be in Wilmington, Delaware by now, but we were delayed by weather and had to land here. Tell Jessel I'll call him as soon as I get to Delaware."

"Sure thing. I can understand about the weather. It's raining and blowing pretty hard here now, but he should be back within the hour," Betty said cheerfully.

"I hope to be in the air by then, Betty. Talk to you later."

In the lounge, Keith found a newsstand. He settled gratefully into a comfortable chair with the *New York Times* to catch up on the news. A lot of the front page was devoted to the weather. The latest hurricane, Frank, had blasted the Florida coast, causing wind damage and dangerously high water. There was a large color map of the storm-affected area in the weather section. An article followed with statistics on the hurricane, which was now ravaging the Mid-Atlantic coast.

Next, Keith searched the foreign news, looking for any reference to the trouble in Austria. Apparently, the suspicious death of an elderly war hero didn't rate any mention. Keith was relieved, but not completely surprised.

There was a coffee shop in the pilots' lounge. It was nearly full with crews waiting for the weather to clear. Keith found a single vacant seat at a table for four. The man across the table was reading a message with the haggard look of an old seafarer.

"Mind if I have a seat?" asked Keith.

"No, we don't," he said, barely looking up. The others moved slightly to allow Keith to sit down.

A short blonde waitress of about seventeen approached, took Keith's order, and departed.

"You look as bad as I feel," said Keith with an engaging smile.

"I guess I do. I've had one hell of a couple months. We work for the U.S. Weather Department, airborne hurricane watch," he said pointing to his two companions. "These two guys are Bill Simpson and Duke Monroe. Bill is my navigator and copilot. Duke is our instruments technician. The name here is Jackson, first name Tom."

Bill was an average-sized man, about five-foot eight with a handlebar mustache. Duke was short, slightly overweight, with a double chin. The faces of all three men had traces of sunburn.

"Mine's Keith," he said, leaning forward and offering his hand. "I run a charter agency out of Aspen, Colorado. Glad to meet you. Bet you've had a rough season."

"You're right about that," replied Bill with a laugh. "Tell him about it, Tom."

"You remember the first hurricane, Alvin? I damn near lost our old P-3, not to mention Bill here, and old Art Simpson," Tom explained as he leaned back in his chair. "Barely managed to limp into Lauderdale on three engines. Worst flight we've ever had for turbulence and lightning. All our navcom gear was out from lightning. When we landed, Art quit flat out. That flight shook him up so bad, I doubt the guy will ever fly again. After that, we got a decent piece of equipment. We're now flying the new Orion," said Tom proudly.

"Even so, we keep Tom out of the center when those babies are building up," added Bill.

"Yeah, I made that mistake only once. After they leave the Caribbean, that's a different story. They start to taper off. I don't mind flying in 'em then, but not ever when they're building, almost as if all the forces of hell are concentrated in a fifteen-mile radius," said Tom, finishing his iced tea and draining the sugar from the bottom of his glass.

"Must take a lot of courage to keep doing that kind of work week after week," said Keith.

"This year is one for the records," Duke continued.

"How many records have been broken?" asked Keith.

"I don't know for sure, but we've never had so many hurricanes in such a short period. To make matters worse, the satellite boys aren't doing much good at predicting these things. That's put a lot of burden on us hurricane watchers. We get a lot of flying time in weather systems the birds have trouble predicting, lots of time to gather data. Then the computer jocks keep trying to improve their model using our data … Am I boring you with all this weather talk?" asked Duke.

"Not at all. Pilots have a vested interest in weather predictions," chuckled Keith.

The waitress returned with Keith's club sandwich and iced tea.

"I guess with all this flying you don't get much time to lie on the beach. Funny, you all look pretty tan," Keith looked from one to the other.

The weather pilot grinned.

"No, I don't take much stock in sunbathing. Don't have the skin for it. Every time I get the slightest burn on my back, two days later I'm driven almost crazy by 'the itches'. Something to do with histamines I've been told. But my tan isn't from the beach, it's from high altitude flying. Something similar to the problems on the beaches here in Bermuda."

"What problems?" Keith frowned as he took a hungry bite.

"Haven't you heard? They tried to keep it quiet for a few weeks, but finally they couldn't deny it any longer. There was a rash of severe sunburn cases here, some of which were nearly fatal. At first, the medical guys thought it was just the turkey tourists too dumb to use the proper sunscreen. Then some of the residents started turning up in the hospital. They just couldn't deny it. They asked us to do a study. Bunch of our folks arrived two weeks ago with boxes of our radiation equipment. Got ourselves a real surprise, all right. Best we can tell, there is a local tear in the ozone layer causing a threefold increase in ultraviolet radiation. You know, for every one percent reduction in the ozone layer, there's a two percent increase in ultraviolet light. A threefold increase means a lot of people are going to get skin cancer," Bill announced in a low voice.

Despite the warm humid air in the coffee shop, Keith felt a chill.

"Any idea about the cause?"

"Nope, but the physics boys are working on it," replied Duke.

The three men had finished their sandwiches. The blonde returned with their bill. After a short discussion over payment, Tom left two dollars on the table and the three weathermen prepared to leave.

"Well, I think we're about to get clearance, so we'd better be getting the latest weather bulletin. Been nice meeting you ... ah, Keith. There, I remembered," Tom smiled proudly.

"Thanks for the information and good luck to you guys. I hope the hurricane season ends real soon," Keith said, shaking his head.

"You and me both," sighed Tom as he left.

That does it! thought Keith as he finished his sandwich. *Lebedev was right! I wonder how bad the damage to the ozone layer is already. Worse yet, is the damage permanent?*

Keith wondered if Jessel had found Lebedev's violin.

• Chapter 10 •

MONDAY, SEPTEMBER 16

Charlie Durr was still half asleep. It was a dreary, cold morning in Cherry Hill, New Jersey. The previous weekend at the shore had been a long and tedious one. He had spent much of Saturday getting his twenty-four-foot fishing boat out of the water and into the yard in the back of the shop where it would remain until spring. On Sunday, he closed up the bungalow on Long Beach Island. This morning, it was drizzling. Charlie was not looking forward to winter.

Thirty years ago this fall Charlie had married his wife, Eve, when he left the Marine Corps. He put his life's savings, all five-thousand dollars, into fixing up an obsolete corner gas station. Eve sold groceries out front before there were convenience stores. Charlie never did well in the service business, but soon the word spread that he had a knack for sheet metal work, a trade he picked up working in the Marine motor pool. He started restoring classic cars, then branched into custom work. Every speed freak within miles wanted his services. Charlie expanded and converted the garage and convenience store into a body shop. Eve was relieved of the tedious work out front just in time, because Charlie Junior and his sister Evelyn had arrived and were a lot to handle.

After twenty more years of honest effort, Charlie's business now occupied a six-bay facility on two fenced-in acres with a proper front office. The year he moved the shop, Charlie Junior joined the business. Now Durr and Son was doing fairly well. The family business was fully paid for. Eve finally could buy some of the clothes and jewelry she had gone without for so many years. Charlie had five years left on his house mortgage, and in ten years the beach house would be theirs. He then planned to retire and let his son run the business, if he was ready.

His greatest joy was spending time with his grandchildren. His son had a boy and a girl, Jason and Megan, ages three and five. They were quite a handful to watch, but a joy for short periods of time.

Evelyn was a different matter. She was the bright one. From the beginning, she had been in the gifted program in school. Now she was going off to college, to Princeton of all places. Eve always said he was soft on Evelyn. It was probably true because it was hard for him to deny her anything. Now it was a car she wanted. No way could she go off to college without one, she had said with those clear blue eyes staring up at him. He finally found one for her. A nice low-mileage Nissan. Never mind that it had a little sheet metal damage from some freak accident. It was sound and Dewey, his trusted service manager, would have the motor purring like a kitten. Charlie planned to surprise her with the car when she came home for the weekend.

Charlie entered the office. His desk was neat and clear just as he had left it the previous Friday. His son's desk in contrast was the same mess it had been when he quit estimating the work on the Ford van, which was towed in on Thursday. *Good luck there, Junior,* thought Charlie. He would have to deal with Lou Lattorney from National Insurance. If there was ever a guy who wanted to kill the body shop business, Lou was it. Charlie kept his costs down by speculating on parts he would need and buying in volume. He stocked the parts in the shed out back. In a few years, the value of the parts tripled. Problem was, Lou knew it and insisted on forcing his price down, even below guide. Lou couldn't understand free enterprise and was just a jerk, no other way to put it.

Charlie checked his calendar. There were two cars scheduled

for completion today. He had better review the progress with Junior before the customers started calling. Somewhere down the interstate, there was a siren blaring. He rose from his desk and got the ingredients from the cupboard above the office sink for the morning coffee. When the coffee system started to drip, he headed for the garage. Dewey was just rolling out from under the Nissan.

"She looks good, Boss. I think we will be done in plenty of time for this Friday," said Dewey, standing up and wiping his hands with a rag.

The sirens outside were getting louder. Charlie was about to ask Dewey how his weekend had been, when he suddenly realized the siren was coming from the parking lot out front.

"What the hell?" shot Charlie as he burst through the door to the front office. To his surprise, there were no less than five large men dressed like plain clothes cops entering from outside. Before he could ask any questions, the lead man showed his identification.

Charlie was astounded.

"What does the FBI want with my business? We run an honest shop here," replied Charlie, his mouth hanging open.

Before him stood agent Jack Miller, who was in a big hurry.

"Did you purchase a Nissan Stanza from Price Auto Sales recently?" Miller demanded.

"Yes, but..."

"Where is it?" shot Miller, not waiting for Charlie to finish.

Charlie pointed into the garage. Four agents sprang for the door, barely missing each other in their haste. In seconds they had surrounded Dewey and demanded the keys. Before Dewey could find them one of the men picked up a crowbar and threatened to pry the trunk open. Finally, Dewey found the keys and the four men stepped aside. Dewey opened the trunk and four heads thrust inside. With a quick look around, the lead man shouted to Miller.

"Jack, there's nothing in the trunk!"

Agent Miller turned to Charlie.

"Did you clean out the trunk?"

Charlie hadn't. He glanced at Dewey. That was enough for agent Miller. He moved in front of Charlie.

"What did you find in the trunk?"

"Well, I just found an old violin with the wood busted up some, that's all."

"Where is it?" demanded agent Miller, his eyes narrowing on the black man.

"Now wait just a minute!" started Charlie, his face getting red.

"Stay out of this, mister!" warned Miller. "I want to know where that violin is." Then in an attempt to justify himself, "It's important to national security."

"I dunno, it was just a piece of junk. I think I threw it out," said Dewey, his voice shaking slightly.

"Throw it out you say, where did you throw it out?"

"In the dumpster out back," stammered Dewey.

Four bodies scrambled outside in unison. Charlie came to the realization they were heading out back. He hadn't gotten his guard dog, Rex, in his cage yet. Rex was a German Shepherd and a refugee from the dog pound. He was as mean as anything found in a junk yard and definitely a one-master dog.

Before he could get into the backyard, Rex was already giving chase to the two lead officers. The first one saw Rex coming and jumped into the dumpster and out of harm's way. The second wasn't so lucky. Rex had already chewed through his back pocket and had a vicious clamp on the exposed cheek inside his pants. The other two had wisely jumped back inside and closed the door. It took Charlie a good five minutes to get Rex off the poor guy, calm him down, and get him into his cage.

Charlie turned to the man whose trousers were shredded. Already the telltale signs of blood were showing. "Sorry about the dog, but you guys should have asked! I'd have been glad to cage him," said Charlie, shaking his head. This was going to be a morning for the record.

With a sudden whoop for joy, the man in the dumpster raised triumphantly a battered and slightly broken violin. "I got it, Jack, and it looks like the objective is still inside!" the man shouted as he bounded out of the dumpster.

Everyone headed for the door at once. Charlie couldn't believe his eyes. The bitten agent seemed completely unconcerned in his hurry to catch the others. As he climbed in the car, Miller looked back at Charlie. "Sorry to disrupt your morning, but we got what we were after. We won't be bothering you again sir," shouted Miller, and then they were off with the sirens blaring.

Dewey stood next to Charlie as the men watched the two police cars disappear down the street. "How about that! Police escort and all. What do you suppose they were looking for in that old violin?" asked Dewey.

"I don't know and I doubt I ever will," shrugged Charlie.

A red Corvette rounded the corner and sped through the gate. It was Charlie Junior. He parked the Corvette next to the fence out of the way of traffic, as was his custom. He must have thought it strange for his dad and Dewey to be standing out front. "Well, what's with you two?" asked Junior.

"You would never guess. You would never f—ing guess," said Charlie as he turned for the door to the office. *There were some mornings,* he thought. *Some mornings that just weren't right until that first cup of coffee. Well, better try two cups because this morning is starting out weird!*

TUESDAY, SEPTEMBER 17, MOSCOW

It was a cold, gray morning in Moscow. Outside the office on Marshal Zukov Avenue snow covered the sidewalk. From his window on the fifth floor, Victor Gerisimov could see an old woman on the concrete struggling to sweep the light coating into the gutter. Her back, bent from age, strained with each motion, but she continued with stubborn determination while her breath hung in small wisps of condensation about the black scarf wrapping her face. Snow was still in the air, the promise of further accumulation. Winter had arrived early in Moscow. Already there were skaters gliding on the ice rink in Gorky Park. *It will be another long and cold winter,* thought Gerisimov.

Turning from his window he reread, the urgent message from

the agent in Florida. The information was passed from a computer technician at the John F. Kennedy Space Center who had a particularly good nose for small items of import.

> *"Significant possibility exists Americans suspect Russian involvement in weather. Recent computer simulation running successive iterations strongly suggest Harvest Program is the stimulus. Program now has level five security."*

Gerisimov knew full well the significance of level five security measures. Not since the day before the invasion of Grenada, and before that the Cuban missile crisis, had he seen such security measures. Obviously, the Americans were planning something. But what? Had they cause to suspect?

It did not help that Pronin had gone incommunicado just after his arrival in Montreal a week ago. Was the American activity an indicator he had failed in his attempt to prevent the exposure of the Harvest Satellite by the traitor Lebedev? Or was this just a routine increase of security as they prepared to launch a new spy satellite? Either way, he would have to inform General Tuzov of the news, a task that brought with it a feeling of dread. He had come a long way over many years from when he was a border guard for his career to be damaged now. Clearly, the responsibility weighed heavily on the hands of Teslov Socknat, who had placed so much trust in Captain Pronin. Wasn't there evidence Pronin was a questionable choice? Hadn't he been involved in that dissident affair? Weren't his methods resulting in the victim's death under investigation?

This last thought brought a smile to Gerisimov's face – he, who many years ago had personally ordered the shooting of Hungarian refuges sneaking across the border in '57. Somehow, he felt his actions were justified, while Pronin's methods were outdated compared to those used elsewhere in the KGB, CIA, and for that matter, the Israeli Mossad and MI-6. Why wait to get information wrung out of an almost senseless victim when, with the proper use of drugs, the information could be quickly and undramatically obtained. No, if the project is uncovered because Pronin failed to stamp out the treachery of Lebedev, then it would be Socknat's head that would roll. He had cleverly not objected to Teslov's support for Pronin, knowing it would provide an out for himself if he failed.

Gerisimov had previously scheduled a briefing with General Tuzov. He picked up the phone to give Tuzov the courtesy of a phone call and to assure himself the general would be available.

After a moment's wait, Larisa answered for the general. Just listening to her voice in his ear caused Gerisimov to visualize her sensuous body. But he shut the image out and concentrated instead on the issue of the moment. The general was in and would see him as scheduled.

With grim determination, Gerisimov put the message in the tattered folder around which he tied the retaining cord, and then placed it in a small briefcase he kept behind his modern teak desk.

He rose to prepare to leave. Carefully, he put on his heavy wool coat, placed his fur hat firmly on his head, walked a few steps, and shut the door to his office, leaving the lights on. After a brief conversation with his secretary, he headed for the basement where Sasha had the black Chaika waiting with the heater running.

WILMINGTON, DELAWARE
THURSDAY, SEPTEMBER 19, 8 A.M.

Keith walked briskly across the concrete to the terminal building near the Midlantic Aviation Hangar. The sky was clearing with the sun beginning to break through after a heavy rain.

Immediately inside the terminal was the reception area. Keith asked the young woman behind the desk where he could find a phone. He was directed upstairs to the pilots' lounge.

On his way up, he had difficulty seeing the steps. He realized the power was off.

At the top of the stairs, he found the pilots' lounge and walked into the anteroom. Fortunately, the light coming through the window made it possible to find the phone.

Keith hurried over and picked up the receiver. To his relief, there was a dial tone. He dialed Jessel's Washington number. After several clicks, the phone responded with a busy signal. He dialed again, but the result was the same. Next, he tried the local operator. After what seemed an endless wait, an exhausted voice answered. "Operator, may I help you?"

"Yes, please, I'm trying to place a call to D.C. and I get an immediate busy signal," Keith hurriedly explained.

"I am sorry sir, but the trunk lines to Washington are temporarily out of service. They should be repaired within the hour," she responded.

The call to Jessel would have to wait. Jessel had a plane waiting in Washington, but he was stuck and that was that. Thinking of Anna, he dialed Jim Dawson's number. He wanted to hear her voice again. This time the call went through. After four rings Jim answered. "Jim, this is Keith, is Anna there?"

There was a momentary silence at the other end. "Keith, I'm glad you called. We haven't seen or heard from Anna since she left to pick up some things in your cabin. Last night we thought she must have decided to stay for the night, but she didn't show up this morning. We've called, but only get your answering machine. We also checked with the sheriff's department, so we know she wasn't in an accident. She was expecting to fly to New York this afternoon, but she missed her flight."

Keith felt an uneasy stir in the pit of his stomach. This was bad news. He hadn't given Anna any thought since he left La Guardia. Now he wished he had.

"I don't like it. I'm going to do some checking from this end. Maybe she had to leave early for New York. I'll call you back."

Keith hung up. Where the hell was Anna? He dialed her apartment in New York. The phone rang fifteen times, no answer. On the chance she might be in the cabin, he dialed his number.

In a few seconds, he heard the beginning of his recorded message. If Anna was there, she hadn't turned the machine off. He pushed the access keys on the phone pad. The recorded message stopped and the machine began to play his messages. Several people had called, but they left no message. There were three routine messages of little importance. Then the loud voice of Marty, his partner, broke in. "Keith, where the hell are you? I'm getting nasty phone calls. The Austrian authorities are real mad! I don't know what kind of a mess you got yourself into there, but give me a call as soon as you get this message. I'd damn well appreciate it!"

Keith was about to hang up to give him a call, when suddenly a familiar voice with a Russian accent broke in. The voice on the other end was that of Nikolai Pronin! "So you made it back to the States."

"Maybe," Keith said, as he tried to stay calm. "When did you arrive and what are you doing in my cabin?"

"I will ask the questions! You were very lucky in Austria. You were quick, but I have been quicker and have had better luck in Colorado. So stupid of you to leave your business card in Halperin's apartment. My men found your cabin and watched it. Of course, your girlfriend showed up. In case you don't believe me, listen."

In the background Keith could hear the sound of a struggle. Then Anna broke the silence.

"Keith," Anna's voice was weak. "I'm sorry. I shouldn't have come to the cabin. There's three of them be—"

Keith could hear Anna being dragged away from the phone.

"If you ever want to see your Anna alive again, you will not try to get help. Instead, you will bring both the music and the violin here. You do have them with you?"

"Yes, I do," lied Keith.

"Very well, then bring them to me and, Maddox, this time no tricks. How soon can you be here?"

Keith thought for a moment. He didn't know the flight or shuttle schedules to Colorado from Wilmington. A lot of things could go wrong.

"The earliest I can get there is late tonight," he replied.

"Good ... I want you to be at the phone booth outside the Redstone Inn this evening at six o'clock. I will call you. I will arrange for the exchange."

The phone went dead. Keith was still holding it in disbelief when it started to beep loudly. The timing would be very tight. He wasn't sure he could make it.

Pronin had killed before. He wouldn't think twice about killing Anna. He was desperate, with a blind desire to achieve his mission. Didn't his presence in Colorado prove it? The thought of Anna in the hands of the Russian butcher was infuriating. Keith wanted to contact Jessel immediately, but was it worth Anna's life? He had to get to Colorado. In the next few minutes he booked a flight from Philadelphia to Denver and arranged for the Airport Shuttle to pick him up.

GLENWOOD SPRINGS, COLORADO, 4 P.M.

An hour after Keith arrived in Denver, he took the short commuter hop to Rifle, west of Glenwood Springs, and a little out of the way in case Pronin's men were waiting for him. The plane was almost filled by a Texas hunting party. Keith was fortunate enough to get a standby seat the last minute. He knew Marty was in Denver, so he called Jim Dawson for help. Jim arrived full of questions shortly after Keith landed. Keith explained that Anna was in serious trouble, and did his best to relate the events in Austria leading up to her capture in Colorado as he hastily left Rifle airport in Jim's car. Jim was particularly curious about the music and its secret message. Keith let Jim read it while he drove to Glenwood Springs, a town whose name was derived from an old and famous hot spring resort.

They rushed to the Hot Springs Hotel and Pool, where Keith rented a locker, placed the music inside, and together they left on State Highway 82 for Redstone. They had to get there by six o'clock. It was well after five-thirty already.

On Highway 82, Keith paid no attention to the speed limit. At the fork in the road near Carbondale, he turned onto State Highway 133 and crossed the Roaring Fork River. On the other side of town, Keith accelerated again as they passed through green pastures under the view of snow-capped Mount Sopris. There was almost no time to formulate a strategy.

Of one thing Keith was sure: At six o'clock he would be alone at the phone booth. If anything looked suspicious, Anna wouldn't live long. He would have to get a plan set with Jim, and Jim must keep out of sight.

REDSTONE, COLORADO, 5:50 P.M.

On the second floor of the Redstone Inn, a lean man with cropped black hair lay stretched out on the bed next to the window with his binoculars focused on the parking lot of the General store across the boulevard. His name was Anatoly Melnikov, a Russian agent living in New York who had recently killed an old man in Philadelphia to keep a State secret. It was risky for him to remain in America, but as soon as he finished with Pronin, he would return to Russia. He had waited an hour for the American to arrive. The quaint but narrow street was not empty. Redstone was hosting a flea market for the weekend. Shoppers were strolling down the street in small groups. A man alone in a Chevy Camaro rounded the turn from the highway and parked near the phone booth. The man did not get out, but remained inside. Was this the American they were waiting for?

In the distance, the jingle of the pay phone could be heard. Pronin was calling. The man in the Camaro climbed out and ran to answer it. There was a brief but heated conversation, and the man hung up.

The American left the phone booth and got in his car. A second later the lights came on, the engine roared, and the Camaro lurched up the street toward the Inn. It turned right, crossed the Crystal River bridge, turned left, and raced south. At no time did Anatoly see anyone make contact with the stranger.

He picked up the phone, dialed, listened for an answer, and then spoke a few words in Russian. He listened for a second, grunted in agreement, hung up and prepared to leave.

Farther up the valley inside a neglected garage next to a ramshackled miner's cabin dating back to the early mining days of Crystal City, Pronin waited impatiently. The American was alone. Anatoly had confirmed that. They would carefully watch him as he came up the valley. His girlfriend was securely tied up inside the rental car. This would be a simple trade of the girl for the music and the violin, but afterward he would not let them escape. He would then make his exit using the helicopter Andrei had contracted.

He climbed into the Blazer with Andrei, a technician who ten years ago was recruited in Colorado Springs. Andrei did maintenance work on the computer systems at the North American Aerospace Defense Command or NORAD. His information on the vast electronic network comprising the American early warning system was particularly interesting to the Russians. For a few dollars he had traded secrets the Russians couldn't buy for millions elsewhere. Andrei had a weakness for gambling and women. Occasionally, he spent weekends in Las Vegas. Sometimes he was a big winner, but more often he was not. For the past ten years the Soviets had bankrolled his losses and supplied him with women. Besides his other vices, Andrei had a great appreciation for food. His weight had always been a problem, but now in mid-life he could no longer squeeze into the small computer spaces where maintenance work was required. After failing at several attempts to diet, management took pity on him and promoted him to scheduling supervisor. In his new position, he no longer had access to classified information. The Russians felt Andrei had eaten himself out of a job. Now Andrei was trying to prove he could be useful in other ways, but despite his effort, he was considered expendable by the KGB.

Pronin sat behind the wheel and fiddled with the keys nervously. His mind drifted back to Natasha. "I love you anyway, my sweet," were the last words he remembered. How brave she had been. The surgeons had told her she would live only a few hours without the surgery, but with it her chances were slightly better. He had remained in Austria trying to catch the American. She must have felt quite alone that cold morning before her surgery. The memory of their last phone conversation tore deep in the pit of his stomach. Despite the best medical services available in the USSR, after four hours of surgery she never regained consciousness. The chief surgeon conceded her heart was very weak and the surgery was simply too late. He had not been there when she needed him most and now he was missing her funeral—all because of this damn American.

Andrei was concerned. The man behind the wheel frightened him. Not only was he intimidating by his physical size, but he seemed to be a demon possessed. Why else was Pronin risking so much to recover an old violin and some sheet music? Andrei was not familiar with these mountains, nor was he by any means in shape for physical activity. At this altitude, any exertion resulted in immediate breathlessness. He had an uneasy feeling about the UZI between the car seats. He, too, carried a small pistol, but he doubted he could use it.

At first the operation had been simple. Hadn't he done well finding the woman alone in the cabin and arranging for the helicopter to be waiting in Schofield Park? After such immediate success, he could only think of the bonus he deserved from the Russians. But that was before things turned ugly, before Pronin arrived. Now that he was here, what was to become of the woman bound and gagged in the back? Would this abduction lead to murder? This was not work for a fat technician, and definitely not worth the few dollars the cheap Russians offered.

Twenty miles down the valley toward Carbondale, Keith sped south along Route 133 toward Marble. Jim had hidden behind the seat while Keith waited for the phone. At a sharp bend in the road near Keith's cabin, he had slowed and Jim had jumped out. Jim would get Keith's Jeep and take a different route to the location where Keith would meet Pronin.

Keith continued on Route 133 until he reached the turn for Marble that was ten miles farther up the county road. After passing Marble, Keith would drive slowly on the dirt road to Crystal City. The road was bad and had many ruts. That would give Jim time to take the other route through Lead King Basin and reach the Crystal City bridge where the exchange was to take place. Jim would surprise the Russians from behind. Keith had Jim's Colt 45 revolver and a box of ammunition under the seat of the Camaro. Jim had Keith's deer rifle in the Jeep.

Farther up the valley on a prominent outcropping of granite, a man crouched in the shadows and carefully surveyed the road.

Alexis Drinov was the other Russian with Pronin. His specialty was space technology, not covert operations. He was comfortable in this rugged mountain terrain because he grew up on a collective farm near the Caucasus. Despite his peasant background, he became an exceptional student at an early age and was selected for an engineering education. Eventually, he achieved a position in the KGB. This was his first operation abroad. America had been quite a shock for him. He had not realized Americans had so many of the consumer goods sought after in the Soviet Union. Alexis had waited for an hour, occasionally scanning the road with his field glasses. There had been no traffic on the dirt road since sunset. It was much colder now. He stamped his feet impatiently to keep them warm. It wouldn't be long now.

Almost on cue, a set of headlights came slowly into view as a compact car made the bend in the road. Alexis waited ten minutes while the car slowly wound its way up the valley. He gave the road one final glance, then took the powerful flashlight out of his utility pack. Its reflective lens was focused to produce a pencil thin beam of light. He pointed it toward the small town where Pronin was waiting. In the cool dry night air, the beam was almost invisible as he flashed a short pulse, followed by a long pulse, and then two short pulses of light. The road was clear. It was time to close in.

Keith was having difficulty keeping the Camaro out of the ruts in the road. After a summer of hard use, they were so deep they could easily high-center the Camaro. He was not in a hurry. It would take Jim a lot longer to get to Crystal City by going the other way.

Keith passed the small parking area where he could see the Crystal Mill (or the Lost Horse Mill as it was originally called), probably the most photographed structure in the Crystal Valley. The Crystal Bridge was around the corner. He knew Pronin would be there. The moment was near. The twin shafts of the Camaro's headlights cut a swath through the cold mountain air and fell upon a Chevy Blazer parked on the other side of the bridge. Sure enough, Pronin was standing behind the Blazer next to a fat man who held a small pistol to Anna's head.

Keith stopped the car, left the lights shining, and slowly got out. In his right hand he held key to the locker. "OK, you Russian asshole, hand her over," he challenged.

Pronin chose to ignore the insult. "Show me the music."

"No chance, not until Anna is free!" Keith countered.

"You can see the woman. Where is the music?" Pronin continued.

Anna's hands were tied behind her back. The fat man holding her surrounded her body with his heavy arms. Anna did not look well. Her face was ashen, her eyes were puffy, and Keith could see fear in them.

"I've brought you your woman, Maddox. Now give me the music and the violin or she dies!"

Where the hell was Jim? Hadn't he gone slowly enough? What was taking him so long? Keith heard the sound of Andrei cocking his gun. He stretched his right hand out over the rushing water of the Crystal River.

"I don't have the music here," Keith began slowly and deliberately. "It's in a locker in Glenwood Springs. The key is in my right hand. If anything happens to Anna, the key will fall in the water. You can be sure there are folks in Washington who will soon be here, and they won't need to wait for the key."

Pronin was furious, another complication. For once couldn't this be a simple trade? Did the American have to try these silly tricks? The authorities in Washington must not get the music.

Keith stood defiantly with his hand over the water while Pronin stared at him in silence. He knew time was running out. Where was Jim?

"Get your hands up!" came Jim's loud voice from the scrub oak behind the Blazer.

"Jim, you made it!" shouted Keith. "All right, Pronin, you and your buddy get your hands in the air!" Keith scrambled to get Jim's revolver out of the car.

"So much like a cowboy, Maddox. Aren't you forgetting that we have your girlfriend? Perhaps you will enjoy seeing her die?" snarled Pronin. He turned to Andrei, who had a tight grip on Anna's shoulders. The pistol in his hand was pressed hard against the side of Anna's face. Andrei's finger was on the trigger. "Perhaps, Maddox, it is best you and your friend calm down and lower your weapons. Obviously we can kill her if this silly act of yours continues any further," Pronin said confidently.

Andrei was nervous. His heavy breathing could be heard in the cool night air. He had no stomach for physical violence, and doubted he could kill the girl even though his finger could easily pull the trigger. His right knee was shaking. He shifted his weight to his right leg to stop it. The woman moved forward slightly.

Anna sensed her obese captor was apprehensive. She was terrified by the gun pressed firmly against her temple. She tried to move her weight forward. The ground was uneven. She weighed far less than Andrei, but she displaced his mass slightly, forcing him to step forward to restrain her. Unable to see the ground below, Andrei clumsily stepped on a small round rock and twisted his ankle as it rolled under his foot. He groaned and tried to shift his weight to his left leg. Too late. He lost his balance and started to fall. He grabbed Anna by the waist and toppled on his right side. The impact would have smashed Anna's shoulder had she not twisted her body at the last second. Andrei went down hard. Anna pushed the gun from her temple and smashed her elbow into Andrei's ample stomach. Andrei groaned and released her. In a second, Anna was sprinting for the bridge.

Andrei dropped his gun. He awkwardly reached for it. Pronin darted out of the light of the headlights. There was a loud report from Jim's rifle.

Keith had seen Anna and the fat man go down. The instant he heard Jim's shot, he extinguished the headlights. Everything was dark. Anna got into the car. Jim followed quickly. Keith had the motor running and the wheels spinning wildly in reverse. He tore off the exhaust system on a rock and spun into a turn, reversing his direction. He slammed the Camaro into first and powered down the road. A second later, he risked turning on the headlights and swerved to miss a tree. There was a roar of automatic fire from behind. Pieces of bark flew from a nearby tree, and the rear window collapsed under impact. Keith stood on the accelerator. The heavy eight-cylinder engine roared, and exhaust poured up through the floorboards. Keith shifted into second after he rounded the first turn. They were free! Keith turned to Anna. "Nice going! If you hadn't gotten free, we'd be back there still,"

Jim was untying the rope that held Anna's wrists together.

"Shit, Keith, this has all been so horrible. I wish I had never gotten involved with this mess. That Pronin is such a bastard! I'm so glad you're here." Anna put her arm around Keith's shoulders and hugged him tightly.

"What are we going to do now?" Jim asked, relieved to be rid of the Russian.

"Soon as we get to Marble, we'll call the Sheriff's Department and get a few deputies up here. Pronin can't get far. Not at night," Keith declared.

"We could double back and try ourselves?" Jim said with a grin.

"No, I don't think so," finished Keith grimly. "Anybody who wants to take Pronin better have a lot of help."

The road climbed toward Lizard Lake. Ahead, there was a narrow and dangerous turn. Suddenly, Keith slammed on the brakes. A large tree had fallen, completely blocking the road!

"I don't like this," Keith declared as he turned to look behind them. There was a glow in the distance. Pronin would soon catch up. "We'd better get this damn tree out of the way, and fast!" Keith announced as he got out.

The rushing water in the river could be heard far below. Jim took the rifle and started down-grade to find a good position to hold off the Russians. Anna ran to help Keith. Up the valley, the headlights of Pronin's Blazer could be seen.

There was no room to go around the tree. Keith and Anna tried to push it. The aspen rolled easily, too easily. He stared at the tree trunk. Someone had chainsawed the aspen! There was a dull thump from behind the car and a groan from Jim. Keith and Anna turned and suddenly found themselves looking down the business end of a Russian Tokarev 9mm.

Alexis had waited patiently until the two men separated before moving from behind the large boulder where Pronin had instructed him to stay. Something had gone wrong with the exchange. He had been ready, and rightly so. Now he had recaptured the Americans. When he arrived, Pronin would be pleased with his performance.

Keith and Anna faced the determined man as he shouted something in Russian. They both raised their hands slowly. The Blazer soon stopped behind the Camaro. Pronin and Andrei got out.

"Good work, Alexis. You have done well, much better than Andrei," said Pronin, and then to Keith he said, "So we meet again, and so soon! Too bad you could not make good on your escape."

He walked over to Jim, now lying on the ground behind the Camaro, and kicked him in the ribs. "Looks like this one will have a real bad headache." Pronin turned to Andrei. "Search these two. See if they still have the key," instructed Pronin.

Andrei searched Keith's pockets and found the key.

"Alexis, help Andrei get this one into our car," Pronin instructed, pointing to Jim. "Then we must push the tree over the edge and get moving."

In a few minutes, they had the tree clear and the Camaro out of the way. Both Keith and Anna had their hands and feet tied with heavy rope and were shoved into the back of the Blazer. Pronin drove. When they reached Marble, they met Anatoly in a Honda Accord. Pronin stopped to talk to Anatoly for a moment and gave him the key to the locker. Anatoly departed for Glenwood Springs while Pronin drove up the six-mile road to the marble quarry.

Keith was furious. The odds had been grossly in Pronin's favor. There were four of them. How had he ever thought he could be successful? The ride to the old marble quarry took twenty minutes. There they were unloaded and Keith and Anna's legs untied. Jim was still unconscious, and was carried from the Blazer. He was pale and bleeding from an ugly knot on the back of his head. When his men were finished with Keith and Anna, Pronin faced them with the UZI.

"I have sent Anatoly to Glenwood Springs to try the locker. You should all be dead by now, but just in case the music and violin aren't in the locker, we'll wait by the quarry until he returns. Now, walk up the hill, and this time, Maddox, no tricks or your girlfriend will get it first!"

Pronin turned to his stout assistant. "Andrei, carry the injured one."

Andrei was shocked. He could barely make the climb up the final grade by himself. How could he make it carrying another man? He started to protest. One threatening look from Pronin was enough. He would carry the man. He hoisted Jim to his shoulders in a fireman's carry and started up the hill after the others.

Keith followed Anna toward the mouth of the large quarry. They had barely begun climbing before Andrei started wheezing audibly. Before they were halfway up the steep hillside, he was sweating profusely and panting like a great bear.

Pronin found satisfaction in the fat man's suffering. Good that he should feel pain. Hadn't he screwed up at the bridge? How he despised this fat traitor who sold his country's secrets for a few rubles. It would do him good to work for once. It wouldn't have a lasting effect, for soon they would all be at the bottom of the quarry. This location was perfect.

Four times on the path Andrei stopped to rest. On the fourth stop, Pronin became so impatient he fired several rounds into the ground at Andrei's feet. The soft earth flew in gritty chunks against Andrei's legs. He desperately lunged forward, forgetting his pain. His breath came in loud rasping pulls as he kept pace with the others. Andrei was in trouble. He was more than completely out of breath. His chest felt like someone was standing on it. When he reached the top, he dropped Jim and collapsed in complete exhaustion. Now the pain in his chest was so severe he doubled over, clutching his chest.

Pronin was amused by Andrei's predicament, but there was business to be done. His prisoners must be disabled. First, they would tie Anna's legs together. That would keep her immobile. He looked around and found a heavy piece of metal pipe and tied it to Keith's leg.

"That will keep you from running into the jungle, Maddox," Pronin said proudly.

"Don't be so quick to write us off. We're not finished yet," said Keith defiantly.

"We'll see about that when Anatoly returns. It will be better for you if he has the music," Pronin sneered.

An hour passed waiting for Anatoly, and Keith developed leg cramps from sitting on the cold ground. Anna wasn't faring well either. She lay in a fetal position on the cold rock next to Keith. Jim mumbled something two or three times. Andrei cowered by a rock near where he had dropped Jim. Andrei's groans were replaced by occasional whimpering.

There was a dim light from down the valley. The light grew until Anatoly reached the parking lot. Five minutes later, he made it to the quarry, carrying a sack.

"What took you so long?" asked Pronin.

"There was some trouble at the Hot Springs. They were closed for the night, but the maintenance man let me in when I explained I was a foreigner and not aware of their policy. I found music, but no violin."

Pronin turned to Keith. "Well, Maddox, where is the violin?" he demanded.

"You'll never get it," Keith replied defiantly.

"Is that so? Haven't we been here before? Have you forgotten what happened to your friend Winn?" snarled Pronin.

The mention of Allen brought the memories rushing back.

Pronin drew a cigarette from a pack in his jacket pocket. He lit it and took a deep drag. The two men stared at each other.

"You see, after all these years you haven't learned how much I delight in torturing people." Pronin exhaled slowly, enjoying its flavor as he stared off in the distance. He returned his stare to Keith. "Have you ever experienced how a cigarette can burn? Perhaps I should show you."

Keith stood his ground. Pronin took the cigarette from his mouth and pressed the glowing end against Keith's cheek. The smell of burning flesh and the sudden sharp pain shocked him. He tried to move away from the pain while twisting his face. Pronin, his face in a frozen grin, stared at Keith. Though his eyes watered, Keith rallied and kicked savagely with his free leg. Pronin anticipated his move and neatly sidestepped the attack. Keith lost his balance and went down hard, hitting his head. He rose, shaking, as the world seemed to spin wildly. Anatoly grabbed Keith from behind and held him firmly.

Pronin stepped back, grinning. "Maddox, you have caused me so much pain. Did you know that my wife died while I was chasing you in Austria?"

"No. How could I? I didn't even know you were married," replied Keith.

"She died alone in the hospital. Thanks to you, I was not there. Oh, it would give me such pleasure to see you suffer. Do you know I could make it last for days? With your strength, it might last a week. You'd be surprised by the foul tricks I learned in Afghanistan. Sadly, I haven't enough time. I need answers now. Therefore, I must rely on what I know works."

Pronin turned to Anna. She tried to shrink back, but Pronin grabbed her arm and forced her to a sitting position. "I understand she is a model. I wonder how you would feel if I messed up her face a little," said Pronin, raising his cigarette.

"Don't you dare touch her, you bastard!" shouted Keith.

"And what can you do about it?" Pronin smiled.

"Make no mistake, if you hurt her the slightest, I guarantee you'll never see that violin, ever!" challenged Keith.

"Really, we'll see about that." Pronin relit his cigarette. He grabbed Anna's long hair firmly in his left hand and pulled it back sharply. Her torso was thrust backwards, exposing the lower portion of her firm belly. Taking his cigarette out of his mouth, he held it over her navel. Anna shrieked with terror and twisted hard against Pronin's grip on her hair. Slowly, his hand descended. Keith bellowed helplessly while Anatoly struggled to restrain him. Anna sobbed fitfully as his hand lowered. The burning end of his cigarette glowed brightly in a light breeze. The descent ended with the sickening hiss of burning flesh. Anna gave out a high-pitched scream, and her face turned bright red. The cigarette continued to burn as Pronin pressed harder. In a few seconds, it mercifully extinguished. Anna uttered a short gasp, then went limp, collapsing at Pronin's feet.

Pronin was disappointed, but he turned to Keith. "She doesn't have any tolerance for pain, but mark my words, I will remove every finger and toe on her body, and if you still insist on defying me, I will work on the larger joints until there is nothing left intact!"

Keith choked with rage. Pronin grinned at Keith. "Shall we begin?" He laughed and turned to Anatoly. "Get some water and pour it on her."

Anatoly disappeared with a plastic bucket over the edge of the quarry, and descended the steps Jim and Keith had partially restored. Some mischievous children must have removed the barricade, for it was not in sight. He returned with the bucket and splashed the contents in Anna's face. The shock and cold did not bring her around. Keith knew this was only the beginning. Pronin would revive her and continue his sadistic torture. He had no option but to give in.

"OK, Pronin you win. Don't hurt her any more. You can have the violin," Keith said quietly.

Pronin expected the American to give in quickly. After all, hadn't he done so before? This was too easy! Too bad though, it was just getting to be fun. Then it occurred to him that the American had tricked him once before by appearing to give in.

"Where is the violin?" asked Pronin.

"I hid it where you will never find it, that's where," Keith replied firmly.

"If you're suggesting you will lead us to where it is hidden, save your breath. You've tried that before. None of you are leaving here," snarled Pronin.

"OK, have it your way, but I hid it in an abandoned mine shaft. There are hundreds of mine shafts in this area. You don't have time to search them all and you'll never find it without my direction," shot Keith.

"You can draw us a map," Pronin said.

"Then give me something to write with," Keith replied.

Anatoly took a note pad and a pen from his jacket pocket.

"I'll need my hands free to draw," Keith said.

Pronin nodded, and Anatoly untied Keith's hands. Keith slowly rubbed them together. He took the pen and note pad. It was from the Redstone Inn. He held the notepad up in the distant light and began to draw, but he could not see the lines on the paper.

"This is the route. Can you see where the highway stretches north from here?" Keith asked.

Pronin squinted at the paper. He could not see a thing. "No, we need more light," shrugged Pronin.

"Then let's move under the light," Keith suggested.

Pronin nodded in agreement, and started for the light over the ancient platform.

Alexis and Anatoly followed Keith as he struggled with the metal pipe. Alexis held the UZI aimed at Keith's back. "Could I untie my foot? It would make it much easier to follow you," Keith pleaded.

"It would also make it easy for you to escape. No, Maddox, not this time. This time you can carry it. I don't want any heroics," Pronin replied matter-of-factly.

Keith struggled with the iron pipe. It must have weighed a hundred pounds. Pronin was already under the light over the platform. When Keith stepped on the platform, he felt it give slightly. In a flash he remembered he and Jim had removed the beams. With the combined weight of both of them and the weight of the pipe, he might be able to make the platform collapse, but he would have to find just the right location. The platform jutted out over the quarry water. Keith had heard the old timers say that the water was hundreds of feet deep with tunnels leading in all directions. If he could bring the platform down, he wanted something substantial to grab. Keith moved toward Pronin. Suddenly, he dropped the pipe.

Pronin felt the motion of the platform and looked up from the map just in time to see Keith release the pipe. Suddenly, he realized the platform was collapsing. There was a creaking and snapping sound from the ancient timbers underneath as the platform broke away from the solid rock.

Keith dove for the edge of the platform just in time to see it separate from the quarry's edge. Desperately crawling forward, Keith grasped the fractured end of a rotted beam anchored to the marble rock. He was barely able to wrap his arms around the stub before there was a tremendous jerk from the rope on his right leg. The strain was almost unbearable, but he held on as the planks of the platform sank from under him. The platform crashed into the water below.

Pronin jumped clear in the last instant before the platform plunged into the water. He hit the water in a sideways belly flop. There was a crack in the marble wall a few feet away. He reached the crack and jammed his hand inside, then shouted to Alexis and Anatoly above.

Anatoly and Alexis stood in shocked silence, peering over the edge of the quarry wall. Anatoly was the first to react. He set the UZI down and grabbed a loose rope from the temporary barricade and tossed the end to Pronin. Pronin grabbed the rope and started pulling himself hand-over-hand up the wall. Alexis assisted Anatoly by also holding the rope.

Anna had made progress in the last few minutes. In desperation, she had faked passing out from Pronin's cruel cigarette burn. A few seconds after the platform collapsed and the two Russians were distracted, she worked the rope loose around her hands on a sharp piece of metal. She then quickly untied her feet.

She stood tentatively. She could see the two Russians standing at the edge of the quarry, straining at the rope. She was terrified, but knew she had to do something—anything that would make the difference. She took a deep breath and lunged forward. Before either knew she was free, Anna was airborne. She smashed into Alexis, knocking him forward. Alexis clawed at the air to regain his balance. With a terrified scream, he fell head-first into the quarry. Anatoly reached for the UZI. As he swung to level it at Anna's stomach, she nearly lifted him off the ground with a savage kick to the groin. Anatoly groaned and dropped the UZI. Anna lunged forward with her head down. She hit him in the midsection, knocking him over the edge. He clawed at Anna to prevent himself from falling. His fingernails caught her wrist and dug in. She jerked it backwards and out of his grasp. Anatoly stared at her in disbelief as he slowly toppled over the edge and fell to the water below. Only a large cloud of bubbles remained on the surface where the men had disappeared. Neither man had ever learned to swim. Pronin clung to the rocks below while Keith hung desperately to a fractured beam.

Pronin knew when he saw Alexis and Anatoly fall that the tables were turned. He stared in disbelief at Anna.

"You bitch!" he snarled. He reached into his jacket and grabbed the Russian pistol he always carried in the field. He pointed the weapon at Keith.

"This time, Maddox, you will not escape!" Pronin declared resolutely, his finger beginning to squeeze the trigger.

Anna was horrified. The sight of the pistol in Pronin's hand was too much. She was shaking all over, her breath coming in short gasps. She saw the UZI at her feet. She had no idea how to use it. She reached instinctively for it. In one motion she grasped and pointed the weapon at the Russian assassin. Her fingers found the trigger, a burst of fire erupted from the weapon, and it jerked upward out of control. She dropped the gun, the smoke blurred her vision and her eyes filled with tears. Anna bent over, her body racked with sobs. Only rising bubbles remained below.

"Are you all right?" Keith called out.

There was silence from above, but Keith thought she might be crying. After a moment, Anna replied weakly, "I think so."

"You did great, Anna!"

"Oh, Jesus, Keith, I did great? I've never done anything like this before! I just killed three men, and you think that's great? I think it's pretty close to murder, that's what I think," Anna's voice shook.

"OK, OK, I apologize. I'm sorry this had to happen. I'm sorry I got you into this mess, but I'd be grateful if you cut this damn pipe off my foot," said Keith.

It took a couple of minutes for Anna to find a sharp enough rock, climb down to where Keith was hanging, and cut him free.

"I don't know if I'll ever be able to walk on this leg again after what it's been through," Keith said ruefully, as he hobbled out the quarry entrance. Jim was conscious, but barely able to walk. Andrei seemed relieved that the Russians were gone, but he remained quiet.

"We've got to get Jim to the hospital pronto," said Keith, as he limped alongside Jim toward the Blazer. Anna was silent, and Keith was completely exhausted.

NASA LANGLEY RESEARCH CENTER
HAMPTON, VIRGINIA
MONDAY, SEPTEMBER 23

Dan Pedicone shook his head and reluctantly put down his notebook. Then he stretched his arms and yawned deeply while arching his back, all in an effort to fight the urge to fall asleep. With his attention momentarily broken, he thought of his wife Penelope and their young son Danny Junior. Danny was nine months old and growing fast. Already, he had two lower teeth and four upper teeth showing. The upper four had just come in. Their emergence made Danny a very fussy and restless baby. It was a particularly rough time for Penelope because she had to face most of it alone, with Dan spending the better part of the last ten days at the laboratory.

The last time he was home was the morning he turned in the preliminary report to Ron. That afternoon, Colonel Canning and a retired Admiral named Jessel had shown up for a thorough review. That night, the emphasis had shifted from the canister itself to the contents he had carefully pumped out. Dan stifled a yawn, trying to get back to his notebook, but his eyes refused to focus and his handwriting appeared to be just a blur.

Funny how that standard pressure tank had suddenly become so important. The previous week he had practically stumbled over it once or twice while coming or going from his office, never giving it a thought. He remembered he had some trouble getting the vacuum pump to work while evacuating the contents of the black canister. A leak developed, and it appeared as if the contents would be lost, but his technician had replaced a seal and the pump began working perfectly. The contents were pumped into a small pressure cylinder and he had taken it to his office for safekeeping. There it remained until that retired admiral, Jessel, insisted the secret to the purpose of the canister lay in the gas contained inside.

While he was having trouble with the pump and some of the gas was escaping, he remembered the strange fragrance. It was oddly familiar, while mysteriously unique. Later, when he carried the pressure cylinder to his office, he noticed it had become quite warm. He expected it to be warm because most gases give off heat when they are compressed, but this was warmer than usual. Then again, when the gas was exposed to a heavy concentration of ultraviolet light and compressed, as Admiral Jessel suggested, the effect was tenfold. Apparently, a lot of the ultraviolet light energy could be stored temporarily in the strange gas.

Dan had shut his office door to keep the noise of the cleaning crew from disturbing his concentration. Suddenly, there was a knock. He rose stiffly and realized he had been sitting for hours trying to unravel the mystery of the strange gas and its purpose in space.

Opening the door, he was immediately bathed in Ron's tired but happy smile. In one hand he carried two mugs of steaming coffee, and in the other was a bag filled with donuts from their favorite donut shop a mile away. "Good morning, Dan. I thought I would get us a treat. I feel lucky today. The SVR team just reported this morning that they are back on schedule, so, by God, we are going to make it!" said Ron with a jubilant smile.

That was great news, although Dan had hardly given thought to their progress all week, what with all the testing he had personally conducted. Ron was unusually helpful. They had worked around the clock, with each getting three to four hours of sleep whenever there was an opportunity. Under these circumstances, they found they worked together well. Somehow when he was completely fatigued, he found less energy to criticize and more energy to appreciate the assistance from another.

Ron passed Dan a mug of coffee, black as Dan liked it. Then Ron opened the bag, took out a cinnamon donut, passed the bag to Dan, placed his donut over his mug, dunked it into his coffee and took a bite.

"Dan, I have a theory about this stuff and how it works, and I want to try it out on you, OK?"

"OK, since you paid for breakfast, go ahead,"

"One thing that we know about the black tank is the material the Russians used is unique. I don't think they copied it from anyone else, so they probably poured lots of resources into its development. Of all the materials we know of, I'll bet this is the most expensive. Therefore, they would only use it where it had a clear performance advantage, right?" began Ron.

"Sounds good so far. Go on."

"The most obvious advantage is its invisibility to radar. So, you can be sure it would go into their spy satellites."

"Yeah, but we have no record of any such satellites..."

"We don't have any record of anything maybe because they haven't been discovered yet," said Ron.

"Bingo! Because they can make them invisible!"

"That's right. Now why does this black can get the same treatment? Because the Russians don't want us to see it either, that's why. Judging from what Colonel Canning showed us, they had a whole lot of the cans up in space. Probably they had a big delivery vehicle, but something went wrong. Like maybe they had a rocket failure and they all came down to earth at once, not like they were supposed to. Then the Russians, afraid we might get our hands on some of the material, scrambled to recover the remains. They were right to try because that's exactly what happened, we did get our hands on it! Are you with me so far?"

"So far," nodded Dan, sipping his coffee.

"OK, what troubles me is its purpose in space. I've been doing a lot of thinking and now I think I know what it is. Suppose they put up a second vehicle. Yesterday, I got a follow-up call from that Admiral Jessel. You remember, the guy who was here two weeks ago when Colonel Canning showed up? He said they think it has something to do with affecting our weather."

"No, not that old theory again?" asked Dan, obviously disappointed. "Seems every time we or the Russians mount a major space program, some nut accuses us of messing with weather."

"Yeah, that's right. Both sides have been accused of working on weather systems for so long it seems ridiculous, so I had to ask if he was joking. He got considerably worked up and insisted he wasn't. I didn't think the theory had much weight, so I didn't even mention it to you at the time, preferring to wait until you finished the ultraviolet testing."

"I passed that test off as some kind of professional intuition. Why did you suggest it?"

"It wasn't a hunch, but a suggestion from Admiral Jessel. Now, with your results showing the gas' ability to store ultraviolet energy, I felt his theory might have real merit. I suspect the Russians release the gas in the outer atmosphere where it absorbs plenty of energy from ultraviolet light. Then, because it is slightly heavier than air, the gas begins to settle. Settling brings with it compression and that would involve the release of great quantities of heat. I expect the gas would then rise, being buoyed up by the heated surrounding air. It could then again absorb more ultraviolet radiation, cool, and settle. You can see that for a while the process could repeat itself before the gas would dissipate. The rising air heated by the gas could create a low-pressure zone. You know low-pressure systems involve storms, right?"

"Right."

At that moment there was a shrill alarm. Both Dan and Ron recognized the signal for an evacuation. Simultaneously, Ron looked at his watch while Dan glanced at the office clock. At eight a.m. each Monday the evacuation alarm was tested. An announcement on the public address system always preceded such testing, but because Dan's office was in an out-of-the-way location in the back of the building, it couldn't be heard. After both men realized there was no emergency, Ron continued.

"Now for the big IF. If the right conditions exist, could this stuff trigger a tropical depression? That's the question."

"Now hold on, Ron. I agree all the heated air would probably create a local low-pressure area, but it is a big leap from a small local low-pressure area to a full blown storm,"

"I know that full well. I called a meteorologist friend of mine at JFK Space Center and discussed the theory with him for the past three hours. After considerable discussion, he fed the heat dissipation data you acquired yesterday and our best guess of how much of the gas they could deliver into his computer. We then put it all into their tropical storm model and, letting the numbers crunch for about an hour, we came up with a bona fide storm. He's got all the curves coming out now. It goes without saying, but he agrees it would be possible."

"You mean they actually use the gas to create tropical storms?"

"Yeah, just think of it. There is tremendous energy stored in the moist tropical air in the Caribbean this time of year. All it needs is a trigger to get a low-pressure system started and a hurricane begins to build up. Yes, I believe they use the gas to get it started."

"If they repeatedly stimulated the atmosphere, say every hour or so, maybe it might be possible, but it has one problem."

"What's that?"

"Well, it won't work at night, because it relies on absorbing ultraviolet light, and that implies daylight."

"Yes, but I already checked. All the recent storms began early in the morning and gathered immense strength mainly in the first day. That adds more strength to the story. Then at night the storm relies on the heated tropical air to continue till morning."

"You're not implying the Russians have systematically created this year's disastrous east coast hurricanes? Why?"

"Yes, I am, and I think it might be to slow down the deployment of the Global Climate Survey System. Possibly, this isn't the first time the Russians have been messing with weather. After all, it's been rumored for years. Perhaps they have something to hide."

Dan stared at Ron, dumbfounded. The possibility made all too much sense.

"And there's one other thing you'd better check," added Ron gravely.

"What other thing?"

"Jessel says the gas breaks down into chlorine among other things."

Dan remembered the strange fragrance of the gas. A subtle suspicion rose in his mind as to the source of his memory. It smelled a little like the public swimming pool where he once was a lifeguard.

"That could be. I'll check it out immediately,"

"You better hope it doesn't."

"Why?"

"Because if it does, the Russians may have put enough chlorine gas into the outer atmosphere to severely damage the ozone layer."

Dan's whistle was low and slow as the thought made its impact.

• Chapter 11 •

RUSSIAN IKI RESEARCH CENTER
FRIDAY, SEPTEMBER 20

Yuri Lichev, the Russian Defense Minister, entered the spacious office of Arthur Savelin inside the IKI Research Center Central Office Building. It was not customary for Lichev to make calls on subordinates, much less to call at five a.m., but these were unusual circumstances. For several weeks, the treacherous actions of Lebedev had been known. Every possible effort was expended to stop the flow of information before it reached Washington. Fortunately, his good friend General Tuzov warned him of the deteriorating situation before Foreign Minister Savitsky could make use of it.

He had just come from a late night meeting with Chairman Panfilov. There was news from America that they were becoming wise to Soviet tampering with their weather. Given the possibility the Americans might discover the existence of the Russian Harvest Satellite, Panfilov and Lichev agreed the satellite was to be disposed of immediately. This was to be done in an inconspicuous way.

He considered sending a coded message to Savelin, but in view of the sensitivity of the situation, he chose to go immediately himself. It was two hours before dawn when he arrived. He had stopped for some refreshment in the all-night cafeteria at the IKI Research Center to help him keep a clear head before meeting with Savelin.

Savelin had been aroused from deep sleep at his apartment by the phone in the room he affectionately called his den. It was a room that he allowed his wife and children in only on rare occasions. He excused his behavior by saying he kept important state secrets there and it would not do for them to snoop. In fact, he was a collector of books, having many volumes from foreign sources.

At Lichev's request, Savelin departed for the office, knowing he would arrive well before Lichev. The time would not be wasted. Prior to leaving his apartment, he called Ustinov to be sure he would be waiting when he arrived. Savelin suspected something was wrong with the Harvest Satellite program. He didn't know just what, but why else would Lichev want to see him at this time of day? There wasn't any new snow on the road, and the traffic at this early hour was all but non-existent. His driver made good time, almost beating Ustinov who lived close enough to walk.

For the past hour, Ustinov had been briefing Savelin on the progress of the program. So far they had created a succession of five hurricanes, each about two weeks apart. Time was required for the moist tropical air to build up before there would be sufficient stored energy to sustain a tropical depression. Each storm was created in a calculated location where its approach to the American shore would lead to southern Florida. There was considerable difficulty determining the best location. Two of the five storms had missed the Florida coast completely, but the three which hit had had a real effect. The Americans hadn't had but one launch of the space shuttle since the program began.

Finally, Savelin was satisfied. Ustinov was delivering the bad weather just as Defense Minister Lichev wanted. He concluded further trouble with the crisis started by Lebedev was the reason for Lichev's visit. This increased his concern, as it reflected badly on his judgment. It was known that Lebedev was unreliable before he committed this treachery, so why had he been so lenient? Fortunately, in his defense, it could be argued he alerted the authorities. He considered this argument, forgetting it was Ustinov who had arranged to have Lebedev followed. After all, he continued, Lebedev was under observation when his treachery began. The authorities were alerted; they should have caught him in the act. He had done his part. The blame couldn't be put on him.

Savelin took Lichev's hat and coat and hung them in a closet built into the back wall of the office. Lichev sat down heavily in one of the leather-covered seats in front of Savelin's desk. Deep lines showed on his face. Savelin guessed he hadn't gotten any sleep the night before.

"Would you like some tea?" asked Savelin, turning to a pot warming on the shelf behind his desk.

"No, thank you. I've already had some on the way up," replied Lichev, shaking his head.

Savelin took a sip from his cup, waiting for Lichev to speak.

"I regret to inform you that the security of our Harvest Satellite program is in jeopardy," began Lichev.

If Savelin was surprised by the news, his face didn't show it.

"How did this happen?" Savelin asked.

"We have lost contact with our agent in America who was courageously trying to stomp out the evidence which the traitor Lebedev had provided," answered Lichev, looking directly at Savelin.

Internally, Savelin winced. He was well aware Lebedev had confessed everything, including his theft of the security device from the prototype. He didn't feel comfortable knowing the traitor was once one of his closest friends.

"And what is the status of the security device?" asked Savelin.

"Unknown."

"That is indeed bad news."

"Worse yet, we have information that indicates the Americans are fast unravelling the secret of our Harvest Satellite, and may be preparing the security device for use." Lichev wasn't sure of the latter, but it was his gut feeling. "I have just come from the office of Chairman Panfilov. We have agreed you must make the system un-operational and send it into deep space where the Americans can't find it."

Savelin stared at Lichev in shocked silence.

"That's not possible. The system has only small maneuvering rockets, and though we can send it farther out in space, the orbit will decay and the satellite will eventually fall into the atmosphere, spreading its debris as the first system did."

This was a problem Lichev hadn't considered. He had left Panfilov's office assuring him the satellite would shortly be in deep space and safely out of the reach of the Americans. He should have conferred with Savelin first. Now that was impossible. He was committed to disposing of the satellite. He decided to try a different tack.

"Can you send it into the atmosphere so sharply it will burn up?"

"It is possible, but risky. You may remember what happened to the first rocket. We lost control of it in the ionization layer, and for some unknown reason it deployed its canisters before we regained control. I don't advise it. It is better we use all the canisters first, then let the deployment vehicle self-destruct on reentry."

"If I let you continue making storms, how many can you make?" asked Lichev.

"Two, or possibly three, if we are conservative. It all depends on how long we wait between storms," replied Savelin.

"How long will it take to make these storms?"

"We could start soon, but it would take two to four weeks."

"We don't have any time. We need a solution now." In Lichev's mind a different tactic was emerging.

"What if you make one really big storm? Could you dispose of it all?" asked Lichev.

"Oh, yes! But the resulting storm would be so large we couldn't possibly be sure what it would become or where it would go," replied Savelin.

"Never mind that, just dump the whole load! If we get lucky and the storm is really big, it might hit their facilities so hard it will put them out of action until after February. That way we will accomplish our objective," concluded Lichev. "When can you start?"

"The day after tomorrow would be best."

"How about you start the first thing this morning? Considering the time change between here and the Caribbean, that will be in about eight hours. Your people can be done with it this evening."

Savelin considered for a moment. It was not to his liking, but if it ended this embarrassment created by Lebedev and put it safely in the past, then so be it!

"I don't recommend it, and I don't take any responsibility for the results, but if you insist, we will dispose of the satellite's cargo, and on the next pass it will then self-destruct over Siberia," responded Savelin.

"Then let the preparations begin, and be quick about it!" said Lichev as he rose from his seat.

In a moment, Lichev was out of Savelin's office with his hat and coat. As he stepped outside the reception area, he glanced at the sky. There was a faint glow coming from the east, indicating it would soon be sunrise. When he let the door shut behind him and started down the steps in front of the Central Office Building, he suddenly felt very old.

• Chapter 12 •

MARBLE, COLORADO SATURDAY, SEPTEMBER 21,1991

After the events in the quarry near Marble, Keith and Anna rushed Jim to the hospital in Glenwood Springs. The Emergency Room staff immediately examined him. Because a head injury with possible complications was involved, Jim was flown by helicopter to Denver General. The doctors hoped Jim would recover without complications, but the next forty-eight hours would be critical.

Anna had waited patiently while the doctors examined Jim. When they were finished and Jim was on his way, they treated Anna's burn and scratches. An hour later, after receiving several bandages and an ankle brace for Keith, they left.

Outside, Anna faced Keith with tears in her eyes.

"Keith, when we first met, you were so wonderful. My mountain man." She wiped her eyes with a handkerchief. "I loved you completely and without reservation. But this business with Jessel and the Russians is horrible. I'm not used to guns and killing and I don't want any more of it!"

Keith put his arms around Anna and held her tightly for a long time. "I'm sorry, Anna, I really am. But don't worry, we're going to the sheriff. It'll be over soon," Keith soothed.

"Keith, when we finish with the sheriff, I want to go with Vicki to Denver. She needs to be with Jim and I don't want her to go alone," Anna said.

Fifteen minutes after they delivered Andrei to the sheriff's office, Keith called Jessel. His secretary answered, but it took only a few seconds to get the retired Admiral.

"Where the hell you been?" was the initial response. Jessel sounded both surprised and relieved.

In the minutes that followed, Keith explained how Pronin had kidnapped Anna, how they had been held captive by Pronin, the technician Andrei, and two Russian agents, and finally how they had escaped. Now there were only Andrei and the bodies in the quarry.

"Quite a story, Keith. It must have been tough on Anna, but she showed a lot of courage using that UZI."

Jessel filled Keith in on his progress. "We checked out that ozone theory. Lebedev's information about the damaging effects of xzhylene may be correct. The Weather Service has been closely monitoring the ozone layer over the North Atlantic. They found a large tear from the equator north of Bermuda. If the Russians are responsible, and I believe they are, they're just pounding the hell out of it. The president is on the hotline with Moscow now. So far they're denying everything, but the evidence is mounting," Jessel declared.

"Did you find the violin?" asked Keith.

"Yes, the car you left it in was sold to a body shop. We sent a team to Cherry Hill and shook the owner up somewhat, but we got the violin and rushed it to Travis Air Force Base. They are trying to ready some countermeasures at this moment," replied Jessel quietly.

"What are they going to do?"

"Well … I'd rather not say over the phone." Jessel changed the subject, "Could you read Gustav's translation again?"

Keith read the partial message.

When he finished, Jessel asked, "How much of the message remains undeciphered?"

Keith shut his eyes thinking. "It's hard to tell, but I'd guess about a third."

"Did Gustav have any idea what it said?"

"No, not that he mentioned," Keith replied immediately. "I

can only guess, but I'll bet it's important. Everything that preceded it is brief and to the point. I doubt he wasted anything at the end."

"Is there any way you can decode it?"

"Oh, I know how to decode it, but I don't know the piece of music it is derived from. If I had the source, decoding it letter by letter would be easy. Then we'd translate the German into English. But Gustav didn't mention the piece, so I don't know the source. Anyone who did is dead," added Keith.

"So the problem is, we have to find the source. Do you think it's foreign?" Jessel asked slowly.

"Yeah, we'd probably have to search through music books popular in my father's time. That would take forever, not to mention possibly all the music popular before their time," answered Keith.

The phone was silent for a moment while Jessel considered the problem. "I'm not sure about that. Not yet anyway. Let me do some phoning. I'll get back to you in an hour. While I'm doing that I'll have someone in my office get a team up to the quarry to recover the Russians' bodies. Meanwhile, you keep Andrei at the Sheriff's office," instructed Jessel.

"Yes, sir," replied Keith, then laughed at himself. Old habits were hard to break.

Keith explained the events at the quarry to Sheriff John Parker. The sheriff agreed to hold Andrei until Jessel's men arrived. Keith and Anna were free to go. Anna left to accompany Jim's wife to Denver. Jessel phoned Keith and barked instructions to meet him early the next morning at the airport in Colorado Springs. From there, Jessel promised they would have a good shot at decoding the music. Keith was skeptical.

CUBA, THURSDAY, SEPTEMBER 19

Captain Fedor Terehov, Operations Officer, took the cassette from the safe in his office and entered the Operations Control Room. There were three men on duty, each manning a console situated on a raised floor at the front of the room. On the wall there was a modest color display containing a world map with the location of several satellites projected on it. Concentric circles about their location indicated the limits of their transmission capabilities.

The Operations Officer moved closer to the largest console and passed the tape to the Control Officer, Yuri Latovitch, who inserted the streaming tape into the console in front of him. Immediately, the CRT indicated the loading process was in progress.

In a few seconds, the three rows of lights changed from red to green, indicating the console was ready for use. Now the computer under the console began directing the large receiving dish antenna in step with the trajectory of the approaching satellite. He listened to his headset for the first response from the Harvest Satellite. A moment ago, his console computer began transmitting a special numerical sequence that was the access code for the deployment system of the Harvest Satellite. It was at this moment that Latovitch realized he should have relieved himself before the Harvest Satellite made its Caribbean approach. Now the pressure in his bladder was building. There was no time for a break. The console computer would continue to initiate the sequence until the satellite responded. When it did, he had to be at the console.

The access sequence was complicated and did not repeat itself, so as to make access to the Harvest Satellite from hostile forces impossible. Months ago, when the vehicle went aloft, it carried with it a secret set of codes. The code would change to a new one in the sequence every time it was accessed. Unless the sequence was known, the Russians were confident the code couldn't be broken. Latovitch expected a delay of several seconds before he would be online with the vehicle in his complete control. Until then, he could relax for a moment. Once online, he would begin the deployment countdown.

He sat in the Operations Control Room of the modest complex in the base of a mountain in a valley twenty miles southeast of the Cuban port of Mayari. The complex occupied a nickel mine that was abandoned during the Cuban Revolution. The mine was situated in a broad fertile valley that produced sugar at its lower end in the north. Farther south near the mine, the major crop was coffee. The stream that flowed through the valley had its source in the pine forest farther to the south.

Outside the underground complex, the tracking and transmitting antennas were cleverly blended into the existing, but decrepit, buildings and machinery. In early 1982, the Russians obtained permission from the Cuban government to install the advanced electronics outpost. It had a twofold mission: the first to provide surveillance of the American Naval Base at Guantanamo Bay, the second to provide a control station for the Soviet Space Program. Almost overnight the Soviet engineers had an advance team covering the area with camouflage before the earthmoving equipment and machinery arrived. All the work had to be completed without attracting the attention of the American spy satellites.

The first objective for the Soviet engineers was to reestablish the narrow gauge railroad that originally brought the ore down the valley. It was on this railroad all the supplies for the complex would be transported. Next, a large diesel generating station was installed at the base of the hill in what had been the ore loading station for the railroad. This station was to provide power for the complex. Afterward, the mill buildings were literally blasted apart overnight and fiberglass facsimiles built in their place by the following morning. In the months that followed, the engineers erected two large dish antennas under two of the fiberglass buildings. Under a single but larger building near the ridge above the mine, they erected several fully rotational low band antennas. It was these antennas that constantly monitored signals emanating from Guantanamo.

Operations personnel, such as Latovitch—of which there were thirty and the maintenance crew of fifteen—were quartered in the mine complex of tunnels. Their spaces were cramped, poorly ventilated, and infested by a variety of tropical insects. But underground, it was cooler and there were good food, supplies, and entertainment brought by the railroad.

Once a month, Latovitch and several of the operators spent their weekend away, usually in Havana. He and his companions frequented the restaurants, casinos, and the bars. Late nights were spent dancing and drinking heavily.

On several occasions, he had not spent the night alone, but never twice with the same woman. This bothered Latovitch somewhat. After all he had experienced during his five years in the army, he still hadn't become accustomed to this Latin way of life.

Despite the many amenities in the complex and the extra pay for foreign service, Latovitch did not like Cuba. The humid climate, which was often miserably hot and seemed never to change, made his being away from home harder. He was due for rotation back in a few months. Secretly, he counted the days.

Suddenly, there it was! He was online, the green light indicating he could send the preconstructed command from his console computer. By using the fingers of both hands, he deftly switched to the appropriate channel and stroked the keyboard to begin the command transfer. All this was done with little thought because it was the tenth time in the last twelve hours he had deployed a portion of the Harvest Satellite payload. At the bottom of his CRT was a command packet sequence number that decremented as each element of the command was sent. During ideal conditions when reception was good, the sequence took about fifteen seconds. When conditions deteriorated, the decrement was slower. Conditions over the past three days had steadily grown worse, but the transmission was going through, the entire sequence taking perhaps thirty seconds. When it reached zero, the transmission would be complete.

What surprised him was the quantity involved in this operation. In the last three days he had nearly exhausted the supply of xzhylene gas canisters. This revolution would complete that delivery. The command packet sequence number reached zero, indicating the command had been sent. Now he waited for the confirmation message indicating the command had been completely received. While waiting, Latovitch tried to keep his mind off his swelling bladder.

Suddenly, there was a momentary flicker in the lights. The panel before him, which previously showed all green lights, showed a confused array of yellow and red lights, and the CRT was blank. He swore under his breath. This was no time for a momentary loss of power! Someone must have switched power improperly between generators. Idiots! *Don't they know we have an operation in progress?*

Out of the corner of his eye, Latovitch saw the Operations Officer heading for the Maintenance Officer's office. There would be some sharp words there. Interruptions in power were not permitted during these operations, and the maintenance crew was well aware of their responsibility.

Again, he loaded the tape. He advanced the access code by one, and when the console was again green, he began the sequence. Twenty seconds later he was again online. Valuable time had been lost in the interruption. There was barely enough time to send the sequence once to the Harvest Satellite before it would be out of range. It would have to go through with a minimum of retries. Again, the sequence began. Latovitch held his breath. Despite the air conditioning in the control room, Latovitch began to sweat. Again, his deft fingers stroked the keyboard. The command packet sequence number started to decrement at its usual speed, but then slowed. *There must be difficulty in transmission or reception,* thought Latovitch. He glanced at the world map and found the Harvest Satellite. In seconds, it would be out of range! Again, he held his breath as the numbers crept toward zero. Now there were twenty packets to go. He felt helpless, unable to make any adjustments in the computerized operation to improve transmission. Then only ten packets remained. Then five. But the numbers seemed to stop. Then in a sudden burst the last five were transmitted and the received message light was green. Latovitch let out a slow exhale.

Latovitch took off his headset and wiped the perspiration that had accumulated underneath. He had not had a break for the last four hours and felt quite stiff. The pain in his bladder was by now unbearable. He caught the eye of Vitaly Marchenko, who came over and assumed control while Latovitch hastily strode down the hall.

Latovitch made it into the tiled bathroom, pushed the door open with more than enough force, and tore at the zipper of his trousers. Standing in front of the urinal, he was just getting below the threshold of pain aftermath when the lights started to dim.

"Damn the engineers! What the hell's the matter now?" shouted Latovitch.

Outside the bathroom, he could not be heard for all the swearing and groaning. The operations crew was madly switching all the electronics gear off so that when power was restored, it could be protected from power surges until the engineers got the generators under control. Latovitch waited for the lights to come on. They didn't. Instead, the emergency circuit illuminated the minimal emergency lights. Fortunately, one was installed in the bathroom and Latovitch could make his way into the Operations Control Room. There was a shout from down the entrance corridor. Several of the operations' crew left their posts and began heading for the doorway. Latovitch chose to follow.

When the operations crew reached the outside entrance, Latovitch realized it was day outside. But it looked like night. The sky was almost pitch black and there was a very strong wind blowing torrents of water horizontally across the ground. The water was fast collecting and flowing down the hillside. Where it found a weakness, it carved deep ruts in the brown clay and rock of the mine tailings. Farther down, Latovitch could see the river had risen and was overflowing its banks. Latovitch realized it must have been stormy outside for some time. Being inside, he had been protected from the storm's effects. Now he could see the problem that the engineers were battling. The river had entered the generator room at the bottom of the hill. Several of the engineers were inside the building waving their arms. Latovitch realized they were trapped!

"Hurry! We must help them, or they will be swept away!" shouted Latovitch, as he sprang through the door at the mine exit and began running down the hillside.

Several other personnel, Vitaly Marchenko among them, followed suit. They were all sliding and struggling to keep their balance on the slippery clay as the wind blew relentlessly, threatening to knock them down at any moment.

Latovitch reached the muddy water's edge. He looked across

the ever-widening gulf between the new shore and the generator building. The water was a dark and evil brown with an abundance of debris floating about and rising rapidly. Latovitch guessed it was a meter deep at the most between where he stood and the generator building. The trouble was that the water was moving rapidly, too rapidly to make the transit for the generator crew safe. Three men stood clinging to the railing leading from the doorway into the dark water. Latovitch recognized them all. Each was a good man. Their leader, Chief Antonofsky, a tall and somewhat overweight electrician, was trying to rig a line from a discarded electrical cable. The other two were eager to try their luck with the water. Only the experience of their chief kept them from plunging headlong into the water. Somehow, Chief Antonofsky knew the water would be treacherous, despite its shallow appearance. Latovitch watched the rising waters and thought the Chief was right.

"Come! We must make a human chain!" shouted Latovitch.

Latovitch grabbed the hand of Marchenko and started out into the water. Marchenko grabbed the hand of the man next to him, and so it went until all five men on the shore were strung out across the water.

"Grab my wrist and I'll do the same!" shouted Marchenko.

By grasping each other's wrists, they doubled the strength between the two men. Latovitch was now almost ten feet from shore, finding the current very strong. There was very little time.

"Throw the cable quickly!" shouted Latovitch to Chief Antonofsky.

The chief made a wide circle out of the cable and, while still hanging on to the railing with his left hand, placed one cable end in his mouth and tossed the rest of the coil in the direction of Latovitch. The coil fell short and was caught by the current, almost tearing the other end out of the chief's mouth.

Chief Antonofsky grabbed the cable with his free hand and readied the coil again. The water continued its rise. The railing was beginning to submerge. Soon, Chief Antonofsky would have to retreat inside the building. Latovitch was beginning to lose his balance. The water was tearing the loose tailings from around and under his feet. Latovitch could see others leaving the mine entrance to join in the human chain, but he realized they would be too late.

Chief Antonofsky wrapped his legs around the railing and prepared for a final desperate toss. This time, he held the free end in his left hand. The chief let out a loud grunt and tossed the cable high in the air. The coil unwound in mid-air, the far end sailing over Latovitch's head, but he was able to grab it with his free hand before it disappeared into the swirling water. Latovitch wrapped the cable around his left arm while he tightened his grip on Marchenko's wrist.

"Tie your end off to the railing and start coming across one at a time," shouted Latovitch.

Quickly, Chief Antonofsky tied the end and began helping the first man to cross. Latovitch was appalled by the sudden strain on the cable. His fingernails dug into the flesh of Marchenko. Marchenko's fingernails did the same. Each man groaned under the strain. Slowly, the first man half crawled and half swam across the gap. When he reached Latovitch, he released the cable and groped his way past each man until he reached shore.

The second man started across. Again, each man in the human chain groaned under the strain. He made his way across hand-over-hand. The wind was rising again and the rain drove hard before it. Latovitch turned his face away from its force. The second man was making his way past Latovitch. Somewhere upstream, there was a low crunching sound, barely audible above the sound of the wind and rain.

Now it was Chief Antonofsky's turn. Latovitch anticipated the strain would be great, due to the chief's bulk, but he was surprised by its actual magnitude. The water tore at the chief's clothes, increasing the effect of his bulk. Latovitch's grip was slipping on Marchenko's wrist. The sound from upstream grew louder. Latovitch shot a glance in the direction of its source. To his horror, he saw a large tree had broken off and was sliding along in the river and twisting as its limbs snagged on the bottom.

"Quickly, a tree!" screamed Latovitch.

Chief Antonofsky saw the danger and began to move with surprising speed. In seconds, he reached Latovitch, but the tree was fast approaching. The chief was behind Marchenko when the tree passed Latovitch.

No one observed exactly what happened next. The official report listed it as a freak accident. Somehow, as the outstretched limbs of the tree passed Latovitch, his leg must have been entangled in the branches of a submerged limb. Before Latovitch could react, he was swept away from Marchenko. Latovitch subsequently freed himself from the tree and, being a good swimmer, began frantically stroking his way toward shore. Getting there required swimming along with the current for some distance. Unfortunately, the railroad bed, which served to channel the rising water, had three underpasses downstream of the generation station. It was underneath the second of these underpasses that Latovitch was swept.

Days later, his lifeless body was found among the twisted debris. Latovitch was one of two Russians who lost his life in Hurricane Gail. The second was a sailor who fell overboard shortly after midnight from a trawler trying to outrun the storm.

COLORADO SPRINGS, THURSDAY, SEPTEMBER 19

Bright and early in the morning under clear skies, Keith met Jessel's plane. Jessel was not alone. Keith was introduced to Jeb Wilson who, he soon learned, worked for The Radio Company of America. Jeb was on loan to the Smithsonian Institution heading a three-year project in musical history. After introductions, they moved immediately to the military complex, NORAD.

On the way across town, Jessel explained the plan was to search through an immense music file that Jeb's project had assembled. This file was so vast it nearly encompassed all the music man had devised since the dawn of creation. The plan was to use computers to search through the massive file. Keith doubted Jessel's confidence at first. After all, wasn't it an impossible job? All the music on file would have to be entered into the computer.

How many years could that take? Jeb produced a volume of eleven compact digital discs.

"This is the latest in CDROM technology. Trust me, a lot of people worked a long time to input a heck of a lot of sheet music. The team just completed this set and, believe me, there are literally millions of works on these discs. It is truly an international musical history pressed on the latest technology," boasted Jeb, holding one of the discs up in the sunlight.

Keith was amazed by their miniature size and high density. He also noted the colored patterns generated when sunlight passed through the translucent discs. He began to suspect there was a possibility the right music could be found.

NORAD is located deep inside Cheyenne Mountain on the outskirts of Colorado Springs. It is intended to be the central location for American Military Command in the event of nuclear war. To be secure, it was designed to withstand a direct nuclear hit. To that end, it is located a mile deep underground.

In order to gather, assemble, and display the collective information gained by all the satellite, geo-sensors and air and surface search radars in the American defense system, a large computer complex was created. With it was installed the largest uninterruptable power supply in the world. Situated at the center of the computer complex are two super-cooled computers. Their raw horsepower probably measures in the very high megaflops/second numbers, but their specifications are a classified secret. In order to channel and organize information flow to these central computers, a large array of 32 bit mainframe computers was installed. In the room above, known as the "War Room", an elaborate assortment of electronic image processors convert the computer information generated from below into three world status displays, which are projected on three walls in front of the "War Desk".

For obvious reasons, more computing power is available in the complex than is used on any given day. To assist in making excess capacity available for defense-related work, the military planners provided a Special Applications Room with a variety of input and output devices.

Keith, Jeb, and Admiral Jessel found themselves a long way from the surface in the midst of a sizable collection of consoles, plotters, disk and tape drives, and video displays. The task they presented for the computer complex was simple in concept yet the operations were so redundant that it gobbled computer capacity.

Though the job might be large in scope, it was not difficult for Jessel to find the right experts and arrange for them to meet at NORAD. Five professionals were waiting when they arrived. Each man and woman was an expert in the use of the software and systems available at NORAD. Keith was amazed Jessel could arrange for such expertise on short notice.

Forty-five minutes later, they had assembled the necessary hardware and software to read the discs. Next, a searching algorithm was developed to compare the music provided by Lebedev against each piece of sheet music stored on the digital discs. When near-matches were discovered between two pieces of music, the differences were tabulated and decoded by the same method Gustav had explained a week before. All of this was done by software.

The team leader, Chief Robin Martinson, took the time to explain to Keith how they used a high level language very much like English to generate the software.

"The neat thing is, most of the work can be done in parallel using our mainframes. That will greatly speed the process. Each mainframe will be assigned a part of the music data. Once a partial match is identified by one of the mainframe computers, we can use the translation scheme you described to get the old German dialect. Then we can directly convert the German into English using our universal language translator. Everything is automatic. All you have to do is wait," said Robin enthusiastically.

Keith was amazed by the technology. Even Jessel seemed impressed. After the discs were read and the data stored in NORAD's incredibly large storage bank, the search process began. The team immediately crowded around the console, waiting for the results.

Unfortunately, most of the day was spent waiting. Every five minutes or so a possible match would flash on the console, but when translated into English, the messages appeared meaningless.

Eventually, Keith, Jeb, and Jessel retired to the break room outside the Special Applications Area. There, they studied printouts of the last twenty possible messages hoping to find some clue. The appearance of Communications Specialist Abrams suddenly broke their concentration.

"Sir, I have a message from Travis," said Abrams, passing an envelope to Jessel.

Jessel opened the envelope, read it, and frowned.

"Well, let's have it," said Keith.

"Bad news. The Air Force attempted to locate the Russian Weather Machine at the orbit coordinates you got from Lebedev."

Jessel lowered his voice and leaned forward before continuing. "They deployed the anti-satellite system we aren't supposed to have anymore. The shot went off perfectly. Although the security device you recovered appeared to function flawlessly, it failed to make contact with its Russian target. After a brief period in space, the rocket fell into the atmosphere and burned up. I'm sorry, but that's it. Without the security device, we won't get a second chance. The Russians are probably wise to us and have moved their weather machine by now anyway," whispered Jessel.

Abrams had started to leave, then abruptly turned back. "Sir, I thought you should know, there's a new tropical depression building up rapidly southeast of Cuba. This one could be epic! The winds are already at hurricane force and intensifying rapidly."

Jessel and Keith looked at each other. Both felt the impact of the news simultaneously.

"From what we know about the destructive after-effects of this Russian weather system, my guess is we might be witnessing the end of the world's protective ozone layer," said Jessel gravely.

Both men understood the importance of the ozone layer. Its primary benefit is to shield earth-bound occupants from the harmful effects of ultraviolet radiation. Without the protection of the layer, many species of plant and animal life would be threatened. The total effect could not be completely estimated, but certainly without it the world would change for the worse.

"The prospect is really bleak," agreed Keith. After a pause he continued. "Let's hope the rest of Lebedev's music offers some hope. Otherwise, the world as we know it may well be history."

"Well, there's not much we can do with these old printouts. Let's go back to the Applications Room," suggested Jessel.

They returned, gathered around the laser printer, and waited for more output. From time to time, a garbled message would flash on the console. Each time the result would also be printed. Each printout was examined carefully in the hope some sense could be made of it. For a long time, nothing proved worthwhile. The boredom was getting to Keith, and he was beginning to suspect he was right to believe decoding Lebedev's music to be an impossible task. It was approaching 1600.

"I hate to be a party pooper but we're about to have a shift change. At 1600 each day we do a system backup. That means we'll shortly be out of business for about two hours," said Robin.

Keith groaned in disappointment when there was a flash on the console. At first, it seemed to be only another decoded message with the usual gibberish. But the letters split into words, and then the words, translated into English. Suddenly, the printer came to life. Keith grabbed the output and read it.

IF ALL ELSE FAILS. THE BREAK DOWN INTO CHLORINE FROM XZHYLENE CAN BE COUNTERACTED BY SPREADING PULVERIZED ESTER OF SODIUM AT 20000 METERS IN THE VICINITY OF THE STORM'S CENTER. FORMULA FOR COMPLEX ESTER FOLLOWS;

Keith's limited chemical background wasn't much help with the brief text that followed. He passed the printout to Jessel. The retired Admiral looked at it for a moment. His eyes squinted slightly, and he lapsed into thought for a second, sitting back in his chair.

"I think I'd better get on the phone. There might be a way to get some of this stuff, and it better be in a big hurry!" said Jessel, picking up the Applications Room phone.

MONDAY, SEPTEMBER 23

Admiral Jessel hadn't had but two hours sleep in the last thirty-six hours. Most of the time was spent on the phone trying to locate a supplier with the right expertise and materials available. After a slow start, Jessel was beginning to make progress. He had contacted the White House to brief the president on their success in decoding Lebedev's message.

The complicated job of finding the resources to produce and transport the chemical compound to the storm center had begun. It was a long and fruitless search, until they discovered a small chemical company in Mississippi. Keith had helped make calls when he could, and get sandwiches and coffee for the group. Next, Jessel chose the transport facilities at Dover Air Force base.

"Why are you using Dover and not the Cape? We could use the space shuttle and deliver a larger payload," suggested Keith.

"First of all, we don't need that much altitude. That tidbit of information we got from the boys at Langley. They're the folks who developed the model for the Russian Xzhylene system. Although they continue to refine their model, they believe the optimum altitude is fifty thousand feet. Dover has transport planes capable of delivering the stuff, so they were the logical choice," replied Jessel.

"But aren't they a little out of the way?"

"It might not be apparent a mile below ground in Colorado, but there is a monster hurricane approaching Florida. It will hit Cuba tonight and may kill several thousand people. After skimming by the north shore of Cuba, the weather boys think it will pick up again over the water. No airport within four hundred miles of the storm is open. By using Dover, the transport planes can get airborne before they enter the storm and climb over it."

Keith remembered his conversation with the pilot Tom Jackson. He didn't envy the pilots who were to fly over the storm.

"We're hoping to get the compound in the air during the next twelve hours. Let's hope we do," concluded Jessel.

That afternoon, Keith called Denver General. It took him a good half hour to track Anna down. She sounded far away on the phone. Jim was doing better and would soon be out of ICU. When he tried to fill her in on their progress, she interrupted.

"Keith, I'm sorry, but I don't want to think about what happened right now. I'm having trouble rationalizing what I did back in the quarry. I don't want things to be as they are. I want things to be as they were," Anna began in a quiet voice.

Keith was caught short. He had only been thinking of himself. "OK, Anna, you're right. I'm sorry."

"I don't want you to be sorry. I just need you with me. Can you come here?" Anna's voice was strained.

"Right now there is something I have to do, but I can be there this evening," Keith promised.

Anna was disappointed, but she tried not to show it. "OK, I'll be waiting."

Keith hung up, and twenty minutes later he left NORAD and headed west at high speed. There was one thing he had to find out for sure.

FOUR HOURS LATER, YULE MARBLE QUARRY

Water was pouring out of portable pumps, one at each of the three entrances. It was clear and very cold. Inside it remained cold enough for ice to form year around. Keith knew it would make exploration of the many tunnels treacherous. Below, men were spreading sand on the ice as they explored each tunnel. The process was safe, but slow. Keith asked one of the operators who was refueling a pump where the team leader was. He pointed to the middle entrance.

"You'll find him inside one of the tunnels to the left," he said, and went back to work.

Keith climbed down from the entrance. He passed the remains of the platform that had collapsed before they saw the last of Pronin. In contrast to his last visit where there once was only a single lamp, there now were dozens of lighting circuits feeding power to temporary lights strung throughout the tunnels. Keith found the team leader in a side tunnel studying a blueprint from the county engineer's office taped on the marble wall. The print was brown with age. As Keith approached, he looked in his direction.

"Ah, you must be Keith Maddox. I'm Doug Landon. We've been expecting you," he said.

"Hello," said Keith, offering his hand. "Had any luck?"

"We found the first two agents you described right away, but not one you described as their leader. Every hour or so the water lowers enough to explore another tunnel, but we haven't found any sign of him. You know, there are so many small openings and fissures with so much water coming in, we may never be able to get all the water out."

The possibility that Pronin's body might not be found did not sit well with Keith.

Keith reluctantly left the tunnel. He went out the middle entrance and descended the path toward the parking lot. The trail passed an immense mound of marble rubble and then rounded a curve by Yule Creek.

Keith's eyes left the entrance above and, as he lowered his gaze to the trail below, a dark shadow caught his attention. A fat brown marmot scurried and disappeared under a rock.

Keith moved closer to the rock wall. Was there an opening where the marmot had disappeared? As he got closer, he could make out the entrance to a very low passage. Bending down, he prepared to enter.

Keith knew too well how easily old tunnels collapse. This tunnel was indeed low, and carved out of solid rock. Crawling soon became difficult. There were no rotten support timbers because they weren't needed. After venturing forward about twenty feet, the tunnel appeared lighter ahead. Soon, Keith could clearly see light at an opening ahead. Suddenly, the tunnel burst through the rock wall and into the quarry works. Keith stood on the small ledge and looked around. At the edge there was a chunk of ice. He must be just above the original level of the water! He looked carefully around his feet. There was a small brown patch to his right. Was it a smear of blood? He couldn't be sure. Keith shouted for Doug. His head appeared at the end of the tunnel that led to his makeshift office.

"Have you explored this tunnel?" asked Keith.

There was a momentary silence from above. Doug moved to a better vantage point where he could see Keith.

"What tunnel?"

"This tunnel," replied Keith pointing to the opening through which he had just come.

"No ... We hadn't seen it. I'll get someone right away."

"This one leads to the outside and, there is a brown stain here. You better get someone to look at it." Doug disappeared. Keith returned through the tunnel to the entrance.

Outside, Doug and one of his men met them, and together they crawled back. Doug's assistant examined the brown patch for a moment and then began collecting a sample. Keith crawled back out to the Colorado sun.

A shout from the parking lot startled him. He recognized Wade Ericson, the owner of the Marble General Store. Wade was waving his arms as he came up the path. Keith hurried down the rocky slope to the wooden bridge.

"Some fellow named Jessel's on the phone. He says it's mighty urgent!" shouted Wade excitedly.

It took twenty minutes to reach the store in his Jeep. The dust stirred up by Wade's Blazer made breathing difficult all the way. Jessel was still on the line when he picked up the phone.

"We got real troubles here, Keith. There's a deadline we have to meet to still have any effect with the compound. The people at Langley say we've got ten hours. The only people who manufacture the compound are in Pascagoula, Mississippi. The problem is, the stuff won't be ready until about three hours before it must be delivered to the storm center. Worse yet, the delivery aircraft must be modified to spread a thin dusting of the compound. Neither the Air Force, Army, or the Navy has such an apparatus readily available. What we need is a good short runway aircraft with the proper dispersion system installed. You've got it."

"Got what?"

"You've got a rebuilt Lear 35 modified to seed clouds."

Keith was surprised. He had never mentioned Marty's pet project to Jessel. How had Jessel learned? It seemed he knew everything.

"How do you know that?"

"Never mind how I know. I just know." There was a wicked chuckle from Jessel's end. "Can it fly?"

"Sure, but there must be better options."

"No, we've investigated several scenarios, like using helicopters, but we either can't get them there fast enough, aren't equipped properly, or we will probably lose them in the storm. You're our best chance. I assume you want to try?"

"You had to ask?"

"It seemed only the right thing to do."

Keith knew it would come to this. He had never refused Jessel before. Now was no time to start.

"So where do I pick up the stuff?"

"First things first. I want you to pick up an application pulverizer at Fort Riley, Kansas. I'm having them modify the apparatus to fit the specifications of your aircraft."

Keith realized Jessel just assumed he would volunteer. His having ordered the modifications proved it.

"Next, proceed to Pascagoula and pick up two tons of the compound. It will be in sealed drums under oil. How long before you can be airborne?"

"In about an hour. It will take a half hour to get out of the mountains, and if I remember correctly, about an hour to get to Fort Riley," said Keith.

Suddenly, he wasn't so sure of the idea. What was it Tom Jackson had said about flying into the center of the storm? Wasn't he crazy to take an old refurbished Lear 35 into it? And then another thought struck him, could he fly the plane with his ankle in a brace?

"There is one other thing I'll need."

"What's that?"

"Well, I probably can get my partner, Marty, to operate the seeding equipment. He's in Denver. I can pick him up on the way,

342

but when we start seeding, I'll need a copilot. Marty will have to operate the equipment. The guy I would like most is with the weather service. His name is Tom Jackson. I met him in Bermuda. He's been flying into these storms for years. If anybody knows how to get in and out of one of those babies, he does."

"I'll look into it. He might be available. Is there anything else?"

Somehow, Keith had a feeling Tom would be joining them. Could anyone resist Jessel's persuasive ways?

"No. I'll call you from Fort Riley if I do."

"Fine, good luck and good flying!"

Keith hung up. The airport at Aspen was an hour away. Surprisingly, the Lear 35 was waiting when he arrived. Steve Lawton, a new pilot, was completing the pre-flight check. Keith climbed aboard.

"Hey, Keith, what's going on? Some guy called me an hour ago, asking about the plane with cloud seeding equipment. Then he tells me the U.S. government wants it for a few days and that you're on your way over."

"That's right, Steve. We're working for Uncle Sam now. I'll need you to fly to Denver with me to pick up Marty. Then you can return on one of our charters or stay the night in Denver."

Steve requested and received clearance to Denver and a few minutes later they were airborne and climbing sharply. Once above fifteen thousand feet Keith dropped the right wing and swung the Lear east, headed for Denver.

Marty was another story. He was still dealing with the aftermath of Keith's Austrian visit. He was direct and to the point when Keith arrived.

"Jesus, Keith, what a hell of a mess you left me! The Cessna was impounded in Israel. I still don't have the vaguest idea why they ever let us have it back. Do you know what jet fuel costs in Israel? Next time you want to borrow one of the company planes, why don't you bring it back yourself! You can face the flak from the FAA too! If we operate like this, we'll get our license pulled, dammit!"

Throughout Marty's onslaught, Keith kept smiling. Finally, Marty calmed down. It took Keith ten minutes to convince Marty he was serious about needing the Lear 35, but after he confirmed the U. S. Government was paying, he agreed to accompany Keith to Fort Riley.

Keith had to make one phone call. He closed the door to the company office and dialed the hotel where Anna was staying. Two rings later Anna answered, "Hello?"

"It's Keith. I'm in Denver, but I can't come over, I've got some flying to do."

"What do you mean? I thought we had a date," said Anna.

"Anna, there's no other place I'd rather be, but this is very important! I've got to try to stop the hurricane from ruining the ozone layer."

"Do you know how crazy that sounds? Don't tell me you're going to fly in that storm!" exclaimed Anna.

"I know, but yes, I am," Keith conceded.

"You're crazy. This is no business of yours. Why don't you let Jessel do his own work? Why are you so anxious to jump at his every request?"

"You don't understand, do you? Jessel once saved my life. I'm indebted to him and like it or not, I'm flying!" retorted Keith.

"OK, then you've made your choice. When you're done don't come looking for me here. I've had enough. I'm going home to New York," Anna said, sobbing into the phone.

"I'm sorry, Anna. I really am." Keith hung up the phone, turned the office light out and shut the door.

During the flight, Keith had time to explain the Russian system and how they were attempting to remedy the ozone situation. Marty was somewhat skeptical, to say the least.

An hour later in a remote hangar at Fort Riley, a team of army engineers was waiting with a pulverizing mill modified to fit inside the Lear's small cargo compartment. The team attacked the job the moment they arrived. Marty was impressed by the speed with which they installed the apparatus, and said so.

"OK, Keith, up until now I suspected all this ozone stuff was the product of you and your old Navy buddies' overactive imagination. After watching the Army at work, I can see they take it seriously. So ... I'm beginning to believe it too!"

"Good, now we'd better find out how to operate this equipment, because you're going to have to use it."

The operation of the mill was quite simple, as Staff Sergeant Miller explained; the compound was to be fed into the upper hopper, then the pulverized output was to be fed into the cloud seeding apparatus. The pulverized material was pumped through tubing in the wings and out the nozzles; and the rate of pumping would be slower but similar to the cloud seeding compounds they were familiar with. There was one thing that Miller hadn't explained, and that was how volatile the sodium compound would prove to be. That would be learned in Pascagoula.

TWO HOURS LATER

The sky was dark and ominous, with strong, gusting winds and low clouds scudding close to the horizon. The runway was wet and there was a ten knot crosswind when Keith brought the Lear 35 in for a landing at the airport in Pascagoula. His landing was not perfect. At the last second, he felt the Lear lose lift and drop suddenly on its left landing gear. After an awkward bounce and a negative comment from Marty, he brought the jet down smoothly and taxied to the hangar.

Jessel was waiting with a team of chemical technicians when they arrived. Keith parked the Lear 35 just inside a modest hangar. Jessel was first to enter the Lear when Keith opened the door. Keith introduced Marty. They left the plane to the technicians.

In the corner of the warehouse were twenty drums each with a brightly colored label. The technicians immediately began to move the drums into the cabin.

Inside the hangar, Jessel introduced Keith and Marty to Bill Smith who worked for the chemical firm that produced the compound. Bill was short with gray hair, a weathered face, and had a dead-serious manner. His face showed concern as he watched the technicians move the drums. Bill was not one to beat around the bush.

"This stuff is stable inside the sealed drums; that's because they're sealed and the compound is under oil. But open them up, pour the oil off and expose the compound to moisture, and you'll have one hell of a fire. The idea is to have the sodium absorb the chlorine produced by the Russian gas system. When it does, it forms table salt, which is pretty much harmless. It'll do that just fine, but it also likes to absorb water. When it does, it releases hydrogen gas. I don't have to tell you the dangers involved with hydrogen."

He didn't. They all had precise visions of the small cabin in the Lear turning into an inferno.

"Well, how the hell can we use this stuff? It's more like a bomb than an antidote!" said Keith.

Keith could see Marty turning white as a sheet. An uneasy feeling rose in his stomach. Even Jessel appeared somewhat dubious.

"Fortunately, it's not as bad as metallic sodium. For one thing you couldn't pulverize metallic sodium. For another, metallic sodium will self-ignite in free air. This stuff is partially stabilized and will pulverize in the mill the Army has provided. The trick will be to keep the relative humidity below fifty percent."

"That's impossible. We're supposed to drop this stuff into the middle of a hurricane! The whole storm is one big mass of humid tropical air. How can we find dry air in that?" asked Keith.

"Precisely where you're going. At fifty thousand feet in the storm's center, the humidity should be below fifty percent. We're providing you with a means to measure humidity. All you need to do is to wait till it drops below fifty percent before you start seeding. After you do that, you're committed. You must disperse all the compound before you enter moist air again. If you don't, it will burn by itself," replied Bill.

"And us too, I suppose," said Marty.

"I'm afraid so. This stuff just doesn't mix with water. I wish there were an alternative. I'm sorry there isn't."

Marty looked at Keith. Obviously, he didn't like the situation. He next looked at Jessel.

"Keith tells me there isn't any other aircraft available that can deliver this stuff. Is that really true, or did Keith volunteer us?"

"We can't just kick this stuff out the door of some aircraft. It has to be spread in a fine cloud. As I told Keith a couple of hours ago, we don't have any such aircraft in either the Air Force, Army or Navy. Certainly not one modified as yours is, for cloud seeding. It happens you fellows have just the right equipment. In addition, since Keith has been involved with this crisis from the beginning, we don't have to go into any lengthy explanation. We could use other civilian contractors, but by the time we finished explaining the situation it would be too late. Now, Marty, you don't have to go. We have several technicians who have volunteered, but if you do go, we can save time by not waiting for you to show them how to use the equipment."

Marty considered Jessel's remark for a moment, then turned to Keith.

"I assume you're in, Keith?"

"Yes, I'm in."

"OK, partner, you stood by me when I needed you. I owe you one. If you're in, I'm in!" said Marty.

Jessel interrupted.

"There's one other thing. Until we choose to go public on this story, the whole mission is secret. Is that understood?"

Both Keith and Marty nodded in agreement.

The technicians were about finished loading the drums. The last item aboard was an empty container into which the oil would be poured. Soon, they would refuel the Lear and be ready for takeoff. At that moment, a gray pickup truck with U.S. Navy written on its right door pulled up in front of the hangar. A tall man wearing a flight jacket got out. A moment later, Keith recognized Tom Jackson. The small group moved forward to welcome the weather pilot.

"Tom," began Keith, "Two weeks ago we met in the pilots' lounge in Bermuda."

"I ought to remember! Aren't you the guy who requested me for this job?"

"Yes, I thought of you because your background was ideal. I'd like you to meet my partner, Marty, and my former boss, Admiral retired Robert Jessel."

Tom shook hands with Marty, then faced Jessel.

"You don't have to introduce this guy," said Tom. "I met him a half hour ago. He twisted my boss's arm real hard. That's why I'm here. That's aside from the fact I've suspected something was very peculiar about these crazy storms. Now we know why."

"Tom was fully briefed on the mission before you arrived," said Jessel.

"Yes, I heard the story. Believe me, I had second thoughts about this stuff, but the consequences of doing nothing are too severe. If there is any chance we can stop it, we've got to try," said Tom.

"You don't have to sell us on that. We already decided we're in," said Keith.

"Good," said Tom. "Do you have any survival gear aboard in case we have to ditch?"

Keith and Marty looked at each other. They hadn't considered ditching.

"No, we don't," replied Keith honestly.

"Well, that's OK. I assumed you might not. so I've got a raft and survival kit in the truck. Let's get it aboard," suggested Tom.

In a few minutes, they got Tom's gear aboard and the refueling was finished. There was barely room for Marty to sit due to the equipment, survival gear, and drums of compound inside the stripped cabin of the Lear 35. Keith took the copilot's seat.

"Tom, you drive. My ankle is sprained. You can fly her better than I if things get rough. I'll take her off and you can fly her from then on. You're more experienced with this kind of flying than I am anyway. Besides, when we get into the storm's center, I'll have to help Marty with the equipment."

Jessel took a moment to wish the crew the best of luck, shaking the hand of each man. Then he made his way toward the door. He paused, reluctant to leave. "Seems like we've parted like this before, Keith. I'll be on the edge of my seat till we hear you are safely out of the storm. Good luck."

From old habit, Jessel saluted the crew, and then left. Marty closed the door behind him.

Keith went over his checklist as he started the engines. He contacted the control tower for clearance, then called the flight service station for the latest weather report.

SUDDEN STORM

Hurricane Gail was seventy-five miles south of Fort Myers on the Florida Gulf Coast and heading north at fifteen knots. Winds were at 180 miles and intensifying after lashing the Cuban coast. Keith looked at Tom. The outlook was grim.

Jessel walked back to the hangar. His thoughts were with the crew. It's easier aboard taking the chances than waiting in the pilots' lounge, he thought. Behind him he heard the roar of the jet as Keith taxied out to the runway. The wind was strengthening and there was a light rain. To the east, the sky was getting dark.

As he opened the main door to the hangar, there was a flash from lightning, followed by a roll of thunder.

Inside, Jessel made his way toward the lounge. At least they could communicate with Keith as the crew approached the storm center.

Neither the crew of the Lear 35, nor any of Jessel's men noticed the van parked just outside the airport gate as the jet passed by. Had they noticed, they would have seen the Channel 35 news vehicle with its video recorders running. The reporters were acting on a tip from one of the base technicians who had the habit of talking too much after drinks in a local bar.

THREE HOURS LATER

Although he expected the worst, Keith was surprised by the immensity of hurricane Gail. Weather conditions for their takeoff at Pascagoula were marginal at best. Once airborne, Keith gave control to Tom.

Tom was a seasoned pilot. This was not his first time in a Lear 35 either. Five years ago, while on temporary assignment in the Pacific, he had logged about fifty hours. Keith was much relieved and felt confident Tom could handle the plane in almost any situation.

Tom requested clearance and climbed to thirty-eight thousand feet for their approach on Gail. By doing so, they were above the severe headwinds found at lower altitudes. As they progressed, the storm clouds grew denser and more imposing. What really impressed Keith was the ominous black clouds that towered above forty thousand feet near the eye of the storm. He had never observed such lofty thunderheads. Caught by the setting sun, the scene was artistically impressive.

"Must be some effect from the Russian system pulling the warm humid air farther up than normal. Whatever it is, it also increases the incidence of lightning," said Tom.

They both studied the electrical light show. Internal to the massive vortex of swirling black clouds was the almost constant flicker of white-hot lightning.

"How far from us is the storm's eye?" asked Tom.

Keith was acting as navigator. He checked the weather radar for a moment and then looked over the charts.

"About seventy miles due east," he replied.

"Our immediate problem is that black mass of clouds just outside the eye. It might be calm inside, but it's tricky getting there."

Suddenly, the Lear dropped altitude and slid to the left. There was a sharp crash, followed by a groan in the back of the cabin. Tom reacted quickly and brought the plane back to level. From the back came a shout over the noise of the engines.

"Hey! How 'bout a little warning! I'm getting bashed by these damn drums every time you hit a downdraft!" called Marty.

"You better tie everything down back there. We have to get over the wall to get inside this bugger. It's not going to be a pleasant ride!" shouted Tom.

Keith headed aft to help Marty tie things down. They found a rope in the survival gear. In a few minutes they had things fairly well secured. It was then they noticed one of the drums was leaking.

"Hey, Tom, do you remember what that chemist fellow said about this oil? Was it flammable?" asked Keith.

"I don't remember him saying anything about it. I'm on the radio now. Should get an answer soon," replied Tom.

Keith and Marty placed the leaking drum in an empty container. For the time being, the problem was under control.

"Sorry, guys. The oil is flammable, kind of like kerosene. They say be careful with it."

Keith shot Marty a glance. Great, now all they needed was for the compound to catch fire.

SUDDEN STORM

"You'd better get up here, Keith, and Marty better tie himself down! We're about to go over the wall!" shouted Tom.

Keith hurried forward and strapped himself in the copilot's seat. Ahead and somewhat below them towered the massive cloud formation that comprised the outer ring of Gail's center.

"If we were ten thousand feet lower, I doubt we could make it. The hail and lightning are so intense there that you either get struck till all your electronics gear goes or you lose the windshield. Believe me, I know! I only tried once. I won't try again. Fortunately, with this baby we can climb above it and just sail over the top into the center," said Tom.

Keith could see the dark clouds illuminated internally by frequent streaks of lightning. For a moment, he felt a shiver go up his spine by the thought of such turbulence. The clouds below seemed to reach up as if to grab the Lear and pull it down, but the plane was clearly going over the top.

They were hit by a driving updraft. Keith felt his buttocks hit bottom in the seat cushion. "Hang on, after the updraft comes a real bummer downdraft!" shouted Tom.

Sure enough, as suddenly as the updraft hit, it quit and the Lear leveled off in relatively calm air.

"Get ready," said Tom, gritting his teeth.

At first nothing happened and then the Lear dipped and, with roller coaster acceleration, dove downward. Tom struggled to keep the nose up. Behind them, Keith could hear Marty struggling with the cargo. Beneath them, the swirling clouds were coming closer. Tom brought the nose of the Lear up, and in a few seconds they were in the clear with the wall of the storm behind them. They were in the eerie calm of the center of hurricane Gail.

"Keep her in a circle at forty thousand feet while I check the humidity," said Keith as he unbuckled himself and went aft.

Keith switched on the electronic hygrometer. Back at the hangar in Pascagoula, he was not surprised to learn the system relied on the same old principle of a wet bulb and a dry bulb thermometer. Bill Smith had said the only difference with this equipment was the electronics that did all the calculations providing an accurate readout automatically. For a moment, Keith studied the readings. It was at sixty-one percent but falling. There appeared a good chance it would drop below fifty percent before bottoming out. While waiting for the readings to fall, Keith studied the storm outside. He could see the edge of the wall of Gail pass by as Tom kept the Lear in a tight circle. In the eye of Gail, the air was smooth and almost surreal. As Keith watched the meter fall another five percent, it was time to help Marty get the drums in position. By the time they had the drums free of the rope and ready to open, the meter was reading forty-nine percent and still dropping.

"Time to get started," said Keith, pulling the tabs up on the rim of the leaky drum.

After three of the tabs were bent upwards, Marty stripped the lid off. Cautiously, they both looked inside. Under a thin film of oil was a yellow chalky substance. Marty put on a pair of rubber gloves and picked up the scoop the technicians provided for removing the compound. Keith opened the hopper. Marty poured off the oil, then took a small scoop of the compound and placed it in the hopper. As he brought the compound through the air he could hear it sizzle. Apparently, there was enough moisture in the cabin to get the chemistry started, but not enough for it to catch fire. Marty continued to scoop the compound until the drum was empty.

"OK, here goes," said Marty as he flipped the switch on the mill.

Inside the mill, there was a grinding noise. Shortly thereafter, a fine yellow powder began to fall out of the exit chute. As the powder fell it began to smoke slightly. Marty switched the mill off, then attached the rubber tubing to the output chute and draped the other end into the dusting equipment input hopper. If everything worked, they were ready to go.

Marty crossed his fingers and threw the switch again. The mill responded immediately. Soon the fine yellow powder leaving the mill was making its way into the seeding hopper. He next switched on the seeding equipment. The seeding suction fan caught the powder, then blew it into the plumbing leading out to the underside of both wings.

Keith looked out the window. At first there was nothing exiting the three nozzles on the wing, and then slowly a stream of yellow dust emerged. Keith looked aft. Normally, when they were seeding clouds over the western Rockies, the chemicals formed a thin haze that descended slowly into the clouds below. This yellow powder appeared to drift almost upward. It was then that Keith noticed a peculiar odor.

"Do you smell something?" asked Keith.

"Yeah, I noticed it about five minutes ago. Do you think it's from this stuff?" Marty responded.

Tom interrupted. "I've smelled this odor every time I've been in these storms lately. Smells kind of like a pool locker room, doesn't it?"

"Yes," agreed Keith.

"Say, Keith, have you ever had any trouble with your port engine oil pressure? Looks like either the gage is faulty or your pressure is fluctuating."

Keith suddenly remembered his last flight to Denver a month ago. He looked at Marty. Marty shook his head. Keith knew with all the excitement he had caused in Austria, Marty hadn't had time to check on it.

"Yes, the last time I flew her I noticed the gage flutter every so often, but it's been steady all the way out here," he replied.

"Well, it ain't steady now. You guys better make haste back there so we can be on our way home," said Tom.

"OK, we'll expedite things here. How about you try to raise Jessel and advise him of our situation."

"I'll give it a go," replied Tom, switching on the transmitter.

Keith helped Marty empty the drums one-by-one. With each drum emptied, the cabin filled with a little more smoke. With three drums left, they were all beginning to cough.

"I'm not having any luck on the radio. Too much interference from lightning. I don't think there's any way to get through. Also, the gage pressure is falling slightly. You'd best hurry," reported Tom.

Marty and Keith renewed their efforts. Marty was stuffing the last drum's compound into the hopper. When he finished, Keith turned to the window. Now a considerable cloud of powder hung in the air in the tight circle Tom had flown. It was at that moment the readout from the hygrometer caught his eye. To his disbelief he realized it was reading fifty-five percent!

"Oh, shit! We've got tr—" Keith began.

There was a blue flash and a loud explosion. The Lear was soundly rocked. Keith could feel the searing heat of the fire rise out of the seeding equipment and into the cabin. Marty was in front of him. He had been leaning over the equipment when the explosion occurred. In an instant, Marty's face was burned. When Keith looked at him, he found Marty's eyebrows and part of his hair had vaporized. The sickening smell of burnt hair filled the cabin. Fortunately, after a few seconds of blinking, Marty was relieved to find he could still see.

Up forward, Tom was having difficulty. In the seconds that followed the explosion he was contending with multiple problems. First, he momentarily lost electrical power probably due to a short circuit in the seeding equipment; second, the port engine lost all oil pressure and shut down; and third, the cabin was rapidly losing pressure. Fortunately, he still had control of the Lear.

"We're losing cabin pressure. I'm taking her down!" shouted Tom to Keith.

Keith and Marty were having their own problems. The empty drums were scattered all about the cabin. They were now floating in the almost weightlessness of Tom's dive. Keith grabbed the lid for the waste oil container and managed to fasten it down securely before much of the oil spilled out. Tom suddenly brought the Lear out of its dive. The drums were no longer floating, but Marty and Keith were thrown to the floor. In the confusion that followed, they were knocked about by the drums, though they produced little impact being empty.

Keith and Marty got to their feet and hurried forward.

"What's the situation?" asked Keith.

"Bad. Port engine out with no hope of restarting. I'm able to keep her flying using the rudder all right but we can't climb high enough to get over the wall," reported Tom.

"We'd better survey the damage. If we've lost cabin pressure there could be other problems," said Keith.

Keith surveyed the port side while Marty surveyed the starboard side. Keith could see where the explosion had damaged part of the seeding equipment on his side. Apparently, the powder had built up enough hydrogen inside the tubing to ignite. The resulting explosion had blown the three nozzles off. The wing looked slightly damaged around the seeding hardware, but worst of all there was a thin haze forming aft of the wing.

"We got real troubles on this side!" said Keith. "Looks like we're losing fuel!"

"I can see the port wing tank gage is dropping!" called Tom.

"There's some damage on this side, but I don't see we're losing any fuel," reported Marty.

"I'll try to call Jessel again if I can get the Navcom gear working. I'm not sure it'll make any difference with all the lightning. While I try, how about figuring our range and coming up with some way to get this plane out of here," called Tom.

Keith studied his chart. By his last calculation they were twenty miles off the Florida Gulf Coast. The eye of Gail was moving north east toward the coast. The eye would be over land in the next two hours. They could probably keep the Lear airborne, but they could never get her up to forty thousand feet again. Keith guessed they could barely make twenty-three.

"What's the chances of making it through the storm to the other side at about twenty thousand feet?" asked Keith.

Tom stared at Keith for a moment. "Zero! No way we can keep her airborne. It just can't be done. We don't have enough power," replied Tom.

Keith studied the fuel situation. There was enough fuel to last another hour and a half, maybe two hours. If they stayed in the eye, they might reach land. Were there any airports nearby? Keith could only find one. It was Fort Myers.

"If we can stay airborne for another two hours, remaining in the eye, we might make it to Fort Myers," said Keith.

"We might be able to make it, but it's possible they won't be open."

"Do you have any other ideas?" asked Keith.

"No, even if we could fly into the storm, we don't have enough fuel to get out far enough for the winds to be reasonable, and I certainly don't want to try to land in one hundred-mile plus head-winds. It's better we wait it out till we get close to land. If we can, we'll land. If not, we'll ditch," said Tom.

That was it. Their course was set. Not much to do but wait, to wait and to plan for the worst.

ONE HOUR AND FORTY-SIX MINUTES LATER

The Lear was circling at five hundred feet above the ocean. Keith estimated they had less than ten minutes of fuel left. He be-lieved they were near the Gulf coast, but they hadn't sighted any-thing. In the last hour they had decided what to do should they have to ditch. Each man now wore an inflatable life vest.

"I guess we'd better get ready," said Keith.

"Looks that way. I'll bring her down a little," said Tom.

Keith moved aft with Marty. They had positioned the empty drums where they could be thrown out once they opened the door. In a few minutes, Tom had the Lear about four hundred feet above the ocean and had throttled the starboard engine back as much as he dared. Now the Lear mushed through the air so slowly she was about to stall.

"OK, Keith, open the door!" shouted Tom.

Keith got the door open, and almost fell out as a hundred mile-per-hour gust blew through the opening. Fortunately, they had tied Tom's rope across the opening. Light objects were swirled throughout the cabin in the wind. Tom advanced the star-board throttle to compensate for the additional drag. The Lear was not designed to fly with its door open.

Keith moved the first drum into place. When it caught the rush-ing air, it was fairly torn from his hands and sucked out the door. Marty was next with a drum. His luck was no better. One by one they dumped the empty drums out the door, then the oil container. Keith dragged the survival gear toward the door. He checked the raft and the survival kit carefully to be sure they were both secure.

"We wait till just before we hit, then we toss the raft," said Keith.

"Do you think we'll make it?" asked Marty.

"I'm not sure. One thing is for certain, this old Lear will sink like a rock. Our best chance is to jump immediately after we stop bouncing. By then the water should be pouring in," replied Keith.

Keith and Marty stayed by the open door, studying the dark water below. The only light came from the stars above. Ahead, the Lear's landing lights pierced the darkness. In all directions off in the distance, Keith and Marty could see the almost constant flashes of lightning.

"How long after we land do you think it will be calm?" asked Marty.

"Not long, probably fifteen minutes, no more," replied Keith.

"Well, buddy, here's hoping we make it."

"We will, we'd better, I'll owe you one if we don't."

At that moment the starboard engine began to lose power.

"Here we go. Brace yourselves!" shouted Tom.

Tom turned the Lear in the direction of the Gulf Coast and began to edge out of the eye of the storm. His intent was to use the headwind to reduce their speed over the water. Doing this on the north side of the eye might give them enough time to get the raft inflated. Eventually, the starboard engine lost all power after exhausting the Lear's fuel. Now they were only a few feet above the waves. Marty moved the raft closer to the door. Suddenly, the plane hit a wave with tremendous force. As it bounced an enormous shaft of water entered through the open door. Marty and Keith scrambled and managed to boost the raft out just before the Lear settled into the water permanently. Then they were clinging to the equipment forward of the door. The impact of the waves was much worse than they expected. Keith and Marty slammed against the mill, but didn't travel farther. Meanwhile, the Lear buried its nose in the waves and began sinking rapidly.

Keith shoved Marty toward the door. He thought he made it, but he couldn't be sure. There was a lot of water coming in now. The cabin was almost inundated. Keith looked forward; he couldn't see Tom. His immediate instinct was fear, fear of drowning, but he fought it back. Where was Tom? Keith swam forward. The cabin was almost full of water. He grabbed for his last breath and swam farther forward, or was it down?

He found Tom slumped in his seat. Grabbing for his belt he released the weather pilot. Then, taking a grip on his collar, he began swimming his way backward. There was a sharp pressure building in his ears. He knew the Lear was sinking fast. He was kicking hard with his legs and stroking with his free arm as he struggled for the door. He had to feel his way each foot of the distance. His lungs screamed for air. There was precious little time left. The pain increased, until in desperation, he began to slowly release air. This tactic briefly worked; by then he was at the door. He pulled the cord on Tom's life vest. It inflated. Then he pulled his own. He didn't remember what happened next. There must have been the inevitable search for the surface and the tremendous desire to take a breath with no air available. He only remembered how good it felt when he got to the surface.

He was struggling with Tom. Keith couldn't be sure, but he thought he wasn't breathing. He began to apply mouth-to-mouth resuscitation. He was rewarded when Tom regurgitated in his face. Despite the choking stench, Keith kept at it. Shortly, Tom coughed and began to come around.

By now the wind had died down. Somewhere, Keith heard a shout. It was Marty! Keith shouted back. In a few minutes, Marty appeared out of the darkness, paddling the raft.

"We got lucky, Keith, the raft's in good shape!" shouted Marty.

"First, we'd better get our shoes off. Don't want to damage the raft," said Keith.

Keith grabbed the lifeline attached to the raft's perimeter. Quickly he had his, and then Tom's, shoes off. Then he climbed in. With Marty's help they got Tom aboard. Keith looked back toward the Lear and saw only waves.

"I guess she's gone, Marty. We'd better start for shore while we still have time. You take the oars, I'll see what I can do for Tom."

Marty took up the oars. "What direction?" he asked.

Keith looked around. He couldn't tell east from west. They should go east. A few stars were showing but they were rapidly fading. Lightning flashed all about in the distance, followed by the almost constant roll of thunder. If he knew their position relative to the storm, he could guess by the wind which way to go, but he didn't. Then he remembered the survival kit. Quickly, he opened the waterproof container. It was too dark. In frustration, Keith put the container down.

"That way!"

It was a guess, but Marty didn't hesitate and began madly stroking in the direction Keith pointed. For the next few minutes, he continued before fatigue set in and his pace slowed. Keith propped Tom on his side where he was resting for the moment. Next, he sought and found the flashlight in the container. The wind was rapidly picking up, the gusts buffeting the waves with ever-increasing force. The waves around them were choppy and confused, but becoming more organized by the wind. Keith searched the container with the flashlight. Suddenly, he found the object he sought. He studied the compass for a moment.

He pointed to his left. "No, that way!" he shouted over the rising wind.

Keith assumed they had started in the wrong direction, but soon it became apparent Marty was pulling harder with his right arm. That had turned them southward. Keith kept Marty on course by pointing to the east.

Keith sniffed the air. The smell of land filled his lungs. It must be nearby, but could they make it? How much longer would they be in the eye before the wind and rain picked up and the waves capsized their fragile raft?

Marty was exhausted. His hair was wet with sweat and salt water, and he was breathing hard. Keith took the oars. The steady hard wind whipped the sea. All around were white caps, the foam luminescent in the darkness. The spray from the cresting waves sprayed their faces, making it difficult for Keith to stay on course. He was straining at the oars, his breath coming in hoarse gulps. The wind was stronger now, and salt water lashing his face made it difficult to see and breathe. Somewhere in the distance, he thought he heard the sound of breakers crashing on a beach.

The lightning was coming much closer. With each flash, Keith caught glimpses of the swollen waves. They were very high, dwarfing the three men in the raft. Keith was still stroking hard, but was rapidly becoming fatigued. A massive wave approached, illuminated by a brilliant flash of lightning; it looked like a mountain. To Keith's horror, he realized the wave was cresting. He bent forward to stroke using every ounce of strength. Too late. The wave was upon them, its crest already a vertical wall of water. The curl was forming. The raft was going over. Keith dropped the oars and grabbed for the lifeline. Suddenly, the raft capsized and he was under water being driven downward by the smashing force of the falling wave. Keith struggled for the surface, but he wasn't sure he was going to make it.

KALISPELL, MONTANA, TUESDAY SEPTEMBER 24

Main Street was busy with townspeople getting an early start on Halloween by shopping after work. Leaves had fallen early this season, and piles of them rested in the gutters next to the sidewalks. The air was cool and clear, and the sun was setting in the west. The maintenance crews would spend the next two months clearing the streets of leaves and filling potholes before work began hanging Christmas lights until the grand illumination the day after Thanksgiving. In a half hour, the temperature would drop sharply as night approached. In the distance, music played and someone was ringing a bell to its rhythm. On the street corner below a bright string of lights stood the Kalispell Home Electronics Store.

Ted Brown, the store manager, recently had rearranged the display window. Three new nineteen-inch flat screen TVs from different Japanese companies were in front. Each was tuned to the same channel. The sound from one was playing on the outside speaker loud enough for the small gathering in front to catch the early evening news.

Locally, there had been a fire and a suspected murder, but the big news was Hurricane Gail. She was pummeling the states of Florida, Mississippi and Georgia. Gail was statistically the worst hurricane ever to hit the mainland, and there was plenty of damage to show for it. Despite most people having taken the warnings seriously, there was heavy loss of life due to high water, wind, rain, and lightning. Property damage was estimated to total in the billions. The network had plenty of footage to show the Montana audience just how bad things were back east.

The last item was a late-breaking story of a mystery plane that took off from a small airport near Pascagoula, Mississippi. The story made reference to a previous report from the weather bureau indicating a tear existed in the ozone layer over the Atlantic. The local reporter claimed a government employee, who wished to remain anonymous, stated the plane's mission was related to alleviating the problem, but declined to furnish further details. The present whereabouts of the plane was also unknown, but there were unconfirmed reports it was overdue on its return.

The news ended with the sports wrap-up. Around Montana, football was big news. The sportscaster began reeling off the weekend scores. No one noticed the tall stranger among the group lose interest and leave. Had anyone watched carefully, they would have seen his right hand inserted between the second and third buttons of his dark trench coat, pressing the left side of his abdomen. They might also have noticed he walked with a limp. The group remained until the college scores were finished, then they drifted away. Two blocks away, the stranger started his car and turned onto Main Street, heading north toward Canada.

FORT MYERS, WEDNESDAY, SEPTEMBER 25

The scene outside Mt Sinai Hospital in a suburb of Fort Myers was chaotic, but improving. Teams of men and women were busy cleaning up after the hurricane of the previous night. On the ground, a team of men was clearing the uprooted remains of the tall palms that bordered the immense parking lots surrounding the hospital complex. The constant buzz of chainsaws came from several directions. The maintenance crew was replacing broken plate glass windows on the second floor with plywood. The sound of their hammers beat a constant rhythm that carried well in the dense humid air. On the ground, palm fronds, trash, and broken glass were strewn everywhere. Water filled all the low areas and fog hung in the air. A team of electricians from the power company had just arrived to bolster emergency power to the main building. In this neighborhood, and for several miles inland, there was no electrical power. Telephone service was completely disrupted. Much of the damage to the utility system was the result of lightning and high winds.

In every direction one looked, there was work to be done. The crews would be cleaning, clearing, and repairing for months before all the damage and debris disappeared.

The surrounding parking lots held only a few automobiles. Many of the hospital staff from the previous afternoon shift were still at work under the code yellow emergency plan. Several ambulances stood in a neat row in front of the Emergency entrance while tired orderlies moved patients into the building.

Just outside the entrance, but out of the way of traffic, a group of men and women had set up a tent in the middle of a collection of pickup trucks and vans. A generator was running behind one of the vans.

Robert Winfield sat behind a bench that served as a make-shift desk under the hastily erected tent. He wore a baseball cap that touted a famous scout camp in New Mexico, jeans with a wide belt and silver buckle, and a navy blue Ft Myers Amateur Radio Club's jacket. In front of him was a message log. In one hand he held a pencil, and in the other a microphone. That morning, according to plans they had made years in advance, Robert and his club established their support station in front of the hospital shortly after Gail's winds slackened. The sole purpose of their operation was to provide communication when telephone service was interrupted. A whole network of amateurs stretched across the country was passing on messages from local residents to friends and relatives in distant locations.

Robert was in his element. The club had practiced for this emergency. After all their training, this was his first opportunity to show what they could do. He was important. He was helping others and it felt good! Already he had logged 135 messages. A large portion of the content was good news, but some messages were from the hospital, and occasionally the news was bad. He was trying for the fourth time to make contact with Cleveland, Ohio, and having no luck. It was cool in the tent and his folding chair was uncomfortable and made his back stiff. Soon, he had to be relieved. His wife, Ruth, was just passing him a cup of coffee when there was a loud disturbance from behind. Robert turned to find three men approaching the tent. One had a bandage on his head and wore a blanket over his shoulders for a coat, the second's face appeared burned, while the third walked with a limp. Despite their physical condition, the men seemed elated. Robert suspected they had been drinking. His attention returned to his radio. He finally had a contact from Ohio.

Ruth was busy with an elderly couple from Maryland. They were trying to get a message to Washington, D.C. Ruth took their message and logged it on her clipboard. The couple was trying to contact their daughter. That could be difficult. Washington was experiencing severe flooding and wind damage. Only a few amateurs in the area were active and they were overloaded with urgent message traffic. She promised her husband would be working on it soon. The couple moved off toward the refreshments the club had made available.

The trio came forward. Their clothes did not fit well, but they were dry. The tallest one spoke first.

"We'd like to get a message to a man in Pascagoula, ma'am," he said.

"OK, what's the name?" replied Ruth.

"Robert Jessel, Admiral Retired."

"His address?"

Keith gave Ruth the airport address.

"The message?"

"Successfully completed objective. Lost plane. Crew OK. Expect bill."

Ruth didn't flinch, but copied down the message and then turned to the next in line. Keith, Tom and Marty moved off to look for a meal. Not far down the street the arches of a well-known fast food restaurant came in to view. Keith started down the street, but stopped a moment. He turned back and limped to Ruth.

"Ma'am, I'd like to send another message, please, to New York City. It should read:

"Bottle of St. Julien waiting for you. I am too. Keith."

Ruth smiled at him, her blue eyes twinkling, and wrote the words on her pad. When she gazed into his eyes, she saw worry and a possible suggestion of tears, but he smiled back warmly and limped off to join the others.

THE END

Clark W. Heckert has a BSEE and MSEE degree from Case Western Reserve University and two years U.S. Navy experience during the Vietnam war from 1969-70 as the Electronics Material Officer on the Wallace L. Lind (DD703). He spent twenty-seven years in equipment development with the DuPont Company in the Engineering Physics Laboratory, Medical Products, Electronic Imaging and Printing, and Publishing departments. He was an independent consultant for ten years before retiring to Colorado with his wife Pamela. In addition to his Navy experience, Clark has traveled to many parts of the world. Now he spends his time tinkering with his refurbished Jeeps and communicating on amateur radio (K3NI), along with hiking and skiing in the paradise of Redstone, Colorado.

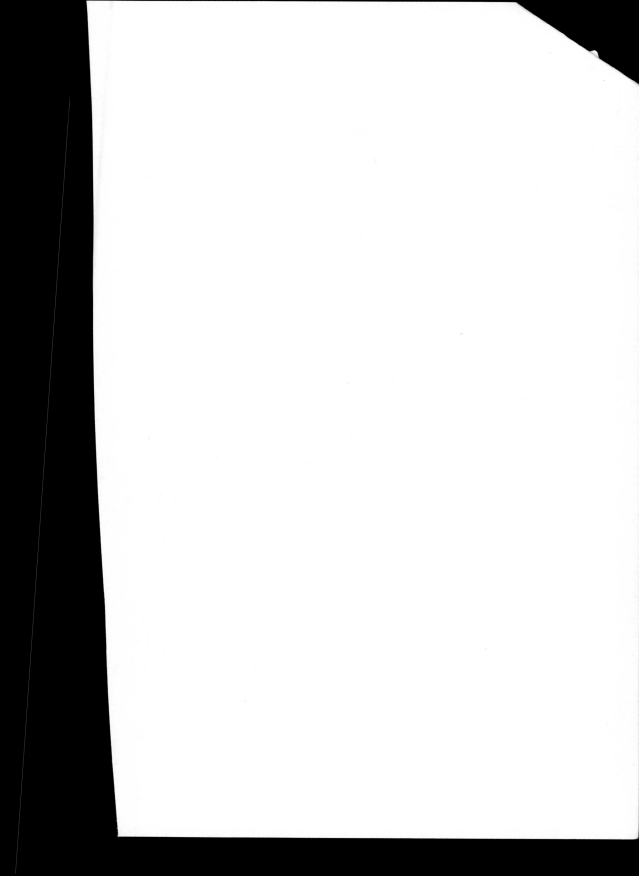

Made in the USA
Columbia, SC
05 July 2018